Crimson Liberty

George W. Morrison

Georjes Press

Spokane, Washington

Published by Georjes Press, P.O. Box 8283, Spokane, Washington, 99203. First printing, December, 2012. You may contact the author at MorrisonGW@aol.com

Cover Art by Lynda Ellis.

Publisher's Note: This is a work of fiction. All names, characters, places, and incidents are the product of the author's imagination or are used fictionally and any resemblance to actual living persons (except Vic Lambert), business establishments, events, products, or locales is entirely coincidental and is not intended as an endorsement or disparagement of any business establishment, event, product, or locale.

ISBN-13: 978-1479153800
ISBN-10: 147915380X

DEDICATION

This book is dedicated to Jessica Margaret Bair Morrison-Dahl, my wife, an English teacher early in her professional career, who continues to believe everyone has a novel to write, for supporting and encouraging me in the writing of this one.

ACKNOWLEDGEMENTS

For sharing their knowledge and experience in theater and in the performing arts, I thank Richard Alderson, Michael Weldon Allen, Dennis Ashley, Lance Goss, Bill Greely, Vic Lambert, Jim Lucas, Peggy O'Neal, Norman Treigle, and Dianna Trotter.

I thank the literature-loving folks who worked with me on various drafts of this manuscript: Debra Adams, Marcia Brandes, Jessica Morrison-Dahl, and Patty Wieser.

I thank the faculty of the Book Passages Mystery Writer's Workshops for helping me develop my talent, and I thank literary agent Kimberley Cameron for encouraging me to believe this book would find a home.

I particularly thank Frances Morrison for assisting me with the construction of Madame Claire's Tarot reading. For its interpretation in this novel, hold me, not Fran, accountable.

EPIGRAPH

To be, or not to be? That is the question.
Whether 'tis nobler in the mind to suffer
The slings and arrows of outrageous fortune,
Or to take arms up against a sea of troubles,
And, by opposing, end them? To die: to sleep;
No more; and by a sleep to say we end
The heartache and the thousand natural shocks
That flesh is heir to, 'tis a consummation
Devoutly to be wished! To die, to sleep;
To sleep: perchance to dream: aye, there's the rub,
For in that sleep of death, what dreams may come
When we have shuffled off this mortal coil,
Must give us pause....

William Shakespeare, Hamlet, Act 3 scene 1

PROLOGUE

I look out upon the grounds of the lamasery and watch the monks rake gravel and tend plants. These Buddhists are gentle men. They revere life and would not take one. I had always considered myself to be a gentle man who reveres life.

Had you ever told me I would knowingly and deliberately take someone's life, I would have politely laughed in your face if I hadn't simply ignored you. I don't even believe in capital punishment. I might have engaged you in brilliant repartee in an attempt to disarm you with my charming wit. Or, depending on how the argument went, I might have agreed that I would take up arms, reluctantly, against the soldiers of a madman bent on enslaving the world as did my father in the Second World War, but that's not my nature.

I am a creator, a lover, and a negotiator—not a killer. Or so I thought.

Chapter One

"Ham's dead and Al's dying; it's in your hands now, Spearman."

Alex only called me Spearman when he was pissed. He wanted me to take an assignment in New Orleans, complete my thesis, and leave the young ladies alone.

"It's a jump start for your career," Alex said, working up to a dramatist's climax, "and at your age, you need it."

You can take the theater department head out of acting, but you can't take acting out of the theater department head. Alex studied acting at the Royal Academy of Dramatic Art in London. I was half-expecting him to pull a Henry V and order me, in iambic pentameter, 'Once more into the breach....' But, since I studied acting at graduate school in Memphis, Tennessee, my orders came in prose.

"Teach drama and produce a student show at Gudrun Hall, produce *Macbeth* for a semi-professional theater, get academic and directing credentials, get paid, and live four months in the French Quarter. What's holding you back? Your harem? You're a bit long in the tooth to be bedding women half your age."

Like the actor he was, Alex stepped into the light of the late afternoon sun that was pouring through the domed ceiling of The Globe, our Elizabethan replica theater, to deliver the last line of his speech. He caught me just as I finished teaching my last class of the summer refresher course on stage combat for drama teachers and was on my way to rendezvous with my latest ingénue, Fiona Brenan, for dinner and recreational sex.

I doubt Alex knew it would be Fiona tonight, but I'm sure he knew it would be someone. It was common knowledge that, after twenty-some years of marriage, I was vigorously enjoying my renewed bachelorhood.

"I can't help it if you don't have any single women my age in the MFA program, Alex, and few in the entire graduate school. I date people I know. I know graduate students, most of whom are younger than I. At least I avoid undergraduates."

"Thank God for small favors, Dewy."

We were back on a first name basis. That's always a good sign.

"Frankly, Dewy, I'm desperate. I promised Dean Halberstam I'd find someone for the first term and you're the best candidate I have."

"Are you sure I'm not the only candidate you have?"

"You don't know everyone, Dewy. No one still on campus is a candidate, but there are a few recent graduates and other students not on campus who are all-but-thesis like you who could do it."

"Like Molly Aldridge?"

"Yes, like Molly. But she's not my first choice. You are. Look, it's a matter of ABC's—academics, balls, and con. Molly's got the con and, Lord knows, she's got the balls, but she's weak in academics. She'll set a new low record for grade point average of anyone who ever earned an MFA from this institution, if she ever graduates".

"I don't think a teaching career was her goal, Alex."

"Right, and one thing you can learn from Molly, Dewy, is to let go once you get the show into performance. Let your stage manager take over. Molly's stage manager called the shots to recover from the curtain screw-up in *Seven Brides* she took on the road for the Muni. Molly's intense when she's in rehearsal and gets overwrought when things don't go her way, but she's out there doing professional theater while you're still in graduate school screwing around with women half your age."

"So how did this vacancy at Gudrun Hall come to be?"

"You're stalling, Dewy."

"O.K. I'm stalling. Tell me anyway."

"All right, but let's get out of this damn sun," he said, as he hooked my arm, moved into the lobby, and started walking in the direction of the exit to the faculty parking lot.

"Stupidest idea they ever came up with," he said, slipping into his famous diatribe against our Globe, "putting on a clear dome. If it were open like the real Globe, at least we could get a breeze. This air conditioning doesn't cut it when it's ninety-five degrees outside. Open air and fans would do better. I wish the trustees understood that Memphis is a thousand miles further south than London and a hell of a lot hotter, especially in summer."

"I tell you, Dewy, we should tear this down and rebuild it like the theater at Oglethorpe University in Atlanta. The roof's solid, but the sides go up and down for natural ventilation."

"Yeah." I agreed with Alex hoping he would keep going and forget the question to which he had demand my answer, but he didn't.

"Damn it. You've got me blathering on about my pet peeve instead of hearing you tell me you'll take the job."

"You were going to tell me how the opening came to be."

"O.K. You're still stalling, but I said I would, so I will. Hammond Laidlaw was the longtime artistic director at Théatre Vieux Carré as well as a faculty member at Gudrun Hall. He died unexpectedly in mid-March. Dean Halberstam called us for temporary staffing for this academic year while they begin a faculty recruiting search. Radu Lupeşçu, Ham's colleague at Gudrun Hall, was willing to give up half of his scheduled sabbatical to fill in for first semester, but his grant came through to work with Theater Budapest and he's already gone."

"So you called on Al Driscoll?"

"Yes, I called Al and he agreed, but his health took a turn for the worse; he's in no shape to teach or direct anywhere, even part-time."

"I knew he was HIV positive, Alex, but I didn't know it was that bad. Is he receiving visitors?"

"He went home to his parents in Savannah to die. So, are you going to New Orleans or not? Don't disappoint me further. You won't like the consequences."

Alex put his hand on my shoulder to arrest my motion and we hesitated by the exit door to finish talking in the comfort of the air-conditioned lobby. Outside was steaming hot.

"Why me? What makes me so special?"

"Fishing for compliments, what? Well, here it is, my lad. Remember the ABCs."

"Academics, balls, and con?"

"By George, I think he's got it!" Alex exclaimed. "Not only do you have one of the best grade point averages in recent memory, you've got balls. And you know how to con people when conning is what it takes to get the job done."

"That's a sterling recommendation? Con men end up in prison."

"Not if they're good, Dewy. Not if they're really, really good. Besides, I don't mean in a criminal way. You're good at making people feel like they're listened to, making them feel important, schmoozing. You hardly ever rub anyone the wrong way—except for me. You're such a strong schmoozer it's almost a weakness."

"Another one of my character strengths, huh? Keep going and you'll talk yourself out of sending me."

"One of your challenges will be to rub someone the wrong way when that's what's required for artistic integrity. You'll grow into that in due time. Here's the crux of it, Dewy. I need a director who can put on a student production where the utmost of tact is required to keep the innocent darlings showing up for rehearsals and performances and who can praise even tepid improvement in a way that sounds sincere. Does that sound like Molly?"

"Frankly, no. She could freeze a glass of water just by mean-mugging it. Lord knows what would happen if she started yelling. That might slide by in the professional theater, but it hardly seems useful in working with kids."

"Or with volunteers, which is what most of the folks at TVC are. And then there is the minefield of theater politics which I doubt Molly could navigate without numerous blow-ups. TVC is run by a woman you'd best think of as a dowager duchess. She controls both the board of directors and the purse strings. She also imposes great influence on artistic direction. She even has her no-count son working as business manager."

"She sounds like a handful."

"Because of her and the Boudron Theater Trust, TVC exists. In spite of her, it often does good work. Your job is to produce the Scottish play at TVC without creating any waves and then to whip a bunch of enthusiastic, but undisciplined, college students into a creditable production of *Four Plays for Coarse Actors*, in reverse order."

"That's quite a challenge, Alex."

"Quite. What ideas do you have about putting a new wrinkle on the Scottish play?"

Visions of Macbeth as Macheath from *The Threepenny Opera* flashed before me. I could get Lady Macbeth up as Polly Peachum. Macduff could be the policeman. Crookfinger Jake would be one of the assassins. No, that wouldn't work. For whom could Victoria's Rider bring a reprieve? Macbeth? No, Macbeth has to die. Scratch that idea. I once saw *The Merchant of Venice* done as warring Mafioso. How about Macbeth as Capone? Capone died, but it was from syphilis. It wouldn't work, and I was drifting.

"Your offer tempts me, Alex, but what I'd like to know is what I don't know that I should know. What aren't you telling me?"

"There's a woman at TVC you must stay away from—period. You'll be bollixed if you even lift your eyebrow in her direction, much less attempt to lift her skirt."

"Is she a ball breaker or something?"

"The word is that she's O.K. Not so, her man, and he's always around. She's a looker and he's a possessor. Radu said her man will have your guts for garters and your balls for breakfast if you make a move on her. Apparently it's happened before."

"Gee! Thanks a million, Alex."

"I know it's cruel to warn you off the young ones and then put you at risk of having an arse-over-teakettle affair with one closer to your age, but the stones come with the farm. Keep it on a professional level and everything should be right as rain. The real challenge is navigating your way through the minefield of theater politics with Clotilde Boudron."

"She's the dowager duchess you told me about?"

"Spot on, lad. She wears the trousers at TVC. Just be sure to give the devil her due, as it were."

I usually got a kick out of Alex Righetti's Briticisms, especially since he was Italian on his father's side and French-Canadian on his mother's, but this Briticism gave me shivers.

"Come on, Dewy. I've got to know by first thing tomorrow morning so I can attempt another solution if you fag out on me. I simply must let Dean Halberstam know who'll be coming. School starts in two weeks."

"That soon?"

"Let me remind you of what I said when we began this conversation, Dewy. The consequences of your refusing to go are that you will not get your MFA from this institution and you will not get a reference from me. The theater world is surprisingly tight, Dewy. Reputation counts. References, too. So what do you say?"

"Duress. That's what I say. You're bullying me into doing something I don't particularly want to do," I said, lying. I was intrigued with the idea of bracing the battleaxe and seducing the siren even if I did have to leave my comfortable nest in Memphis to do it.

"Duress, schmuress. Get off your bum. Do something. You're already in your forties. Are you going to fish or cut bait? If you don't do this, you'll have to do something else because you've done everything there is to do here. It's time to go somewhere else."

"I'm happy here."

"All threats aside, Dewy, you've got to move on sooner or later. In your case, it is sooner. Students come and students go. So far you've done a lot of coming. Now it's time for you to go. You've got to make way for those who come behind you."

"I get your point, Alex."

"I'll have your answer in my office by nine o'clock tomorrow morning, Dewy. No answer will be taken as a 'no' answer. If you choose this assignment, I can promise it will vex you, perplex you, and maybe even unsex you, but you can grow your professional wings, make your bones. That was a pun about unsexing. Lady Macbeth's speech, you know."

"I know."

"It all boils down to one choice, Dewy. Accept this opportunity and go with my blessing: refuse it and go with my curse. But, one way or the other, you will leave this campus."

Chapter Two

Alex got in the last word because he walked out before I could think up a clever riposte. I followed him into the parking lot into the liquid heat of late August, but when he turned right toward the faculty parking lot, I turned left toward my neighborhood bar and hot-footed my way to meet Fiona. Graduate teaching assistants didn't get free parking and you couldn't buy a decent parking place, not even during Summer Quarter.

Why was I hesitating? I wasn't hurting for money and my family no longer depended on me financially. Martha and I split our joint assets when we divorced to which I added about half a million by inheriting it. That gave me the cushion to chuck my civil service career and pursue my passion—theater.

Everyone was successfully launched. My firstborn, Elizabeth, was in Chicago completing her doctoral thesis on mythology and living with her husband who was completing his medical residency.

My son was in the third year of his six-year hitch with the navy.

My ex-wife, Martha, needed nothing from me and was happily doing the horizontal lambada with her flute-instructor boyfriend with whom she traveled. She was generally out of touch with all of us which created some unhappiness for my daughter, but not for me. I was busy with my own interests.

With money in my bank account and my family grown up and gone in three directions, I was footloose, fancy-free, and off in my own direction. I still had my looks, my teeth, a full head of reddish-brown hair that I kept short most of the time, and a vigorous sex life.

With about 175 pounds on my six-foot frame, I was in decent shape. I was only a master's project away from having my academic and professional credentials, a Master of Fine Arts in theater, more commonly known as an MFA. Or, as we thespians put it, I'd be "A mighty fine actor."

I'd put in two and one-half years on campus, directed two student productions, and directed a community theater production in Germantown. Eventually, I'd have to cut the umbilical cord and work in the professional world of theater to make my bones.

So, why was I hesitating? Sure, there were the benefits that came from being older and more worldly-wise than most graduate students, not to mention richer. Sort of like being cock of the walk. I never claimed to have a harem but I seldom lacked for willing bed partners who were, as Alex pointed out, occasionally as young as my daughter, like Fiona, who was waiting for me in our usual booth with a scotch for me and a Heineken for her.

"Hi, Dewy," she said as pulled her guitar case onto her side of the booth. "How's the Old Man of the Theater doing this evening?"

"Wonderful, now that I'm here with you."

"Cool. You look somber. Something's on your mind."

"Alex wants me to go to New Orleans for a semester to be visiting professor and direct a couple of shows."

"Great. That's what you've been prepping for, isn't it?

"I guess so."

"Then what's the prob?"

"It's so sudden. I'd have to leave everything and go to New Orleans almost immediately."

"What have you got going that you can't leave for four months?"

"Memphis barbecue, my river-view apartment, and you, among other things. Wouldn't you miss me?"

"Hell's bells, Dewy. Half of the single women in graduate school would miss you. For the past two years you've been wining and dining us like romance was going out of style. Of course I'd miss you, but I'm not going anywhere," Fiona said, as she flipped the back of her hair with her right hand.

"I've got another year on campus before I can even think about starting a dissertation. Besides, I'm not sure you'd miss me all that much. I'm just your babe *du jour*. How many women have you been out with over the past couple of years? Two dozen? Three dozen?"

"Well...."

"Don't try to figure it out, Dewy. Even if you've been keeping a journal, from what I've heard, you'd need a personal secretary like Don Juan's Laparello, or a CPA to come up with an accurate number. Face it; you've earned your reputation."

"What as? A dirty old man who's good for an evening of flattery and good food?"

"And good conversation, and a good time between the sheets, too. Don't underestimate yourself, Dewy. Besides, you're not really old. It's not like you're in your fifties or anything."

"Wouldn't you miss me?"

"Stop fishing. Of course I'd miss you, but I'm not some dewy-eyed debutante who's looking to marry you. I'll get over it. It's time for you to move on. You can't stay a graduate student forever, particularly at your age. You're older than half the faculty. It's time to get going," she said, flipping the back of her hair with her left hand.

"You can always come back to Memphis to see me. It's only three hundred and ninety-five miles. Hey, if you end up staying down there for second semester I'll come down and hang out with you for Mardi Gras. That'd be cool. Now finish you scotch and take me to dinner. I'm starving and broke."

"How about we dine in this evening. I've learned how to make coconut soup."

"Cool. I love Thai."

We left the bar and walked two blocks to my riverfront bluff apartment. The heat from the languorous, late-August day radiated from the pavement and swirled sinuously about our bodies making me sweat and Fiona glow, molding our clothing to our damp forms, heightening sensuality but dampening enthusiasm. Where was crisp November when you needed it?

My eighth-floor apartment was air-conditioned as was nearly any place you would want to be in Memphis in August, but Fiona insisted on hanging out on my private terrace overlooking that Ol' Man River, the mighty Mississippi.

The lowering of the sun into the Arkansas haze conspired with the breeze, the elevation, and the shade of my two potted crepe myrtles to make the terrace barely tolerable.

Fiona sang Celtic songs while I worked in the kitchen. I left the door open despite the heat so I could hear her. She was good. In honor of her chosen songs I poured two Jameson's and took hers to her when I went out to fire up the grill.

Back inside, I struggled to balance the proportion of lime juice to the chicken broth and coconut base, and I remembered to add a dash of cayenne pepper just before I served the soup.

We took our soup and whiskey on the balcony and followed with grilled rib-eye steaks, rice, and steamed broccoli. We passed on dessert. Fiona cleared the dishes and then she sat beside me on the chaise lounge.

"That was delicious, Dewy. In return, may I sing for my supper?"

"You already have."

"I was singing what I wanted to sing. I'd like to sing something you want to hear. Give me a request. Something you really like."

"Can you sing *Scotch and Soda?*"

"I've never heard of it. Who does it?"

"Dave Guard. One of the Kingston Trio."

"I don't think I've heard of them. Are they a new group?"

"No. They had their heyday about thirty years ago."

"I'm only twenty-three, Dewy. I don't want to burst your bubble, but it's only been a few years since I found out Paul McCartney started out singing with a group."

"Yeah, the Beatles."

"My goodness, them too? I was thinking of Wings."

"Boy am I old."

"I was kidding. Everyone knows about the Beatles. Shut up and kiss me." She laid down her guitar and snuggled up beside me.

"Don't fret. Just kiss me. Take off all your clothes. We're going to make love on your terrace. I'll put your condom on for you."

And she did, and we did, and it was good. But it wasn't great. In fact, sex hadn't really been great for much of the entire two plus years I had been in graduate school dating much younger women. It's not that I have anything against sexually willing young women. I'm fond of them of them in many ways. But something's missing. Mostly they seem either to be almost totally uninvolved in the art of making love or, like Fiona, so adept that they seem to require little contribution on my part. I believe I prefer women of a certain age.

Women about my age who are still in the game are far more exciting. They know what to do; they know the right moves for seduction. They know how to experience the thrill of the chase, how to say what gives them pleasure, and how to ask what gives you pleasure. They seem to know that each experience is unique and must be appreciated on its own merits and that some nights are better than others.

At our ages, I suspect their nights were often better than mine. If only I had the recovery power I had at twenty with the wisdom I have now; and, if wishes were horses, beggars would ride.

"What's on your mind, Dewy? It seems like you're afraid to let go. Haven't you ever read Kierkegaard? You know, the existential philosopher. You're afraid to take a leap of faith."

"Spare me, Fiona. I took my leap of faith years ago with Martha. I made a bad landing and fractured both ankles."

"Poor baby. What went wrong?"

"I don't know. Maybe Martha grew up or decided to follow her bliss. We were barely out of our teens when we met and married. Twenty year-olds think they're being emotionally honest but what they're good at is emotional self-deception."

"Women my age have developed a greater desire to be honest— particularly emotionally honest. Forty-somethings may be into minor deceptions such as padded bras, cosmetics, wrinkle creams, and eye lifts, but they are fully aware they have put on their rose-colored glasses. As in the theater, they engage in a willing suspension of dis-belief. I believe as Martha grew in consciousness, she realized she hadn't been true to herself. Her newfound sense of emotional hon-esty wouldn't let her continue to cheat and remain in our marriage. She left and took up with her flute instructor. Now they tour the country making and selling wooden flutes and giving concerts."

"Look at yourself, Dewy. You left, took up with women half your age, and started directing plays."

"Yeah. At first, I was bummed out, but I've come to appreciate the gift she gave me—the freedom to be the me I am instead of the misery of trying to be a me I am not in an attempt to please others."

"I'm confused, Dewy. If you weren't 'you' in your twenty-something year relationship, how do you know you're 'you' now?"

"What I'm trying to say, Fiona, is for me, most twenty-something year-old women present mostly the challenge of seduction. Can a forty-three year-old man seduce them? So far I've been generally successful, but where's the thrill beyond sex?"

"No commitment, huh?"

"No, and not much connection. Please don't take this unkindly, Fiona. You are the most self-aware twenty-something I know; but by and large, except for the thrill of the chase, and I haven't had to chase that hard, seducing young women is getting boring."

"Chicks just glom on to you like cockleburs to corduroy, right? Like you were a magnet and they had iron filings in their panties— and shit for brains."

"That's harsh, Fiona. I am fond of you."

"Listen to you, Dewy. It's not a big deal. Most of the girls you've been dating don't look at you as a prospective mate. They see a well-off, interesting guy who doesn't lie, treats them with gentleness and respect, and knows how to show them a good time despite your being glib, self-absorbed, chauvinistic, and wishy-washy."

"That's way harsh, Fiona."

"Oh, Dewy, lighten up. Don't take yourself so seriously. You aren't the only one in your relationships—unless you're a narcissist." She mooned up her face and feigned puppy-love.

"I don't believe you are a narcissist, Dewy, although, as a lowly psychology graduate student, I'm not licensed to make a diagnosis. If you want commitment and connection, commit and connect. That's more likely to happen with a woman closer to your own age."

"You know, Fiona, that's what I've been thinking, too. A woman of a certain age knows much of what I know, has experienced much of what I have experienced, and has a greater chance of touching my soul. When I'm naked with a woman of my years, I am truly naked, vulnerable. I think that's why I'm hesitant to leave and go back out into the real world."

"Now you're talking, Dewy. Now you're getting down to your fear. Even so, it's time for you to move on. It's time to 'Screw your courage to the sticking place.' Is that right? I haven't looked at *Macbeth* since high school."

"That's right on, Fiona."

"Dewy, you've spent the last couple of years doing—doing graduate school, doing graduate students, doing plays, doing whatever. Now it's time to be. Be someone who makes a difference. Be actor. Be director. Be producer. Just be what you will be, and then you will do what comes from that."

"That's really existential, Fiona."

"It's like this, Dewy. If you don't take that assignment in New Orleans, I'll spread a rumor about you that will cause mothers to make their pubescent daughters turn away when you pass, twenty-somethings to cross their legs when they see you coming, and rude boys to point at your crotch and laugh," she said, arching her back and flipping her hair with both hands. I knew what was coming next.

"Now, shut up and ball my brains out one more time. It's your going-away gift. Then I'm going to take my guitar over to the County Cork Pub. The Pennywhistle Rovers said I could sit in with them for the eleven o'clock set."

We made love under the hazy harvest moon. It was not boring, but it was the end.

When Fiona left it was still early enough for me to call Alex at home. I wasn't ready to let him know my real hesitation was my fear of being vulnerable, so when he answered, I attempted a stall.

"Alex, Maybe I could go down second term."

"Dean Halberstam has spring of '98 covered, Dewy. She needs someone to teach and direct now and TVC needs someone to direct *Macbeth* in December. This December. 1997. They'll be looking for a permanent replacement for Hammond. It could be you. They don't pay well, but you don't need the money so much, and it would give you a platform to work from."

"Tell me a little more about the TVC, Alex, especially about that femme fatale and her jealous husband?"

"Most of what I know I got from Radu. Stella Maris has been wardrobe mistress for donkey's years, at least a decade. Recently she's been acting, but this Vladimir guy, I don't think they're married, has never been happy about her involvement in the theater and he particularly resents anyone who pays close attention to her."

"You're telling me to stay away from Stella Maris?"

"Actually, you can't stay away from Stella, old boy. Just stay out of bed with her. Rely on your natural skills and abilities. Do what's right and let the chips fall where they may. I presume you accept this temporary assignment?"

"Not so fast, Alex. Why can't you advise me to stay away from Stella? Because she's my wardrobe mistress?"

"No. Because she's your Lady Macbeth."

"For real?"

"Yes."

"Can she act?"

"She got rave reviews for playing Madge in *Picnic*."

"Well, she can act and she can play a young woman. That's great, but can she play a mature woman? And what about my master's project? I need to get that done so I can get my degree. I don't want these last two years to count for nothing."

"Dewy, Dewy, Dewy, you offend me by suggesting that two years of study at our venerable institution is nothing. No, don't fence with me. Listen. Your master's thesis will be something about *Macbeth*. Staging *Macbeth* without major mishap would be worth a master's degree all by itself, but that won't happen. All productions of *Macbeth* are cursed."

"Think about this. You could show the Weird Sisters to be projections of Macbeth's psyche. Or, if you want something both subtle and profound, direct it so Lady Macbeth is shown as the victim of her husband's vaunting ambition instead of the other way around. I've long thought it could be played that way without changing one word of dialogue. It would be in the acting and in the directing."

"However you work it, Dewy, my lad, videotape your production and turn it in with your director's notebook to supplement your formal thesis. It should be a piece of cake. Now, do you have any other pusillanimous protestations to proffer?"

I was torn between my desire to charge headlong into a challenging production with a dangerous woman and my fear of leaving my cozy nest. Unfortunately, Fiona had taken some of the coziness out of it and Alex was going to take out the rest, but I strained for one more rational objection.

"I'd have to be there in about two weeks. I doubt I'll be able to find a place to live in that short a time."

"That's it? That's all that's holding you back? Then, my boy, have I got news for you. You'll sublet Radu's apartment in the French Quarter completely furnished, sheets and all. He'll sublet it to you while he's in Budapest. I know you can afford it."

I was both out of excuses and warming to the project, anticipating the twin challenges of working with a woman I had been commanded to leave unseduced and directing *Macbeth* without serious mishap.

I got shafted in college when Cap Pickett cast Geoffrey Bales as Macbeth and gave me Macduff. So what if Geoff was six feet and two inches tall and I was a half-inch shy of six feet? So what if Geoff outweighed me by fifty pounds? He moved like an ox, put the emphasis on the wrong syllable, and had an emotional range that ran from A to B.

So what if I was the one who could range from tender weeping when Macduff learns Macbeth's minions slaughtered his wife and children to near-berserk outrage when he learns Macbeth usurped the crown, and then show the chutzpah to call out Macbeth, a much larger foe?

So what if I won the best supporting actor award and Geoff got panned, never to darken the stage again?

At least Geoff didn't score with Melanie Witherspoon, the student playing Lady Macbeth, either. If I ever made such a huge casting mistake as Cap made, I hope I would have the courage to replace the actor. Even if replacing an actor were never necessary, if I accepted Alex's offer, I would have the opportunity to produce a better *Macbeth* than Cap did and maybe even score with Lady Macbeth this time.

"Yes, Alex, I'll do it. When do I leave?"

"You can leave anytime you want as long as you're there by the third of September. Registration starts the Thursday after Labor Day and classes start Monday. I told Dean Halberstam you'd be there."

"You have more confidence in me than I have."

"I have more faith in you than you have. I've never seen you lack for confidence. Remember the ABC's? What you take for self-doubt is really just your fundamental lack of arrogance. You don't doubt your own perceptions but you're willing to accept that someone else may have a different, but valid, point of view. You slow down and think when you stop to listen to others' points of view, Dewy. Don't lose that. Otherwise, you really would be just another arrogant asshole director. We have too many of those as it is."

"Thanks for the affirmation, Alex. There's just one more thing."

"Make it quick. My wife is calling me. It's date night."

"How did Hammond Laidlaw die?"

"Drowned. Radu said Hammond left the cast party for *Picnic* about one A.M. and wasn't seen again, at least not alive. A week later they found his body caught on a snag in the river on the Algiers side. They figure he drank too much, fell in the drink, and drowned. No witnesses. Ruled accidental. End of story."

"Was Hammond involved with Stella?"

"Gotta' go. The little lady is threatening to put me in the doghouse. Goodnight."

"Was Hammond involved with Stella?"

"Don't worry about Ham, Dewy. He's out of the picture. Just stay away from Stella. I'd hate to lose you, too."

Chapter Three

I had a few last-minute details to take care of about subletting my apartment to a couple of graduate students, so it was noon before I left Memphis. The drive south was unremarkable. It had been remarkable in my youth before the interstate system opened and cars routinely had air conditioning, but those days have long since passed.

The ripening cotton in the Mississippi Delta would soon be ready for picking. What had been lush, green vegetation around Jackson last April and May was now yellowed and browned by the unrelenting heat of summer and the inevitable ripening of seed. In mitigation, days were getting shorter.

The four o'clocks, their chemical clocks triggered by the shortening days, were popping open as I stopped near Brookhaven for a box of greasy fried chicken, Cajun-spiced, of course. Why is fast food greasy food? I couldn't keep doing that. My cholesterol and blood pressure were fine, always had been, but recently I started to notice a thickening around my middle. If this chicken would just get me through to New Orleans, I promised myself I'd never eat deep-fried food again, or movie popcorn.

By the time I reached Metairie, the elongated shadows had nearly merged into one dark pool and bats were dive-bombing the insects flitting around street lamps. It was a warm, clear, hazy evening, the kind you generally see in late summer in the humid parts of the South which is any part of the South below the fall line.

Warm, because it was barely the beginning of September. Clear, because there was no significant accumulation of clouds. Hazy, because the prevailing weather pattern brought warm, moist Gulf air swirling up in a slow, giant cyclone from Key West to Brownsville and moved it north until it collided with the cooler, drier, jet stream, anywhere south of Manitoba to north of Memphis creating an airborne micro-droplet miasma.

What humidity fell out of that moisture-laden air in afternoon thunder showers immediately evaporated back into the atmosphere and added to the surface haze, like the haze I had moved through as I crossed Lake Ponchatrain and headed into New Orleans.

That's like the way I thought of New Orleans, warm, clear, and hazy, something warm and welcoming, completely open to be experienced, yet illusive and slightly out of focus. I had always visited New Orleans in the wettest months, May through August. Maybe by late September, after the autumnal equinox, the clearer, drier atmosphere would help keep things in focus. Or, maybe not.

I made my way to the French Quarter easily enough and tried to navigate my way to St. Phillip Street which was not at all easy. The French Quarter's regular grid of one-way streets was made irregular by temporary street closures, some less temporary than others, like Bourbon Street. If those city blocks weren't closed to automobile traffic during peak tourist times, too many people would get their hands run over as they crawled out of bars.

I expected things to be quiet on a Wednesday evening, but it was not so. Maybe this was the last hurrah of the college crowd.

The most popular three blocks of Bourbon Street had been completely given over to pedestrians, but I managed to work my way back around to St. Phillip Street and locate Radu's apartment which was mine through the end of December. I hoped I would get his parking permit too, if he had one, because all the parking places on the street were marked for local permit holders only.

I had to go all the way down to the intersection of North Peters and Ursuline to find a quasi-legal parking space on the edge of a construction site at the French Market and walk back to the Wicca Shop on St. Phillip to get the key from Radu's landlady, a Madame Claire.

I entered the shop and asked for Madame Claire. The clerk informed me that Madame Claire was in her reading room with a client but would be available shortly if I cared to wait, or I could make an appointment and come back at my appointed hour.

I asked what kind of reading Madame Claire did and was informed that she most often read the Tarot. In addition, I learned that she was a gifted psychic, palm reader, numerologist, and astrologer. She was often clairaudient and sometimes clairvoyant.

I told the clerk I came to get the key to Radu's apartment. She looked disappointed, probably at not having an opportunity to sell me something, but she said that if I cared to wait, there was a chair in the back corner where I could sit until Madame could see me. Instead, I browsed and kept an eye on the clerk to see when she went into the Reading Room to inform Madame Claire that I was waiting.

I wandered among aisles abundantly and tightly packed with unusual and fabulous items. Crystals, Mardi Gras masks, pewter figures of witches, wizards, and dragons, stuffed baby alligators, voodoo dolls, candles, powders, crucifixes, statues of Buddha, statues of Jesus, statues of Mary, Stars of David, packages of incense, jars of unguents, vials of aromatic oils, I Ch'ing coins, packets of herbs, yellowroot, sassafras, chunks of white clay, Tarot decks, and a small library of books from *Edgar Cayce, The Sleeping Prophet*, to a recent best-seller, *Embraced by the Light*, numbered among the many native and exotic items on the shelves.

I browsed *Embraced by the Light* and found the experiences the author described to be generally consistent with accounts I had read from cultures spanning two millennia including Sumer and Babylon which she had interpreted through her present-day experience with Protestant Christianity.

Interestingly enough, the author said that all religions were more-or-less valid for some people at some stages of their spiritual development. Her idea of heritable memory storage in body cells seemed to fit in with both Cayce's akashic records and Jung's collective unconscious.

I heard people come out of the reading room.

"Monsieur Spearman."

I found myself looking into a pair of dark brown eyes, widely spaced, set in an oval face with high cheek bones. An olive complexion and a fringe of black, curly hair escaping from a multihued head scarf led me to presume this woman was my landlord.

"You are Madame Claire?"

"In person."

"And you knew who I was because you are clairvoyant?"

"No, I know who you are because my clerk told me the man who will sublet Radu's apartment waits to see me."

"I must have been distracted. I didn't see her go in."

"It is not always necessary to be in the same room or even to open your mouth to communicate, is it Monsieur Spearman? You are an actor, no?"

"Sometimes. Now, I'm mostly a director."

"Communication is not always only by words spoken aloud, no?"

"No, I mean yes, it is not only by the spoken word."

"Good! We have that straightened out. Now, I'll set you up in Radu's apartment. Here are your keys," she said, producing a pair of keys from a pocket in her voluminous green silk skirt. "If you lose keys, come by my shop and tell me. We will have to change the lock. We will not put Radu's photographic print collection at risk of theft."

"You may pay rent for September now and then pay on the first of each month. Rent is late on the sixth. The late fee is ten percent. Both the driveway gate and the person door on the street open with one key. The other key opens the apartment. One parking space in the courtyard is for you."

"Apply at the police station for a resident parking permit. Ask the officer to call me to say you are tenant. They know me. If you have guests, you park legally on the street with your permit; your guests can park in your space in the courtyard."

"Get a Louisiana driver's license since you will be resident more than sixty days. Louisiana law is inherited from the *Code Napoléon*. Among other things, that means the tenant is responsible for all repairs to the inside of a rented domicile. Even so, I have a personal interest in Radu's apartment. If anything happens, do not rely on my clairaudience. Come to the shop and make your report."

"I will."

"Do you have any questions, Monsieur Spearman?"

"Don't you know what they are?"

"Yes, I have Middle-European ancestry, Hungarian and Romanian. My mother is French. Probably a little bit gypsy, too. I am Radu's cousin. Please don't cross the lances with me, Monsieur Spearman. My gifts are gifts, sometimes without joy. I weary of people who toy with me."

"If you want to play with me as a person, Monsieur Spearman, make an effort to know me as a person. If you have courage enough, step into my space. Let me decide if I will step into your space as a human being, as a child of God who lives and loves for her allotted time and then passes on."

"What do you theater people say, Monsieur Spearman? 'Out, out, brief candle. Life is but a walking shadow, a poor player who struts and frets his hour upon the stage and then is heard no more,' no?"

"Yes, 'A tale told by an idiot, full of sound and fury, signifying nothing.' It's from *Macbeth*, Madame Claire. Forgive my rudeness.

I'm uncomfortable with the idea of psychic gifts. I certainly deserve reproof, but, if I may make a rather poor pun, you've given me the sound and fury of an entire *Tempest.*"

"Ah, Monsieur Spearman, you have decided to test the waters, to take a small step into my space, no? Yes, I think I will learn to like you even with your sharp edge that wants softening. Not too much. There's no call to make the silk purse from the sow's ear. Since now you know you do not have to be what others want, you have leave to be what you want," she said, tapping her hand over her heart.

"Forgive me, Monsieur Spearman. You know that already and you wish to retire. When you leave the shop, the courtyard door is the next door on the right. Walk upstairs to the balcony to find the door to number three, an auspicious number."

"No permanent harm will come to you in number three as long as you live in the light. Be careful walking up the stairs. They are as safe as steps can be, but misfortune happens most when we leave one plane for another. But, I talk too much, and you haven't even crossed my palm with silver."

"I'm sorry. Let me write the rent check."

"That was a joke, Monsieur Spearman. Never mind. Yes, you write your rent check now. Leave it with Mademoiselle Parker at the cash register. *Bon soir,* Monsieur Spearman. Oh, Radu asked me to tell you to read the Elday book."

"What's that?"

"I don't know, Monsieur Spearman. I am only the messenger. Now, go with God. Give my regards to Dr. Fellows."

"Who?"

"A dear friend. It will become clear. *Bon soir.*"

I walked up the street and found the person door and the drive-way gate into the courtyard. There was one empty place in the parking area. I retraced my steps to the French Market, got my car, and parked it in the courtyard. I grabbed my luggage, jogged up the steps, and opened the door to number three. Fortunately, the air conditioner had been left on.

Radu's furniture was simple, functional, and neutral. The only obvious splashes of color were provided by a few color photographs among his large collection of black-and-white photographs that hung on nearly every square inch of wall that was more than two feet off the floor. A first glance suggested that half of them were fine art prints, some from photographers I could identify including Walker Evans, Edward Weston, and at least one pint by Diane Arbus.

The other half looked like cast photos from theater productions, probably ones Radu had directed, except for one color photograph of Alfred Drake, the actor who created the Petruchio role for *Kiss Me Kate*, full front, standing slightly behind a redheaded woman in three-quarters profile. Both wore pseudo-Elizabethan costumes.

The photo had an inscription, "Kiss Me, Stella," and was signed by Cole Porter. That must have been a preview or original cast publicity photo from *Kiss Me Kate*. I didn't think Radu was old enough to have seen the original production of *Kiss Me Kate*, much less to have worked it. It opened on Broadway about 50 years ago.

The photograph was well-executed and looked like a publicity shot, not an art composition. Clearly, it didn't belong with the art prints. Even though the man and woman were dressed in clothing that appeared to be Elizabethan, their costuming looked as if it also belonged to the 1940s or early '50s instead of, say the '20s or the '70s. As with current fashion and hairstyles, theatrical period costumes and hairstyles reflect the style of the times in which they are re-created as they attempt to be faithful to their antique roots.

Alfred Drake's hair looked about the same as it did for his entire career. The woman's hair had a late '40s influence on a Restoration not Elizabethan, style with her long, curly tresses cascading seductively over her shoulder, gently caressing her breast, and spilling over the top of her low-cut, push-up bodice, and '40s or early '50s judging by the bubble perched on top.

Even her makeup showed styling more modern than in Shakespeare's day. Her red lipstick and brown eyebrows were several shades too dark for her apricot hair and alabaster complexion. That styling was in vogue around the halfway mark of this century.

It reminded me of Judy Garland's makeup in *Meet Me in St. Louis*. The story was set in 1903-1904. Miss Garland was made up with an over-abundance of lipstick in a hue far too red for modern tastes, woefully out of place for 1903, but fashionable in 1944, the year Vincente Minnelli directed the movie. The woman in the photo had a Marilyn Monroe beauty mark. Like Miss Monroe's, her beauty mark was a bit too dark to seem real. At least her green eyes were undated in their appeal. That publicity photo definitely had come from another time and was out of place.

None of those show photographs were signed, but all of them had show titles and dates. I found cast pictures from shows as diverse as *Carousel* and *Hair* and as alike as *Picnic* and *Pygmalion* starting in 1968 for *Pygmalion* and as recent as this year for *Picnic*. Théatre Vieux Carré produced *Picnic* last March, but Hammond directed it, not Radu.

If these photographs were cast shots from Radu's productions, Radu must have started directing regularly in 1968. That would have made him, at most, an infant when *Kiss Me Kate* ran on Broadway. Why, then, did Radu have the publicity photo from the 1948 production of *Kiss Me Kate* and the cast photo from *Picnic*, which Hammond Laidlaw directed at TVC last March, mixed in with the collection of shows he directed?

Something was off in the *Picnic* photograph, too. I couldn't find Madge. I found one juvenile female who must have been Madge's kid sister, Millie. No one who looked that young would be cast as Madge; she had no chest. All the other women were mature adults including Madge's mother and her next-door neighbor. There was no young woman, no Madge. And next to the picture was a photocopy of a charcoal sketch of the woman in the *Kiss Me Kate* publicity picture. It was a puzzle.

In addition to a modest bedroom with two windows, Radu's apartment included a small kitchen with a table that sat three, a small bathroom with an old-fashioned footed bathtub, and a tiny office or study barely large enough to fit a six-foot library table across its width under the room's only window. Filing cabinets flanked the door.

The study was deep enough to open a file drawer with three feet to spare between it and the library table. Narrow shelf units stood on top of the library table on both sides of the window, their shelves filled with play scripts and a set of well-worn volumes hand-lettered from A to L.

The windows in the study and bedroom and the French doors in the living room opened onto a balcony above the alley that separated this building from the French Quarter Hotel. My balcony looked onto the hotel's balconies, an occluded view.

Indeed, this was my New Orleans, warmly inviting, open to be experienced, and yet puzzling, ambiguously accessible, and slightly out of focus.

Chapter Four

I rose early and made my way to campus. Classes hadn't started so I had no trouble finding a parking place. The departmental secretary said that would soon change. I filled out form after form, one of which would get me a faculty parking sticker, and was ushered into a brief meeting with the academic dean, Dr. Halberstam.

"Welcome to Gudrun Hall, Mr. Spearman. I hope you have settled in without difficulty."

"Thank you, Dean Halberstam. I moved into Radu's apartment without difficulty but I have yet to find my way to his office. I came straight here."

"That is completely understandable, Mr. Spearman. Dr. Righetti may not have told you, but I am also one of the five members of the board of directors of Théâtre Vieux Carré. We pride ourselves on our relationship with TVC, as we call it among ourselves. We expect you to represent Gudrun Hall well when you direct *Macbeth* just as we expect you to have an excellent production of *Four Plays for Coarse Actors* here."

"I shall strive to meet your expectations."

"I am aware, Mr. Spearman, that theater people do not always adhere to the highest standards of personal conduct regarding intimacy. I freely acknowledge that I have been accused of having excessively high standards; nevertheless, we have no graduate students on our campus and the undergraduates are strictly off limits."

"Duly noted, Dean Halberstam," I said, feeling like I had just been punched in the gut.

"Frankly, Mr. Spearman, had we not been desperate for a last-minute substitute, you and I would not be conversing today. Your reputation has preceded you heralding both your high competence and your low morals. Mr. Spearman, I require professional and academic excellence from our faculty. I will accept nothing less."

"I am fully committed to both academic and professional excellence, Dean Halberstam. I believe I will do well at Gudrun Hall."

"I also expect exemplary personal conduct, Mr. Spearman. If you intend less, please leave now."

That was another sucker punch, but I recovered with aplomb.

"I left those intentions in Memphis, Dean Halberstam."

"See that they remain in Memphis, Mr. Spearman. We have no room for misunderstanding or error on this. However, I am mindful of your favorable reputation as a director. It is your production for Gudrun Hall that I wish to discuss this morning. Inform me about the play you are producing here. I am no prude, Mr. Spearman, but I wonder if *Four Plays for Coarse Actors* is suitable for young people. We have our reputation to consider. Mr. Lupeșcu assured me last spring this production would be appropriate. I require your reassurance."

"Actually, Dean Halberstam, the word 'coarse' doesn't mean vulgar in our modern sense although there are a few sight gags that border on tasteless. It means coarse as in rough, unfinished. These four short farces are quite funny."

"Good. We like to present compelling drama and uproarious comedy and we like to include as many students as possible in the productions. However, I wish to impress upon you the gravity of my concern that we not offend our community or the parents of our students with vulgarities. I expect you will excise all profanity."

Since I hadn't read the script, only its summary in the Samuel French catalogue, I didn't know if there were profanities, so I addressed one of her previous concerns.

"With supernumeraries, we could easily cast fifty people. Add large production and front end crews and this can be a huge production with many opportunities to impress parents with their children's performances."

"Excellent, Mr. Spearman, that's what we like to hear. I shan't have an opportunity to read the script and I have no more time for this interview today. Will you be good enough to come to my office tomorrow at ten o'clock and review with me these four plays?"

"Of course, Dean Halberstam."

"I am particularly concerned with the one called '*Il Fornicazione*.' If it means what I believe it to mean, it will be unsuitable. Be prepared to address this particular concern tomorrow."

"Yes, Dean Halberstam."

I have asked two of your colleagues to call on you this morning. Dr. Bridges is an Oxford scholar and head of your department. Dr.

Fellows is an adjunct professor. Mrs. Collins will show you to Professor Lupeșçu's office which is yours for the semester. I shall see you again at ten o'clock, tomorrow. I value promptness."

Prudence dictated that I have no questions, so I exited, followed Mrs. Collins to my office, and sat down to read the entire script of *Four Plays for Coarse Actors*.

At eleven o'clock, two men stopped at my door.

"Spearman, I presume?" said the younger, thinner man who, despite the steamy heat, was dressed in a three-piece, tropical-weight, wool tweed suit. "Please allow me to introduce the Reverend Doctor Chandler Fellows and myself, Maurice Bridges," he said, with a tinge of British accent.

"Mr. Spearman, I am pleased to make your acquaintance," said the shorter, older man who had a decidedly yellow complexion and looked Asian. He was dressed in a gray suit with a black shirt and white clerical collar. "Madame Claire told me yesterday that I would soon meet a tall, fair, and handsome stranger. That must be you."

"How could she know?" I asked. "Is she prescient, too?"

"I jest, Mr. Spearman. Madame Claire, my esteemed friend, would not need to be prescient to know that you and I would meet because we are fellow faculty members. But, yes, she is prescient. I honor her insight and her wisdom."

"I'll keep that in mind, Dr. Fellows."

"The students often refer to me behind my back as 'Dr. Yellow,' probably because of my Chinese mother. I prefer that you call me Chan." He extended his hand.

I took his hand and shook it, and then the slender man extended his hand and we shook hands.

"Maurice," he said. "I don't know what students call me behind my back, but I wouldn't listen. They are often rude and barbarous."

"You must be the one who studied at Oxford."

"Quite right. I serve presently as Associate Professor of Speech and Drama and chairman of the department. I teach communication theory, debate and persuasion, and rhetoric. Chandler is Adjunct Professor of Public Speaking. He also teaches Greek to religious studies students and comparative religion to philosophy students."

"Yes," Chan said, "I'm only part-time. My real job is pastor of St. Andrew's in Gretna."

"Episcopal?"

"An excellent deduction, Mr. Spearman. I suppose the 'St. Andrew' gave it away. Yes, I'm an Episcopal priest, a rare breed in Catholic New Orleans. But, as you will soon discover, people in New Orleans will tolerate almost anything. That's good for me, Mr. Spearman, because I lived three years in India studying at an ashram and I have a Buddhist heritage on my mother's side. I serve a small parish in Gretna. That takes about half my time. To keep my mind active, I also teach here. With the way things are, I'll likely continue part-time teaching here until I retire in about ten years."

"Have your received your class schedule?" Maurice asked.

"Yes. Mrs. Collins gave it to me when I saw the dean."

"Good. All your classrooms and the theater are in this building. I must toddle off now to my luncheon with the theater department heads from Dillard, Loyola, LSU, Tulane, and UNO. We only do this twice a year and I would hate to miss it. Perhaps Chandler can show you our theater," Maurice said, as he turned and strode towards the front door.

"I would be delighted, Mr. Spearman."

"Please call me Dewy."

"Certainly. Dewy. Named for the admiral or for the librarian?"

"Neither. I was named for the Celtic god of the sea."

"Excellent. Mythology has been a joy in my life. I conduct a seminar on mythology every other year. Once, the late Joseph Campbell met with us. Do you follow it much?"

"Not much, Chan. My daughter is the mythology scholar. I suppose some of her learning rubbed off on me. Much of what we deal with in literature, poetry, and theater is modern adaptation of ancient tales. From that I've gained a backdoor knowledge of mythology."

"The basic stories are universal, Dewy. Their presentations change with the culture presenting them much as you might change the color of your stage lighting with a gel. But, 'Lay on,' McDewy, 'and damn'd be him that first cries, Hold, enough.' Just thought I'd show you I've done a bit of the Bard, myself," he said. "I once played Puck in *A Midsummer Night's Dream*. But, I've rambled on too long. Let me take you to your theater."

It was a large, proscenium arch theater. The arch was thirty feet wide with another dozen feet off-stage left and right. The stage was twenty-six feet deep with an additional six-foot apron in front of the arch. Behind the traveling show curtain was a teaser with a set of accompanying tormentors, all black. Overhead, I counted eight battens. Four battens were hung with sets of tormentors with borders. The other four were electrified and presently hung with lights. The cycloramic backdrop was white and was lit from below.

The battens were hung with a steel counter-balance system with tension blocks centered at three-foot intervals from the arch to the cyclorama on stage left. The arbors for the tension blocks were bolted into the floor and were set about two feet beyond the edges of a line from the arch to the cyclorama. All the battens were hung from a 32-foot fly loft. If we had any desire to do so, we could stage *Peter Pan*, *Angels in America*, or any flying show.

The main floor seated about 600 people and the balcony seated another 150. The light booth and follow spots were in the back of the balcony. A light bar had been hung from the ceiling. A sunken orchestra pit and a three-foot aisle separated the stage from the first row of seats. Access to the under stage, which had about seven feet of clearance, was through the orchestra pit. It was a good performance space for the two shows this term, *Four Plays for Coarse Actors* and *A Funny Thing Happened on the Way to the Forum*.

I wondered if Dean Halberstam knew *Forum* was populated with courtesans, eunuchs, and a procurer. Philia, the ingénue around whom the plot turns, is brought to Rome by Marcus, the procurer, who has a contract to supply Miles Gloriosus, the victorious Roman captain, with a virgin bride. Before Marcus can deliver Philia to the captain, she catches the eye of a lecherous, ageing senator and then falls in love with the senator's stripling son. Both father and son have designs on Philia—the old man to bed her, the young man to wed her—and Miles discovers Philia, his putative virgin fiancée, is his twin sister from whom he has been separated since infancy. The twins reunite with their father who has been searching for them since they were stolen in infancy by pirates.

Maurice would direct *Forum*, but since I hadn't taken the opportunity of informing Dean Halberstam of the *Fourm*'s salacious characters during the third-degree interrogation she gave me over *Four Plays for Coarse Actors*, I wondered if the good dean and I were going to tangle about that, too.

Chapter Five

Chan was the one who had to say, "Hold, enough," and left to tend his flock, but not before he pointed me in the direction of the campus cafeteria. After lunching alone I returned to the office. I made phone calls to Alex and to my daughter to give them the phone numbers to my office at Gudrun Hall and to Radu's apartment.

Radu prepared a public flyer announcing an open casting call for *Four Plays for Coarse Actors*, which I posted on the theater's front door, and a private list of recommendations of whom to cast in various roles. I spent the afternoon combing through the script of *Four Plays* and working on my director's notebook.

At five o'clock, I grabbed a turkey sandwich from the student grill and headed back to the French Quarter. I parked at the apartment and walked the six blocks to TVC. The door was unlocked so I let myself in.

For this show the stage had been set in a square on the floor. The audience would surround the stage on all four sides and be seated on risers that began at floor level beyond a three-foot aisle surrounding the acting space. Three sets of risers were set on three sides of the square and the two open spaces at the common corners were filled in with risers on diagonals to make a solid, squared horseshoe.

The fourth set of risers had been placed at the bottom of the open horseshoe with open passageways at each end as aisles for patrons to make their way to their seats and for actors to make their entrances and exits.

Little was happening at the moment. I sat on the end of the top row of the north bank of risers and counted the seats in the house. I don't know why, but it was a minor compulsion of mine. In social situations, at least ones where people were fairly stationary, and always in theatrical productions, I count how many people are present. Weird, perhaps, but harmless.

The four blocks of seats had six tiers of fifteen seats each. That totaled 360. In addition, the two wedge-shaped risers joining the north bank to the east and the west banks would seat 50 people each for a total capacity of 460 patrons.

With a ticket price of $15 on Wednesdays and Thursdays and $20 on Fridays and Saturdays, *Suddenly* had the potential of pulling in $6,900 weekdays and $9,200 weekends. That could gross as much as $32,000 a week, minus the houses seats of course, making a potential take of $125,000 for the scheduled four-week run.

As I was sitting in the semidarkness calculating revenue, a short, burly man in a dark gray business suit walked across the set coming from the direction of the front office. A tall, gangly, scruffy-looking man dressed in black followed closely behind him.

"No, I told you," burly man said. "Twenty-five percent is it."

"But now I have more expenses. I need fifty percent," gangly man replied.

"No."

"If I don't get fifty percent, you'll be sorry."

"Forget it, Spider. You're a drunk with a bad rep. Who'd believe you? And if you do anything stupid I'll fire your ass in a New York minute. Then you'll get zero percent and be outa' work. Who else would hire a drunk like you? Shut up and get back to work."

Burly man strode up my aisle and headed for the front door without noticing me. Gangly man noticed me.

"Mind your own damn business," gangly man growled, and then he pulled a half-pint bottle of vodka out of his back pocket, took a large slug, capped and pocketed the bottle, wiped his mouth on the back of his arm, and rambled over to the light booth. The lights came up and a chubby, balding man came out of the light booth and made his way over to me.

"Who are you?

"Dewy Spearman."

"Glad to meet you. I look forward to your production of the Scottish play. I'm Pete Vanlandingham, director of this show, board member, and high school drama teacher. I see you met Spider."

"The guy with the bottle?"

"Yes, the bottle. He's rough around the edges and we worry about his drinking. I just know he's going to fall off a catwalk one day. He's not too sociable, but he knows his stuff and he's always here. I think he even sleeps here. Good lighting directors are hard to find. I'm afraid we're stuck with Spider."

"Can he take direction?"

"He works best if you tell him what you want the effect to be and let him deliver it. Just don't expect much in the way of social graces. I start rehearsal in about five minutes if everyone shows up on time. Why don't you stick around and watch."

I watched Pete rehearse *Suddenly Last Summer* which is performed in one act. The show would go up in eight days, so Pete was in the panic stage of rehearsal.

The blocking had been worked out and the actors should have memorized their lines, but the actor who played Dr. Krucrowitz, 'Dr. Sugar,' as Mrs. Venable calls him, kept muffing his.

"I'm sorry, Pete," the young actor said. "I can't keep these lines straight. They're so much alike. 'Yes, tell me more, uhmm,' and more 'uhmm.' I don't get to really say anything. It's frustrating."

"I understand your concern, Lance, but that's the way Tennessee Williams wrote it. 'Dr. Sugar' is using a technique called Rogerian counseling."

"He oughta' be using the Stanislavski technique like I do."

"Dear Lance," Pete said, and paused for a moment. "Listen to me carefully. I'm going to say this one more time. Take notes if you have to, but, for God's sake, get this and get it now. You can use the Stanislavski method, or technique, to play 'Dr Sugar' if it works for you. But, in this play, the character of Dr. Krucrowitz—'Dr, Sugar'—uses a therapy technique called Rogerian counseling to help pull Catherine's story out of her."

"Mrs. V wants to force Catherine, her niece, to have a frontal lobotomy, literally to have Catherine's story cut out of her consciousness, and she's offered Dr. Sugar a new wing at Lyons View Hospital to entice him into doing it."

"Mrs. V will brook no challenge to her delusional belief that her precious son, Sebastian, was an *artiste* who forsook the pursuit of women to pursue literary excellence. She is not able to acknowledge that Sebastian was a dilettante and a third-rate poet who used his literary pretention and her prestigious presence, then Catherine's beautiful presence when Mrs. V's beauty faded, as his entrée into European social circles from which he could arrange clandestine homosexual encounters.

"You mean, like spying?"

"What? Oh, clandestine. No, not spying, Lance. Secret."

"O.K. I get it. Sebastian hadn't come out."

"Hardly anyone had in the 1930s. As I was saying, Catherine was with Sebastian on his last trip made at the nadir of the Great Depression. Catherine was with Sebastian on a secluded public beach in Spain to which Sebastian had lured a large number of urchin boys by offering them candy. To hear Catherine tell it, this gang of destitute children attacked Sebastian and devoured him as Catherine looked on, horrified."

"Preposterous, says Mrs. V., Sebastian collapsed and died of a heart attack."

"Not so fast, says Dr. Sugar. I will not perform a lobotomy on Catherine until I have heard her full story."

"Unfortunately, Catherine is so traumatized that Dr. Sugar has to give her an injection of truth serum to get her to talk at all, and even with that he has to tease the story out of her bit by bit. He's using the Rogerian counseling technique to do it. Catherine's story is what this show is about, and getting it out is your job, Lance. You know that. So do it as Williams wrote it."

"Of course, Pete, I know that. But I still say the dialogue sucks."

"When you write your own Pulitzer Prize-winning plays, you can write dialogue that doesn't suck. In the meantime, pick up your script and use it. After rehearsal, woodshed your lines. Think of it as a professional challenge."

"O.K., Pete. I'm a professional. I'll do my job. But why do we have to do this in the round? I always have my back to someone."

"Olivier, Richardson, Wells, and Burton act with their backs to the audience. Why don't you try it, Lance. Stretch yourself."

No one said anything for about ten seconds.

"O.K.", Pete said, turning to the others. "Everybody take ten while Lance runs through his lines."

Pete shook his head as he walked over to me.

"Lance is such a beautiful boy, but he has difficulty seeing the larger picture. If I can keep him focused on getting Catherine's story out, I can make this work. Good luck when you direct him in the Scottish play."

"He's too old for Fleance. Is he cast as Macduff?"

"No, as Macbeth."

"No!"

"Yes."

"Who did that?"

"Mrs. Boudron, the president and chief benefactor of this not-for-profit corporation. At her insistence the board hired Lance for the season as our first repertory actor. He's also conducting acting workshops for young people. She promised him Macbeth."

"I'm in deep trouble, Pete. I've only seen this little bit of his work, but I'm willing to bet this is about as good as he gets. If he could nail his lines, I could see him playing Chris in *The Milk Train Doesn't Stop Here Anymore*, Brick in *Cat on a Hot Tin Roof*, and maybe Lancelot in *Camelot* if he can sing, any role that calls for a beautiful, tanned, southern California bland, self-absorbed boy-man."

"Yes, Dewy, he does have that kind of arrogant beauty."

"That's what I see, Pete. It's going to be an incredible stretch for Lance to give an authentic performance as Macbeth, particularly the way I want Macbeth played."

"Better you than me," Pete said, as he headed to the lavatory.

I walked down the risers and was met by burly man.

"Who are you?" he demanded.

"Dewy Spearman. Who are you?"

"I'm Ellis Boudron. I'm the business manager. You're contracted to direct *Macbeth*. What are you doing here now?"

His tone was belligerent and he had the same last name as the doyenne of this theater. He must be the 'no-count son' Alex had spoken of. Clearly Ellis Boudron was no real theater person. He didn't honor the superstition about not referring to the Scottish play as *Macbeth* in any theater—ever.

Alex had warned me that Community Theater would be a political minefield. This one was beginning to look like Bosnia. I decided to play it cool and see how things developed.

"I just got to town and came by to look at the theater. Pete invited me to watch."

"Pete," Ellis yelled in the direction of the lavatory. "You invite Spearman?"

"Sure, Ellis," Pete's voice crooned back.

"Well, keep outta' the way, Spearman, and mind your own damn business. When you direct here, you run the actors on the stage. I run everything else. Keep that in mind and we'll get along just fine. But you mess with my business, I mess with you. You understand?"

"I think I've got the pic—"

I didn't get to finish my word because an over-sized crescent wrench hit the floor between us making a solid, metallic bang. Ellis didn't even look up.

"Spider, I know you dropped that on purpose, but that won't make no diff'rence. Everything stays the same. Now get back to the light booth."

I looked up and watched Spider dance gracefully over the open grid-work of beams and planks that made up the overhead structure. I'll give him one thing. He was agile for a drunk.

Ellis continued to focus his attention on me.

"Close call," I said.

"Just mind your own friggin' business or maybe next time that wrench won't miss."

Ellis turned and strode toward the office. Pete and the four actors were drifting back to the set. This seemed like a good time to leave and I started for the front door. I waved at Pete as I went. He called out and told me to be sure to come to the preview in a week.

Before I got to the door, gangly man swung down from the grid.

"You directing the Scottish play?"

"Yes, I am."

"I'm Spider, your lighting director. Tell me what you want and I'll give it a go. But give me plenty of notice. We change equipment a lot and I want to make sure I've got what you need."

"O.K. I'll have my director's notebook done in a month."

"Right. And a word to the wise: don't mess with Boudron. If you need something, come see me, but quiet like."

"What?" I asked Spider, but he had already swung back up into the grid work like a tailless spider monkey and faded to black against the unlit ceiling. I wanted to find out what he was talking about but I didn't want the attention paid to me that would come from calling out after him.

I certainly didn't want to follow him up into the grid work to get a clarification of his remark, so I walked out of the theater, crossed the street to the Lafitte Lounge, and took a table on the balcony where I could see both the front door and the stage door so I could catch Spider as he came out.

As I sipped McLeod's Isle of Skye Scotch on the rocks, I worked on my director's notebook for *Four Plays* with one eye and kept my other eye on the theater doors.

About ten o'clock, Ellis left by the front door followed by Pete and the four actors. Spider left by the stage door which he locked behind him. He turned up the street.

I left money on the table and dashed downstairs to catch up with Spider, but he had a good start and his legs were much longer than mine. I was doing well just to keep pace which I did for several blocks until Spider entered a bar just off Bourbon Street.

I drew up at the door and slipped in. Spider was sitting at the end of the bar and talking quietly to a young, slender, Eurasian woman. He pulled a wad of money out of his pocket, gave it to her, and then stood up and headed for the front door.

That seemed suspicious. I turned to face the wall to prevent Spider from recognizing me. After he passed, I followed him. He walked over to Rampart Street and entered a storefront building. I paused a moment and then I followed him inside keeping my head down to avoid detection. I found myself standing in the back of a meeting hall with a meeting in progress in front of me.

Spider stood on the aisle in the third row and addressed the group. "Hi, my name is Spider and I'm an alcoholic. It's been seven months and four days since I had a drink."

I slipped out the door and walked home wondering why Spider lied. Only three hours ago he had taken a pull from his vodka bottle.

At the apartment, I found a note in the mailbox, an invitation printed on ivory vellum paper and embossed with a gold crest. Clotilde Boudron requested the pleasure of my company at a dinner party to be held in my honor at eight o'clock P.M. on Friday, September 26, at Maison Boudron to allow me to meet the principal persons involved in the Théatre Vieux Carré. Black tie was optional and I was authorized to bring a companion.

I supposed Ellis would be there, too. That could prove disruptive to a social occasion. Sooner or later, Ellis and I were going to face off.

Chapter Six

I posted extra notices of the casting call before my ten o'clock meeting with Dean Halberstam. When I was ushered into her office I had with me my annotated copy of *Four Plays for Coarse Actors* to answer her questions about the material.

The good dean was sitting perfectly composed in her high-back executive office chair. Despite the sultry, early-September New Orleans weather, her hair was flawlessly coiffed. I could not find even one wrinkle on her royal blue, raw silk suit which elegantly set off her pale, Nordic complexion and her flaxen hair. Her rose cravat added and additional touch of color and style.

"Thank you for your promptness, Mr. Spearman. Tell me about *Four Plays for Coarse Actors*."

"Certainly, Dean Halberstam. *Four Plays* was written by Michael Green for production at the Edinburgh Fringe Festival. The four short farces are written to lampoon noted works, authors, or genres, and can all be played in one evening."

"Do you suppose you can summarize all four of them for me in thirty minutes? I have been called to a special meeting on the budget and I must keep our meeting brief."

"Certainly," I said. "The first of the four plays, *Streuth*, is a spoof of British cozies."

"Cozies?"

"Cozies are murder mysteries set in a closed location like a snow-bound inn, locked railway car, or island retreat. In this cozy, the characters are caricatures. The Inspector walks with a heavy step, wears his hat indoors, and presents himself as the image of Captain Ahab on a bad day."

"Mr. D'Arcy, the middle-aged master of the household, is to be played by a very young man who must wear grotesque makeup to appear old enough. Mrs. D'Arcy is to be played by a woman who probably got the role because she was the only member of the acting troupe who had a recreation room large enough to hold a rehearsal."

"Mrs. D'Arcy has no talent and has a 'low-class' accent which she unsuccessfully disguises to appear middle class which leads us to believe she should actually be the cook."

"The D'Arcy son, Hubert, doesn't move from his mark during the entire play and incessantly rocks back and forth with his eyes fixed steadily on the audience, except when he's reading his lines from a cheat sheet inside his cigarette case."

"The Major is a veritable Colonel Blimp with an ill-fitting monocle and ad lib lines such as 'By Jove,' 'what, what,' and 'tally ho,' that he inserts at random."

"So far, Mr. Spearman, that all seems innocent enough."

"Please, call me Dewy."

"I prefer more formal titles of address, Mr. Spearman."

"Well, it is a farce, Dr. Halberstam," I said, echoing her formality by using her credentialed title, but I was not thrilled about doing it.

"It's supposed to be light and innocent, yet it has its gruesome moments. That's why we use a mannequin to play Henry, the corpse whose head falls off. Among other bits, James, the butler, who walks like Quasimodo and speaks like Mr. Smee from the old Disney film version of Peter Pan, spends most of his time holding up the set which appears on the verge of imminent collapse."

"Cook, who wears her cap pulled down and stumbles about, is played as if she were a refined, middle-aged lady who is attempting to speak as if she were low-class."

"Mr. Spearman, since we draw our students mainly from the Southern United States, I wonder if we can accomplish subtle differences among what appear to be British accents."

Did I see the faintest of twinkles in her ice-blue eyes?

"Right, Dean Halberstam, I'll have Cook speak Cajun with perfect diction and enunciation. Mrs. D'Arcy will speak Standard English using only the present tense and dropping many word endings."

"The Vicar, the play's villain, has a bushy black beard, rolls his eyes, and silently, but obviously, mouths other people's speeches. The Prompter, who may actually have to give an errant actor the correct line, is supposed to be highly visible throughout the play waving a script and calling out lines from time to time whether needed or not. And that's the cast of the first of the four shows."

"Let me understand, Mr. Spearman. The Vicar mouths everyone's speeches but does not speak them. The Prompter speaks other character's lines randomly whether they are needed as prompts or not. The point of that is…?"

"Humor, Dean Halberstam."

"Humor?"

"Yes."

"Well then, can you summarize the plot for me?"

"There's not a plot, really—just a series of sight gags."

"Does anyone curse?"

"No."

"Does anyone touch anyone else suggestively?"

"No."

"Does anyone touch his, hers, or anyone's genitals?"

"One stage movement hints at that possibility. Hubert misses his mother's outstretched teacup and absent-mindedly pours a pot of tea into her lap; but, being the lady she is, she keeps her hands in sight and out of her crotch. Will that be acceptable?"

I was beginning to sound irritated, which I truly was, by Dean Halberstam's apparent lack of humor.

"I suppose so, Mr., Spearman," she answered, "but again, I warn you; I will not accept vulgarity. What else I should know about?"

I chose to ignore my irritation and soldiered on.

"Nothing, really, just more sight gags."

"Then tell me about the second of the four plays, *Il Fornicazione*. That is the one I am concerned about. I believe that means 'The Fornicator'. That is unacceptable."

She was irritating me more. I hadn't chosen this. Radu chose it. Why hadn't she given him the third degree?

"Well, nobody gets naked," I replied, perhaps a bit testily.

"I should hope not. There's enough of that in the French Quarter. I will not tolerate nudity at Gudrun Hall."

I thought she was seriously considering that we might attempt nudity, but I wasn't sure.

"My Italian is poor, Dean Halberstam, but Michael Green translated *Il Fornicazione* as 'The Adulterer'. It's not a steamy grab fest. It's a spoof of Grand Opera in general. It plays like a badly written romance novel, a real bodice-ripper."

"Bodice-ripper?

"Yes. A bodice-ripper. The term is a modern one generally applied to formulaic romance novels in which a single woman, initially reluctant to respond to the overtures of a wealthy, powerful man, gives in to her lustful desires and, figuratively or literally, rips open her bodice to show her passion."

"We'll have none of that at Gudrun Hall, Mr. Spearman."

"Allow me to finish, Dean Halberstam. *Il Fornicazione* is a spoof, not an example, and it offers opportunity for a cast of thousands— two dozen, anyway, including six principal players and any number of attendants, huntsmen, and retainers. Everyone who comes for auditions and is not otherwise cast will be one of these supernumeraries."

"Splendid, Mr. Spearman. We like as many students as possible to be involved. Please consult Dr. Bridges to find a less-provocative title for *Il Fornicazione*. Now, tell me about the plot. I trust we will get back to the ripped bodice in a moment, but I shall not interrupt until you have finished."

"Thank you, Dean Halberstam. Basically, while the elderly Count Formaggio is out hunting with his many retainers, the supernumeraries I mentioned before, his younger wife receives her even-younger lover, Alfonzo, who turns out to be the count's long-lost son by his deceased first wife."

"Is there any inappropriate touching?"

"No, except possibly for one sight gag. In a fit of clumsiness, Alfonzo trips and, falling, grabs the countess' gown ripping it open and exposing her undergarments—the bodice-ripper spoof. It'll a take a bit of rehearsal to get it just right."

"As long as she is wearing a sufficiency of undergarments, that's far less salacious than Rhett and Scarlett's famous staircase scene. I suppose we can live with that."

I thought it best not to mention the near-castration scene in which Alfonzo, before discovering his true paternity, boasts that he will kill Formaggio to steal away the Countess and brandishes his dagger to show his resolve. The Countess, who has her own plan, swats down Alfonzo's dagger, unfortunately, into his crotch, and he sings soprano for a while. We'd just surprise the good dean with that bit.

"There's a lot of dying and rising up to sing some more before dying again and a bit with the maid's organizing six men to carry the count's body out, as in Hamlet, which leads to further disaster because the count continually slips off their hands."

"That's quite involved to say the least, Mr. Spearman. Does the production take as long as your telling of it?"

I no longer believed Dean Halberstam had been serious about not interrupting. Maybe she had a control issue.

"Not really, Dean Halberstam. There's much more than I've told you, but it takes longer to explain every bit of business than it takes to do it, after the actors have been schooled to performance level, of course."

"I've little time remaining for this conversation, Mr. Spearman. What difficulties might there be in the other two parts of this play. Is there anything in the other two I should concern myself with?"

"I don't believe so. *A Collier's Tuesday Tea* is a spoof of D. H. Lawrence."

"Not *Sons and Lovers?*"

"Only with respect to the son who, to his father's dismay, refuses to work in the coal mines. There is no sex, no nudity, no grabbing, and no cussing. So we're O.K. there.

"Quickly, I'm out of time. What about the fourth play?"

"It parodies Shakespeare's comedies. All of them. "

"Is it bawdier than the Bard?"

"Not really. Nurse, who continually remarks about her equipage for her profession, is a male stuffed with two soccer balls to show that fitness. One soccer ball falls out and bounces around on stage as Nurse rushes off in embarrassment."

"Bawdy, but not offensive."

"Yes, Dean Halberstam. Another possible concern involves Delia, the maiden who disguises herself as a boy and continually baits her swain, Dronio, to see past her disguise and recognize her as Delia which Dronio is unable to do until the disguised Delia drops her hat and bends over to pick it up. Then he recognizes her."

"That's as raunchy as it gets."

I was surprised Dean Halberstam said 'raunchy.' I would have expected 'lewd,' or something more formal and more pejorative, 'lascivious,' perhaps.

"I'm afraid so, Dean Halberstam. We could replace *All's Well That Ends As You Like It* with something less bawdy, but we wouldn't be able to put nearly as many students on stage." I was hoping the possibility of losing her opportunity to have me showcase a large number of students would override any more thoughts she may have about dropping *All's Well*. It would be silly to print *Four Plays for Coarse Actors* on the playbill and then stage only three plays. With four weeks and two days remaining until opening curtain, I'd have to scramble to get anything to replace *All's Well*.

"Mr. Spearman, how will you ever get four shows produced in one month?"

"I intend to enlist four assistant directors, Dean Halberstam, and Radu left recommendations of whom to cast which make my job easier. I have faith Radu would not recommend incompetent actors."

"May I see the list?"

I handed her the list. She studied it for a moment and handed it back. "Susannah Coumo is not enrolled this term. You'll have to find someone else. I must leave to attend my meeting. I have no more time for vetting these plays."

I rose to leave but she signaled with her hand that she was not ready to dismiss me just yet.

"Frankly, Mr. Spearman, your reputation as a rake has preceded you. Your private life is your own, but I will not have it spilling over into your duties and responsibilities at Gudrun Hall and I will not stand for your seducing my students. I will not hesitate to fire you in the middle of the term, even in the middle of your production, if I hear of any dalliance with our students. You are warned."

She nodded to let me know I was dismissed. Without further words, she ushered me out and we went our separate ways. I guess I knew where I stood. I was a threat to the chastity and morality of the young ladies of Gudrun Hall and my behavior would be closely scrutinized by an ice princess who held my job in her hands.

I spent Friday, Saturday, and Sunday working on my director's notebook and preparing for my classes. On Sunday and Monday evenings I held auditions. In the end, after two nights of auditions, I followed Radu's recommendations for the most part.

Roger Bolen, whom he had recommended to play the Inspector in Strueth, also had not returned to college. I cast in that role D'Wayne Anders, a student from Jamaica who actually had a British accent.

Henry Strebbing, whom Radu had recommended to play Alfonzo in *Il Fornicazione*, just wouldn't do. He sang too well. I asked him to be my choral director and coach the supernumeraries in the Huntsmen's Chorus, which, contrary to the rest of the show, is supposed to be sung well and frequently.

For Alfonzo, I cast Rich Hilley, a non-singing actor who had not been on campus the previous year. Unfortunately, Rich was a bean pole, so we'd just have to make the window from which he enters very small and have him unfold like Mr. Bean to make it funny.

Rich would also give a 'Mutt and Jeff' flavor to the scene by playing against Annie Mirada as Countess. Annie outweighed Rich by sixty pounds. Since she had the height to go with her bulk, I decided to play it Wagnerian and let her sing one really great note at the end.

For Delia, I took a chance on Susan Riley, an entering freshman. As far as I could tell, Susan was shy and had been put up to reading by some of her friends. In her casual conversation she sounded like a crowd-pleasing adolescent, but in her reading voice I heard the solid self-assurance of a girl who was on the verge of becoming a woman, a self-conscious child who could, with proper encouragement, become a self-confident adult, an ugly duckling who could, perhaps overnight, become a graceful swan, a Delia who could flirt confidently with Dronio. Not that Susan was ugly. Quite the contrary.

What was I thinking? I left Memphis resolved to swear off involvements with women young enough to be my daughter, definitely ones who could be my students, but here I was thinking how I could help this one develop into a woman. My challenge would be to help her become a woman without getting into her bed to do it.

I also recruited four director's assistants, one for each of the four plays, with Henry Strebbing assigned to *Il Fornicazione*.

I posted the cast list on the theater door on Tuesday informing everyone that rehearsals would be Sunday through Thursday at seven P.M. beginning immediately.

I went back to Radu's office, mine for the semester, and settled in. I explored his collection of director's notebooks. He had one to match each of the show photographs hanging in his apartment except for *Kiss Me Kate*. He even had Hammond Laidlaw's notebook for *Picnic* which had been produced at TVC last March. I started reading it. It was as much a journal as it was a director's notebook.

I learned Hammond had asked Spider to flood the backyard scene of *Picnic*, which they staged in the round, with a dozen snooded spots, but Spider said they didn't have any. Hammond made a note that they had them the previous year when he staged *The Lark*. According to Hammond's notes, Spider claimed they'd been sold as surplus.

I read what must have been Hammond's draft of a memo to Ellis Boudron requesting, none too politely, that Ellis get busy and apply for a grant to buy new spots. Ellis must have been successful because Hammond noted that eighteen snooded spots had come in on February 15th which would have been just before the show opened.

I hadn't seen any sign of snooded spots on my visit to TVC. I made a mental note to ask Spider about them because I would need several of them to light the banquet scene and one more, fitted with a special gel, to highlight Banquo's ghost. I could use that same special for Macbeth's famous dagger speech, too. Add in some special makeup and I could make both Banquo's ghost and the dagger glow.

Before I left for dinner, I flipped through the rest of the notebook and saw that several entries had been marked with a yellow highlighting pen, but I didn't have time to read them.

I grabbed a sandwich at the college grill and went back to start rehearsal. I had four complete casts with no overlapping players. In the legitimate theater we would have done all four plays with about eight actors. Some actors, like Green's Coarse Actor, would even play multiple parts in each play. In college productions, giving as many people as possible a chance to be on stage is a prime objective regardless of how difficult it makes the director's life.

Promptly at seven P.M., I gave a speech about the way we would work rehearsals. I organized the four casts, assigned them to separate rehearsal classrooms, and instructed each of the director's assistants to have their cast read the script aloud continually until ten P.M.

Before I dismissed them to their respective rehearsal rooms, I issued my challenge. "I cannot make you an actor, but I can help you make yourself an actor. I can't give you more talent, but I can help you develop the talent you have. To do that, I require something of you. No matter how small or great your talent, you can always have great commitment. I require great commitment."

"I expect you to report on time for each rehearsal. I expect you to report by call time for each show. I expect you to memorize your lines. I expect you to master your blocking. I expect you to say only 'thank you' when I give you a director's note. I expect you to be silent while rehearsal is in progress unless your character is speaking on stage. I also expect you to abide by the traditional customs of the theater including the custom of referring to the December production at TVC as 'the Scottish play' when you are inside any theater."

"All of you are capable of meeting my expectations. You have the capacity. I'll help you with the skill. What remains to be seen is whether you have the will. That's up to you."

"If anyone thinks he or she cannot live up to my expectations, see me tomorrow and I'll find your replacement. Otherwise, go to your rehearsal rooms and start woodshedding. We can't get very far until you get the scripts out of your hands, so memorize quickly. Now, go to your rooms and start reading."

The first week of rehearsal went well. I did a rough blocking of each show in turn. I spent most of the weekend preparing props and building the set with the backstage crew. On the third Monday, I had each of the four casts walk through a staged rehearsal of their play once each evening and run lines afterwards.

All the technical problems had been soluble, and I didn't run into my first personnel problem until Friday of the third week, the Friday of Clotilde Boudron's dinner party to be held in my honor, when Susan Riley showed up at my office. She had been doing well as Delia and had seemed particularly attentive to my direction.

"Professor Spearman."

"Please, call me Dewy."

"Dewy, I want to do the show, but I just got a boyfriend and he wants me skip closing night and go to his fraternity party. I can't be in two places at the same time. I want to do the show, but I like having a boyfriend. I've never had one before and I don't want to lose him. What should I do?"

"What do you want to do?" I asked, showing the wisdom of a modern-day Solomon.

"Both," she replied, restoring my humility.

"You've told me you can't do both. Are you sure you can't do both? I don't know how late the fraternity party goes on, but you'll be through with the show by ten-thirty. You'll miss the cast party if you leave then, but you could get to the fraternity party before it's over. I doubt the fraternity party will even start before ten-thirty."

"I think I could," Susan replied, "but he says he doesn't want to miss a minute of the party. Besides, there's a shrimp boil before the party and he wants me to go to that with him, too. He said if I'm going to be his girl I'd better be there with him all evening. I think it's a macho thing."

"You know what happens if you don't show for a performance?"

"Someone told me the stage manager fills in for an actor who isn't there or can't go on, even if he has to do it with script in hand."

"That's pretty much what happens. In our show, I don't think Bubba Phrydas would make a convincing Delia. He'd probably draft one of the women assistant directors or maybe the wardrobe mistress. But that's not what I mean. Do you know what would happen to you if you don't show up for a performance?'

"I'd never act again?" She smiled a coy smile with her eyes half-closed, her mouth half-open, and her lips glistening.

"Not in this theater and maybe not in any other. If you were in the hospital or wracked with contagion, we would adjust and you would be forgiven. If you fail to show simply because you'd rather do something else that evening, we'll still adjust, but you'd be cut, possibly forever. Word gets around. It's the discipline of the theater. Actors act, directors direct, techies tech, and no-shows are shown the door. They aren't welcome back. That's just the way it is."

Her smile turned pouty—a really cute pout.

"I like having a boyfriend. He's my first one. I didn't have boyfriends in high school. I went to a Catholic girls' boarding school. I really like this guy. He's cute."

"How well do you like yourself?"

"I don't understand. What do you mean?"

"It's not complicated. If you respect yourself, you will honor your commitments. If you don't respect yourself, you will bow to the will of others."

"So, you're saying that if I have self-respect, I'll do the show, and if I ditch the show, I'm an ignorant slut who would rather please my jerk boyfriend than please myself."

"I wouldn't put it exactly that way, but you're on the right track. I say that any boy who demands that you conform to his will instead of encouraging you to fulfill yourself is a selfish, lily-livered bully who is unworthy of your love."

"That's way brutal."

"Life can be brutal. Choices can be tough. This choice is yours unless you allow someone else to make it for you. I want you in the show, Susan. I've been watching you. You're good and we need you. But, don't do it to please me. For me, that choice would be easy. An attractive woman like you should have no trouble finding boyfriends. Make whatever choice you need to make to honor who you are, Susan. Be true to yourself. If you don't do the show, I'll adjust, but you'll never perform here again."

"I'm not sure what to do."

"I invite you to consider, Susan, whether you want a boyfriend who demands that you meet his needs while denying yours. Please don't answer me now. Go and think about it. Don't tell me whether you will or won't show up for the last performance. Either do or do not, and learn from the experience. O.K.?"

"I thought you'd try to talk me into it."

"Life is full of surprises, Susan."

"O.K.," she replied, "I'll do what you ask. And if I lose my boy-friend over it, you can escort me to the cast party." Her smile had returned. Even her eyes were beaming. She was dangling her hook.

"Thank you for your invitation, Susan. It's not seemly for me to date my students."

"My older sister is a graduate student in Memphis. She says you dated plenty of students there."

"I was a student, too. Yes, the students I dated were younger than I, but they were graduate students, not undergraduate students, and they weren't my students. You are both."

"Well, I'll see you at rehearsal, Dewy. Keep an open mind on es-corting me to the cast party," she said, tossing her auburn hair in both directions as she left my office. I couldn't help noticing her der-riere sway seductively as she walked.

She'd baited her hook. Catholic boarding school or not, I believe Susan knew exactly how to set a hook and expected to reel me in.

She was cute enough to tempt me.

Chapter Seven

I invited Chan to be my companion for Madame Boudron's dinner party. He picked me up in the Quarter and drove us to Maison Boudron in the Garden District. I wore my tuxedo with the appropriate black tie. Chan wore a tuxedo with his customary black shirt and white clerical collar thus exercising his option for black tie by not wearing one.

Maison Boudron was fairly typical for a Garden District mansion—large, white, and fussy. Chan told me it had been built by Arnoud Lafitte Boudron, our hostess' deceased husband, who made his fortune as a young man running bootleg whiskey. In his middle-age, he married Clotilde Fournier, a debutante, for social reasons. Arnaud was personally wealthier than the entire Fournier family but lacked social standing. He bought it by marrying Clotilde.

According to Chan, Arnoud died at age seventy-five, about thirty years ago, and he left part of his fortune in a marital trust for his wife with his children as beneficiaries and the other part in a second trust to benefit Théatre Vieux Carré. Arnoud had been a patron of the theater during his life and continued to fund it after his death.

Chan and I were met at the door by a liveried butler who escorted us to our hostess, Clotilde Boudron. Clotilde looked to be about seventy-five years old but she dressed as if she were still a debutante in her first social season. Mutton dressed as lamb was a Briticism I once heard Alex say. Now I understood what he meant.

She wore a winter-white, floor-length gown made from some stretchy fabric. The three-quarter length sleeves were attached in a way that left her shoulders bare. Her shoes matched her gown. Except for the small area of her body covered by an emerald pendant and two narrow shoulder straps that held her gown on her body, everything above her deeply plunging neckline was bare. Unfortunately, the line of her gown did little to disguise her fire-plug figure.

Clotilde didn't look much like her son, Ellis, whom I had met at TVC. Unlike Ellis' nearly-black hair, Clotilde's hair was a silver-streaked golden-blond color and cut in a pageboy style. Even her button nose looked nothing like Ellis' hawk nose.

Clotilde greeted us and summoned a servant to take our orders for cocktails. She didn't have McLeod's Isle of Skye scotch so I asked for Jameson's Irish whisky on the rocks. Chan asked for white wine. After Clotilde sorted out the drinks requests and dispatched a servant to fetch them, she turned to me and said, "My dear Mr. Spearman, I insist that you call me Clotilde. I was named for a Sixth Century queen of France. You have noticed that it rhymes with Hilda which, in French, is spelled with a terminal 'e' that sounds like 'uh,' as in Hildegard of Bingen, the 12th Century abbess, poet, and composer."

She offered me her hand, palm down, with her fingers extended in a downward curve as if she expected me to kiss her ring. I took her hand but I did not bow to kiss it.

"Thank you, Clotilde, for hosting a dinner party in my honor," I replied, and dropped her hand.

Clotilde exchanged brief pleasantries with Chan and then summoned a thirtyish, slender woman who walked over to us with the aid of Lofstrand crutches, the forearm crutches that were popular during the polio epidemic of my childhood. She also wore a metal brace on her foot and lower leg. Even in her flat shoes, she was a head taller than Clotilde.

"Laura, please say hello to Mr. Spearman and Dr. Fellows, and then show Dr. Fellows my new William Bennington watercolor, the one next to the oil Jackson Pollock did for me. Clotilde turned and looked at me. "William paints down in the Quarter, *n'est-ce pas?*"

Laura expressed her greetings and then retreated with Chan to another room.

"Laura is my daughter, Mr. Spearman, a bonus baby. In fact, she was Arnoud's last act, *extremis in delicto*. He had a massive stroke at the height of passion. Arnaud was much older than I, *n'est-ce pas?*

Clotilde turned her head and nodded in the direction of a life-size portrait of a standing male. "That's Arnaud looking down on us. We are pleased Laura did not get her father's nose," she said, gesturing at Arnaud's portrait, "and we are at a loss to explain her height. It must be a throwback to some distant ancestor. Arnaud was only five feet seven inches tall and you can see that I am petite."

Clotilde was petite in height, yes, but in girth, not so much. In sharp contrast, her daughter, Laura, was tall and slender. Laura's hair was blonde, but it was a lighter shade of blonde than her mother's and had no silver in it. Except possibly for hair color, Laura looked little like her mother and less like her brother. Laura's Roman nose must have harkened back to another distant ancestor because it looked neither like her mother's nor her brother's remarkable noses.

I surveyed Arnaud's portrait, the image of a middle-aged, dark-haired, dark-eyed, heavy-browed, burly man dressed as an Eighteenth Century pirate who looked like a smaller version of Ellis, hawk nose included. He certainly looked nothing like Laura.

"The portrait was Arnoud's little joke," Clotilde said. "He claimed he was a lineal descendent of the famous New Orleans pirate, Jean Lafitte, from whom he inherited his commercial acumen. Arnaud made his fortune early and married late. In life, my beloved husband loved his family and he loved his theater. In death, he has provided well for both. Come, Dewy. Let me introduce you to some of the other important people at our theater, at least the ones who have arrived. Val and Stella never show up before dark."

The servant returned with my drink. Clotilde took it from his tray, placed it in my hand, and then wrapped her hands around mine.

Clotilde held my gaze for a moment. "Come; let me introduce you to Lance Sterling, our first repertory actor."

"We've met," I said, a little more coolly than I should have, given the politics of the situation.

"Lance is such a dear, and so beautiful. I'm largely responsible for his being here."

"So I heard."

"We have many rooms at Maison Boudron, yet the dear young man insists on living in a garret in the Quarter, like an artist pursuing *La vie Bohème, n'est-ce pas?*"

"I'm afraid I know little of the Bohemian life, Clotilde. I'm pretty much an ordinary guy." I lied. I had been living the Bohemian life for the past two and one-half years—just not the poverty part.

"Not Lance, Mr. Spearman. Lance is not ordinary in any way. Lance is special. He is an *artiste*. He brings a breath of fresh California air to our theater, don't you Lance, darling?"

"Yes, Clotilde," Lance said as he joined our conversational group. "New Orleans is such a dreary place. I'm bringing a ray of California sunshine to this Louisiana haze, but I wish you'd have a word with Vanlandingham, Clothilde. I'm the male lead in *Suddenly* and he's treating me like I'm a bit player. Catherine already has the best lines, and now Pete's giving her the best staging, too."

"It's Catherine's story," I said.

"See, Clotilde," Lance said. "Director's always side with each other against actors. I hope you'll straighten Spearman out before we go into rehearsal for *Macbeth*."

"Don't fret, Lance," Clotilde said, patting his arm, "it will spoil your looks. I'm sure Mr. Spearman is a fine director who appreciates this opportunity to debut his professional directing career at Théatre Vieux Carré as well as to have the opportunity to complete his master's thesis, *n'est-ce pas*, my dearest Dewy?"

I didn't answer.

"I'm sure Dewy will appreciate our artistic sensibilities, dear Lance. After all, without the Boudron Theater Trust, TVC would not survive, *n'est-ce pas?*"

Deciding that wisdom was the better part of valor, I tempered my tongue as I greeted Lance.

"Pleased to meet you, Lance. It's a pleasure to work with a professional actor. Unlike amateurs, who often have no talent and yet believe they know more than the director, professional actors willingly accept direction. How long have you been a professional actor?"

"Long enough, Spearman," Lance replied, with a look on his face that suggested he thought I was up to something but couldn't figure out what it was.

"Then, my dear Clotilde, as long as Lance behaves like a professional actor, we should have no difficulties at all," I said, but I didn't believe it. I didn't believe Lance could take direction or, for that matter, had any great acting talent.

As I was wondering how I could turn Lance into Macbeth, Clotilde interrupted my thoughts.

"Here is my son, Ellis, dearest Dewy. He is business manager for TVC. It's a big job for no salary but it keeps him out of trouble."

Ellis glared at me, downed his drink, and ordered the servant to bring him another double Wild Turkey, straight up.

"Ellis is slow to warm up to strangers, dearest Dewy," Clotilde continued. "Permit me, then, to introduce you to our box office manager, Wendy Bridges, and to her husband, Maurice."

"Yes, and Dr. Bridges and I have also met." Addressing the woman, I said, "I'm pleased to meet you, Mrs. Bridges."

"I am pleased to meet you, Mr. Spearman."

"Please, call me Dewy. That's who I am in the theater."

"Thank you, Dewy. You may call me Wendy."

"Thank you, Wendy. I'd like to chat with you soon to see how we coordinate our efforts for the Scottish play."

"Talk to me, Spearman," Ellis growled. He was standing directly behind Wendy. "I'm the business manager. Wendy works for me."

Wendy looked at her feet.

"Sorry, Ellis. I'm not familiar with local protocol. When can you and I meet to talk about coordinating our efforts for *Macbeth*?"

"Later," Ellis said. He turned and walked out of the room.

"Please excuse Ellis," Wendy said. "We'll chat soon, Mr. Spearman, Dewy. Excuse me for a moment while I speak to Ellis," she said. She left the room following in Ellis' footsteps. On her way out, she passed Chan and Laura who were on their way back in.

Chan joined Maurice and me. Clotilde sent Laura to the kitchen. Lance studied his reflection in the French door. Laura returned from the kitchen and whispered something to Clotilde who then announced that dinner was served.

"Stella Maris," Clotilde said, from her place at the end of the table, "wardrobe mistress and sometimes actress, and her royal consort, Val Von Dragon, are delayed. They will join us shortly." My dearest Dewy, you shall sit to my right. Wendy, please sit next to Mr. Spearman. Laura, sit at the corner. Val will be seated between you and Wendy when he arrives. Ellis, sit on the end opposite me, at the head of the table. Ellis is the man of the house, *n'est ce pas*?"

"Knock it off, Mama," Ellis growled.

"So far," Clotilde continued, apparently oblivious to Ellis' rude remark, "that preserves the customary man-woman arrangement. Lance, dear, sit on my left. Stella, when she arrives, will be seated next to you. Maurice, you take the next chair, and Dr. Fellows...."

Clotilde paused for a moment, scanned the line-up of guests, shook her head from side to side, and then addressed Chan. "Dr. Fellows, it seems you have compromised the arrangement. I shall seat you anyway between Maurice and Ellis."

"I am so sorry to inconvenience you, Mrs. Boudron," Chan said. "I had considered a sex change operation as recently as last week, but my wife won't let me do it. She's afraid I'll start wearing her clothes."

"Really," Clotilde said in a dismissive tone.

"I ain't gonna' sit by Laura, Mama," Ellis said from his seat at the end of the table opposite Clotilde. "Laura, switch places with Wendy and sit by Spearman. Wendy, sit down here," he said, slamming his flat hand on the table next to Laura's place setting. The force of the blow lifted the plate and knocked the silverware askew.

Wendy moved tentatively toward the seat next to Ellis. Laura moved more swiftly than Wendy to the seat next to me.

"Ellis," our hostess said, sharply, "where are your manners?"

"Where they always are, Mama. Now, everybody sit down so we can eat. You still have your boy-girl arrangement, Mama, except for the Gook, here."

"You must pardon Ellis, Dr. Fellows and Mr. Spearman," our hostess said, nodding toward Chan and me as she spoke our names. "I'm afraid Ellis picked up some bad manners when he served in the war and he can't seem to get rid of them. He was decorated for his service in Viet Nam and earned a field commission, *n'est-ce pas?*"

"Were you in the infantry?" Chan asked.

"Special Forces," Ellis said. "I was a LERP. We ran long range reconnaissance patrols against Gooks like you. I'd talk about it, but then I'd have to kill you and that would upset Mama."

"Even after all these years Ellis still won't talk about it," Laura said quietly to me.

"Or learn to distinguish a Chinese-American from a Vietnamese national," I replied, equally softly, to Laura.

"I am not amused," our hostess said, but I couldn't be sure if she had overheard me, was responding to Ellis's rudeness, or was still clucking over Chan's clever riposte about wearing his wife's clothes.

With sparrow-like movements, Wendy divided her attention between her plate and my eyes as she addressed me from her new seat beside Ellis.

"Maurice served, too, Mr. Spearman. He was in the U.S. Air Force. He was stationed in England. That's where we met. He was their competition marksman, rifle and pistol."

"A real straight-shooter, huh?" Ellis said.

Wendy blushed, and then she gave her plate her undivided attention as conversation momentarily ceased.

Clotilde broke the silence.

"Tonight, we are having a meal typical of the plantation dinners of the Ante Bellum Era. This is truly a feast from the Old South."

Between the squash bisque and roast venison courses I managed to have an extended conversation with Laura because Clotilde, seated on my right, focused her full attention on Lance who was seated on her left, across from me.

Laura, I discovered, had graduated nine years earlier from Gudrun Hall with a major in English and a minor in speech and drama. She presently worked as a volunteer at the library and occasionally put on small plays with children's groups.

"Forgive me, Laura, if I am intruding on your privacy, but have you ever held a public job?"

"Heavens no, Mr. Spearman."

"Dewy."

"Dewy. Mother would pitch a hissy-fit. It's beneath our station," Laura whispered to me, sounding quite like her mother.

"Mother says we are wealthy and socially prominent, so it's beneath us to work. But we're wealthy in a strange way. Except for a sizeable trust for the theater, my father left everything else in a marital trust for Mother and named the children of his union with Clotilde Boudron, née Fournier, as heirs."

"As a child of that union, I am an heir, along with Ellis, even though I wasn't born when Daddy died. As long as Mother lives at Maison Boudron and does not re-marry, the trust pays all expenses for running the house and lets Mother draw down part of the trust each year to maintain her lifestyle. If there's anything left when Mother dies, Ellis and I will inherit it."

"Daddy's will also provided each of those same children a yearly stipend of $10,000, after taxes, upon achieving their majority, if they were unmarried, not employed, and continued to live at Maison Boudron. Daddy set that up when Ellis was born. That was a lot of money then, but not so much now."

"By living at Maison Boudron with the household expenses paid by the trust, I can make it on $10,000 a year. Any job I took would have to pay enough for me to live in the real world without my stipend. I don't think Mother would help me out."

"You don't sound content."

"Not entirely. I get bored. Sometimes I feel like taking on something more challenging than reading to children and putting on occasional children's plays at the library, but I can't think of leaving. Besides, I'm handicapped."

"And Ellis?"

"He tried once. It was a disaster. Mother uses Ellis as an example of why Boudrons shouldn't work."

"What happened?"

"I might as well tell you. You'll hear it from someone else if I don't. Ellis was in Viet Nam right up to the end. When he got back he tried to use his yearly $10,000 as seed money to turn deals. After a while, he took up commercial real estate and stock brokering, and then he moved out on his own."

"Ellis gave up his $10,000 stipend?"

"Yes. He was struggling at first. Then he started pulling in lots of money. Some years later he was indicted for aggravated assault, bribery, extortion, real estate fraud, multiple counts of securities fraud, and wire fraud. That would be about fifteen years ago now."

"The aggravated assault was committed on the federal marshals who came to serve him papers. The prosecutor didn't take too kindly to that. Mother was able to fix the state charges. Ellis pled guilty to two counts of assault on a federal employee and one count of securities fraud to stop prosecution on the other federal charges."

"Ellis received a sentence of ten-to-fifteen years and he is forever barred from working in securities and real estate. Since it was a federal case, it took Mother a bit of doing, but eventually she got him out on parole after eight years."

"Is he still on parole, Laura?

"He finished his parole last summer. Mother says she's working on getting him a pardon. I think she's just using that to keep him in line. He's the business manager at TVC, but he doesn't get paid."

"Your mother has considerable influence at TVC. Why?"

"Daddy's money. The trust helps fund the theater as long as a Boudron is on the board of directors. Since the trust provides about one-third of the theater's operating expenses and Mother is the Boudron who sits on the board, she has a lot of say. Mother's been president of the board ever since I can remember. Nearly everyone refers to her as 'Madame Boudron,' but no one says it to her face."

"'Madame Boudron.' I like that. What do you do at TVC?"

"Nothing. I stay out of Mother's way."

"Well, Laura, I don't want to create strife between you and your mother, but I need a volunteer director's assistant for *Macbeth*. Will you consider being my assistant?"

"Why me?"

"You have training in speech and theater, experience in directing children's plays, and you're bored. I need an assistant and you need a challenge. Please consider my offer."

"Don't waste your time flirting with my daughter, dearest Dewy." Clotilde had turned away from Lance and was looking straight at me. "Your reputation as a Lothario has preceded you, but I assure you Laura is not in the market."

Laura neither answered me nor responded to her mother's put-down other than to fall silent and look down at her plate.

"I feel slighted, dearest Dewy, and jealous. You have lavished all your attention on poor Laura and haven't looked in my direction once since we sat down."

"Please forgive my rudeness, Clotilde. I was offering your daughter—"

"Mr. Spearman was offering me an opportunity to show him the sights of New Orleans, Mother," Laura interrupted, "but I told him I don't get around very well."

"Laura. How rude of you to be so inconsiderate of our guest. Rest assured, dearest Dewy, that Laura will assist you in any way she is able, what little that may be."

"I'll keep that in mind, Clotilde," I replied.

"Her abilities are limited, but let's not speak further of it."

I was spared Clotilde's continued attention when she turned to the butler who whispered in her ear. After receiving a nod from Clotilde, the butler announced the arrival of Prince Val Von Dragon and his consort, Miss Stella Maris.

"Val," Clotilde said, beaming at the man. "I'm so glad you could join us, even if it is only for dessert. And Stella, too. Val and Stella, may I present our guest director, Dewy Spearman. Dewy, may I present our wardrobe mistress and sometime actress, Stella Maris—"

I looked up and faced the living image of the woman in Radu's photograph, the beautiful redheaded woman with the emerald green eyes, pale complexion, and Marilyn Monroe beauty mark.

I was stunned. I couldn't breathe.

Chapter Eight

"—and her royal escort, Prince Vladimir Von Dragon."

"Pleased to meet you," I said, when I resumed breathing.

"Pleased to meet you, Mr. Spearman," she replied.

"Pease, call me Val," the man said, addressing me. "I'm stuck with the family title, but I prefer not to use it. Really, Clotilde, I wish you wouldn't announce me that way."

"But Val, New Orleans has so few members of the European nobility left."

"True, Clotilde, but unimportant. My ancient hereditary title, plus $25, would get me a fairly decent lunch in the French Quarter. So would $25. Please, Clotilde, let's hear no more of it."

I looked at the man momentarily as he sat down where Madame Boudron directed him to sit, between Laura and Wendy. He was a mature man but I could not place his age. His skin was smooth. His hair was white but seemed prematurely so. His complexion was as fair as hers. I couldn't tell the color of his eyes because he was wearing tinted eye glasses and he presented only his profile to me.

His well-tailored cutaway fit his lean, athletic frame practically like a second skin. He exuded an aura of power as he was introduced to Chan, whom he apparently had never met, and exchanged pleasantries with everyone at the table while he toyed with the Peach Melba a servant had brought him at Clotilde's command.

I turned my attention to Stella who was seated next to Lance, across from me, and was far more pleasing to regard.

"You are the wardrobe mistress," I said.

"Yes, for nearly the entire time I have been in New Orleans."

"And, you're an actress."

"Of a sort; lately more and more. In fact, I'm doing two shows at TVC this season, back to back. First, I've been cast as Wilhemina in *The Passion of Dracula.*"

"Yes, just in time for Halloween. How very cute," Val said, his sarcasm clearly surpassing mine and sounding so unattractive.

"It's not enough that your precious theater would stage a show demeaning all Romanians and anyone of Middle-European ancestry, they must also stage it at Halloween, a particularly pathetic holiday."

"You are of Middle-European ancestry?" I asked. "I would have thought 'Vladimir Von Dragon' was Dutch or German."

"Val changed his name, Dewy," Madame Boudron said. 'Vladimir' gets in the way what with our former Cold-War attitude toward Russians and our unfortunate present-day characterization of them as heavy-handed hoodlums, *n'est-ce pas?*"

"Von Dragon is Russian?" I would not be put off by Madame Boudron's overbearing ways.

"No, my dear boy," Val answered with an edge of hostility in his voice. "Von Dragon is the best your feeble Western tongues can do with my Middle-European family name. Westerners have never thought much of my part of the world. Alexander the Great came from nearby Macedonia. He was the son of Phillip of Macedonia, yet in the West, Alexander is thought of as Greek, as if there were no civilization anywhere except in ancient Greece or Rome and their successors. No, everyone thinks the Balkans are where boobies are hatched, so anyone who comes from the Balkans must be a booby."

"Watch your blood pressure, Val," Stella murmured, but her caution served only to inflame him.

"The best you Westerners can say about my part of the world is to write silly novels and sappy plays about vampires, one of which you are about to produce at TVC with Stella playing Wilhemina against my wishes. She should confine herself to making costumes, if that."

"Who else would we have for adult female leads?" Maurice asked.

Val ignored him.

"And then, to add insult to injury, you have cast this pretty boy here, Lance Sterling, to play the Count. Such a travesty offends everyone of good taste anywhere, Romanian or not."

"Val!" Stella said, sharply. "You've gone too far."

"Wait, what?" Lance said. "Wait, Von Dragon. I think you're insulting me. I'm a professional actor. I can play Dracula. But I'd rather play Harker. Clotilde, don't you think I'd make a better Harker? After all, he is the male lead."

"Another example of Western arrogance," Val shot back. "I am quite certain that Lance would make a better Harker, that insipid young journalist who falls madly in love with Wilhemina and attempts to interfere with the real passion of the play, the passion of Wilhemina and the Count, the true male lead. It's only because of your silly ideas of romance as beauty and light that you fail to see beauty in the passion of darkness. That is why young Lance sees Harker as the male lead and that is precisely the role he should play."

"That's what I've been saying," Lance said. "Clotilde, fix it so I can play Harker."

"Then, my darling Lance," Clotilde replied, "who would play Count Dracula?"

"I don't know," Lance replied. "I don't want to do it. It gives me the creeps. Vanlandingham or Spearman can think of someone."

"I may have thought of someone, indeed," I said, as I struck upon a way to cast the role and have a bit of mischievous fun.

"Perhaps the role calls for someone with a feeling for the beauty and passion of darkness, someone with a feeling for the heroic nobility of the Romanian soul, perhaps someone like…" I paused for effect and Lance bought into it.

"Who, Spearman? Who?" Lance asked.

"Someone like Val," I said to everyone in general, but I kept my eye on Val.

Val smiled.

"Ridiculous," Madame Boudron said.

"Wait, what? That would be great," Lance said. "Then I can play Harker. Fix it, Clotilde. I'd be ever so grateful."

"Yes," chimed in Maurice. "I think Lance should play Harker. It suits his talents better."

Ellis joined the conversation. "Then our pretty boy wouldn't have to spoil his looks by dyeing his hair black, would he Maurice?"

"Ellis!" Wendy said, and then she fixed her gaze on her plate and shrank in her clothing.

"That settles it," Lance said. "I'm not dyeing my hair black to play some silly vampire. Let Val do it. Let him dye his hair black."

"I think it could be done with white hair, don't you, Spearman?"

Val spoke to me, but he was looking directly at Madame Boudron.

Stella looked at Val from across the table and said, quietly, "Val, I wish you wouldn't."

"I don't know," Madame Boudron said. "I had my heart set on seeing Lance in that role. But, if he'd rather play Harker, I suppose he can. We'll have to get someone else to play the Count, someone who is willing to have black hair. The audience expects black hair on Dracula. It's part of the tradition, *n'est-ce pas?*"

"Which is precisely why I insist on doing it with white hair," Val said, his words oozing down the table, "to show the power and majesty of the Romanian soul without cheap theatrical stereotyping."

"That's just great, Val," Ellis said. "Now, why don't you put your money where your mouth is?"

"Quite right, Ellis. Quite right. I'll do it. I'll play the Count."

"So you'll play the Count. Whoopee! Now put your money where your mouth is."

"I'm afraid I don't follow you, dear boy."

"Put your friggin' money where your friggin' mouth is. Give us a donation so we can afford to put on the friggin' play."

"Ellis!" Mrs. Boudron barely suppressed a scream. "I'm mortified. We have always taken excellent care of Théatre Vieux Carré. To suggest that a role must be bought is unthinkable. Apologize!"

"No. TVC always needs money; Von Dragon has plenty."

"Please, Clotilde," Val said, his voice as thick and sweet as tupelo honey, "I will consider it an honor to double my annual donation to TVC. Stella finds such delight at TVC when we are in residence, and now I will have a rare opportunity to share that joy with her as she spends untold hours at the theater. Otherwise, I see so little of her."

"Didn't TVC get an Arts Council grant?" Stella asked.

"Whoopee," Ellis said, with a distinct lack of enthusiasm. "That don't mean we don't need Von Dragon's money."

"Well," Maurice said, "I'm glad that's settled. *Passion* starts in rehearsal day after tomorrow. Lenny will be in for a bit of a surprise when he finds out about the casting changes, but I think Lance's talents will work better as Harker."

"Yeah, and he won't have to spoil his looks," Ellis muttered under his breath but still loud enough for everyone to hear. Maurice colored and Wendy stared at her plate again.

"Now that we have that settled, what's the second role in which you have been cast?" I said as if I didn't know.

"If I survive *The Passion of Dracula*, I have been cast as Lady Macbeth in your production of the Scottish play. I hope you will be satisfied with my performance."

"I hope you can play old and not so pretty. You look far too young and beautiful to play Lady Macbeth."

"You flatter me, Mr. Spearman. I'm older than I look."

"Please call me Dewy."

"Stella."

"Stella, did you ever work in a production of *Kiss Me Kate*?"

Val shot her a quick glance—quick—but electrically charged.

Stella blinked several times. "No, why do you ask?"

"Radu has a color photograph of you from publicity shots for *Kiss Me Kate* signed by Cole Porter that must date from about 1948 or '49. That would make you considerably older than you look."

"Oh, that," she said with a laugh. "I can see how you might be confused. I didn't know Radu had one of those pictures. That was my aunt, also Stella Maris. Aunt Stella retired from theater shortly after that picture was made."

"You certainly look young enough to play Wilhemina in *The Passion of Dracula*. I hope you can play old enough for Lady Macbeth."

"I have to get through *The Passion of Dracula* first."

"I suggest," said Madame Boudron, "we adjourn to the drawing room for brandy and cigars now that they have become fashionable again. Until tonight, Salvador Dali may have been the last person to smoke a cigar in my drawing room."

"Norman Treigle, that dear man, used to smoke cigarette after cigarette, but no cigar. I begged Norman to stop, but he would laugh that wicked laugh he used when he sang Mephistopheles and continue lighting one cigarette from another."

"Didn't they both die from smoking" Chan asked.

"You are being tiresome, Dr. Fellows," Madame Boudron said, waving the back of her hand at him in a gesture of dismissal. "Perhaps that's why you have never been a guest at my salons. Most of the literati have attended me, particularly the great Southern writers and artists. Whenever a great person comes to New Orleans, he comes to my salon. I coached Burl Ives on how to play Big Daddy. I attempted to coach Tony Franciosa on using an authentic southern accent when he was filming dear Tennessee's *Summer and Smoke*, to little avail I might add. And Van Cliburn—"

"Careful, Mother," Laura said. "Mr. Cliburn is still living and might not support the story you are about to tell."

"Yes, Laura, I suppose it would be indelicate to reveal the identity of all my callers and some of their confidences, but many of the great ones have been here: Ernest Hemingway, William Faulkner, Truman

Capote, James Jones, Roy Orbison, Marlon Brando, Hume Cronyn, Roddy Mcdowall, Michael Rennie, Tennessee Williams, even Andy Warhol, all the great people of literature and the arts."

"All of those people were men," Chan said. "Are there no great women of literature and the arts?"

"No," Madame Boudron said, simply, clearly, and as if she meant it, which she most likely did.

"Well," Chan added, "I guess that kills that conversation."

"I admit there are a few women who can sing," Clotilde said, "but only two or three women write passably well. None of them, except for Harper Lee and Eudora Welty, are Southerners. It takes a man like dear Tennessee to have a soul tortured enough to be a great writer. He was often a guest at my salons and in my home. He used my garden as the play's garden when he wrote *Suddenly Last Summer*."

"I'd love to see your garden, Clotilde," I said, "and see how closely it matches my memory of the garden from the movie. I must have seen it a dozen times. Elizabeth Taylor was great in that movie, not to mention hot."

"Unfortunately, dearest Dewy, Camille devastated that garden. We rebuilt it as a courtyard. I can understand your fascination with Elizabeth Taylor and her see-through bathing suit, but Montgomery Clift was the star attraction. He was a guest in my salon, too. Tennessee despised the movie but he thought highly of Montgomery. He said so, right here in this room at one of my salons."

"You seem fond of Tennessee Williams."

"But of course. Tennessee was such a dear man. He is responsible for my daughter's name. My beloved husband always said that if we ever had a daughter we would name her Marie Lafitte after his mother. Arnaud died before our daughter was born and I never did like his mother, bless her heart, so I chose 'Laura,' after Tennessee's character in *The Glass Menagerie*, because of her leg. Tennessee loved Laura when she was little."

"Pease, Mother," Laura said.

"Of course, dearest Dewy, Laura was too young then to remember Tennessee now, but he loved her. And, I don't care what others say, I dispute the belief that he was a homosexual—at least not exclusively. Tennessee was a highly sensitive man with a tortured soul."

"Maybe Tennessee Williams wasn't no faggot," Ellis said, "but lots of theater people are, particularly out in California."

"Wait, what?" Lance interrupted. "Are you talking about me? You've been on my case for weeks and now you're saying I'm gay."

"I'm saying you're a stuck-up California actor who loves himself more'n anyone else. Draw your own conclusions."

"If I wasn't here as an invited guest, I'd kick your ass for saying I'm a pansy."

"Go ahead, Lance, if you're man enough. I tell you what. You kick my ass good and I'll leave this house. I kick your ass good and you'll leave this town. Fair enough? Let's just you an' me step outside and settle this man to man—if you are one."

"Ellis!" Madame Boudron shouted. And then slowly and monotonically she said, "You are out of line. Apologize to Lance, now."

"No, Mama."

"Then leave this room."

"Never mind, Clotilde," Lance said. I'm going down to the Quarter for fresh air. Can somebody give me a ride?"

"I'll give you a lift, old boy," Maurice said. "Wendy, you can take a cab when you are ready to leave. I'll probably stop for a brandy with Lance. The dear boy looks a little peaked."

"She won't need no cab," Ellis said. "She's gonna' stop by TVC with me. I'll give her a ride."

"I'm certain you will," Maurice said beneath his breath.

"And I shall take my leave, Mrs. Boudron," Chan said. "Thank you for the evening. Don't think it hasn't been wonderful. Are you coming, Dewy?"

"Uh, yes Chan. Laura, think about my offer. Stella, Val, Wendy, Laura, a pleasure to meet you," I said as Chan hustled me to the door close on the heels of Lance and Maurice.

"Mr. Spearman, Dewy," Madame Boudron said in a commanding manner that caused me to interrupt my exit. "Laura will not be able to accept your invitation. However, I will take great pleasure in showing you the sights of New Orleans, particularly the night spots."

I could think of few things less pleasant than spending an evening alone with Clotilde, so I demurred.

"You're too kind, Clotilde. Except for wanting to hear a bit of jazz, I expect I'll be too busy working on my productions and my thesis to do much sight-seeing."

"I love jazz, too, Dewy!" Stella said. "I'll go hear jazz with you. Starting Sunday I'll be tied up with rehearsals, so shall we say tomorrow at dusk at the Court of Two Sisters down on Royal Street? I'll see you there. *Ciao*."

As I was nodding my head and saying "Yes," Chan shoved me out the door.

"Chan," I said, as we got in the car, "I believe you just insulted Madame Boudron."

"When I said, 'Don't think it hasn't been wonderful?'"

"Yes."

"You can take it either as an insult or as a compliment. I believe she took it as a compliment. It's her choice anyway. That's a Buddhist thing."

"But you're a Christian and you meant to insult her."

"You can learn a lot from Buddhism, Dewy. I did. Besides, she is an insufferable and insulting bore. About the only thing she has going for her is her husband's money."

"She has her daughter. Laura seems to live in her mother's shadow and suffer from low self-esteem, but I believe she's a good and strong person. Ellis seems to be a rougher version of Clotilde, even if he looks more like Arnoud, but Laura is different. It's as if she doesn't belong in that family."

"Maybe she doesn't?"

"Are you suggesting that Boudron is not Laura's father?"

"On the bayou, the Cajuns say, 'Mama's baby, papa's maybe.'"

"If Arnoud Boudron wasn't Laura's father, what would that do to the trust?"

"Likely cut her out if it were true and if it were known."

"Could it be true?"

"That is an interesting question. Ellis looks like Arnoud's portrait but Laura doesn't. Old Boudron was about seventy-five when he died some thirty years ago. Clotilde was about forty-five. They say it was a massive stroke, which is likely, and that he died making love to Clotilde, which seems unlikely. Not that she was too old, but who would want to?"

"Since Clotilde was pregnant, obviously she'd been having sex with someone. Whoever that was is Laura's father. If it wasn't Arnoud, then I doubt Mrs. Boudron would advertise it. That would be a scandal even in New Orleans."

"Well, if Laura doesn't look like Arnoud, who does she look like, Tennessee Williams?"

"I don't know, Dewy. I never met Tennessee Williams."

"I guess it's not really important. Laura is Laura whoever her father is, and I hope she finds herself. Meanwhile, Chan, what can you tell me about Stella and Val? Are they married?"

"I don't think so. They have never represented themselves as being married. Other than the fact that Stella's been active with the theater for about ten years, I know very little. I had never met Val until this evening although I have certainly heard about him. Stella's beautiful and she has talent. I've seen her perform. I hear that she and Val go away every spring and come back every fall. He dabbles in the market and makes business deals, mostly import and export. As one might suspect, he has a reputation that would be considered unsavory were he not wealthy and connected."

"That's it?"

"I've told you all I know."

"O.K. what don't you know that you can tell me?"

"You're sharp, Dewy, but I will not cast aspersions based on hearsay. You chastised me for possibly insulting an insufferable woman. I'll not have you think ill of me for repeating common gossip about a beautiful one who has caught your eye."

"You don't miss much, Chan."

"Out, Dewy. You're home. Go hear jazz with Stella. Just watch your back."

Chapter Nine

Had thoughts of the events of the last month, particularly the events of last night, been cream, sugar, and vanilla on salted ice, they would be ice cream now from all the churning going on in my head. When I completed my morning grooming, I decided to pay a professional call on Madame Claire. Maybe she could help me get a better grip on things. At least a reading should be worth a laugh or two.

I went down to the Wicca Shop. Miss Parker collected my fee and made my appointment for about an hour later. I went over to The French Market and bought café au lait and a strawberry napoleon for breakfast. I carried my coffee and napoleon out to Jackson Square and watched performance artists for a few minutes.

When I returned to the Wicca Shop I was ushered into Madame Claire's reading room. What a letdown. The room was small. There were no votives, no fringed lamp shades, and no crystal ball.

Madame Claire was seated on the north side of the table. She bade me sit across from her.

"Good morning, Monsieur Spearman. You wish to know the future, no?"

"No, not really. I wish to know the present. I'm not sure what's going on in my life right now and I would appreciate a little insight."

"Insight is my business. Seeing. I make no promise. I only read the cards. Sometimes I see clearly. You are Celtic, no?"

"Yes, if you mean Scots and Irish."

"And maybe a little bit Scandinavian, no?"

"A bit Scandinavian, a little German, and a little French, too."

"We do the Celtic cross. It is good for three months. That keeps us in the present. Let us begin. You are on the quest, no?"

"I suppose so."

"The Fool is the naïve seeker of truth," she said as she laid the Fool's card on the table. That is you. Hold your question in mind, and shuffle the cards. Statisticians say seven shuffles make a random deal, but we do not believe in random, do we Monsieur Spearman?"

"No, I guess not."

"Then shuffle as you will. When you are finished, place them face down on the table, cut them three times, and stack them as you will. Since you are of the theater I give you my Shakespeare deck."

I fixed my question in my mind. I would find it difficult to speak it aloud, but I could say it silently with no embarrassment. Then, without really knowing why I did it, I shuffled the cards exactly seven times before I cut and stacked them.

"Now, with the cards remaining face down, fan them out, pick exactly ten cards, and make them into a stack."

I did as she asked, and she turned over the first card.

"This first card you draw, the two of orbs, cups in standard decks, is the Lord of Love. I place it over the Fool. See, Romeo and Juliet. Young Juliet had to choose to stay or go. She must choose to leave forever her Capulet family and go with the man she loves, Romeo, a Montague, or choose to forever leave Romeo, marry County Paris, and stay in the good graces of her family, Capulet. The Montagues and Capulets have bad blood between them, no?"

"Yes," I replied.

"You will choose, too. Soon. The nature of this choice I don't see. Think three times before you choose."

Turning over the next card, she said, "Crossing you is the three of orbs. It goes sideways over your first card." She placed the three of orbs on top of the Lord of Love at a right angle, not straight up.

"Right side up, this is the card of celebration, wedding, or birth, or a warning not to indulge in the excess of celebratory pleasure."

"Upside down, it warns that pleasure, excess pleasure or promiscuity, yours or someone else's, is the challenge to your question. Since the crossing card is laid sideways, it is neither right-side up nor upside down, no? We will decide the meaning of this card from other cards."

"You saying I'm a lecher?" I thought of my harem in Memphis.

"No, Monsieur Spearman, I say nothing. The cards speak. Whatever your question is, too much pleasure or fear of pleasure is the challenge to your question. Do not break my concentration, please. Let us turn the third card."

"The Lovers. This represents the past. See, here Romeo and Juliet meet the holy man. Right side up, this card tells the tale of Romeo's putting on a disguise and sneaking into the Capulet's costume party to see his present girlfriend, Rosalind, and then his falling in love with Juliet and wooing her in secret. Together they persuade the holy man, Friar Lawrence, to marry them. They defy both their families by their forever love for each other."

"In their case," I said, "forever came the next day."

"When reversed, as it is here, this card suggests conflict, disillusionment, and the breakdown of relationships in your past."

"I don't claim to have led an exemplary life, Madame Claire. What about the present?"

"The next card, the three of scepters, is Fate. The Three Sisters. This is the card of now, the present. By itself, this is the card of power. In this position, it says the meaning of the other cards cannot be altered. These things will come to pass."

"The Three Sisters, like the Weird Sisters in *Macbeth*?" I said.

"The same," Madame Claire responded. "'The weird sisters, hand in hand—'"

"'—posters of the sea and land, thus do go about, about, thrice to thine, and thrice to mine, and thrice again to make up nine. Peace, the Charm's wound up,'" I said, completing the line from *Macbeth*.

"Very good, Monsieur Spearman. You know the material."

"So, you're telling me, because of the Weird Sisters' appearance, the meaning of the other cards cannot be altered. It is fated."

"That is so, Monsieur Spearman. May I continue?"

The hair on my neck was standing up. Maybe this was more than a joke. But, once begun is half done, so I told her to continue.

"Card number five represents your immediate future. You have the two of scepters. Alliance is the meaning of this card. Here, from the opening scene of *Romeo and Juliet*, are the two Montague retainers, Sampson and Gregory. Sampson boasts he shall strike quickly if he is moved to strike, and Gregory, a smartass like you, reminds Sampson that he is never quickly moved to do anything. You know the scene, no?"

"Sampson: 'I strike quickly, being moved.' Gregory: 'But thou are not quickly moved to strike.'"

"Very good, Monsieur Spearman. Then what do they do?"

"They collude to provoke a fight with the Capulet retainers which gets both families into big trouble with the Duke."

"This they do together as allies. They balance one another, no?"

"Yes."

"In the near future, you will make an alliance, find a balance. This may lead to good or to trouble. Whether you balance two forces within yourself or join with something outside you, I cannot see."

"For the longer future, this next card, the Hermit, shows that you will follow the path of solitary meditation, the inner way. You will gain wisdom from personal experience. From Shakespeare you would be King Lear, with his fool, crossing the desolate moor in darkness with freezing wind driving into your face, realizing that your follies are you own."

Madame Claire looked directly at me. I attempted to cover my discomfort by quoting Shakespeare. "As King Lear, himself, put it, Madame Claire, 'The gods are just, and of our present vices make instruments to plague us.'"

"Very good, Monsieur Spearman."

"Let me see if I understand. You're saying, I mean, the cards are saying I'm going to be a hermit in the near future? How near?"

"This reading is good for about three months."

"So, within three months I'll make an alliance and then become a hermit, right?"

"This is what the cards say. Shall I continue?"

"What different will it make if I don't see the rest of them?"

"No difference to the cards but perhaps a great difference to you. As your Shakespeare said, 'Forewarned is forearmed,' no?"

"You said the appearance of the Weird Sisters makes everything inevitable. What difference will it make for me to know what's going to happen if it will happen whether I know or not?"

"How you react to what happens is shaped by your preparation for it, Monsieur Spearman. Events are foreordained. Reactions are not. You are your own master unless you give your power away. May I continue?"

"Yes, continue."

"Card seven is the King of Orbs. From Shakespeare I see Oberon. If Oberon gives his word, he keeps it. In mythology, this represents Bran the Blessed, who brought the Cauldron of Regeneration up from Lake of the Basin. He is also known by your name, Dewi, the Celtic sea king who is also known as David, the Patron Saint of Wales, famous for Davy Jones' Locker, a place of safety for souls of drowned sailors. Dewi once married the Moon Goddess, Queen Mab in her English name. Yes, Monsieur Spearman, you are the

Fisher King, a character of ageless power and strength who suffers a wound that will not heal to make others whole."

"Aren't you laying it on a bit thick, Madame Claire? I already paid for this reading."

"Do not insult me. I read the cards, I do not write them."

"Yes. 'The moving finger writes, and having writ, moves on: Nor all your piety nor wit shall lure it back to cancel half a line, nor all your tears wash out a word of it,' or something like that."

"Omar Khayyam, no? You have much learning, but little wisdom, Monsieur Spearman. It will come. May I continue?"

"Yes. Please forgive me. This is strange and discomforting."

"The environment that surrounds you is represented by this card, the nine of orbs. In Shakespeare, when Prince Hal becomes King Henry V, he sends away his old partner in drink and debauchery, Sir John Falstaff. Prince Hal tells Falstaff he has changed, he can no longer go whoring and carousing. Now that he is named the king, he must be the king."

"'Presume not that I am the thing I was.'"

"Very good, Monsieur Spearman. Unexpected things happen. What they are, I cannot see. You will be tempted to keep something you find. Do not, or you will be called to account for stealing."

"Stealing? Like boosting a car?"

"Perhaps. There are many forms of stealing, Monsieur Spearman, including stealing someone's time. Under the Napoleonic Code, there is such a thing as stealing by finding. The issue is not that you find something. The issue is what you do with it. The cards do not say you are a thief. They say actions will be taken against you for taking something another claims. May I continue?"

"Please do. With only two cards left, how bad can it get?"

"Your hopes and fears are represented by this ninth card," she said, turning it over. She blanched, and then she crossed herself.

"The Devil."

Chapter Ten

"This is not a cheerful card, Monsieur Spearman. In your Shakespeare, this would be Iago. Iago whispers in Othello's ear and lies to him about his lieutenant, Cassio. Iago lies to General Othello about his innocent wife, Desdemona. Iago tells Othello that Desdemona is faithless, that she has cuckolded him, and that his troops laugh at him behind his back. Iago inflames Othello to lethal fury."

"Iago has no clear purpose for his deceit and he is never called to account for his malevolence. This is the card of your present hopes and fears. You create illusion and fear it at the same time. You fear you will doubt the truth and believe the lie. It is an apt card for a theatrical director, no? You daily deal with truth and lies, with reality and illusion. You create illusion to tell the truth, and yet you know truth is illusory."

"This, also, is the card of carnal lust. It may be that your devil is of the flesh. More than that I do not see. Let us turn the last card," she said, as she placed her hand on the last of my ten cards.

"We've come this far, Madame Claire. Why not?"

"Your last card shows the final outcome of your question," she said as she turned over the Hanged Man. She frowned. "You will be baffled, like Hamlet, here. To be, or not to be. That will be your dilemma to resolve. You will be called upon to choose, to give up something precious so something precious may be gained. By the end of three months' time, Monsieur Spearman, you will make great changes in your life and in your beliefs."

My sarcasm, aroused by Val's performance last night, decided to pay a visit. "That about as clear as a glass of Mississippi mud in the middle of a moonless night, Madame Claire."

"Monsieur Spearman, this is a difficult reading. In time it will become clear. You are a strong and powerful person. You will find what you need, but you will find it by losing what you have found. You will be in constant danger. Do you have questions about this reading?"

"Yes, what kind of danger? An auto accident? Am I killed?"

"It is not clear, but I do not see your death. This concludes my reading, Monsieur Spearman. Beyond what I have told you, I see no more. I hope this proves of value to you."

She waved her hand to dismiss me and then changed its direction and waved me back.

"Wait. I have a vision. I see the letter 'L.' I don't know what it means. Ponder it. Maybe it will become clear to you."

She took a piece of paper from a drawer in her table, wrote on it, folded it, and handed it to me.

"If you are troubled by this reading, come again in few days. Now, I must light a white candle. Please give this note to Mademoiselle Parker on your way out."

On my way out I unfolded the note and read it. Madame Claire instructed Mademoiselle Parker not to disturb her for ten minutes before sending in her next client. When I handed the re-folded note to Mademoiselle Parker, I asked, "Does Madame Claire often take a ten minute break between readings?"

"Only when the Devil's in the deal."

I left the Wicca Shop and headed to TVC. When I got there, *Suddenly Last Summer* was in technical rehearsal. I set aside my unease with my Tarot reading and went to the light booth to speak with Spider. He was busy talking to the Eurasian woman I had seen him with at the bar. I sat on the risers until she left and then I went in.

"Spider, I need to talk to you but I didn't want to interrupt."

"You watchin' me man?"

"I saw the woman up here. She your girlfriend?"

"Let it go, man. Whatcha' want?"

"Good lighting for the Scottish play."

"O.K., man, but let me get through with this rehearsal."

"Sure."

I sat in the light booth and watched the run-through for *Suddenly.* I saw nothing to change my opinion of Lance Sterling's acting skills, but, to be fair, this rehearsal was to benefit the technical crew, not to hone the acting. After a while a blue light came on over the telephone and Spider nodded to me to answer it.

"Light booth," I said, and held a brief conversation with a man from the Lafayette Players. After we established that I was Dewy

Spearman, a guest director, he told me his name and asked me to give Spider his message. He wanted to buy a salvaged, high-wattage follow spot at half of list.

"What was that?" Spider asked after I hung up.

"Some guy named Bud A. Bear from Lafayette who wants a salvaged follow spot for half of list."

"Bud Hébert?"

"Could be." I had forgotten that many names in Louisiana were pronounced in French.

"I'll take care of that, Spearman. Don't say nothin' to Ellis. And be sure to mind your own damn business."

"Sure, man."

"Now, whatcha' want for the Scottish play, gloom and doom?"

"Not entirely. Let me start with the easy things first. I want to fly the dagger for Macbeth's speech. I'll need a special for that. You can use the same special for Banquo's ghost. Then, I'd like to fly the Weird Sisters and have some tricky lighting to make it work."

"The flying's gonna' be more of a problem than the lighting. You can fly the dagger from the rigging. Just drop a line. Flying three witches is going to be a bitch. There's only one fly harness and assembly. The beams can't support any more. I heard you were going to build a thirty-inch high thrust stage for the show. You won't be able to fly anyone over the thrust at all."

"Well, maybe I'll fly one witch and have the other two enter and exit from traps. Can we put traps into a thirty-inch high thrust and light them from underneath?"

"Maybe. You'd have to have flexible actors to crawl around with only twenty-six inches of headroom, but the technical part can be done if we got the instruments. The ones I'd need to light that got water damaged a while back when we used them for an outdoor jazz festival. They're marked for salvage. I gotta' talk Ellis out of some money for more instruments."

"Well, maybe you're in luck. I heard at Madame Boudron's that Ellis just got a grant."

"When'd you hear that?"

"Last night."

"The Arts Council grant was approved?"

"I believe that's what I heard."

"Son of a bitch!"

"I beg your pardon."

"Nothing, man. Just stay out of it. Lighting's my job. Directing's yours. What else you want?"

"I want directional lighting casting sharp shadows for Macbeth and diffuse lighting casting indistinct shadows for Lady Macbeth."

"That could be a problem, man. Why you want that?"

"I'm trying to play Macbeth as a usurper, an angular man, sharp and hard, and his lady as a victim of his vaunting ambition. Lady Macbeth, for herself, is not a power-hungry, blood-thirsty virago. She is a funhouse mirror that distorts and reflects her lord's vaunting ambition, a frosted looking glass in which Macbeth sees himself, sees his ambition and his cruelty reflected with all of his own moral self-doubts distorted and unrecognizable to him, masked by the frost, distorted by the mirror of Lady Macbeth. She is a window to his soul, a special window which she uses to filter out all of his humanity that might stay him from carrying out his deadly deeds."

"That's heavy, man."

"It's usually played to have Lady Macbeth spur Macbeth into action when his own conscience appears to get the better of him. I want to play it so during the course of their marriage he strips her of her personhood and makes her an instrument of his own ambition to seize power without compunction. He makes her the tool he uses to stir himself to action. She co-dependently saves him from his own doubts and fears at the ultimate sacrifices of her sanity and her life. Long story short, I want him lit hard and her lit soft. Can you do it?"

"Do 'gators shit in the swamp?"

"I guess so."

"If we got money, I can do it. But don't bug me about it, man. I got some jawin' to do to get the instruments you need. Just stay out of my way and mind your own damn business about who's buying and who's selling. Don't tell Ellis about the phone call. It'll screw things up, O.K.?"

"Sure, Spider. Just come through for me."

"No sweat. I always come through, man," he said, as he pulled his half-pint vodka bottle out of his back pocket. "An' don' worry about my drinking, it don't get in the way."

On his way out of the light booth, he uncapped his bottle, took a long pull, and then recapped and pocketed it. He grabbed a high rung on the wall and pulled himself up into the grid. With his black clothes against the black paint of the ceiling, he faded to the point of invisibility. From what I was seeing of the technical rehearsal of *Suddenly*, I had no doubt that Spider could design the lighting for my show. Whether he could come up with the instruments to light it the way I wanted it lit remained to be seen.

I picked up a key to the stage door from Wendy Bridges so I could come in on Sunday and work out my plans for staging the Scottish play, and then I left to meet Stella at the Court of Two Sisters for an evening of jazz. I stopped by the apartment and picked up a University of Tennessee pullover in case it got cool after dark.

Our date was for dusk. I was early, but not by much. The restaurant was nearly full so I went in and claimed a table. Since I didn't want to tie the table up and keep the waiter from making his tips, I ordered dinner. Our date was for jazz, not dinner, but if Stella was hungry when she arrived, she could order then.

The Court of Two Sisters actually was a courtyard, at least where I was sitting. The fading early autumn light played on the courtyard's eastern wall and on the roof of the building next door.

The courtyard was slipping into light gray and lavender twilight and was illuminated by pools of soft yellow from candles glowing gently on each table which highlighted the orange coloring of my UT pullover. A three-piece ensemble belted out Dixieland jazz.

As the gray and lavender dusk deepened into charcoal and aubergine night and the hue of my pullover shifted to burnt orange, my waiter removed the remains of my jambalaya, a succulent, spicy concoction of shrimp and andouille sausage, and brought Irish coffee. As I raised my cup to take a sip, I looked over the rim and saw Stella standing in front of the courtyard's massive fountain and illuminated from behind by the flaring gas flames that suddenly erupted from the water. For a lingering moment, Stella's hair was limned with a tongue of near-copper flame and her sinuous form was silhouetted through her muslin jumpsuit.

I was so distracted that I burned my tongue on my Irish coffee, coughed to keep from choking, and bumped the table as I stood up, partly as a courtesy to greet Stella and partly to spew hot coffee without getting any on myself, the table, or the patrons at the next table.

"Relax," she said as she slid into her chair. "Take a sip of your ice water. Take three deep breaths and then sit down."

"I must have bitten off more than I could chew," I said, trying to be cool, but my voice was up about an octave.

"I hope not; otherwise, I'd be wasting your time and mine."

"Excuse me?"

"Why did you accept my invitation?"

"I want to hear good jazz."

"You can hear jazz all over this city—by yourself. You don't need me for that. Why did you accept my invitation?"

"I am fascinated."

"I thought so. I am fascinated. Now that we've acknowledged our mutual fascinations we may be as coy as we please. I like seduction and I haven't been seduced in longer than you could imagine. You seduce me and I'll seduce you. At the end of the evening we'll see who is a better seducer."

"What about your, er, husband?"

"Val? Val isn't my husband in any sense of the word. He is my one-time lover, my former liberator, my present consort, and my forever curse. Don't ask. It's complicated. But I do have a husband. At least, I may have a husband. Last I heard, he was still alive and in a nursing home."

"Wouldn't he be young to be in a nursing home?"

"How old am I, Dewy?"

"I make it a firm policy never to guess a woman's age or weight. Whatever answer I give, I'm almost certain to offend. Let's just say that you're younger than I."

"Don't cop out on me. How old do I seem to you?"

"Well, I have a feeling that you're close to my age, but you don't look a day over thirty and could play for twenty."

"So you say. I won't disabuse you of that notion, but is there any reason I couldn't have an old husband?"

"I guess not. I read several years ago about an old woman who was still drawing a pension from the State of Alabama as the widow of a Civil War Veteran. She'd been fourteen years old at the turn of the Twentieth Century when she married a very old Civil War veteran. You could have married an older man."

"Something like that. Anyway, my invalid husband was and still may be in a nursing home. I haven't seen him in ages. His family was old-line Philadelphia. Mine was dirt-poor Appalachia. His family was against our marriage from the start."

"I was young and knew little of such things, and they coerced him into getting me to sign a prenuptial agreement in which I renounced any claim to his family's money."

"After his stroke, they managed to cut off everything except my right to live with him in his house and my right to a hundred-dollar monthly allowance. I also had rental income from my brownstone."

"Before his stroke we had started a small publishing business for him to play with. After his stroke he couldn't handle it. He just wandered around the house like a well-educated, well-behaved child. He had no drive, no passion, and very little interest in sex, much less any capacity for it."

"His family had the trustees doling out his trust funds for his care. I could still live with him in our home, but the lawyers wouldn't give me a penny beyond the hundred dollar monthly allowance that had been written in our prenuptial contract. So I took over the publishing business and made it into a commercial success."

"Even though William and I owned the publishing business jointly, his family's lawyers didn't mess with me on that. And, fortunately for us, William had defied his family about how he used his money."

"Before his stroke, William had used a good chunk of his trust income to create a trust for my much-younger sister who was living with us. William treated her like he was her father."

"When William had his stroke, Leona was still young and she couldn't touch the money in her trust until she became an adult. I stayed with William for nearly ten years after his stroke but it was not a good time."

"After Leona turned twenty-one and came into her trust funds, I sold the business, gave half the proceeds to William's family's lawyers, and left."

"You left?"

"I left. William was having serious health problems so I made sure his trustees put him in a supervised care home. I visited him from time to time. Over the past several years he's slipped further and further away. He no longer recognized me so I stopped visiting. Since I have no contact with his family I'm not certain he's still alive. Not that it matters. I'm not really alive myself these days."

"You sound sad. What about your sister, Leona?"

"Leona's doing well."

"How long ago did your husband have his stroke?"

"Don't try to add it up, Dewy. It won't come out right. It was a long time ago."

"How did you meet?"

"Let's save that story for later, Dewy. I think they'd like to turn the table so other tourists can have an opportunity to dine at the Court of Two Sisters tonight. Let's take a walk. We can hear jazz all over the Vieux Carré."

I paid my bill and we left. We didn't get far. We went into Pat O'Brien's and ordered their famous Hurricane Punch.

"So, where did you and William meet?"

"He saw me on stage and fell in love."

"And you?"

"No, not at first. But I was very fond of him."

"Then why did you marry him?"

"I was young, relatively poor, and the sole support of my young sister. I'm not proud of some things I've done in my life, Dewy, but I made decisions as they came. Some turned out well; others didn't. William was an older man with a secure income from his family trust. He was a nice man, a dreamer and a dilettante, but a nice man. His family never understood him and they hated me. They were against us all the way."

"What made the relationship work?"

"He loved me and I liked being loved."

"What did your family say?"

"Nothing. I doubt if they know even to this day that I married William. I grew up in poverty in the mountains of western Virginia. My father worked coal by day and he'd come home drunk every night and work my mother over until he passed out."

"When I was thirteen, Ma died. She just wore out. She couldn't take any more. When Pa decided I should take Ma's place in his bed, I cold cocked him with a cast iron skillet and lit out. As far as I knew I had killed him."

"And you took your sister with you?"

"Not right away. I got her later. Anyway, when William and I married, Leona was still young. William and I never had children, but he wanted to adopt Leona."

"That was a kindness."

"I wouldn't let him adopt her. I didn't want Leona enmeshed in his family. They barely acknowledged me; Leona, not at all."

"You were an actress when you met William."

"Yes."

"Using your aunt's name."

"Yes. I took on her stage name."

"That didn't give you any trouble with Actor's Equity?"

"No."

"They don't let one person use another actor's stage name even if that's the person's legal name. It would get confusing."

"Well, I never made it big so Equity never heard of me. I was only working for a little while and never on Broadway. I only worked in amateur productions after I married. After William's stroke I didn't even do that for a long time. I just stayed home with William and Leona and made a success of the publishing business."

"You must have been proud of that."

"Yes, I was. And it wasn't easy. I had no one to turn to, no emotional support, and few outlets for my passion. After a while I had a brief affair with a literary agent who was having a rough time with his marriage. That didn't last long. We burned out fast and he worked out the problems with his marriage."

"I had a few more affairs, one with a young author we were publishing. Our affair was hot, passionate, and mercifully brief."

"As Leona got closer to adulthood and could keep an eye on William, I started getting out more and I volunteered in theater. That's where I met Val, at a theater party. He became my lover and my liberator. When I left William, I left with Val."

"That must have been a big decision."

"Some decisions are bigger than others, Dewy, and some are more difficult to overcome."

"I'm sorry. I don't understand."

"There's nothing to understand, Dewy, nothing at all. Look, you've finished your Hurricane. Think you can finish mine?"

"Who's driving?"

"Not you. You're staying in Radu's apartment and it's only a few blocks from here. We can walk that far. Finish my punch," she said, pushing her drink toward me, "then we can walk over there. Maybe you'll invite me up to see Radu's famous photographs."

She raised her right eyebrow. "I've heard so much about them."

"Why don't you come up and see my etchings," I said, raising my left eyebrow. I never could raise the right one by itself.

"You decadent theater director."

"That's me."

"I'm counting on it."

I finished Stella's Hurricane Punch and started feeling punchy my-self. I understood why when I read the recipe and discovered that each one contained four ounces of rum. So, I had the four ounces of rum in my drink and I finished Stella's drink. I don't think she had more than a sip. That would make almost eight ounces of rum I drank.

Despite the rum, I managed to walk with Stella on my arm the short distance to Radu's apartment. We climbed the stairs in silence at Stella's suggestion which she made by putting her index finger to her closed mouth, a gesture that called my passionate attention to her rouged lips.

As we entered the apartment, I pointed out the publicity picture.

"Oh, Dewy, that looks almost just like me except my mole is real. Aunt Stella must have painted hers on, and in just about the same place."

"Looks like exactly the same place," I said, as I put my hand to her face, touching her mole.

She moved her face so my fingers were on her lips. She opened her mouth and gently nibbled my fingers. With her hand, she pulled my fingers out of her mouth and, after kissing each one, took my hand and placed it on her breast. She traced the outline of my lips with her finger.

"I don't want to talk about that, Dewy. I want to kiss you," she whispered.

Chapter Eleven

The air was fresh and crisp as I walked to the theater. It was my mind that was fuzzy. An autumnal cold front had moved through overnight clearing the air. What would it take to clear my mind? I chose a route that took me by the French Market to get beignets and café au lait for breakfast. That might not clear my mind, but it was worth a try.

At seven in the morning tourist activity was light. Few sidewalk artists and street performers were out and stirring. I stopped for a moment at Jackson Square to watch a street performer who was out but hardly stirring, a woman I thought of as Crimson Liberty. She wore a crown and a flowing gown like the lady in New York harbor, but her crown and gown were crimson, not green. Her face, arms, and hands were covered in silver body paint. On her fingers she had glued three-inch nail extensions that were painted teal to compliment her crimson crown and gown. Every now and then she would change her pose.

That was the sum of her performance and the tourists loved it. One would walk up and pose beside her while a companion would take a picture, presumably to show the folks back in Andover or Zebulon how fabulous life was in New Orleans. Almost always the tourists would deposit a tip in a metal box, painted teal, she had attached to her ankle with one of those specially-hardened bicycle cable locks that students love. A thief would have to take the woman to get the box.

I didn't always see Crimson Liberty when I walked through the square, but she was often there, never speaking, hardly moving, and always ignoring the tourists she allowed to pose with her. I had never seen her come or go; she was just there.

Life's like that sometimes. You don't always notice the coming and going, just the being there and the not being there. Like last night with Stella. That rum hit me harder than I expected. I've never passed out before, but I've never drunk nearly eight ounces of rum before, either. That's nearly twice the DUI blood-alcohol limit for a man my size.

I remember Stella's being there but not her getting there. I know she wasn't there when I woke up, fully dressed except for my shoes. Strangely, I was dressed in the black turtleneck jersey I often wear when I'm working in the theater, but last night I had worn my orange UT pullover when I went out to meet Stella. I must have put on the turtleneck jersey after I came home, but I had no memory of doing it.

Stella left a note, a physical trace, a confirmation that she had been there. I pulled it out of my pocket and read it again.

Dewy,

I had a wonderful evening. I'll be terribly busy rehearsing The Passion of Dracula for the next three weeks. Don't try to reach me. I'll be free to be your date for the cast party for Four Plays. I'll meet you at the campus theater on the 11th. Love, Stella.

I put the note away and watched my Crimson Liberty for a few minutes as she performed to a nearly-empty square. I pulled a ten-dollar bill out of my pocket, stuffed it in the slot in her metal box, and headed off toward TVC. There's no such thing as a free lunch and even street performers need to be nourished.

The street cleaning crews had swept through earlier, the horse-drawn carriages hadn't started yet today, and only one drunk importuned me for a dollar to buy a beer. If I put aside the minor irritations of a stiff, sore neck and of not being able to recall dressing myself, it looked like it could be a good day.

I quickly changed my mind when I walked into the theater and came face to face with a dead chicken hanging two feet in front of me, a fighting cock by the looks of it. He must have been a splendid specimen when he lived. Now, with his eyes dull and cloudy as he hung by his de-spurred feet, wings akimbo and feathers ruffled away from his body by the unrelenting force of gravity, he looked like a mare's nest of russet feathers with a few streaks of silver and teal.

I looked for visible wounds but saw none, nor did I see blood on the floor. Gently I lifted him and turned him upright. His head lolled to the side. Clearly his neck was wrung. Broken. That kind of injury does not happen in the wild. This was human work.

I went to the green room and called 911. An operator responded.

"What do you need at the Théâtre Vieux Carré?" Obviously they had installed address location equipment.

"I'd like you to send the police over."

"What's the problem?

"I've got a dead cock here."

"How do you know it's dead?"

"It's limp as a dishrag."

"Hey, my frien', that happens to every guy now and then. It'll be O.K. when you sober up."

"Look, there is a dead cock hanging from the rigging. A rooster. It has a broken neck. I don't need the paramedics and I'm probably more sober than most judges. I'd like you to send someone over to investigate. I'm Dewy Spearman and I'll be waiting here."

"O.K., Mr. Spearman, we'll send somebody. But why don't you wait outside. The cock killer could still be lurking in the shadows, you know what I mean?"

"Why do I think you aren't taking this seriously? There might really be someone in here."

"It's O.K., my frien'. We'll send someone over. It's not every day we get to investigate a chicken crime. Wait outside. We'll have someone over in a few minutes."

I hung up and went outside to wait. In a few minutes two men came around the corner on foot. Somehow they just looked like cops. The taller one, a black man, was wearing brown slacks, a green plaid, light-weight sports coat, a white shirt, a purple tie, and a tan, straw fedora with a purple hat band. The shorter one, a white man, was wearing mustard slacks, a royal blue t-shirt, and a denim vest. The tall man opened his jacket and the shorter man opened his vest to flash badges and show guns. The taller one spoke.

"I'm Lt. Thibodeau and this is Officer Landowski," he said, tilting his head toward the white man."

"He's our token minority. Are you Spearman, the guy with the limp cock?"

"Yes," I said, irritated with the way he put the question.

"Landowski said, "Would you like us to take you over to Big Ethel's to get it fixed," and then he grinned. He was missing a tooth.

I could see that both men were on the edge of laughter and I had to admit, grudgingly, that the situation was tailor-made for humorous bantering, so I let my irritation pass and jumped into the game.

"No thanks. This cock's definitely a goner. Not even Hurricane Hattie could blow it back to life. You want to come in and see?"

"O.K., Spearman, but if you're pulling our dicks, a limp cock will be the least of your worries."

"Look, officers, I don't know what's going on here, but when I walked in this morning I found a dead rooster, a fighting cock by the looks of him, hanging from the rigging. His neck's been wrung. I don't know who did it, or why, or how they got in, or even if they're still here. Now, if you'll step inside you'll see what I mean."

The three of us walked in and, as I had done earlier, they immediately spotted the cock.

"Well, I'll be a son of a bitch," Thibodeau said. "It's a friggin' cock. No blood. Looks like his neck's been wrung. Spearman, you step outside. Landowski and I will check the building."

I stepped outside. I didn't have to wait long. In a few minutes Thibodeau and Landowski came out.

"There's no one lurking around where we can see but there's a coupla' locked doors," Thibodeau said. "You got keys?"

"I've got a key that opens the stage door. I don't know what else it opens. I'm just a guest director so I don't know the key arrangements around here. It might open the prop room and maybe the light booth, if it's locked. I doubt it would open the box office. That would be a poor management practice."

"Well," Thibodeau said, "I'm not sure what we've got here. It's not against the law to kill a chicken. People have been killing chickens for thousands of years. My Grand'Mère used to wring their necks. I couldn't stand to watch."

"It's funny, you know, since I was in the army and I became a cop where I'm trained to use lethal force against people, but I can't stand to see a chicken get its neck wrung. But Grand'Mère, she could wring a chicken's neck five ways to Sunday and make one hell of a chicken pot pie. Nowadays you can't even get a conviction for cruelty to animals for killing a chicken no matter how you do it since the Supreme Court ruled that the Santa Ria people could sacrifice chickens as part of their religion. You into Santa Ria, Spearman?"

"No."

"Voodoo?"

"What's that got to do with anything?"

"You must not be from around here, so I'll tell you," Thibodeau said. "From my vast experience, people who hang dead chickens do it for someone else to find, to intimidate or spook them. A lot of voodoo is involved with putting on curses or taking them off. It's mostly just plain intimidation, like in The Godfather when the mob guys stuffed the decapitated head of mouthpiece's race horse in his bed to let to let him know that his being a lawyer didn't mean he couldn't be reached. Is somebody after you to keep quiet about somethin' or to keep your nose out of somethin'?"

"It's the story of my life, officer. Theater directors are always sticking their noses in everything."

I didn't think they picked up on my sarcasm, so I switched direction. "Of course not, officer. Maybe it wasn't even meant for me."

"Yeah, Spearman. Got any ideas?"

I had a few ideas, but nothing that could be proved. Maybe it was meant for me. I had been told to mind my own business more than once since I came to New Orleans. Maybe Susan Riley's boyfriend thought I was competition. I didn't want to get into that with Thibodeau, so I took the easy way out.

"It's probably just somebody's idea of a joke."

"I'll put that down as the official report, Spearman, unless somebody confesses. We don't have time to investigate somethin's not even a crime. If I was going to put any time into investigatin' anything about this here theater, I'd be investigatin' the death of that director who worked here, Hammond Laidlaw."

"I thought he drowned."

"Coroner said he did but he didn't. Weren't no water in his lungs except for the little bit that seeps down when your corpse has been underwater for a week or so."

"So, what did he die of?"

"Exsanguination, they call it. Bled out. Puncture wounds to the carotid artery, the big one in the neck."

"Why did the corner say he drowned?"

"Public relations. Mrs. Boudron didn't want bad publicity and the coroner, Doc Sacristan, be her cousin. Doc didn't say he drowned, exactly. Said it was 'death by misadventure.' Means Laidlaw was stupid enough to fall in the Mississippi and not smart enough to crawl out. Doc mostly jus' ignored the blood loss. Said Laidlaw musta' injured his neck on the way in."

"So why don't you investigate?"

"Case is officially closed. But I tell you, my friend, there's plenty of people right here in this theater to investigate for a whole bunch of things. Your business manager is a felon. Your electrician is a drunk with no fixed address. Your costume lady cruises the truck stops out on I-10 pretty much all winter."

"What costume lady?"

"The redhead. And that boyfrien' of hers, Von Dragon. What a sleaze. He must be into every legal racket in town and some illegal.

"Are you talking about Stella Maris?" I said, feeling suddenly hollow in my gut.

"She the one who sometimes acts on stage here and lives out in the Garden District with Von Dragon?"

"I don't know where she lives, but she's a redhead, a wardrobe mistress, an actress, and she's with Von Dragon. I want to know about her hanging out at truck stops," I said, sharply.

"You theater people just kill me," Thibodeau replied. "Give me pimps and whores any day. At least everybody know what they be up to, and why. Lord knows what you theater people be up to—much less why."

My face warmed and my ears got hotter.

"What about the truck stops?" I found it difficult to keep my voice under control.

"Later, man. My pager vibrated three times while we've been standin' here flappin' our lips. I'll get Landowski to file a report. We sent him to literacy class last year so he can write pretty fine. That'll be the end of it unless something else happens."

"Cut that bird down and toss it in the rubbish or take it home and cook it. If anyone threatens you directly, call me at the station. If you have any more problems with a limp cock, try Big Ethel's. She can straighten out a limp cock quicker than a politician can take a campaign contribution. Come on Landowski."

Thibodeau and Landowski left and I went back inside to cut the cock down, but it was gone. All that remained was two feathers, one silver, and one teal. Like my Crimson Liberty, I hadn't seen the cock come or go, but it had been there. Two feathers confirmed it. Like Stella. I couldn't remember how she got there and I didn't see her leave. Yet she'd been there. Her note confirmed it. But Stella had come and gone of her own volition. Not so, the cock.

I heard the front door slam. That was all I needed. My preplanning for *Macbeth* could wait. I went out the stage door locking it behind me. I didn't mind being in the theater alone. What I minded was being there un-alone, or being there alone except for whomever killed the cock and then removed it.

If I came back on Tuesday during rehearsal for *The Passion of Dracula*, I could count on other people being here, people I knew. I definitely didn't want to be here without at least a small crowd, so I walked back to the apartment.

I sat in Radu's study with no particular plan in mind except, perhaps, to make notes for *Macbeth*. As I mused on the strange events that happened to me since I had come to New Orleans, I found myself staring at the collection of bound volumes.

Each volume had a gold-embossed letter on its spine starting with A and ending with L. I picked up the A volume and began reading at the first page.

"In the spirit of the great photographer, Edward Weston, although presumptuous of me to compare my limited talents to his genius, I begin with A, the first volume of my own daybooks."

Radu had begun his daybooks with the A book. On the shelf, the next volume was the B book, and then the C book. At the end of the row was the L book. The L daybook. Was this the "Elday" book Madame Claire told me to read? The L volume of these daybooks?

I returned the A volume to its place, removed the L volume, and began reading. The first entry was dated about a year ago and was an account of a run-in Radu had with Ellis Boudron. I was comforted to know that Ellis hadn't singled me out for his rude behavior.

I had difficulty concentrating on the book and spent the next hour or two alternately reading and catnapping.

Between catnaps I read Radu's daily concerns, mostly about the theater, how his shows were going, and whether anything would come of his application to be a visiting director at Theater Budapest.

I perked up when I came to a passage in which he described how irritated he had become at Hammond Laidlaw for "mooning over the wardrobe mistress who was playing Madge." That must have been Stella from last March's production at TVC.

I read a few more references interspersed among his accounts of his own daily activities about Hammond chasing after Stella and Von Dragon warning Hammond off.

I came to a page about Stella. Radu wrote, "Actors Equity informed me that Stella Maris joined in 1947. She had various off-Broadway credits including understudy for Kate in out-of-town tryouts in Philadelphia for *Kiss Me Kate*. She was replaced before the New York opening. No reason given. No credits since. Membership lapsed in 1950. Date of birth listed as 1926 but actresses often lie about their age. Next of kin was listed as Leona Yellin."

I wasn't sure I understood what I had just read. If my arithmetic was correct, that would make Stella Maris as old as Clotilde Boudron, maybe older. Radu must have been doing research on Stella's Aunt Stella. The Stella I knew was probably 40 years old although she didn't look a day over 30.

I dozed off again and woke up with just enough time to make it to this evening's rehearsal for *Four Plays* if I didn't stop to eat. The rehearsal went well, but I still felt groggy and not particularly hungry. I skipped eating and went straight home.

I had hardly settled in to finish reading the L Daybook when the door bell rang. I replaced the L volume on the bookshelf and went to the door. Through the peephole I saw Stella. I opened the door.

"Stella, what a surprise. I thought I wasn't going to see you until my cast party on the 11th."

"I've been thinking about you all day, Dewy. I just couldn't stay away. May I come in?"

"Of course. Please do."

"I've already eaten, but I brought you a famous New Orleans oyster po' boy sandwich and a bottle of mineral water."

"Yeah. Sorry about last night. I must have had too much rum. I can't remember much. Did we—"

"No."

"—make love?"

"Yes. We made love all evening. No, we didn't have sex."

"It was the rum. Remember the Porter's scene from *Macbeth*?"

"Tell me."

"The porter, slow to answer a late-night knocking at the castle door, admits Macduff and Lennox and kvetches to them about the consequences of drink. 'What three things does drink especially provoke? Marry sir, nose-painting, sleep, and urine. Lechery, sir, it provokes, and unprovokes: it provokes the desire, but it takes away the performance. Therefore, much drink may be said to be an equivocator with lechery; it makes him, and it mars him; it sets him on, and it takes him off; it persuades him, and disheartens him; makes him stand to, and not stand to; in conclusion, equivocates him in a sleep, and giving him the lie, leaves him.'"

I waited for Stella to say something clever about drinking and sexual performance, but she surprised me with her plaintive request.

"Hold me," she said, putting down the sandwich and the water and standing there, arms open, fingers splayed. "Just hold me."

I held her. She reciprocated fiercely. I thought she was going to squeeze the life out of me until she relaxed her hold, turned her shining tear-runneled face up to mine, and kissed me—long, wet, and passionately.

As if we were sharks in a feeding frenzy we became a blurred mélange of hands, kisses, squeezes, rubs, tickles, nibbles, and naked bodies until, at last, we became a two-headed beast heaving and moaning on the floor, and then we shrieked, shuddered, and collapsed, nearly immobile.

Stella stroked my head and neck as I traced the tracks of her tears down her cheeks.

"Why so sad, little one?"

"I'm happy, Dewy. Really, I am. I just don't want to talk about it. Tell me about your plans for *Macbeth*."

"Can we move to someplace more comfortable?"

"In a few minutes. Right now I just want to lie here and feel the pleasure of your warm body. Shush. Don't talk. Just lie here."

Sometime later I awoke. Stella had placed a pillow under my head and spread a blanket over me. She was sitting on Radu's love seat, wrapped in blanket, watching me. Her clothes were strewn across the floor and intertwined with mine.

"Did you have a nice nap?"

"Yes, and I had a nice time working up to it. This time I can remember everything. I didn't know eight ounces of rum could wipe me out that way. I must have bumped into something, too. I have a tender bruise with broken skin on my neck."

"Don't worry about it. Wrap yourself in your blanket and sit with me. Your sandwich and water are waiting for you. So is your lady."

"You are my lady?"

"Your Lady Macbeth."

"I play the Porter. Lance is going to play Macbeth. So, that would make you his Lady Macbeth. I'm counting on you to help make him be a passable Macbeth. Frankly, I have grave doubts."

"Come, sit up here. Eat, and tell me about it. When you've finished, we'll make love again. Then I'll have to go. I really won't be
able to see you again until your cast party on the 11th, but I'll be
there then. Count on it."

I ate my famous New Orleans oyster po' boy sandwich, drank my
bottle of mineral water, and shared my ideas for *Macbeth* with Stella.
We made love again and fell asleep. In the morning, she was gone—
again.

With no prospect of seeing Stella until the 11th, the coming weeks
were going to be long ones.

Chapter Twelve

We opened *Four Plays for Coarse Actors* on October 8th. After three nights of decent performances, the closing performance went down with a few minor glitches which were neatly offset by a few high points. Bill Arquette, who played Testiculo, the unfunny-to-us clown in *All's Well That Ends As You Like It*, apparently had difficulty on the first two nights realizing that he wasn't getting laughs because he was playing for laughs. Tonight, and last night, too, Bill played it straight and the audience roared at his un-funniness.

Yolanda Batterson, who played Prompter in *A Collier's Tuesday Tea*, got continually worse over the four nights. In the beginning the audience laughed at her, as should happen from the way the show was written and directed, but it seemed she wanted more laughs so she played more and more broadly each night. Tonight's audience was bored with her antics, even with her scripted business, like making crippled Grandpa Joe crawl off the stage in the longest direction which usually caused audiences to howl with laughter.

In comedy, often less is more. Yolanda was giving us a lesson that more was often too much. I wanted to figure out a way to give her gentle feedback so she could improve, if she chose to.

Annie Mirada, Countess in *Il Fornicazione*, disappointed me too. With each successive performance, she sang better and mugged more than in her performance the evening before. Spoofs of opera require dreadful singing, and the best comedy is usually played straight, lessons Annie had yet to learn.

Situations are funny. Character reactions that are appropriate to the logic of the character but inappropriate to the audience's expectations are funny. Lines are funny. Timing is funny. But mugging to the audience is not funny. It takes the actor out of the ensemble and attempts to create a personal relationship between that character and the audience. It breaks down the fourth wall.

Breaking down the fourth wall can be an effective technique in drama. Rarely is it so in comedy.

When I saw Annie mugging directly at the audience, I was disappointed. She had attempted to go for laughs at the expense of her fellow performers rather than playing ensemble and sharing the rewards. Unless she was planning a professional career as a stand-up comedian or a vocal soloist, she wasn't going to get far, and even comedians and soloists have to work with writers and producers.

My most pleasant surprise, confirmation really, was Susan Riley. She performed splendidly as Delia, the ingénue who disguised herself in boy's clothing to sneak out of her father's camp and rendezvous with the object of her affection, Dronio.

Her lavender poet's hat with a fringe of auburn hair peeking out, her form-fitting buff tights, and her bleached muslin jerkin with its laces partly undone to expose her unmanly décolletage, fooled all the characters in the scene but no one in the audience.

Susan had the proper mixture of insouciance, petulance, passion, self-absorption, and jiggle to put on a masterful performance. She neither yielded to the temptation to overplay her part nor resorted to the greenhorn's errors of stepping on other players' lines or upstaging them, tricks which, if pulled by experienced actors, would be deliberate attempts to hog the stage and intimidate their fellow actors.

Professional actors can be called before Actors' Equity to answer charges of unprofessional conduct and can be fined or even fired if the charges are serious and proved to be true.

In College Theater there is no Actors' Equity to hold actors to any standard of performance. That job belongs to the director, who can usually ill-afford to replace a student during a run, and to the entire cast to the extent that the ordinary effects of group dynamics and peer pressure come into play.

A college theater director must deal with teaching professional conduct before the show gets to performance. Once a show's on the boards, there's little a director can do if the actors misbehave.

So, on they went as they were wont to go, four productions brought to fruition by four assistant directors, a cast of more than fifty, and a dozen more students on the stage crew and light crew. All in all, it had gone well.

After the final curtain call we cleared the set and began the cast party. By local tradition the cast party was held on the stage and in the green room. I suppose some students would go off later and have private parties, but the one on stage was the official party.

Even though New Orleans seems not to have a minimum age for consuming alcoholic beverages, our official cast party was dry. To top that off, Dean Halberstam was probably lurking about enforcing propriety and spreading gloom.

Official cast parties are generally not among your really great parties and I fully expected Susan Riley would skip ours to attend the fraternity parties with her boyfriend.

I was wrong.

Susan appeared, dressed in her own clothes, green suede, low-top boots, chocolate-brown tights, a white, opalescent, square-neck, belted peasant blouse that hung down about twelve inches below the bottom of her russet suede laced bodice, and a teal beret from which a fringe of auburn hair escaped.

Her ensemble conspired to make her look much like Delia dressed as a boy with much the same effect, only more so. The laced bodice lifted her breasts in a way that her costume jerkin had not.

"Did you like the performances, Dewy?" she asked as she walked up, stopped about twelve inches in front of me, placed her right hand on my left arm, and batted her eyelashes.

"Your performance was outstanding, Susan. I was particularly impressed that you didn't attempt to overplay your role," I said as I gently removed her hand from my arm.

"I was tempted, Dewy, especially when I snuck into the light booth during a performance and saw Annie hamming it up."

"I'm glad you didn't. Your performance was superb."

"Thanks. Will you be directing anything else here?" she said, turning her face up to look at me. Her pupils were seductively dilated and her moist lips shimmered.

"No. This is my only show. Maurice Bridges is directing the other show this semester, *A Funny Thing Happened on the Way to the Forum*, and then I'm gone. You should try out for a part, maybe one of the courtesans. I'm sure you could do it."

"Thank you for your confidence. Are you doing anything off campus before you leave?" she asked as she put her left hand on my right arm.

"I'm directing the Scottish play at Théatre Vieux Carré," I said as I deftly removed her hand again and dodged her attempt to catch mine.

"May I audition?"

"No. There are few roles for females in that show and all of them have been cast."

"May I work on the crew?"

"I suppose you could if any of the crew chiefs could use you, but I think you should do something in *Forum*. Stay here on campus for a while. Learn with your classmates."

As Susan looked down at the floor, I suddenly realized she had made her entrance alone.

"Where's your boyfriend? I thought you'd be going to that fraternity party with him."

She looked up at me again with a renewed sparkle in her eye.

"I dropped him."

"Oh?"

"He was a jerk. He bruised my arm and nearly sprained my wrist arguing about going to his stupid fraternity party."

"Did you report that to the Dean?"

"No. Why bother? What's the point? All guys that age are jerks. They're not like mature men."

She'd baited the hook.

"You chose to honor your will and not to bow to someone else's."

"I guess so. As a result, I don't have a date for this party."

Now she was dangling her baited hook in my face.

Chapter Thirteen

"I do," Stella said, speaking from directly behind me. I had no idea how long she had been standing there but I was glad she was.

As Susan rose up on her toes to see over my shoulder, she thrust her breasts into my chest.

"Right here," Stella said, stepping around to my right side and placing her arm in mine. Susan came down from her toes.

I heard bells tinkling in Stella's voice. She was dressed in a black, boat-neck, floor-length gown, black pumps, and a single strand of pearls—a visual delight to accompany the delightful music.

"Stella," I said, "please meet our talented Delia, Susan Riley. Susan, please meet Stella Maris."

"I'm pleased to meet you, Miss Riley," Stella said evenly, without the accompanying bells. "I enjoyed your performance. Seldom have I seen so much self-assurance and talent in one so young. You have a gift. I hope you use it wisely."

"Uh, thank you. Thank you, Mrs. Maris," Susan replied as she stepped back, apparently confused.

"Miss," Stella corrected her.

"Thank you, Miss Maris. I'd like to continue working with Dewy. He said this will be the only time I get to work with him."

"You never know, Susan." I said. "I might be directing you on Broadway one day."

"Do you think I can get that far?" Susan asked, beaming her dreamy face again in my direction.

Stella gently nudged my ribs with her elbow.

"Child," I said, only half aware of why I had chosen that form of address, "with your talent, if you master discipline you could even play the Old Vic, but you had best take advantage of your opportunities here first. Maurice Bridges is over there talking to Dr. Fellows, the one dressed like a priest. Go over and tell Professor Bridges that

Dewy recommends you for *Forum*. Now scoot. I need to talk to a few other people, too."

"O.K. May I come by your office sometime and talk?"

"I have office hours on Tuesday and Thursday afternoons. Sign up and thirty minutes of my time is your time. Now run along."

I halfway watched as she walked over and joined Maurice's and Chan's group.

"You were brutal," Stella said.

"I know."

"The girl's in love with you."

"She'll get over it."

"And you?"

"Already have. Ready to go?"

"What about the other people you wanted to talk with?"

"What other people?"

"Dewy, that's not nice. I'm going to spend a few minutes speaking to several of your actors praising them for their work. I suggest you do the same. We'll have the rest of the night for each other."

As I watched Stella walk over to Blanche Hoenhold, Mrs. D'Arcy in *Streuth*, Chan detached himself from Maurice and came over to me.

"Congratulations, Dewy. That was a fine performance, the one you just had with Miss Riley. You handled yourself well. Being stage struck as well as star-struck with her director is a tough thing for a young lady. Judging from the reputation which has preceded you, turning her away was perhaps not so easy."

"I've grown up, Chan."

"Congratulations, again."

"I hope I can handle the relationship I'm starting with Stella."

"I do too, Dewy. Frankly, I don't have a good feeling about it."

"Why? Because she's with Val? They're not married."

"A written contract does not a marriage make nor will its absence unmake one. Two people cannot submit their wills to the will of the relationship unless each is free to do so and does so freely."

"Confucius?"

"Perhaps it was Chandler Fellows. I didn't come here to lecture you, Dewy, or to be your moral tutor, but when you want to talk to someone who has your best interests at heart, I'll be there to listen."

The increasing chatter around Maurice caught my attention, and when I looked, Maurice motioned for us to come over.

"Dewy, rescue me from all these hungry actors. I'm afraid if I don't promise them all parts in *Forum*, they'll devour me on the spot."

"Like Sebastian on the beach in *Suddenly Last Summer*?"

"Well, not literally, and not so graphically." Maurice shuddered.

Addressing the students, Maurice said, "Everyone will have a chance to audition. No part has been precast. But if you don't go away and leave us alone for ten minutes, I will make sure I cast you in some small and insignificant role, perhaps a spear catcher."

"There are no small roles, only small actors," said Henry, the two-hundred pound singer who sang too well whom I had talked into being the chorus master instead of playing Alfonso.

"Yeah," added Annie, also a two-hundred pounder who played the Countess, "and neither you nor I are among them, Henry."

"Speaking of rolls," Henry continued, "are any of those dinner rolls from *A Collier's Tuesday Tea* left, ka-boom, ka-boom," imitating the vaudevillian's rim-shot effect.

"Yeah," a voice called from the food table. "The marmalade's not bad either."

The knot of actors moved off toward the food table making such quips as, "Look at the orange Mama laid", "We would have taken her to the psychiatrist but we needed the oranges," and, "How about a roll on the table?"

"It's nice to see so much enthusiasm," Chan said.

"Yes," Maurice replied. "But I prefer to see more self-discipline."

I must have registered some form of negative reaction because Maurice quickly interjected, "I don't mean to suggest that your production was out of control, old boy, only that these young people could profit from tempering their exuberance with a bit more self-restraint. I know how difficult it is to get them to concentrate on their roles and not become distracted by each other."

"Maurice has great experience with concentration and control," Chan said. "Do you recall the conversation at Mrs. Boudron's dinner party about Maurice serving in the Air Force? He was a crack shot with both rifle and pistol. You know, breathe, relax, aim, sight, and squeeze. He would have represented us at the Moscow Olympics if President Carter hadn't boycotted them."

"That's true, Chandler, old man," Maurice said, "but hardly to the point. That kind of concentration and control is good for perfecting one's own performance. It does little to promote ensemble work. I suppose that's why I'm better at rhetoric than acting. I can concentrate mightily on my own performance and bring it off with great precision, but I'm not as effective at interrelating with a group. Spearman, with only one or two rough spots, has done marvelously well getting these immature actors to perform ensemble. Bravo!"

"Thank you, Maurice. I'm unhappy with a few bits of actor's ego that broke through, but—"

"Say no more," Maurice interrupted. "I'll guess Countess in *Il Fornicazione* and Prompter in *Collier's*, yes?"

"Yes."

"Rest assured, I shall keep that in mind as I cast *Forum*."

"Oh," I added, "about Susan Riley. I am fully convinced she could play a courtesan in *Forum* and I did send her over here to tell you I recommended her to be cast in the show. I didn't tell her that I was thinking of her for Philia because I don't want to presume upon your prerogative to cast whom you please."

"Relax, Spearman, old boy. From what I saw tonight, unless some hitherto unknown talent emerges in the next ten days, Susan Riley is a talent I would want for Philia. We'll have to put a blonde wig on her. I don't know nor do I care whether she can meet the technical requirement for a virgin, but I'm sure she can play one. She seems to have a good balance of boldness and ensemble."

"I'm sure she'll be glad to hear that, Maurice" I said. "I wonder if she'll think I had anything to do with it."

"Why should that be a problem?"

"I wouldn't want her to be grateful for something I didn't do."

"Under the circumstances," said Stella, speaking from behind me again, "isn't that better than her being grateful because it's something you did?"

"But, I didn't," I said. "It would be unfair for her to think otherwise. She did it on her talent, alone."

"Who are you trying to convince?" Maurice asked, "Me, you, or Stella? Hello, Stella, dear. So good to see you again."

"And you, Maurice," Stella said. "I presume Wendy missed the show because she's burning the midnight oil at TVC?"

"Of course," Maurice replied, rolling his eyes. "She's a virtual slave to the box office."

"I was hoping to see her here tonight," I said. "I need to talk to her about managing the house for the Scottish play. It's rather late to still be at the theater for a show that opened at eight o'clock. The box office is usually wrapped up by intermission."

"*Suddenly* has no intermission, but this is the last night of the run," Maurice replied in a tone that led me to understand this part of the conversation had come to its conclusion.

"What about *Macbeth*?" Chan asked.

"Please, Chandler, old man," Maurice said, "remember, while we're in the theater, any theater, refer to it as 'the Scottish play.'"

"Oh, yes. Sorry I forgot. How's the Scottish play, Dewy?"

"I haven't started rehearsals yet since I'm just closing this show. My notebook is coming along well. Next week I'll have some time to come over to TVC and plan the set. I was thinking about flying one or more of the Weird Sisters but Spider is dissuading me."

"That's a wise decision, Dewy. Were you to perform the Scottish play in this theater, you could fly half of the cast if that struck your fancy. It's too risky to fly more than one person at a time at TVC and it's wiser to forgo flying anyone."

"If I can't fly anyone, I'll want to build out a thrust stage so I can have trap doors for the witches. I believe I can make a decision on that if I can get back into the theater to think about it. If I'm allowed, I'd like to sit in on rehearsals for *The Passion of Dracula*."

"Oh, Dewy," Stella said. "I'm sorry, but you can't. Val made a big stink about rehearsals being closed and he got Madame Boudron to agree. Frankly, I'll be glad when *Passion* is over. It consumes my evenings and keeps me from other enjoyable activities."

"I thought Lenny Skavinski was directing? What did he have to say about closing the rehearsals?" I asked.

"He is directing, old boy," Maurice chimed in, "but you know who calls the shots. That's why I won't work there."

"Wendy works there," I said.

"Wendy has her life and I have mine. It's been nice chatting with you, really it has, but I must toddle off now. I'm taking the debate team to a competition tomorrow and I must get my beauty sleep. Good evening Chan, Dewy. I'll see you on campus on Monday. Stella, it's been a pleasure as always. I'll come see you in *Passion*. I'm eager to see Val perform and I am so grateful that nice boy, Lance Sterling, got to play Harker. It's a role better suited to him."

"Your wishes may be granted," Stella said. "I have for you and for Dewy and for Dr. Fellows complimentary tickets to the preview next Wednesday. I will be pleased to have you in the audience. I'd like to give tickets to some members of your cast, too, Dewy."

"Of course you may, Stella."

I watched her move from group to group exchanging a few words with various members of the cast and handing out tickets to some of them. She avoided Susan Riley.

"Spearman, old boy," Maurice said, "before I leave, forgive me for intruding into your private life, but I want to tell you this. In my five years of being peripherally associated with Stella Maris, I've never seen her so animated. Take care. Val is a jealous man and a powerful adversary. I'd sooner cross Madame Boudron than cross Val."

"Did I hear someone mention my family name?" Laura said, as she joined our group.

"Quite," Maurice said. "I was telling Spearman why I prefer not to work at TVC."

"Mother can be overbearing."

"From your mouth to God's ear," Maurice responded, rolling his eyes for the second time this evening.

"Please, Laura, do not think for even one minute that I don't enjoy the pleasure of your company. You are the Boudron whose company I do enjoy. But, alas, I have made my *adieux* and I now must leave. Toodleoo."

Maurice took Laura's hand, kissed it, and left.

"Does Maurice always do that?" I asked.

"He does have certain flair, doesn't he? Usually it's more British than Continental. I liked your shows, Dewy. How did you manage to get all four of them to performance in only four weeks?"

"Assistant directors. One for each play."

"With the Scottish play you only have one show to produce. What would you use an assistant director for?"

"I was thinking more of a director's assistant than an assistant director, but if that's the title it takes to get you to do the job, you are now assistant director."

"I hope you're not counting on having me in the production making things go better with Mother. She's made it abundantly clear that she doesn't want me involved with TVC or with much of anything, for that matter."

"Laura, I have no desire to become enmeshed in the Boudron family's domestic issues. Frankly, I'm not worried about dealing with your mother. Thomas Jefferson said, 'Worry is interest paid in advance on a debt you may never owe.' Whatever comes up I shall deal with at the time. I refuse to worry in advance."

"Something has come up."

"What's that?"

"Mother says if I become your assistant she'll tell the maid to stop cleaning my room and the cook to stop preparing my meals."

"Why doesn't she just threaten to throw you out?"

"My father's will and the trust. I probably could get a court order to continue to have my meals prepared because it's covered in the trust, but I've already planned to eat out."

"Does this mean you'll do the show?"

"Since you have given me billing as assistant director, yes."

"Thanks, Laura. I hope you won't have occasion to regret it."

"I hope you won't have occasion to regret it either, Dewy, but I'm not as sanguine as you are."

"Doubts or not, Laura, I'm sure you'll do a fine job."

"I wasn't thinking of that, Dewy. I was thinking of Mother. When Thomas Jefferson said not to worry about troubles you don't already have, he hadn't met Clotilde Boudron."

"Wouldn't your mother be interested in having the show be successful?"

"Not if it diminished her glory as queen bee. All Mother has left is TVC. She's growing old. The writers, artists, and musicians she consorted with are too old to come around much anymore—or too dead. Much like Mrs. Venable in *Suddenly Last Summer*, Mother's an anachronism. I wonder if Tennessee Williams hadn't looked thirty years into Mother's future when he wrote *Suddenly*. All she has left is her theater. I believe she intends to be Grande Dame until she dies even if she runs the theater into the ground. By the way, you are now on her enemies list and it looks like I'll soon join you there."

"Then why have you agreed to be assistant director?"

"To uphold the honor of the Boudron name."

"I'm afraid I don't understand, Laura."

"I'm not sure I can explain and I'd rather not try. You invited me to be your assistant and I accepted your offer. For the moment, let's leave it at that."

"That's good enough for me."

"Fine, then. What is my first assignment?"

"Read the script, memorize it if you can, make notes for props, and show up for the first rehearsal. We'll work on it from there."

"I have one request, Dewy. Don't announce my appointment as assistant director until I have first broken the news to Mother."

"O.K. by me."

"Good night," Laura said, as she clanked away toward the exit. One would think that she would clear a wide swath swinging her crutches alternately to each side, but she seemed to walk fairly normally bearing her weight on her feet and using the Lofstrands more like walking sticks than crutches.

"Already lining up your next conquest, I see," Stella said from behind me.

"You keep doing that."

"Reading your mind?"

"No, slipping up behind me. I assure you, Laura isn't my next conquest. She's—oops, I can't say anything about it yet."

"Now that we've become intimate you begin keeping secrets from me."

"This is nothing like that. It has nothing to do with you and me. And don't we both have secrets ourselves, you and I?"

Stella's eyes opened wide as if she were frightened.

"What do you mean, Dewy?"

"Aren't we having a secret affair?"

Her look of fright melted into a coquettish smile.

"Of course we are, darling. But if we continue talking so intensely and privately to each other in the midst of a party, it won't be a secret for long."

The worried look returned to her face.

"Dewy, be discreet. I am not entirely a free woman and Val is not a nice person. I'm going to leave now. I have something I must do that has nothing to do with you. Meet me at your apartment in an hour or so, around midnight."

She turned and glided out of the theater. I really didn't want to wait and started to follow her but I was cut off by Dean Halberstam.

"Mr. Spearman."

"Dean Halberstam," I replied, mirroring her formal address.

"I've heard favorable reports of your performance in the classroom and your production of *Four Plays* was outstanding. I can see now what you meant about 'coarse' meaning 'rough' instead of 'vulgar'. I must admit my heart leapt into my throat when Alfonzo ripped open the Countess' gown until saw that it wasn't sexual in any way and that she was appropriately under clothed."

She blushed. "That doesn't sound right, does it? "Let me say, she was wearing a sufficiency of undergarments."

I said nothing. Dean Halberstam screwed up her face but she did not break her silence.

I stood, also silent, doing nothing to ease her discomfort. I supposed she was having an inner dialogue about the relative merits of propriety versus the value of connection.

Finally she spoke. "That's what is meant by 'bodice-ripper.'"

"Well, a spoof of one, anyway."

"I commend you on your professional conduct, Mr. Spearman. Frankly, you remain on my probation list for personal conduct. I witnessed you giving a close audience to Miss Riley. She's infatuated. Was your exchange anything more than praising her for her performance? I trust not. I shall continue keeping my eye on you. I certainly hope you keep your eyes, and your hands, to yourself and continue to do well for the remainder of this term."

"Thank you, Dean Halberstam," I said, thankful that she hadn't shot me down for some of the raunchy bits I hadn't disclosed to her in advance. "I'm pleased to know that my efforts have satisfied you."

"I am satisfied with your directing, Mr. Spearman. However, you were not entirely forthcoming about funny business in the show. Character will have much to do with your success here. Make sure you keep yours above reproach. Your teaching position and perhaps your theatrical directing career depend upon it. I extend my best wishes for your production of the Scottish play. I shall attend."

"Thank you, Dean Halberstam," I replied.

"You are welcome," she replied. "If you will excuse me, I will make this an early evening. My presence may inhibit the students. This is their triumph and yours. I prefer that everyone feel free to celebrate. Good night, Mr. Spearman," she said, and she left.

I wandered around from group to group saying at least one encouraging thing to each actor and crew member. Rich Hilley thanked me for giving him the opportunity of playing Alfonso. Yolanda Batterson surprised me. She told me she had figured out she got more laughs when she played Prompter straight than when she hammed it up.

Nothing remarkable happened until nearly eleven-thirty. As I was about to leave, Susan Riley approached me again. She had ditched the bodice and, from the contours of her silk peasant blouse, I could see she had also ditched her bra. Her nipples were standing at attention.

"Where's your date?" she asked.

"She left."

"Now you don't have a date, either. Walk me to the dorm."

"No, Susan. I won't walk you to the dorm. If you're concerned for your safety, walk with a group of students or call the dormitory escort service. You're an attractive, intelligent, and talented girl, Susan. I appreciate those qualities. I recommend you find a boy who appreciates those qualities, too, and loves you as you are. I am not that boy. I am a middle-aged man. Good night, Susan."

I turned and walked away into the cool October evening.

I moved my car to the street so Stella could park in the courtyard, but she pulled up in a cab. As she had done before, she laid her finger on her lips to call for silence.

With Stella in her black gown, her white pearls not visible, her apricot hair, pale arms, bare neck, and lovely décolletage covered by a black pashmina, and me in my black trousers and black turtle-neck sweater, had anyone been able to see us creep up the black wrought-iron staircase, we might have been taken for evildoers. Stealth and darkness conceal those who come with ill intent. I couldn't recall the source of that thought but I didn't like thinking it described us.

When we stepped inside and closed the door, I asked, "What happened to your pearls?"

"Why don't you find them?"

Stella removed her pashmina showing me her string of pearls depending into the wide neck of her gown. She leaned forward to improve my line of sight.

I turned her around, pulled her close to me, and reached down her gown to pull out her pearls, but my hand strayed to her breast and to the fastener of her front-closing bra. I unsnapped it one-handed."

"I am shocked, shocked, I tell you, and I'll give you five minutes to stop that," she murmured.

I cupped her breast in my hand and gently massaged her nipple which, even now in the present darkness, I knew to be pink, slender, and under appropriate conditions, surprisingly long. With my other hand, I ran my fingers through her hair.

"The zipper's in the back," she said. "Undo it."

I undid it and she shrugged away her gown, her chemise, and her bra. Except for her black pumps and white pearls, she was standing now in the palest of light, naked.

I replaced my left hand on her breast and ran the fingers of my right hand through her copper-red thatch.

"It's not fair," she said. "You're still clothed."

"Fix it."

Slowly and competently she undressed me, sitting me down on the floor to pull off my shoes and trousers.

"You seem to have risen to the occasion."

She traced a line with her tongue 'from nave to chops,' and then she pulled her legs up, straddled me, and gently guided me inside.

We continued making love until I was spent. Stella was stretched out on top of me, sated. After a while, I gently rolled Stella aside, got up, poured two glasses of wine, and beckoned Stella to follow me. We walked naked through the darkened apartment toward the moon-lit bedroom. I closed the curtains cutting off the moonlight as I lcd her to the bed. So pale was she in her nakedness that even in the dark she was easy to find. I lay down next to her. She snuggled up.

"Dewy, you can't imagine how good it is to lie here with you just touching."

"I love you, Stella."

"Don't, Dewy. Don't love me. I'm not free to love."

"I won't judge you. All I want is to love and to be loved."

"I'm afraid to love you. I'm bound to Val in ways I couldn't begin to explain."

"Why don't you just leave him?"

"It's not as simple as that."

"Do you love him?"

"No."

"Do you love me?"

"Yes."

"All I ask is that you love me each day as you love no other. The day you can't do that, say so and I'll go. It's that's simple."

"If only it were. I love you Dewy. I didn't want to love you, but I do. But this is not forever."

"Nothing is forever."

"I mean it. Forever is longer than you realize. You need someone, but I'm not the one."

"Well, I like what I have now."

"I, too. I haven't felt so alive in years. More than you realize. Do you have any idea how old I am?"

"You've asked that before. I don't even want to guess."

"Why not?"

"It's not important."

"Are you sure?"

"Are you trying to tell me something?"

"Not now. Later. I just don't want you to think this will last forever."

"'Only the earth and sky last forever,' according to the Lakota Sioux."

"So I've heard. Now shut up and kiss me. Let's make love."

We made love, and sometime during the dark, secretive night, I fell asleep.

I awoke when my alarm clock went off sometime after dawn.

Stella was gone. Her untouched glass of wine sat on the night stand. Except for a note she left on the kitchen table, no one could know she had been there; she left no other trace.

In her note she said would see me next at the preview for *The Passion of Dracula* on Wednesday.

How could I get her to stay the night?

Chapter Fourteen

The house lights went down and *The Passion of Dracula* opened with a spotlight fading up on Wilhemina, heel to crown, as she stood with her back toward us. She wore only a white, shirtwaist nightgown. Her feet were bare. Her arms were raised to shoulder height and disappeared in front of her into the darkness of her own shadow against the black of the unopened show curtain.

A pair of disembodied hands in pearl-gray gloves emerged from that blackness, caressed Wilhemina's hands and wrists, and crept up her outstretched arms toward her neck.

The animation of these phantasmal, pearl-gray hands, emerging from white French cuffs that, in turn, emerged from black sleeves, suggested the intimate presence of a second body concealed in the darkness in front of Wilhemina.

As black-sleeved arms encircled Wilhemina in a sinuous embrace and pearl-gray hands, fingers widely spread, intermeshed and then locked at the back of her neck, Count Dracula's ruggedly-handsome face sprang from the darkness and stopped next to Wilhemina's head and in the spotlight's circle of light which starkly contrasted his sere white hair with the black of his clothing and the black of the curtain.

The spotlight tightened its circle, now illuminating Wilhemina only from waist to crown. The Count's body was still hidden in deep shadow but his illuminated face, cheek-to-cheek with Wilhemina's, smirked at us. And then, as if Wilhemina were a somnambulist enthralled by her dream lover, she feathered her arm to her sides.

Count Dracula, hissing and showing fangs, in one swift, violent motion stripped Wilhemina's nightgown to her waist exposing her back. Immediately, she rose onto her toes, arched her naked back, thrust her breasts against the Count, and tilted her head, offering her neck and inviting domination.

Exploiting Wilhemina's submission, the Count buried his face in her neck and joined her in ululating feral cries of animal satisfaction.

I gasped. The audience gasped. I don't know if it was the brutality of the piercing embrace or the unexpected exposing of Stella's naked back that gripped us, but we were gripped.

Spider cut the spotlight abruptly casting both them and us into darkness. I couldn't see what was happening in the darkness, but from my knowledge of stagecraft I would expect Val would throw his cape over Stella to prevent her paleness from reflecting any stray light so they both could remain invisible in the blackout as they made their way off stage.

Exiting in the dark is not easy for actors who have just come just come from bright stage lighting, even with phosphorescent tape marks on the floor, but Stella and Val succeeded without mishap.

The show curtain rose and the first act began. As it turned out, the opening scene was the best part of the show.

Lance was sufficiently callow as the young reporter, Harker, who falls in love with Stella's character, Wilhemina. Harker, accompanied by Wilhemina's guardian, and Von Helsing, a Dutch medical consultant, eventually succeed in saving Wilhemina from her malady which, as it turns out, is her passion for Count Dracula.

The audience identified with Harker although I thought Harker to be a priggish fop. Lance managed to nail his lines, as far as I could tell, and seemed to be on the money for blocking, but I had the feeling he was playing to an imaginary mirror in which only he appeared, and he was in love with that image.

Stella did well, but she had little opportunity to work ensemble because almost everyone else seemed to be working alone, except for Renfield. Bert Uhry, the actor who played that poor wretch, was the best of the lot. Renfield was a madman in the service of the Count, so Bert had latitude to play with his role. He did it expertly alternately whining, cajoling, demanding, and disintegrating at appropriate moments and in concert with the other members of the cast.

As individuals, the other members of the cast performed modestly well, too, except for the actor playing Von Helsing. In this version of the Dracula story, Von Helsing is a Dutch medical consultant in withering diseases. It was not clear whether he was an ordained Roman Catholic priest, a friar, or just a cross-dresser, but he wore a brown, hooded robe reminiscent of the Capuchin monks, and he spoke with a poor Dutch accent that made him difficult to understand, not more convincing.

Not even the spectacular effect of Von Helsing's hand-held cross bursting into flame during his confrontation with Dracula could save that actor from the disaster of his own performance.

Val used his natural accent which worked well. So did his white hair, despite Madame Boudron's reservation.

As good as each actor may have been individually, with the exceptions of Stella and Val in the prologue and Bert Uhry as Renfield throughout the show, they were not competent together. They did not play ensemble. It was as if each actor did not like the other actors which, in some cases, I knew to be true.

During the second act I indulged myself in my ritual count of the house. They had arranged the theater to seat 350 people and 303 of those seats were filled. Preview tickets sold for half price and I suspected many people were here on complimentary tickets as was I.

I had been told that theater policy was to give each actor six complimentary tickets to the preview and six more complimentary tickets to be spread out during the run. It seemed odd that the couple who entered the theater in front of me paid cash, half price, for a pair of tickets and were given the same kind of pass I had, passes clearly identified as complimentary. It didn't make any difference for seating. Seating was first come, first served for the preview. Maybe they just didn't print special preview tickets.

After the final curtain, when the actors came out for their curtain calls, Bert Uhry received the most applause as well he should have, but Val got the most reaction.

In addition to considerable applause, Val received a large number of cat calls and boos at high volume. Overall, I'd say he received the greatest audience response of anyone in the show, far greater than the tepid response Lance got from playing Harker.

Chan and I went backstage after the show and joined the cast in the green room. They were congratulating each other and the director, Lenny Skavinski, was congratulating them all.

"Well, Spearman," Val called out. "What do you think of our little dispute? Do you not see that Count Dracula is the hero of the story? It is Dracula, the Prince of Darkness, who turns Wilhemina on to her passion. Harker, that simpering, sanctimonious stripling, merely forces her to return to her dreadfully dreary duty."

Val faced me and said, "Who is the hero, my dear Mr. Spearman?" He paused for a moment, and then he turned to face Stella.

"And, Stella, my darling," he said, hissing like Dracula, "who is the tramp?"

"Drop it, Val," Stella said, speaking softly through clenched teeth.

"I have no intention of dropping anything, my sweet Stella. I have been cast in this role not entirely by my own doing, yet I am doing it well. Even the audience, boobs that they generally are, knows that Harker is a ninny and I am the hero. Did you not hear the wild reaction I got compared to the polite clapping young Lance received for playing Harker? I am vindicated."

"Wait a minute," Lance said in the whine I was coming to believe was his normal conversational voice, "you were playing it for ham and for shock. If I pulled down Stella's gown I'd get applause, too."

"Ah, my dear dunderhead, do you think removing Stella's gown is all that is required to get applause? Then my dear boy, why weren't they applauding Dewy Spearman?"

"Huh?" Lance said.

"Drop it, Val," Stella said *sotto voce*, but not *sotto* enough, because the entire cast and technical crew were looking at us and attending closely. Val noticed this and rose to the occasion.

"My dear Spearman, at Madame Boudron's dinner party you challenged me to play this role, and I have excelled in playing it. You challenged me to prove that Count Dracula was the hero of this story. Judging by audience reaction, I have prevailed. Now, I say to you, dear sir, Wilhemina is a tramp. By the rules of chivalry I challenge you to defend her honor."

Val slapped me across the face with his gloves, threw them at Stella's feet, and stood still, staring into my face.

"If Count Dracula is the hero of this play, the one who unlocks Wilhemina's passion and enslaves her in doing it, then he is a false hero," I said as I bent down and picked up his gloves.

"He seduced her," Val said, his pale eyes fever-bright, "and she begged to be seduced. She chose to be Count Dracula's consort."

"After enslaving herself to her seducer, was she free to leave? I think not," I said as I smoothed his gloves and held them out to him.

Val hissed, showed his fake fangs, stared at me for a moment, and snatched both gloves from my hand. He turned and strode out of the theater through the stage door exit, costume and all.

Stella stood and watched until Val completed his exit. Then she turned and made her exit out the front door, also in costume.

As I hurried after her, I nearly knocked Spider's vodka bottle out of his hand and succeeded at spilling its contents on both him and me. I'd smell like cheap vodka for the rest of the night.

As I left by the stage door exit I heard Lenny say, "I guess we'll do notes tomorrow night before the show. Go home, everybody."

I caught up with Stella on Dauphine Street and called out to her.

"Stella, slow down".

"Go home, Dewy."

"I want to talk to you."

"Go home. Leave me alone; Val knows something. He's livid."

"What does Val know and how does he know it?"

"I don't know. I haven't told him anything. I avoid him as much as possible, but thanks to you I've got to play against him in *The Passion of Dracula*."

"I hadn't thought of that as a negative when I baited Val at the dinner party. I apologize. But, admit it, the audience ate it up."

"They'd have loved a limburger cheese in that role if it could talk. That role is written for maximum audience reaction."

"Even if Lance Sterling played it?"

"I said cheese, not ham."

"See, you're starting to smile. It can't be all bad."

"Dewy, you're impossible."

"No, not impossible. Merely irrepressible. Come on. Let's go out on the Moonwalk and listen to music. You'll have to excuse the way I smell. I had a collision with Spider's vodka bottle."

"You smell just fine."

"It must have evaporated already. Not, it's still wet. It just doesn't smell like anything."

"You go to the Moonwalk if you want to, Dewy. I need to walk around a while alone to collect my thoughts."

"What are you thinking about?"

"About you. And me."

"I like that."

"And Val."

"I don't like that. Phooey on Val. A pox upon his house."

"Don't make the mistake of underestimating him, Dewy. He's a powerful, ruthless adversary and he's called you out. Everyone saw through his charade."

"Can you believe it? Just like in *Camelot*. Val impugned your honor and challenged me to defend it."

"I have no honor, so there's nothing to fight over."

"The last time I fought over a woman's honor, I got a broken arm. Apparently she wanted to keep it."

"Oh, you silly man. You drive me crazy."

"Good," I said, caressing her earlobe.

"I don't mean like that," she said, but she did not move away. "You have no idea what you're letting yourself in for by loving me. I'm not worth it. Go home."

"No. Let me be the judge of what it's worth to me."

"I can't be with you day and night. In fact, we run *Passion* for the next twelve nights and close on Halloween, so nights are out, too. Even Lance agreed to no day off."

"Do you love me?"

"Yes. Against my better judgment, yes."

"And I love you. I'll take what you can give me now. I'll negotiate for more later."

"There may not be more, certainly not until after Halloween."

"I'm ever-hopeful. Come to the apartment. We'll have tonight."

"No, not tonight."

"You have a headache?"

"No, silly man. I need to think. Alone. Val and I are no longer intimate. Although he has mistresses all over the world, he's always been a bit possessive about me; but he's never before been this insanely jealous. He's up to something. What, I don't know."

"I need to think, Dewy. I need to think, now. Go back to the party. Go to the Moonwalk. Go home. I don't care. I'm going to catch a cab to a special place I have, my own little *pied-à-terre* that even Val doesn't know about. I'll go there and think."

"May I go too?"

"No. I must go alone."

"Can I go with you some other time?"

"No. This is my secret place. Only I know where it is."

"I won't tell."

"Of course not. But Val might follow you, or he could hire a private detective to follow you. What was it Benjamin Franklin said about secrets? Three men could keep a secret if two of them were dead?"

"So you'd have to kill me if you told me."

"No. But I'd have to find another secret place and that's not easy. Val is resourceful and relentless."

"Why doesn't he just compel you to tell him?"

"He wouldn't dare."

"Wow! Remind me never to cross you."

"Oh, Dewy! Don't remind me of harsh things. Give me a kiss and then run along."

I kissed her. She was tense at first but she began releasing her tension as I stroked her back and neck.

"Nibble my ear and I'll follow you anywhere," she said, sighing.

"If you mean it, come to the apartment, at least for a while."

"O.K. For a while, but I can't stay all night."

"You never do."

"I still have to think."

"In your secret place?"

"Yes, in my secret place."

We walked down Dauphine Street, turned, and continued on St. Peter's Street until we reached the person door to the apartment's courtyard. As before, we crept silently up the stairs except this time Stella was wearing her costume, an Alice blue, full-length, shirtwaist dress, and I was wearing light tan slacks and a yellow windbreaker. Not exactly camouflage.

When I opened the front door, even without turning on the light, I could see a bare space on the wall where the *Kiss Me Kate* photograph of Stella's Aunt Stella had been.

I heard noise coming from the study.

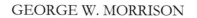

Chapter Fifteen

I motioned for Stella to stay outside and to be silent as I crept toward the study. I stepped to the right side of the open door and poked my head into the room. I snaked my left arm into the room and snapped on the light.

Someone was there, but I barely got a glimpse of him because I pulled my head back to avoid getting clobbered by some object my dark-clad assailant swung at me. By the time I recovered from ducking and jumped into the doorway, ready to attack or flee, my assailant's foot was disappearing out the window onto the balcony.

I rushed around to the French doors to apprehend this villain, but when I stepped out onto the balcony, he was not to be seen. I expected to see him going over the rail to drop to the alley below, a twelve-foot drop, not too difficult if you let yourself down the length of your body and drop the remaining few feet. He was neither hanging from the rail nor running down the alley.

As with most balconies in the Vieux Carré, this one was covered and its flat roof was supported by filigreed wrought-iron columns. After making a quick inspection I decided my assailant could have scaled the wrought iron supports and escaped over the roof, but he would have to be exceedingly nimble and surprisingly swift, or my reaction time was far slower than I realized.

I went inside and joined Stella in the study.

"Are you all right?" she asked.

"Yeah. He swung something at my head but he missed by a good three feet. No harm done."

"This," she said, holding the remains of the J volume of Radu's daybooks, "this is what he swung. Its spine is cracked and pages are falling out. Look, here on the wall, about three inches from the door frame and almost where you head was before you pulled back, here's where it hit. Three feet, indeed."

"Well, he missed, didn't he? And it's a good thing, too. From the looks of the book and the mark on the plaster, I'd probably be knocked out. I'm not so much worried about me, but I feel responsible for Radu's apartment. I guess I should call the police."

"Do we need police for this? Whoever it was has already gone."

"Yeah, but I've already had to call the police about finding a dead cock at the theater. They said to call right away if anything else happened."

I picked up the phone and dialed emergency services. After I explained to the dispatcher that I was subletting from the person to whom the telephone was listed, they said they'd send somebody over.

"Dewy. It looks like it's just not our night. I'm going. I'll see you again, after the run."

"You don't have to go. This won't take long."

"There's nothing I could add to what you'll tell them so don't even mention my name. They'll just pester me for a statement and I didn't see anything. I'm leaving. I need my thinking time."

"A kiss upon our parting."

"No kissing. Look what it led to last time. Goodnight, sweet prince," she said, and then she left. Just like that.

In the next few minutes, as I was awaiting the arrival of the police, I poured a double scotch and sipped it while I surveyed the apartment. Nothing was missing except the photograph of Stella's Aunt Stella and the K and L volumes of Radu's daybooks.

"Spearman," Lt. Thibodeau said as he walked through the open front door. "Landowski's outside looking around. We caught the squeal and claimed it. Maybe we underestimated the first incident. Any calling cards this time?"

"No. Nothing is here that wasn't here when I left this evening."

"Did you look in every drawer, inside the oven, under the bed, even between the sheets?"

"No."

"Do it while I'm here to cover you unless you've got contraband you don't want a cop to see."

"If you find any contraband I'll just say the intruder left it."

"Yeah, man, but I might have to confiscate it. That'd be a bummer, you know. While you're lookin', tell me what's missing, and don't go messin' things up in case we decide to dust for prints."

"Not necessary. He wore gloves. I already know what's missing, a photograph and two volumes of a diary."

"Any commercial value?"

"Not yet. They're Radu Lupeşçu's. If he becomes famous they might be worth something, but not now."

"And the photograph?"

"It was just an old Broadway publicity photograph. Maybe a theater buff would pay fifty dollars for it, but that'd be about it. Funny, he left all the art prints. The Diane Arbus and Walker Evans silver gelatin prints are worth a few thousand, easy."

"Maybe you interrupted him."

"Maybe so, but he'd already taken the photo off the wall and gone into the study when I came in. I guess that's when he grabbed the K and L volumes. He nearly beaned me with the J volume."

"You read them?"

"I looked at the beginning of the L volume. Radu is the guy I'm filling in for at the college. He left me a message to read the L volume. I started reading it but I fell asleep."

"What kind of stuff did he write?"

"A little gossip. A lot of stuff about the theater, problems, complaints, worries, ideas, stuff like that."

"Anybody mentioned by name?"

"Yes, nearly everybody I know from the theater is mentioned there including the director who died last year."

"Hammond Laidlaw?"

"Yeah. Him."

"Did Radu say anything about Hammond Laidlaw?"

"Oh, this and that. You know."

"No, I don't know. That's why I'm asking you."

"I didn't finish it so I don't know everything he might have said, but he did say that Hammond was chasing after a woman who wasn't interested or available. Radu was worried about him."

"Woman have a name?"

"Yes, but I hardly see how it's relevant."

"You got a blind spot big as Biloxi about that woman my friend. Her name would be Stella Maris. That was no secret at the time. We did a preliminary investigation and found out that much."

"O.K., O.K. Stella Maris. What's that got to do with anything?"

"Don't get steamed, my frien'. Be cool. Just checkin' things out. What else that book say?"

"Oh, some stuff about problems at the theater, mostly about lights as I recall."

"They weren't paying the 'lectricity bill?"

"Lights. Lighting instruments. There was too much volatility in the inventory."

"You mean shortages and high turnover?"

"Yes. Oh, I see. You already knew that."

"Preliminary investigation."

Officer Landowski came in and walked out onto the balcony.

"Personally," I said, continuing my conversation, "I think Ellis Boudron and Spider Slidell are running some kind of scam with the lighting instruments."

"You filin' charges?"

"No. It's just a suspicion. Besides, if Spider can light my show the way I want it lit, I don't really care where he gets the lights."

"Hey man, look what jus' fell off a truck."

"Well, I wouldn't want him to be receiving stolen property."

"Or steal them from this theater and sell them?"

"No, not from this theater. Why are you giving me a hard time?"

"Beats the hell outta' me, my frien'. Tell me about the intruder. You said he wore gloves. What else did you see?"

"Very little. Mostly, I just saw black. He was dressed mostly in black."

"Like a Ninja?"

"No, not like that. I think my mind registered a flash of something not black but I can't see any other colors."

"Maybe you saw bare hands."

"His hands were covered. They definitely weren't skin colored."

"You mean pink like yours or mahogany like mine?"

"In Crayola colors, I'm closer to the tan crayon the than the pink one, but his hands weren't a color of any skin I've ever seen. Maybe he had on white gloves. I remember white somewhere."

"O.K., we won't bother with prints. Nothing of value's gone and nobody's hurt. Landowski," he called out to his partner, "what you see on the doors?"

Landowski called back. "No force marks. Probably 'loided the lock on the French door. No marks on the balcony. Slick dude."

Madame Claire had come in silently and was standing in the doorway. Thibodeau spoke to her. "You see anything?"

"Nothing useful as evidence, officer, but I sense evil and desperation. This was no common thief. He took what he came for. He will not return. This is a thing complete. You won't find traces in the alley. This thief went over the roof. This is no common burglary. This is an act of evil. I feel it."

"O.K.," Thibodeau said, shaking his head. "Let's wrap this up. Landowski, you can write the report again. Spearman, just for the record, what was the size and subject of the photograph?"

"It was an 8 x 10 color publicity still for a musical comedy from fifty years ago, *Kiss Me Kate*."

"And who was in it?"

"Don't you know already from your preliminary investigation?"

"You tell me."

"It was Howard Keel, the guy who opened *Kiss Me Kate* on Broadway, and Stella Maris, the original Stella Maris, the aunt of the one we know here in New Orleans."

"How you know it wasn't her broke in here to get it?"

"Because she was with me."

"She's not here now."

"She left."

"Yeah."

"What's that mean?"

"Nothing. Come on, Landowski. We've got a report to file. You get anything on Ellis Boudron, Spearman, you come to me, you hear? Bye now."

Lt. Thibodeau, Officer Landowski, and Madame Claire left the apartment. I was left with unanswered questions and a growing sense of disquiet with things at TVC. Stella hadn't broken in. She was with me. What was Thibodeau hinting at?

Why couldn't people just come right out and say what was on their minds?

Chapter Sixteen

It had been a long sixteen days from the preview of *The Passion of Dracula* until its close on Halloween, longer because I had not seen Stella. She had sent me a note asking me to stay away from TVC while *Passion* was running and promising me a pleasant surprise as a reward for waiting.

Merely seeing Stella at our first read-through for *Macbeth* would be pleasant for me. I could only hope her surprise would be even better. I tried not thinking about the questions nagging me: why was this relationship not moving as fast as I wanted in the direction I wanted it to move, what kind of hold could Val possibly have on Stella, and why couldn't Stella ever meet me for lunch?

I decided without really thinking about it not to think about it. If I asked the right questions I might not like the answers. I wanted much more. Even so, I did not want to risk losing what little I had.

The entire cast had assembled by the seven o'clock call time. In addition to the cast, both Ellis Boudron and Wendy Bridges were present which was unusual. Front office folks hardly ever come to a rehearsal. Even Maurice had shown up and he had no connection to the show except for being Wendy's husband. Maurice and Wendy were sitting together with empty seats on both sides of them. I even saw Spider for a brief moment as he moved around overhead.

I walked onto the stage and sat down on a stool I had preset under a single light at center stage. I was going for effect. Ellis ruined my effect when he walked onstage and explained none too politely that we could use the theater through Wednesday. James Whitmore was coming in on Thursday for ten days to do *Give 'em Hell, Harry*, his one-man show about President Truman. We could come back a week from Sunday. In the meantime Ellis had arranged for us to rehearse at the Gates of Babylon Krewe Hall.

When Ellis finished his announcement he turned the meeting over to me and sat down on the other side of Wendy. Maurice stood up, walked over to Pete Vanlandingham, and sat down beside him.

In less than twenty seconds, Pete rose and asked, "Dewy, is it O.K. with you if Maurice hangs around rehearsal?"

"Sure, Pete. Maurice, welcome. Aren't you busy with *Forum*?"

"Yes, Dewy, old boy, but not until tomorrow. Is it acceptable for me to stay this evening?"

"No problem, Maurice."

Ellis got up and left the theater. Maurice moved back to his original seat next to Wendy.

"O.K., everybody, listen up," I said. You've all probably seen the Scottish play and you may have performed it. At this moment I do not plan to cut or change even one word of Shakespeare's dialogue, but I reserve the right to do that later if I think it's necessary. I will cut Act III, Scene V, where the witches meet Hecate. By all accounts that's a song lifted from Thomas Middleton's *The Witch* and inserted in the Scottish play after Shakespeare's death. It doesn't belong."

"You may have heard that all productions of the Scottish play are cursed. That's superstition. We all are all going to work together to get this show on the boards without serious mishap. You can do it."

"This production will be my project for my master of fine arts degree. I plan to make a video record of at least one performance. I don't expect that will have any effect on your own performance."

"Will that be tape or film?" Stella asked.

"Does that make a difference?" I asked in return.

"I don't film well. Photographs don't work for me. They always turn out badly. I simply won't be photographed."

"That's true," Pete said. "We use a charcoal drawing of Stella in place of a publicity photo. I might start doing that myself. All the cameras I run across lately make me look chubby and bald."

Everyone laughed.

"O.K." I said, "I'll videotape it. If that's not a problem let's get back on task. What will distinguish this performance of the Scottish play from any you have previously seen is the way we handle the relationship between Lord and Lady Macbeth."

"I'm sure you can all recite Lady Macbeth's lines about screwing your courage to the sticking place. You all know she couldn't stab the sleeping King Duncan because he so resembled her father. Macbeth did that gory deed, but he wavered in courage sufficient to replace the grooms' purloined, bloodied knives in their beds and then besmear them with the king's blood."

"Lady Macbeth took the daggers from her husband's hands, smeared the sleeping grooms' faces with King Duncan's blood, and tossed the bloody daggers onto their pillows. This she did, not out of anger, rage, or malice; this she did to do for her husband that which he caviled at doing himself."

"Lady Macbeth became the instrument of her husband's vaunting, but equivocal, ambition. She did the dirty deed but she did it with a clean heart."

"'My hands are of your color, but I shame to wear a heart so white,'" Maurice said, speaking Lady Macbeth's line.

"Thank you, Maurice," I said, attempting to sound any way other than irritated. "Are you in this show?"

"Sorry, Dewy, old boy," he replied. "At prep school we put on the Scottish play. Lacking women, we did as Shakespeare did, and I played Lady Macbeth. I take your points, both about Lady Macbeth's motivation and about my shutting up. I shan't interfere again."

"Thank you, Maurice. Laura, will you pass out the rehearsal and performance schedules? Everyone, please remember, Laura is not only assistant director, she's also stage manager. If you are having any difficulty with meeting a call time, call Laura immediately. Now, let's get on with the show. Tonight we'll do a read-through. Tomorrow night we'll begin blocking. We're going to block in reverse order starting with Act V tomorrow. Any questions?"

"Yeah," Pete said. "Are we going to do this in five acts with four intermissions?"

"No. We'll do this in two parts with one intermission. We'll start the second half with Act IV, Scene 1. That way we start both parts of the play with the Weird Sisters in scenes that Shakespeare actually wrote, and don't give me any of that Christopher Marlow or Earl of Oxford crap. I won't hear it. By Thursday we'll have the whole show roughly blocked. Friday and Saturday we're off. Starting Sunday, either here or over at Gates of Babylon, we'll do run-throughs of Act V until we've got it. Then on to Act IV."

"I expect you will be off book by the end of the second week. We'll put the witches' scenes in at a full run-through on Friday the 28th without special effects. The witches will come in early on that Saturday so we can stage the effects. We'll run the entire show including the witches' scenes the next evening, Sunday, with the entire cast."

"We have a tech rehearsal on that Saturday?" Lance said.

"Yes, with the witches."

"We're working Sunday through Friday with a tech rehearsal on Saturday, and then we're back on Sunday though Saturday for opening week. By Equity rules I get at least one day off a week. I gave up my day off for *Passion*, but I'll be damned if I'll give it up for this."

"If you read your printed schedule you will notice that the only actors called for tech rehearsal on Saturday are the witches. Only the tech crew and the witches show up for that Saturday tech rehearsal. You'll give the tech crew your best at the run-through on Sunday night after your day off on Saturday, Lance. We'll work with the witches on Saturday and then we'll work with everyone on Sunday. Laura and I will stand in for any other actors who might be needed for the Saturday rehearsal."

"The Saturday of the tech rehearsal?" Lance asked.

"Exactly. Thanksgiving week everybody's off on Thursday and on for Friday. After the run-through on the following Sunday, we'll do a full dress with effects on Monday, take Tuesday off, and preview this show on Wednesday. We open on Thursday, the 4th, and close on Saturday, the 20th. You've all had your scripts for weeks so I expect you'll know your lines quickly. Not counting tonight's read-through and the preview, we have nineteen evenings to get this show on the boards. That's twice as long as you have in summer stock."

"In summer stock we did two a day," Lance said.

"Right, but only for one week. Two a day for six days is twelve rehearsals. We have nineteen."

"That's not twice as many," Lance said.

"Please accept my apology, Lance. We have about 85 per cent more rehearsals than summer stock. Is that going to be a problem?"

"Not for me. I'm a professional. But I don't know about these other people," Lance replied.

"O.K. Everyone, how many of you have your lines memorized?"

About a third of the hands went up.

"How many will memorize them by week's end?"

Nearly every hand went up.

"And how many will have them memorized by the 14th?"

All hands went up.

"Good, now I won't have to stick anyone's head on a pike. Are you satisfied, Lance?"

"Hey, I'm a professional. You're the one who's got to worry about people not knowing their lines, not me. You're the director."

"Please remember that and we'll get along famously," I replied, hosting another brief visit from my sarcasm. I'd have to watch that. I didn't want to be just another arrogant, asshole director.

"I've got special plans for the witches. I plan to fly one, have one enter and exit through a trap, and have the third witch appear out of smoke. I'll get Spider to do some specials for that, too. I've got other special lighting plans if Spider can get the instruments.

"Hey, Spider," I yelled in the direction of the light booth. "Are you up there?"

"Yeah, man, what you want?"

"You got my instruments?"

"I'm workin' on it, man. I think we got a deal. Don't bug me about it. I always come through."

Ellis, who had stolen back into the rehearsal space, stood and yelled at me, "I'm not going to tell you again, Spearman, if you need lighting instruments you come see me, not Spider."

Then he yelled at Spider, "Spider, you no-count, thieving, egg-sucking dog, get your sorry ass down to the front office, now!"

Spider took his half-pint vodka bottle out of his back pocket and took a long pull. He replaced the bottle as he danced across the rigging in the direction of the light booth and disappeared against the blackness of the ceiling.

Ellis signaled Wendy to follow him to the front offices, but she shook her head and stayed in her seat. Ellis glowered at her for a full minute and then he turned and stomped his way to the front. No one seemed unhappy with Ellis' departure.

After few seconds of silence Pete said, "I swear Spider's going to kill himself. I wish Ellis could get him to stop doing that."

"Drinking, or dancing around in the rigging?" I asked.

"Either. Both. It scares me. But he always comes through, just like he says."

"He's working on the drinking. Last month I saw him go into…."

I cut myself off as I realized that second A in AA stood for anonymous. I wasn't certain of the AA rules, but it would be Spider's place, not mine, to reveal his membership.

"Into what?" Pete asked. "A convulsion? He pulls at that bottle all day and all night."

"It's not a very big bottle though, is it Pete? And he never seems to be drunk, does he?"

"I guess not," Pete said. "So, what special lighting do you have in mind? Green for the witches?"

"Actually, no. I'm going for red and lavender, hot and cool. I don't want to talk about that now. We'll work on that before the witches come in for their first tech rehearsal."

I turned to the group. "O.K. gang, let's take it from the top."

We had barely started the read-through when Ellis came back in, took Wendy by the arm, and walked her out the stage door exit. Maurice busied himself with a script and didn't look up until five minutes after they had left the theater.

It wasn't a bad reading. Horace Sullivan sounded pompous as King Duncan. Maybe he thought a king should sound pompous. I'd prefer he sound warmer and more approachable which would give more reason for the audience to see his murder as a heinous crime.

The witches cackled too much. I informed them of my vision of the Weird Sisters as seers and soothsayers, not harpies and harridans, and they should be played cool, competent, and confident.

I had to give the second witch, Adriana Dare, a lesson on fillet. In *Macbeth*, the 'fillet of a fenny snake' was a slice taken from a snake that lived in a fen, not a slice taken from a snake with fins, which made a subtle difference in pronouncing 'fenny;' and, in Scots and British English, 'fillet' rhymes with 'skillet' as opposed to the French 'fillet' which rhymes with 'sashay.'

Lance surprised me with his reading, at least when I closed my eyes. Although I missed the angst I was expecting in the murder scene, the fear and anger I was expecting when he sees the phantasmagoric royal issue of Banquo stretching out to the crack of doom and compares it to his barren family tree, and the pathos I was expecting when he learned of his lady's death, he wasn't bad.

Lance enunciated clearly without giving that air of "I'm playing Shakespeare so I have a right to be pompous." He read the lines well paying due respect to the iambic pentameter in which all his lines were written, including the heroic couplets, and equally due respect to the communication value of those lines. He had a good, even delivery. Perhaps too even.

If only Lance weren't so young and so beautiful. Why hadn't he become a news anchor instead of an actor? Maybe I could age him with makeup and coach him to move like a mature man. But would I ever get authentic, mature emotions from him? I had my doubts.

When he got to Macbeth's famous speech, the one that inspired the title of William Faulkner's novel, *The Sound and the Fury*, he blew it. At Dunsinane, while Macbeth is preparing for an imminent English invasion, attempting to quell an insurrection, and fretting about the thick-coming fancies that keep his lady from her rest, his attending officer, Seyton, enters and says, "The Queen, my lord, is dead."

Macbeth replies, "She should have died hereafter; there would have been time for such a word. Tomorrow and tomorrow and tomorrow creeps in this petty pace from day to day to the last syllable of recorded time; and all our yesterdays have lighted fools the way to dusty death. Out, out, brief candle! Life's but a walking shadow, a poor player that struts and frets his hour upon the stage and then is heard no more. It is a tale told by an idiot, full of sound and fury, signifying nothing."

In spite of the sentiment of his moving speech, Macbeth does not act as if it is over for him. He continues to strut and fret his hour upon the stage, the next few minutes, anyway. Moments later, when he learns that Birnam Wood actually has marched to Dunsinane, the harbinger of his defeat, he still calls out for his armor. "Ring the alarum bell! Blow wind, come wrack, at least we'll die with harness on our back!"

Lance got everything from "Tomorrow and tomorrow...." He just didn't get the "She should have died hereafter; there would have been time for such a word." I guess he was so wrapped up in himself that he simply didn't know what it was like to be inextricably involved with a partner, to love a partner, and to be bereft by the partner's departure. Well, it would be my job as director to make him discover that, at least for our performances.

I dislike being a doubter. I'd rather believe that things will come together and will work out for the best. I sometimes even believe a pig can learn to whistle if it wants to badly enough and has an excellent teacher, but I was doubtful, and there was no way around it. I doubted Lance could do a great job of playing Macbeth. Since a great job was not in the cards, maybe the best I could hope for would be a good job. I'd even settle for adequate.

How could he possibly play against Stella? He was so young and buff that he might as well play Ken to Stella's Barbie. No, at least

Stella looked and moved like a real woman, and she could get her voice right. No Barbie, she.

In this first run-through Stella sounded strong but tender toward her husband, strong and resolutely bent toward serving her husband's ambition, and strong but trapped in a relationship which she could leave only by her death, her untimely death, the sticking point for Lance's Macbeth, but Stella's Lady Macbeth's only and final exit.

Ah, Stella. Stella Maris, my star of the sea. Who are you, and why are you in my life? When can I love you? When can I see you? When will you stay?

"Will that be it, Dewy?" Laura asked.

"What?"

"That's the end of the second read-through. It's eleven o'clock. Are we through?"

"Yeah. That's a wrap. Notes tomorrow. Rehearse here until we move to the Gates of Babylon Krewe Hall. Seven o'clock. Laura will be serving as stage manager. Guys, if you have any problem with making your call, let Laura know. O.K. See you all tomorrow night."

Pete and Maurice were the first two out of the stage door. Lance left next accompanied by Adriana Dare. Then everyone else started drifting out. As the others left, Stella passed by me and whispered, "I'll be waiting for you outside."

Laura came over, moved my director's notebook out of the chair next to me, and sat down beside me, a task I thought would be daunting with her brace and crutches but one she negotiated easily.

"I thought I was the assistant director," she said.

"You are," I replied. "You are also the stage manger."

"What do you require of me as stage manger?"

"Manage the show. You are the personnel manager for the cast and the director's executive officer. You keep tabs on who is where, take any notes I give you, make your own notes of muffed lines, and see that things that are supposed to happen actually do happen."

"Such as?" Laura asked.

"During the show, you stand at a desk just offstage and follow the play line by line. If the actors founder and can't recover, you call out lines. You make sure actors make their entrances. If we had any scenery you'd make sure the scenery gets changed. You make sure the property master has all props ready and all actors are in their correct costumes. You monitor sound and light, check them against the script, and call in the cues if that's necessary. You raise and lower the curtain or have an assistant do it on your command. If any problems come up, you solve them."

"In general, the stage manager does anything necessary to keep the show running including donning a costume, grabbing a script, and filling in for any actor who can't go on."

"You don't ask for much, do you?"

"Hey. I didn't make that up. That's what a stage manager does. Is that a problem?"

"Yes. Not for me, Dewy. It's a problem for Mother. She says I'm not up to the professional standards required at TVC. But I am. You'll see."

"I see already. I think you're the one who will see."

"O.K., Dr. Adler, let's not have any ego psychology here. I'm sure I won't let down the honor of the Boudron name. On that note, please accept my apology for Ellis' curt treatment of you earlier this evening. He's still rough around the edges."

"No, Laura, I won't accept your apology for Ellis' behavior. You are not Ellis and you are not responsible for his behavior. Just be responsible for yourself. Forgive me for being indelicate, but if you and your mother always clean up after Ellis, he'll never learn to clean up after himself."

"You are being indelicate. I am attempting to uphold the honor of the Boudron name. Ellis may not be the exemplar of that honor, but he is my brother."

"And if he acts dishonorably?"

"He has already paid his debt to society."

"If he acts dishonorably now?"

"He may need polishing, but he wouldn't do anything to dishonor the Boudron name."

"If he acts dishonorably tomorrow, and tomorrow?"

"If he acts dishonorably, let me know and I will do whatever it takes to see that amends are made."

"Including letting him take the rap for his own actions?"

"You are being difficult."

"You are being evasive. Will you call Ellis on his behavior if it is truly dishonorable?"

"Yes," she said, with great intensity but little volume, as if she were afraid that even she might hear herself.

"Yes," she repeated, louder. "If Ellis behaves truly dishonorably I'll confront him and expect him to make amends. But, I will not be persuaded to confront him over his rudeness. That's just his way."

"Fair enough."

"What do you mean?"

"Just that. Your attitude is fair enough. I'll put up with his rudeness, but if he acts truly dishonorably, I'll enlist you as an ally to lead him to apologize and make amends."

"It sounds so simple when you say it."

"It is simple."

"No. You don't know Ellis, or Mother. They have their ideas of what it means to uphold the honor of the Boudron name. Apologies and amends would not among them."

"Maybe it's time they learned."

"Maybe, but not likely. Are there other duties required of a stage manager. Is there anything else I need to do tonight as assistant director and stage manger before I leave?"

"Make sure we have a key to get into the Krewe Hall."

"I already got it from Ellis," she said, holding up a key.

"Turn on the ghost light and make sure we're locked up here. I'll walk you to your car."

"That's not necessary. I'm quite accustomed to getting around on my own. I want to sit here a while and think."

"O.K., but it's not a good idea for you to be here by yourself. I don't know if you heard or not, but somebody got in here a month or so ago and hung up a dead chicken."

"I think Spider's still here. I didn't see him go out."

"He must live here. O.K. See you tomorrow. I'll set the lock on the stage door so no one can get in.

Chapter Seventeen

I walked out the stage door into the night. Failing to see Stella, I went around the corner and headed to Bourbon Street. Stella was standing outside a bar listening to a Dixieland trio.

"Hi, sailor," she said. "New in town?"

"I bet you say that to all the guys."

"Only the sailors," she said, as she stretched up and kissed me.

"So, what's the surprise?"

"I'm the surprise. I'm here. Just you and me—and hundreds of drunks and tourists—right here in the Vieux Carré. Let's do the tourist thing, maybe take a stroll through the neighborhood, as long as we end up at your place."

"What've you done about Val?"

"Don't worry, he's busy. While we're doing the show I'll be able to see you every night, either before rehearsal or after it."

"Not both?"

"No, not most nights."

"Can you stay over?"

"Maybe. I'm not a morning person. I'm much better off at my own place come morning."

"Stella, I don't see other women. I'm greedy. I want more; I want all of you all of the time. Why can't I have that?"

"Because I have a life, if you can call it that. I have things to do that don't involve you, things you might not find to your liking. I have commitments, agreements I made in the past. I can't give you all my time. Until we finish *Macbeth*, I can give you a large part of most evenings but I can't give you every evening. If you can accept that, I'm yours for that time. If you can't, leave now. I don't want to fight about this later."

"I rarely fight."

"I should never have started with you, Dewy. I thought you'd be a pleasant diversion, a breath of fresh air. I'm getting in over my head. If we keep courting each other, we'll be courting disaster."

"Yeah. Well, Stella, as Macbeth himself said, 'Ring the alarum bell! Blow wind, come wrack, at least we'll die with harness on our back!'"

"You're right, Dewy. I'm killing my own buzz. Let's not look at what we're doing; let's just do it. Let's be ourselves. Come on. I'll show you the famous wrought-iron cornstalk gate on our way to your apartment."

We took a walking tour of the Vieux Carré and looked at decorative wrought-iron fences and gates. Some were outstanding examples of decorative art. The local artisans had a good thing going for themselves. Wrought iron rusts, and it rusts faster in the humid atmosphere of New Orleans. Repairing, restoring, and replacing it means repeat business. As charming and interesting as the fences and gates were, they'd probably look better in daylight, and nothing was preventing me from coming back in daylight to see them.

When we arrived at the apartment, Stella again signaled for silence as we ascended the stairs. When we were inside I asked her why stealth was so important to her.

"I know most ordinary people make allowances for the behavior of theater people," she said, "but I have a reputation to protect and I don't want anyone to tell Val they saw me going into your apartment. It's such a small thing. You don't mind, do you?"

"Yes, I mind. I don't like sneaking around. I want to have an open relationship, one that stands or falls on its own merits, not one based on deception and delusion."

"We have what we have, Dewy. I wish it were otherwise, but this is what I can give you."

She turned away from me and as she spoke, I heard the catch in her voice. "You need someone, Dewy, but I'm not that person. I'm no good for you."

I took her by the shoulders and turned her around. Silent tears slid down her pale cheeks. Against only token resistance I tilted her face upwards and kissed her salty tears.

"Stella, let me be the judge of what's good for me."

"Hold me, Dewy," she said, as her tears found their voice. I picked her up and carried her to bed. She clung to me all the way.

After a while, she stopped crying, and with no words spoken, we made love. When I awoke the day was bright and cheery. I wasn't. My quick survey of my bedroom confirmed lack, not abundance. No wine glass. No note. No Stella. Despite my depression, I crawled out of bed. Tear stains on the pillow and the scent of a woman were the only traces Stella left.

As I brushed my teeth, I noticed the wound on my neck had nearly healed. I started to prepare breakfast but became distracted when I realized I didn't have my director's notebook. I started searching for it, forgetting breakfast. When I was certain my notebook wasn't in the apartment, I attempted to reconstruct the events of the previous evening.

I recalled Laura's moving it when she sat beside me after rehearsal. It was probably still at the theater. I could zip right over there, pick it up, and swing by the Café du Monde for café au lait and beignets for my breakfast. I didn't have to make my presentation on stage combat safety to the Southeastern Theater Conference at LSU until eleven o'clock.

I arrived at the theater about eight o'clock. With trepidation, the residue of my previous early-morning unpleasant surprise, I unlocked the stage door and went in.

I wished I hadn't.

Chapter Eighteen

From the rigging, eerily illuminated from the ghost light below, attended by blue bottle flies, accompanied by the smells of vodka and death, hung Spider's body. I retched, but there were only beignets and coffee in my stomach to expel and they remained in situ and continued to contribute to my discomfort.

It looked like Spider had been dead for some time. He and I were probably the only ones here. If others were in the building, surely they would have attended to him by now.

I was spooked. First, the cock; now, Spider. I stepped outside to call 911. I didn't want to stay in the theater even to use the telephone. After a few blocks of searching, I concluded that street-side telephones are not easy to find in the French Quarter. However, the police are. I walked to the station on Royal Street and told the desk sergeant about the body hanging from the rigging at Théatre Vieux Carré. He waved his hand and two uniformed officers joined us. He told them my story and asked me to accompany them to the theater, let them in, and wait there until the detectives arrived. I agreed.

When we returned to the theater, both officers went in by the stage door. After a cursory glance, they stepped back outside and closed the door. One officer went around to the main door. The other officer waited outside the stage door with me. In a few minutes an ambulance, a fire truck, two squad cars, and a black Ford Crown Victoria with a flashing blue light on the dashboard pulled up.

Lt. Thibodeau and Officer Landowski got out of the Crown Vic.

"You, again," Thibodeau said

"Yes."

"O.K. Stand aside."

Thibodeau, Landowski, and four uniformed officers, flashlights in hands and gun holsters unsnapped, filed into the theater. In no more than a minute Thibodeau poked his head out of the stage door.

"You know how to turn on the rest of the lights, Spearman? We only got this standing lamp to see by."

"There's a switch for a work light eighteen inches to your right about shoulder high. The main panel is stage right, in the wings, under the catwalk."

"Where's that?"

"As you face the audience, look on the wall to your right, close to the edge of the proscenium."

"Which one is the proscenium?"

"It's the open arch between backstage and the audience."

"How 'bout you come in and do that?"

"Is it safe?"

"Don't look like nobody's here but the stiff and he's no threat. I'll cover you anyway."

"Sure. Why not? It's all in a director's day," I said, without enthusiasm.

"We're going to need somebody to make a formal I.D, but offhand, I'd say it was Spider Slidell. You agree, Spearman?"

"That's Spider."

"When's the last time you saw him, alive?"

"About seven-fifteen last night. We were getting ready to start our read-through of the Scottish play and I spoke to him right here."

"That the last time you saw him?"

"Yeah."

"Where'd he go after that?"

"Ellis Boudron yelled for him to get his 'sorry ass down to the front office' and he headed across the catwalk towards the light booth which is directly above the box office."

"Charming man, huh?"

"Ellis or Spider?"

"Yes. So, Spearman, who all was here last night?"

I gave him a copy of the cast contact list and told him Maurice and Wendy Bridges and Ellis Boudron were here, too.

"How long has Spider been dead?" I asked.

"A while. You got an alibi?"

"Do I need an alibi?"

"You never know. Tell me your whereabouts last night."

"Sure. I was here with everybody until rehearsal ended. No, Ellis Boudron and Wendy Bridges left before eight, I think, but everyone else was here until eleven. I stayed after and talked with Laura Boudron for ten or fifteen minutes. Then I went home."

"Alone?"

"No."

"All night?"

I hesitated. I really couldn't say Stella had been there all night because she wasn't there when I woke up, but I hadn't killed Spider so what difference would it make how good an alibi I had?

"Yeah, Lieutenant. All night."

"You wanna' tell me who with?"

"No, not unless I have to. If I need an alibi, I'm sure she'll come forward. Otherwise, I prefer to protect the lady's reputation."

"Too late for that, Spearman."

"What do you mean, Lieutenant? Are you trying to tell me the lady isn't a lady?" I was hot and I guess I showed it.

"Cool it, man. Spider mighta' just fell and hung himself. Then nobody need an alibi. You the last to leave?"

"No. Laura Boudron was here when I left. She said she wanted to think about a few things. I said I didn't want to leave her here alone. She said she hadn't seen Spider leave so she wouldn't be alone. You can't think Laura killed Spider."

"I don't think nothin' yet, Spearman. Mighta' been an accident. Mighta' not. Just doin' a preliminary investigation. What time you leave?"

"About eleven-fifteen. What time do you think Spider died?"

"Hard to say. Wait for forensics. More'n a few minutes ago. I don't think you just did it and then ran to the station to put in the squeal."

"Thanks, but why is that?"

"Who's runnin' this 'vestigation, you or me?"

"I want to know, Thibodeau. I'm really spooked. First, a dead cock. Now, a dead Spider. Maybe he slipped and fell. The way he danced across the grid, it sure seems possible. And he smells of vodka. I know people say you can't smell vodka but I can. I can even smell pure grain alcohol."

"Go on, man," Thibodeau said.

"O.K. I'm certainly no forensic expert, but I'd judge that Spider's been dead for some time. The only color in his face is gray. The blood must have drained down to his feet. I think that's called 'lividity.'"

"Yeah, man, livor mortis."

"And then there are the flies. The only dead humans I've ever seen have been at funeral homes and they were embalmed and made up to look almost alive, but I've seen more than a few road-killed raccoons and such. You don't see many flies on them right away, but after a few hours you see a lot of flies, particularly those blue bottle flies. And the stains, Thibodeau. Look at the stains on his trousers where he soiled himself. They look dry. That would take a few hours I think. And what are those dried stains on his shirt? Vodka?" I said, walking toward Spider's stinking body.

"Don't touch anything man, and don't step in nothin'."

"Nothing to step in. Floor's clean. Whatever vodka he spilled on his shirt is completely dry now. With the alcohol content of vodka, that's hardly surprising. All in all I'd say he's been dead more than a couple of hours, maybe even since late last night, which means I couldn't possibly have done it."

"Didn't suggest you had, Spearman."

"I don't think Laura Boudron could have done it. With her brace and crutches, she'd have a hell of a time chasing Spider around the grid to catch his neck on a loop of cable even if he was drunk."

"You through, Spearman?"

"Yeah, I guess, for now."

"O.K., man. Most likely he was drunk and fell after everyone left. We just have to check everything out. Crime scene boys will do a workup and Doc Sacristan will hold a Coroner's Inquest. Doc says 'misadventure,' no sweat. Doc says 'suspicious causes,' look to your alibi. For now, you got somethin' to do somewhere else?"

"Yeah. I have to teach a class at eleven o'clock."

"Why don't you go do that now? Come by the station later and make a statement. They'll type it up and you can sign it. O.K.?"

"Sure. Tell me. Do you think it was an accident?"

"Can't say, Spearman. He's dead. If somebody saw him fall, maybe it's an accident. If not, we got to wait for forensics. It does seem strange though, two people from this theater meetin' their untimely demise through misadventure. First Laidlaw, now Slidell."

"You'll let me know the results?"

"Yeah, Spearman. You and everybody else. Now beat it."

On my way to the LSU campus I stopped by the Café du Monde for coffee. No beignet. I didn't want to increase my nauseous discomfort. Once I was in my workshop with my theatrical peers, I was able to put aside the earlier events of the day, but that temporary amnesia didn't last long.

I felt like I had to talk to Stella before the police did, if they were going to. In case I really did need an alibi, I wanted to make sure I had one. She had told me not to call her, so I decided I would go see her in person. I had her address in the Garden District on the cast list. I grabbed an extra copy of *Macbeth*. I could always say she left it at the theater and I came to return it to her. It was a flimsy pretext, truth be told, but better than nothing.

I caught the St. Charles Streetcar at the intersection of Canal and Carondelet and rode out into the Garden District. Unlike Maison Boudron, Val VonDragon's house was not in a gated community. It was several streets away from Maison Boudron and stood in the middle of a huge lot surrounded by live oak trees. I rang the doorbell. A servant answered my ring. I introduced myself.

"I've come to return this to Miss Maris. She left it at the theater late last night. Is she in?"

"She don't receive visitors. You can leave it with me an' I leave it for her."

"Will she get it before rehearsal tonight?"

"Can't say. Generally don't see her before your rehearsal."

"Well, maybe I'll keep it and return it to her at rehearsal. If you see her, will you tell her there's been an accident at the theater and she should speak to me before she talks to anybody else."

"You mean the police?"

"Not specifically. But, yes the police, too."

"Two policemens already stopped by today."

"What did she tell them?"

"She weren't here. They left they card an' say for her to call."

"Thank you. I guess I'll just see her at rehearsal."

"Yes, sir."

I turned to go, and then, acting on impulse, I turned around and asked, "Is Mr. Von Dragon here?"

"Ain't seen him since the night after they do that last show over to the theater."

"Did the police ask to talk to him, too?"

"No, sir. Just Miz Stella."

"Thanks," I said, and left.

I took the streetcar back to Stop 0 and walked over to the Police station on Royal Street. I told the desk sergeant that Lt. Thibodeau wanted to take my statement but the sergeant sent me to another detective who recorded my statement on tape and asked me to wait to sign a typed copy. A while later, he returned and read my statement aloud while I read a copy silently. I signed it. He asked me to wait another few minutes for Lt. Thibodeau.

When Thibodeau came in he didn't beat around the bush.

"You get your alibi straight?"

"Do I need it?"

"Lucky you. Looks like not. The assistant D.A. and Doc Sacristan are in a conference but it looks like Spider broke his neck fallin' into the riggin'."

"Then he didn't asphyxiate?"

"No. Broke his neck before he could do that. Presumably fell. It's just as well, too. Most of you'd have a hell of a time with your alibis."

"What do you mean?"

"Nearly everybody was with somebody they rather not name unless they absolutely have to so as not to compromise somebody's reputation, except Laura Boudron. She went home, alone. Her mama is her alibi. She swears Laura was home by eleven o'clock."

"We didn't finish rehearsal until eleven o'clock and Laura and I talked for at least fifteen minutes after that. Even if she had gone straight home she couldn't have been there at eleven. It would be closer to midnight. Check with the man at the gate."

"We did. He'll swear to whatever Clotilde Boudron swears to."

"Why would she lie?"

"To protect the Boudron name and keep Laura from being implicated in case it went down as foul play. Mrs. Boudron don't want no mo' scandal touchin' her or her own. Not her theater, neither. She already been on the phone to the D.A. and Doc Sacristan about it."

"When do they think Spider died?"

"Hard to pin down for certain. Pretty soon after you saw him and at least eight hours before you found him."

"That would be between about seven o'clock and midnight."

"That's what the forensics folks say."

"Since he wasn't hanging there when I left at eleven-fifteen he must have died just after I left."

"Or just after Laura Boudron left. Or just before."

"Surely you don't suspect Laura. Spider's twice her size."

"Take it easy, man. I don't have to suspect nobody on account of Doc's gonna' say it was an accident. Laura's mama might want to fudge on the time Laura got home just to be on the safe side."

"Yeah, I guess so. When's the inquest?"

"You gonna' go?"

"Sure, if I don't have to miss class."

"Should be 'bout one o'clock on a Friday, if Doc holds to form. I'd look for the 28th. Courts are open on Black Friday."

"O.K. I'll be there. I'm sure glad it wasn't murder. I'd get the creeps thinking a killer was skulking around."

"I'm glad it wasn't murder, too. If it was murder I wouldn't know which one o' you to pin it on. Nobody got a solid alibi."

"Yeah, well, that's how things go."

"'Specially with you theater people."

"Maybe so," I said. Maybe so, but it was a cheap shot.

My hunger finally outweighed my nausea, so I stopped at an oyster bar for French bread, gumbo, and a schooner of beer. I topped it off with a half-dozen raw oysters. It was an 'r' month. When I got back to the theater the place was abuzz. Yellow tape marked off the area where Spider had been hanging.

Pete wanted to know if rehearsal was on, Lance wanted to know if he could be released from his contract, and Laura wanted to apologize for misplacing my director's notebook.

I assured Pete that we could continue with our read-through, informed Lance that I would gladly release him from his contract if I could but that was a matter he would have to take up with the Board of Directors of which Pete was a member, and assured Laura that it was not her fault I forgot my notebook.

Laura wondered out loud whether, had she stayed longer, Spider would not have died because she would have been there to help him. Lance said that would have made no difference because disaster always accompanies the Scottish play, and besides, Spider broke his neck when he fell. Nobody could help with that.

Pete said he'd seen it coming two months ago what with Spider's drinking and dancing around on the grid.

Ellis Boudron came in, reminded us that Spider was a drunk, and made an announcement. "I've arranged to have Bud Hérbert come in and work lights, but he's just a techie. Pete, you're the new lighting designer. Spearman, give Pete a list of what you need and he'll go over it with me. Pete, you got any complaints, take 'em up at the next board meeting. Everybody get that? I don't want to have to say it again."

"Sure, Ellis," Pete said. "Is TVC going to do anything for Spider?"

"Why the hell should we? He was just a damn drunk. Anything else?"

"Yes," Laura spoke up. "We'll have a nonsectarian service for Spider on Saturday, a memorial service if the police have not yet released his body. We'll have a real New Orleans funeral, band and all. Everybody's welcome."

Ellis gave Laura a hard look and then turned and walked out at flank speed.

Laura said we could get into the Krewe Hall one night early if we wished to, so we all walked over there and did our read-through.

Everyone was distracted and Lance was whining. I lost my patience with him three times. Pete was inattentive. He was late with his lines and mispronounced even common words. And Stella— Stella, who arrived just on time and not one moment before—kept her head buried in her script.

Only Laura was cool. She sat at my right side and took every note I whispered to her. I tried not to make so many notes that I overburdened her. Also, I didn't want to catch the cast in errors at a time when they were obviously distracted by Spider's death, but I did dictate notes and they were telling. Many of my notes could have been reduced to four words: Lance makes me crazy.

After the read-through, I cut Stella off as she was making her way to the exit. She was not pleased to be stopped. In fact, she confronted me with angry words.

"Why did you come to my house today? I told you never to do that."

"I wanted to talk to you before the police did about our alibis in case we needed them."

"Do you think I would say anything to compromise you?"

"Well, no. But I wanted to talk to you anyway."

"I told you what the terms were. Take them or leave them, but never come to my house or try to contact me there. It's for my good as well as yours. I have my reputation to uphold, and Val is a cruel and jealous man."

"Your servant said she hadn't seen Val since the show ended."

"That doesn't mean anything."

"Stella, I don't mean to push you, or bully you, or hurry you along, but I've fallen in love with you and I want to be your full-time lover. It's that simple."

Her anger softened. When she replied she didn't immediately jump down my throat.

"Unfortunately, Dewy, it's not that simple."

"Come to the apartment and we can talk this over."

"Not tonight. I told you I'd not be able to see you every night."

"Tomorrow night?"

"Maybe," she said with traces of a smile pulling at the corners of her eyes and mouth, if you're especially nice to me at the read-through tomorrow night, and if you won't fret so about Lance. He'll learn his lines the way everyone does."

"It's not the way he learns his lines I'm worried about. It's the way he delivers them."

"You're the director, but this isn't rocket science. Lighten up a little. I've got to go now. 'Bye," she said, blowing me a kiss and hurrying out the door to disappear in a crowd of tourists.

I went home and went to sleep in the same condition I had awakened this morning. Alone. Would it ever be thus?

The next weeks went quickly, or not quickly enough, depending on what I was attending to in the moment.

Spider's memorial turned out to be a modestly large affair. Ellis Boudron was absent. Laura put on a good show. I got there late and missed the eulogies. I was in time for the parade.

Madame Claire told me she had sent a letter to Radu in care of the theater in Budapest to tell him of the theft of the picture and the K and L volumes of his daybooks, but she had not received a reply.

Lance's progress in finding the real man, Macbeth, was agonizingly slow.

My time with Stella was agonizingly limited with little progress in our relationship. I asked Stella to talk about her past some more but she said she had already told me her story. When I pressed for details of how she felt about particular events in her life, she changed the subject or said she would rather stay focused in the present. When I attempted to point to a future that included us as a pair, she definitely wanted to stay focused on the present.

I saw her only every other night. Whenever she came home with me after rehearsal, she was always there when I fell asleep but never there when I awoke.

Once, when I awoke in the wee hours of the morning, she was sitting up in bed stroking my hair and staring at me with tears welling up in her eyes, her languorous liquid emerald eyes.

When I asked her what the matter was, she put her finger on my lips to quiet me. Then we made love, and I fell asleep. When I awoke, she was gone—again.

Chapter Nineteen

I stopped by Chan's office to talk to him on the Friday morning of Doc Sacristan's inquest. Chan said if I ever needed to talk with someone who had my best interests at heart, I could talk to him anytime. I reminded him of that and he invited me in and sat me down.

"Chan, I'm in love, but I'm not happy. What's wrong?"

"Perhaps you should tell me, Dewy."

"Do Episcopalians recognize the sanctity of confession?"

"Do you have something to confess?"

"I'm not sure. I mean, I'm not sure what the sin is here."

"Perhaps what you need is a counselor, not a confessor. I'll treat whatever you say to me with the utmost confidence. What's troubling you?"

"Stella."

"Stella or your feelings about Stella?"

"You're good, Chan."

"It's important to take ownership. No one makes you 'feel' anything. You are the one who feels. Others may provoke, incite, seduce, withhold, or deny, but your feelings are your feelings, no one else's."

"Well, I have mixed feelings."

"Tell me about it, Dewy."

"I've fallen in love with Stella. We have an arrangement but not a partnership. My love for her is not returned in full measure."

"You are not getting from this relationship what you want?"

"No."

"What do you want?"

"Her."

"To own her?"

"No. To have her as my fully-committed partner."

"And what hinders her from committing herself to a partnership with you?"

"Val Von Dragon."

"I think not, Dewy, but tell me how Von Dragon prevents her from doing something, presuming she wants to do it."

"What do you mean, Chan?"

"How does one person prevent another person from doing something?"

"Create doubt, intimidate, and batter. Did you know that more than half of the women who are killed by their husbands or lovers are killed when they're trying to leave them or have just left them?"

"Yes, Dewy. As a pastor, I've studied domestic violence. I've also worked with the violated and with the violators. How does it apply here?"

"I don't know, Chan. Stella warned me about Val. She says he's a jealous man and a 'formidable adversary whom I should not underestimate.'"

"She doesn't say she fears him."

"No, she doesn't say that. She does say he is a man to be feared."

"I repeat my question. What is hindering her from committing herself to a partnership with you?"

"I don't know. She says she hasn't been intimate with Val in a long time, but I know she's beholden to him in ways she couldn't even begin to explain."

"Or chooses not to explain."

"Damn it, Chan. You're not helping me here. Don't be so hard."

"If it were easy you would have solved this already, but I have every confidence that you will."

"O.K. She chooses not to tell me. She chooses not to commit to me. What's wrong with me? Am I not worthy?"

"Why does there have to be anything wrong with you? Could there be something wrong with her?"

"She's beautiful, Chan, and sensitive, and strong. But she's wounded. She's like a bird with one wing down. I think that's part of her appeal to me. She's a woman with whom I can be truly vulnerable and to whom I can give comfort, protection, and healing, but she's keeping me away from true intimacy. It's like she's trying to protect something, probably herself."

"Or you?"

"Me?"

"Perhaps, Dewy. Going by your words, she doesn't seem to fear Val personally, but she seems to fear for your safety. I witnessed

Val's slapping you with his gloves at the preview of *The Passion of Dracula*. He veiled his threat by referring to Wilhemina, Stella's character, but we all got the message. You and Stella may think you're discreet, but the two of you are subjects of common gossip."

"No kidding?"

"No kidding, Dewy."

"Well, if everybody knows, why hasn't Val been around to have it out with me?"

"Good question. What would you suppose the answer to be?"

"He's given up?"

"Perhaps. Or maybe Val has stepped aside so you and Stella can forge a partnership, if you can. If that is so, what's hindering Stella?"

"I don't know."

"Or, Dewy, maybe Val has merely retired to the sidelines to wait for Stella to finish having her fling with you."

"That's not very charitable of you, Chan."

"Or maybe Val left town for Canada, as rumor has it, following his last performance of *The Passion of Dracula*."

"No."

"Why not, Dewy?"

"If Val left town Stella would have said so."

"Would she?"

"Why wouldn't she, Chan. She's been with me every other night since *Passion* closed. Why wouldn't she tell me if Val had left town?"

"I don't know the answers, Dewy. I just know the questions."

I sat in silence. What was Stella up to? She said she could get away only every other night implying she had some freedom of movement, but she was also in some way still accountable to Val.

Now I find out that Val is out of town, or may be out of town. Wait a minute. When I had gone out to their house looking for Stella on the day Spider died, the servant told me she hadn't seen Val in two days, since the night *Passion* closed. That's one I probably could resolve. I could check on Val and find out whether he's in or out of town. Then what?

"Are you still thinking, Dewy?"

"Yeah, Chan."

"Want to tell me about it?"

"No. I don't think so. I've got to check on something, and then Stella and I have some serious talking to do."

"Know what you want, Dewy, and don't delude yourself."

"Thanks, Chan, you've been a big help, even if hasn't been pleasant."

"You're welcome, Dewy. If you need more help, I'm here."

After class I spent half an hour trying to track down Von Dragon without success. At both his office and his home I spoke to underlings who would tell me nothing of his whereabouts. They offered to take a message. I declined to leave one. Maybe Thibodeau would know something of Von Dragon's whereabouts.

Thibodeau was already seated when I arrived at Doc Sacristan's inquest on Spider's death. I sat next to him on the back row of the hearing room and asked him if he knew anything of Von Dragon's whereabouts. He didn't, but he told a bit about the justice system.

Doc Sacristan was a retired obstetrician who had taken the minimum number of courses to be qualified as coroner. The medical examination work was done by others and Doc's main job was to determine the status of the death. Most deaths were attended by physicians who would certify the cause of death. For unattended, unexpected deaths, especially where there was any possibility of foul play, the coroner decided the legal status of death and could convene a Coroner's Jury to bring in a verdict on it.

Doc Sacristan convened his jury, six people, to determine whether Spider's death was homicide, suicide, accident, or death by misadventure which, Thibodeau said, was legalese for an accident where you took stupid risks and failed to survive them.

In addition to the coroner, clerk, jury, Thibodeau, and me, three other people were present. Ellis Boudron sat in the front row. The Eurasian woman I had seen with Spider and a middle-aged man who was with her also sat on the back row at the other end of our bench.

The clerk of the court called to order the inquest into the status of death of one Garrison Lovejoy Slidell, deceased, with the Honorable Lucien Sacristan, M.D., presiding. Doc banged his gavel on his desk and announced that the inquest was in session. He called Lt. Thibodeau to the witness stand and the clerk swore him in.

"Lt. Thibodeau," Doc said. "As investigating officer, will you tell the jury the circumstances surrounding discovery of the deceased?"

"Certainly. At ten minutes after eight o'clock on the morning of November 2, 1997, a Wednesday, I received a call from central dispatch to proceed to the Théatre Vieux Carré where I would find a body hanging in ropes and electrical cables. I arrived with my partner, Officer Landowski, at the same time as two squads of uniformed officers, and we joined them."

"Mr. Dewy Spearman, who had made the original report at the station only minutes before, was also at the scene."

"When we entered the building we discovered a body hanging from the rigging. From its appearance, specifically the angle at which the head was hanging, the lividity of the hands, the coldness of the skin, the absence of a pulse, and the number of flies buzzing around, we judged that the person in question had been dead for at least several hours."

"We took steps to secure the area as a crime scene and we called in the Crime Scene Investigation Team."

"What about you Lt. Thibodeau," Doc said. "Did you notice anything to suggest this hanging may have been the result of foul play?"

"No."

"What evidence might have made led you to suspect foul play had you grounds for suspecting it?"

"Visible signs of struggle, wounds, or graffiti written on the body or nearby surfaces."

"Did you notice any odors?"

"Yes. Other than the customary odors caused by the relaxation of the urinary and bowel sphincters, there was an odor of ethanol."

"And did you find a possible source for that ethanol?"

"Yes. We found a capped, empty, half-pint bottle of vodka in the decedent's right back pocket."

"Thank you, Lt. Thibodeau. Did you find any note or other evidence that might suggest the decedent had committed suicide?"

"No."

At that moment I heard the young woman on the other end of the row speaking softly to her companion as she was nodding her head up and down.

"Can you give information about the time of death?"

"I'm no pathologist, Doc, so I can't say anything about how long he'd been dead. According to reports by witnesses, the part of the theater he was found in had been in continuous occupation from seven o'clock P.M. until about eleven-thirty P.M. and no one reported seeing a dead body during that time span."

"Thank you, Lt. Thibodeau. You may step down."

Thibodeau came back and sat with me.

"I now call Ellis Boudron."

When Ellis was seated and sworn in, Doc continued. "Mr. Boudron, please state your name, occupation, and relationship to the decedent."

"My name is Ellis Sacristan Boudron. I'm the business manager at Théatre Vieux Carré. I was Spider's boss."

Thibodeau leaned over and whispered to me. "Ellis is Doc's first cousin once removed on his mama's side."

"Mr. Boudron, what can you say to this jury that might help them reach a just verdict in this case?"

"I'm sorry to say this, Your Honor, but Spider was a drunk."

The girl at the end of my row began shaking her head sideways at this testimony.

"Spider was a good lighting designer," Ellis continued, "that's why we kept him on; but he was a drunk."

"Mr. Boudron, can you tell us of anything about Mr. Slidell's work habits that might throw light on the cause of his death?"

"Yeah. Sure. He'd just as soon shinny up a rope as use a ladder. He was always runnin' around the grid and pullin' at his bottle."

"Had he ever fallen before?"

"No sir, Doc, but he did drop a big wrench two months back. It fell right between Dewy Spearman and me," Ellis continued, nodding at me. "It liked to scare us to death. Three inches either way and one of us would'a had a broken foot. Six inches and it'a been a busted head."

"Did Mr. Slidell have any enemies that you know of?"

"No sir, Doc. Other than pissin' people off by drinkin', he didn't give nobody trouble. As far as I know, everybody liked him well enough. I heard a bunch of folks came to his funeral."

"Thank you, Mr. Boudron. In your opinion, had Mr. Slidell been despondent lately?"

"No sir, Doc. I've known Spider since we served together in 'Nam. He had some trouble with that posttraumatic stress stuff and went to the V.A. a coupla' times. They put him on some pills a coupla' years back but I think they stopped. Maybe that's why he drank. But he ain't been cryin' in his beer, so to speak. Nope. He's been pretty steady. Jus' doin' his job."

"Thank you Mr. Boudron," Doc Sacristan said. "You may step down."

Ellis went back to his seat.

"Ladies and gentlemen of the jury," Doc continued, "I have before me a report from the pathology service which confirms my own professional opinion. This report tells us that Garrison Lovejoy Slidell, commonly known as 'Spider,' died as the result of a broken neck. Analysis of stomach contents revealed vodka in quantity. There were no contusions, abrasions, or wounds of any kind other than perimortem bruising at the site of his fracture."

"According to the pathologist, the time of death is placed somewhere between eight o'clock and midnight of November 1, the evening preceding the discovery of the body. Lt. Thibodeau has told you the area of the theater in which Mr. Slidell's body was found had been continuously occupied from seven o'clock until at least eleven-thirty. There is no evidence of foul play or suicide."

"The most likely explanation of events is that after eleven-thirty, when everyone else had left the theater, Mr. Slidell, in the course of performing his duties, and while under the influence of intoxicants, lost his footing, fell into the rigging, and broke his neck which killed him instantly. In short, he was drunk, fell, and broke his neck. Therefore, ladies and gentlemen of the jury, it would seem that you will bring in a verdict of death by misadventure. Should you need to retire to consider your verdict, you may do so. Otherwise, Mr. Foreman, if you will tell me that death by misadventure is the true verdict, I will have the clerk enter it on Mr. Slidell's death certificate and we can all go home. Is that your verdict?"

The members of the jury looked at each other and nodded their heads up and down.

"Very well," Doc continued. "The Coroner's Jury rules death by misadventure. So say you all. Let it be entered. Ladies and gentlemen of the jury, thank you for your service. The jury is dismissed and this inquest is adjourned."

Doc Sacristan, the clerk, the jury, and Ellis left the courtroom. I stayed. There were a few things I wanted to say to Thibodeau.

"Tell me, Thibodeau, how is it that you can give testimony from the witness chair sounding like an Ivy League scholar but you talk street punk the rest of the time?"

"You ain't never heard no street punk talk as good as me, homey."

"That's the point. You obviously aren't a street punk. Why talk like one?"

"Street cred. Whose gonna' trust a black detective in New Orleans if he speaks like a Philadelphia lawyer? You want me to use the Baltimore accent I grew up with?"

"O.K. I got it."

"Right, man. Say, what did you think about the proceeding?"

"It was slick, Thibodeau. Maybe too slick. There seems to be no question that Spider's broken neck killed him, but I have trouble understanding the drinking part. It doesn't smell right."

"A couple of weeks ago I followed Spider into an AA meeting and heard him say he'd been sober for months. Another time I saw him fill his vodka bottle with water from the drinking fountain. I've seen him dance across the grid several times. Nobody can do that drunk. That crescent wrench he dropped between Ellis and me was no accident. He dropped it on purpose to show Ellis he was angry with him. I have a hard time believing Spider was drunk."

"Thank you," I heard a female voice say from the other end of the bench.

"Mr. Spearman, I am An Lin Slidell. Spider was my father. This is Jack Singleton, my father's sponsor in AA. My father was an alcoholic but he was not a drunk."

"What she means," Singleton said, "is that Spider was an alcoholic but he was in recovery. He was clean and sober."

"The pathologist said he had vodka in his stomach," I said.

"Yes," An Lin replied, "but did he have alcohol in his blood?"

"What?" Lt. Thibodeau asked.

"Did my father have alcohol in his blood?"

Singleton joined the conversation.

"Spider had some personality problems. Sometimes when you sober up you find out you're ugly, or mean, or lonely, or just a son of a bitch. You know, you find out things that you were using alcohol to keep from finding out. I think for Spider it was fear of intimacy."

"Spider was abandoned by his alcoholic parents when he was a child. In turn, he abandoned An Lin and her mother in Viet Nam during the evacuation. As far as I can tell, except for hanging around with Ellis Boudron, Spider never was close to anyone and I doubt he was really close to Ellis. When An Lin tracked Spider down a year ago, he had a crisis. From dealing with that crisis came his decision to sober up and be a father. He still didn't want people to get close, not even An Lin. He used that bottle to keep people away. He kept up a charade of being a drunk so he could hide in plain sight."

"Like Edgar feigning 'Poor Tom' in *King Lear*," I said.

"So," Thibodeau said, "you're saying Spider wasn't drunk."

"I want to see pathology report," An Lin said. "Nobody see it; just hear what Doc Sacristan say. He is a cousin of Boudron. He will try to make sure nobody point fingers at theater or at Boudrons. I will see report and I will fix Boudrons."

"An Lin," Thibodeau said, "what's in it for you if Spider was sober?"

"My father helps me to set up in business. I study nail technology. I work at bar and save money, open nail salon one day, become independent business woman. My father promise help. Say he will come up with $20,000 to help. Give me $5,000 already."

"Now, father is dead. No more help. He kill himself on purpose, I get nothing. He die by accident, I get as minimum $10,000 insurance unless he is negligent, like work when drunk like Doc Sacristan say. If theater at fault, I sue and collect lots of money, maybe $100,000. If he was murdered, I don't know how much money. Maybe enough to start two businesses."

"Even if he wasn't drunk, An Lin, do you have any idea how hard it would be to prove murder? There is no evidence and there are no witnesses."

An Lin looked hard at Thibodeau and spoke slowly, but strongly, "This is not Viet Nam. This is America. In Viet Nam everybody have hand out. Only wealthy have justice, even with communists. In Viet Nam I am nobody, daughter of foreigner. *Bui doi.* I get no justice. In America I am not dirt of life. I am somebody, daughter of Garrison Lovejoy Slidell. He was not perfect father, but he is my father. He is not a drunk. He not die by accident. He will have justice—without pay off anybody. You help, or you stand in way."

"Well, little lady," Lt. Thibodeau said with what sounded like admiration, "I'll see what I can do."

"You do that, Lieutenant. I go find attorney. Get copy of pathology report and file workman's compensation insurance claim, maybe more."

With that declaration, she nodded at me and left the room with Singleton in tow.

"Well," Thibodeau said. "What do you make of that?"

"Have you read the pathology report?" I asked.

"No."

"Why not?"

"No reason to. Spider broke his neck. No signs of struggle. No witnesses. Everybody have an alibi, more or less," he said, looking at me out of the corners of his eyes.

"Like mine?"

"'Bout, like yours."

"Mine wasn't all that good, you know."

"Thought not, but no reason to press. Looked like Spider fell. Nothing pointed to murder."

"How about vodka in his stomach but not in his blood, like An Lin suggested?"

"He be sober for months and then he drank a lot all at once."

"Yeah, but it has to get into your blood to make you drunk, Thibodeau. I think this stinks. I want to read that pathology report and go where it leads us."

"Case be closed. Jury say 'accident.' I got no authority to reopen the case."

"Do you have the authority to read the pathology report?"

"Sure. We got one at the station."

"Let's go. No harm in reading it. Then we'll see where that leads us."

"O.K., man, let's go. Don't say nothin' to nobody 'bout this or you and I'll be in a world of hurt, and you can count on getting your share of it."

Chapter Twenty

I felt better. My troubles seemed to fade now that I had someone else's misery to focus on. The whole thing about Spider's death troubled me. Finding him had been a shock. And, what about the dead cock? Had that been a warning to Spider instead of to me? What about Spider's putting water in his vodka bottle? The whole thing smelled fishy before. Now that I heard what An Lin and Singleton had to say, it stank, and I was determined to get to the bottom of it.

Back at the station, Thibodeau handed me each page of the pathology report to read after he read it. Unfortunately, he was the slower reader.

From the report we learned that Spider had vodka in his stomach, and even had some in his lungs but none in his blood. We learned that his spinal cord had been separated laterally between his fifth and sixth cervical vertebrae.

"So, Thibodeau, how do you get vodka down into your lungs?"

"It goes down the wrong pipe and you choke on it."

"And you cough it up or you drown in it which would make asphyxiation the cause of death, not spinal cord trauma."

"Yeah. Right."

"You can't be drunk without alcohol in your blood. Some alcohol even gets absorbed straight from your stomach in minutes. So, how do you get alcohol into your stomach and not in your blood?"

"You take a big slug right before you die."

"I guess that's possible, but it doesn't account for alcohol in his lungs. If you swallow it the wrong way, you could get some of it in your lungs, and unless you coughed it all up, you might drown or choke to death, but it wouldn't break your neck."

"O.K. Try this, Spearman. Spider be standin' on the catwalk. He chugs his vodka and gets some down his windpipe. He doubles over in a fit of coughin' and falls. He catches' his neck in the riggin' and breaks it."

"And then he screws the cap back on the bottle and sticks the bottle back in his pocket, right?"

"Probably not, Spearman. Damn. You good."

"O.K., the next thing we need to focus on is the fracture itself. There was a loop of smooth electrical cable around his neck, that's why there were no rope burns. How could you land in a loop of cable in a way that would shove your fifth cervical vertebra sideways?"

"They start counting down from the base of the skull, so the sixth and fifth cervical vertebrae would be the next two right above here," I said, touching Thibodeau's seventh cervical vertebra, the first one that doesn't move when you tilt your head forward, and moving my fingers up to the joint between the sixth and fifth cervical vertebrae.

"I think a hanging would mess you up closer to your jaw, like maybe the second or third vertebra," I said, as I moved my hand to that spot on Thibodeau's neck

"Yeah, man. It is confusin'," Thibodeau said.

"Can we call whoever produced the pathology report?"

"I guess so, but it could get tricky, case bein' closed and all."

"Let me talk to him. I'm not official and I don't have to talk about this specific case."

"That would be Dr. Death, and him's a her, Deidre Lantana."

Thibodeau got Dr. Lantana on the phone and put me on.

"Dr. Lantana. This is Dewy Spearman. I teach theater at Gudrun Hall and my students have presented me with a problem in our play-writing class. We're writing a whodunit. In our play, the dead man is supposed to look like he was hung, but he actually died of a broken neck before he was strung up."

"Well, Mr. Spearman, people who are hung often die of a broken neck. It's common enough that they call it a hangman's fracture. In fact, a good executioner tries to do it that way so death is instantaneous. If you get an incompetent hangman, the condemned person dies of asphyxiation which can take a minute or two of jerking around before the prisoner loses consciousness. It might take several more minutes before clinical death, even longer if the condemned person has a well-muscled neck and the rope doesn't cut off all air flow immediately. It's not a pretty sight."

"Yes, I think we understand that," I said. "It's important to the plot that the victim was actually murdered by another of the characters who attempted to make it look like an accidental hanging. In other words, could a person break a victim's neck and lead everyone to believe it was an accidental hanging?"

"Well, I'm not so sure they could deceive a pathologist. A hangman's facture is like no other."

"O.K. But no one in the country manor—did I tell you they're all snowbound in an isolated manor in the countryside? No one in the manor is a pathologist or medically trained at any level."

"Is that like *Mousetrap*? I think he shot his victim in that play."

"Yes, this is like *Mousetrap*. There's even a policeman there, incognito of course, who's going to solve the murder. What we need to know is how someone could actually break someone else's neck with his or her bare hands and then make it look like a hanging."

"Well," she said, "the breaking part is easy for someone with fair strength. With the victim seated, come up from behind, stabilize the victim's head with one hand, say your left hand, and give a powerful thrust toward the left with your right hand on the right side of the victim's neck, low, just above the shoulder. A swift, powerful thrust should make the vertebra slice right through the spinal cord between the fifth and sixth cervical vertebrae."

"Thanks, Dr. Lantana. Could that kind of injury happen if the victim actually was hung?"

"Low probability. Even if the victim fell sideways into a noose, the weight of the lower body would pull the victim downward. It's pretty hard to hang yourself from your ear or even from your chin. Unless you fall into a closed loop on a slipknot that tightens and arrests your fall, you'd likely just keep falling and not end up hanging."

"If your feet caught on something and gravity couldn't pull you down by the weight of your legs and trunk, the weight of your torso might be enough to lead to a fractured neck if you caught your neck on something hard and unmovable, but you'd see a fracture pattern different from a hangman's fracture and there would be visible trauma to the neck and face and also around the feet or ankles."

"Dr. Lantana, you're saying that severing the spinal cord at the sixth cervical vertebra is unlikely to happen as an accidental hanging."

"No, not by itself, but we had a case a few weeks ago where the victim fell sideways and whacked his neck on an iron pipe while his feet were caught on a platform. The weight of his torso pulled him down. As he fell, he got caught up in some electrical cables that formed a loop much like a noose and arrested the decedent's fall."

"When his butt hung down far enough, his feet pulled free. He fractured his neck and coincidentally hung himself perimortem. That's the way it came down, at least from what we got on it. Frankly, Mr. Spearman, as I said, that's a chain of events with a low probability of happening, but it's possible. That's the way the coroner said it happened, so that's that. Say, you're involved with theater. You might have heard of that event. It was down at the Théâtre Vieux Carré. Thibodeau's probably has the report."

"Thank you, Dr. Lantana. You've been most helpful," I said, as Thibodeau and I both hung up.

"Does the coroner usually tell the pathology lab what to find?"

"No. Chatter back and forth sometimes, but that's the first time I heard about a sideways fall against an iron pipe, and this is my case."

"And no booze in the bloodstream. 'There's something rotten in the state of Denmark.' Who's Doc covering up for?"

"Maybe the theater in general. Doc be Clotilde Boudron's first cousin and a member of the board of directors."

"The theater didn't murder Spider, Thibodeau. A person or persons murdered Spider. Probably only one person. I don't much believe in conspiracies; somebody always talks."

"O.K., Spearman. If Spider be murdered, who you make for it?"

"Ellis Boudron."

"Why?"

"Spider and Ellis ran a scam. They sold off assets and pocketed the money. I heard them argue. Spider said he needed a bigger cut because he had responsibilities. He wanted fifty percent. My bet is Spider started making deals on his own and Ellis found out."

"Ellis had an alibi."

"Wendy Bridges?"

"How ever did you guess?" Thibodeau said, raising his eyebrows in mock surprise.

"You don't have to be sarcastic. It doesn't work, anyway. I tried being sarcastic and it didn't get me anywhere. Truth be told, Ellis' alibi is about as good an alibi as I had, and I know I didn't do it."

"O.K., Spearman. Ellis Boudron is our man. How we gonna' get him? Remember, this case is closed."

"Reopen it."

"Takes the D.A. to do that and we got nothing to take to him. We gonna' have to do this unofficial."

"O.K. The key is to break Ellis' alibi."

"Even then we're just circumstantial."

"I think I can get Ellis on embezzlement."

"For selling lights?"

"Better than that. Tapping the till. I believe Wendy is his accomplice. I'll nail Wendy and then use her to get to Ellis."

"O.K., man, but don't do nothin' too illegal, and I don't want to hear about it if you do. Let me know when you got enough for me to make an arrest."

"O.K.," I said. "It's a deal."

He stuck out his hand and I shook it.

"You all right, my friend. I was worryin' about you, considering the company you keep, but you all right."

That got my dander up.

"Just a minute, Thibodeau. You've been insinuating that my lady, Stella Maris, is unsavory for two months now. I want you to spit it out. What have you got against her?"

"I'm not goin' to say, my frien'."

"That's chicken shit."

"No, that's circumspect. I'm going to let others say. You got a picture of Stella Maris?"

"No. As a matter of fact, I don't."

"Know where you can get one?"

"Right now?"

"Yes."

"I've got a charcoal sketch back at the apartment."

"Never mind," he said, as he picked up the telephone and asked for the sketch artist.

"We'll do it here. First we gonna' start with this identification kit. You just start flippin' through until you find the features that match hers. The artist will take it from there."

In about twenty minutes we had a pencil sketch of Stella Maris. Thibodeau made a copy of the sketch and told me to call Laura and tell her to start rehearsal without me. He told me to tell her I was at the police department seeing about a break-in at my apartment and that I might not be able make the beginning of rehearsal. After I finished my call to Laura, Thibodeau told me we'd eat while we were out. I wasn't too keen about being late to rehearsal, especially in light of the motivational speech I had given the kids at Gudrun Hall, but dinner sounded fine. Even though it was just turning five o'clock, daylight was done and I hadn't eaten since before daylight.

Thibodeau wouldn't say where we were going but we were headed out of town. After a twenty-minute drive, we pulled up at a truck stop off I-10. We went inside and sat down. A waitress with really big hair came up and spoke directly to Thibodeau.

"'Lo, Lieutenant. Is that a .38 long-nose police special in your front pocket or are you just happy to see me?"

"Hi, yourself, Lavonia. This is my frien', Dewy Spearman."

"Hi, Dewy."

Lavonia dropped the menu on the floor, stood on it, and looked me in the eye.

"You can have anything on the menu you want, big boy."

"Can it, Lavonia. We need to ask you a few questions."

"Official business?"

"Not yet."

"O.K. Why don't you boys order something and I'll be back directly. We're kinda' busy about now."

She put the menu on the table, poured two cups of coffee, and left. Thibodeau told me we were going to have the meat loaf special and shouted out the order. We sat and drank coffee in silence until a server brought our meal. We ate in silence until Lavonia came over to ask if everything was all right. Thibodeau pulled Stella's picture out of his jacket and showed it to her"

"Ever see this woman before?"

"Oh, sure, honey. That's the Black Widow."

"What can you tell me about her?"

"I take her to be freelance 'cause she don't have a pimp."

When I got through choking on a mouthful of meat loaf, I spoke, in disbelief.

"She's a prostitute?"

Chapter Twenty-One

"Lots of girls work the truck stop, honey. Trucks these days even got beds in 'em. I've climbed up in one or two, myself. Not with just anybody, mind you, and not for money, Lieutenant, so don't go arrestin' me."

"Outta' my jurisdiction, Lavonia."

"I know, honey. Why you think I'm tellin' you this?"

"How often do you see her out here?" Thibodeau asked.

"Coupla' times a week. Sure as my name's Lavonia Jackson, that lady shows up a half-hour after dark. We call her the Black Widow on account of she's always dressed in black and she likes to bite."

"She go away for the summer?" Thibodeau asked.

"How should I know what she does for the summer?"

"Don't you waitresses run a pool on what day she shows back up each fall?"

"Yeah, but I never won it."

"So," I asked, repeating myself, "is she a prostitute?"

"Honey, how should I know? Maybe she does it for kicks. Why don't you go ask somebody's been with her? Wait," she said, looking out through the window into the darkness. "There she is now, heading toward that Peterbilt with the john in the tan jacket."

I jumped up and ran out the door chasing after Stella and calling out her name, but she disappeared behind a truck. The man in the tan jacket turned around and blocked my path.

"You giving my lady a hard time?" he asked, but not as if he expected an answer.

"I just need to talk to her. Step out of my way, please."

"You're gonna' have to come through me to get to her, sonny." He pulled a sap out of his pocket and slapped it against his hand.

"No need for violence, friend. I just want to talk to the lady."

"She's taken. Now beat it before I beat you."

"Hold on, fella'," Thibodeau said, as he came up behind me and flashed his badge. "This is official police business."

"Kiss my white ass, black boy," the trucker said as he lunged at Thibodeau.

Using my experience with stage combat, I stuck out my foot and tripped the trucker. He fell at Thibodeau's feet uttering curses I haven't heard since I visited my son at his duty station in San Diego.

Thibodeau stepped on his wrist forcing him to release the sap.

"You gonna' be still or do I have to draw my weapon?"

"Eat shit."

"That's a happy thought. Why don't you take a few deep breaths and then we'll have ourselves a nice talk. I'm sure you don't want to be arrested for impeding a police investigation and have me impound your rig."

"Eat shit and die."

"I think we best start again," Thibodeau said, as he kicked away the trucker's weapon. "My name is Lt. Thibodeau. With my own two eyes I saw you conspiring with a known felon who is wanted by the FBI for violations of the Mann Act."

"What's that?"

"The transportation of minors across state lines for immoral purposes. What you crackers call 'white slavery'."

"No shit. I don't know about that; she just come on to me."

"Did she ask you for money?"

"Do I look like George Clooney? Of course she asked for money. Fifty bucks."

"And you took her up on it?"

"Hell yes. I got a thousand ridin' on it."

"How's that, man?"

"Guys in my company are always talking about this classy gal who dresses in black and sometimes hangs out at this stop. We got a pool goin'. Two years now. First one who bangs her and brings back proof gets the whole thousand."

"How you gonna' prove it?" Thibodeau asked. "They gonna' take your word?"

"It's easy, man. Just take a picture of her in the sleeper. Every trucker's got his name stenciled on the back of his crib. We'll know whose it is."

"And nobody's collected in two years?"

"Shit, no. Coupla' guys seen her gettin' in a cab, but guys she got in with won't never say nothin'. Claim they can't remember. One guy rigged a remote control camera, and when he had his film developed, he had pictures with bimbos from Birmingham to Sacramento, but the one from this stop was just him in his sleeper with all his clothes on. He says he can't even remember takin' the picture. Can I get up now?"

"Sure, man. Just be cool. We only want to talk. I'm not here to bust you. We want to talk to the lady. I guess she's gone by now. She take your money?"

"Hell no. My mama didn't raise no stupid children. I always pay after. I'm no fool."

"But you are a cracker. Have a nice day. Let's go, Spearman."

"Hey," the trucker yelled. "What about my sap?"

"Contraband," Thibodeau snapped back. "I'm seizing it. You want it back, you file a claim with the Orleans Parish Sheriff."

The trucker muttered profanities on his way back to his rig.

Thibodeau stuck the sap in his pocket as we headed for his car.

"I'd like to teach that trucker a lesson in race relations, Spearman, but I'm gettin' too old for it. By the way, I was jivin' about that Mann Act stuff. I just wanted to get that cracker's attention."

I said nothing. I was in shock. When we reached the French Quarter, Thibodeau passed the theater and stopped at my apartment.

"You still got half an hour before your rehearsal starts. Go upstairs and pour yourself a stiff drink. If you feel like going to rehearsal, go. If you don't, let your assistant director do her thing. You got somebody you can talk to?"

"Yeah," I answered, speaking for the first time since I discovered the unhappy answer to the question about Stella I had posed to Lavonia. "When I'm ready."

"O.K., man; hop out, and take care."

I trudged upstairs, went in, and collapsed on the love seat next to Radu's bar. I started in on the scotch. Sometime before dawn I passed out or fell asleep. Either way, it stopped me from thinking about Stella's being a prostitute.

Until I woke up.

I dragged myself through the morning. I had a lot on my mind and I was having a hard time keeping one train of thought from colliding with another one. How was I going to expose Ellis? What could I do about Lance? Why was Stella doing this to me?

At noon, I met Laura, the witches, and the technical crew. Laura said nothing about my missing rehearsal last night and I did not volunteer an explanation. I couldn't bring myself to ask if Stella showed.

We ran through the first and third scenes of Act I and the first scene of Act IV with the witches. Laura and I filled in for Banquo and Macbeth so the tech crew could see what they needed to do. That got Stella off my mind for several hours. My plan was to have the three witches' scenes be ethereal, the quintessential element, with the four classical elements reifying the Weird Sisters' forebodings.

When the audience arrived, they would see an empty thrust stage emanating from the proscenium and, behind the proscenium, a pile of blocks of various heights and widths forming tiered platforms on which some scenes would be staged. When the house lights went down, a black cauldron would rise from a trap door in the center of the thrust emitting dry-ice fog to open the show. The primary scene lighting would be the green special on the cauldron from directly overhead combined with lavender side-lighting and yellow fire lighting under the cauldron. The cauldron, which we would use in all the witches scenes, represented water.

My first witch, Bruce Wilcoxin, a dancer, was as tall and lanky as the late Spider Slidell. He controlled his sinuous body to good effect. We costumed Bruce with a dance belt over a green-and-tan camouflage long-sleeved leotard and matching tights. He made his entrances and exits through a second trap door in the thrust, opening and closing it as he went and moving with slow, powerful, fluid movements like a boa constrictor. Bruce's thin beard added fidelity to Banquo's line, "You should be women, and yet your beards forbid me to interpret that you are so." Bruce was earth.

My second witch, Adriana Dare, had been born missing a hand and wrist on her left arm and wore a cosmetic prosthetic hand socially. She volunteered to take it off for the show to add to the eccentricity of the witches' scenes and to lend verity to her line, "By the pricking of my thumbs, something wicked this way comes."

We costumed Adriana in a diaphanous white chiffon empire-style gown with a white feather boa and rigged more dry ice and fans to stir her gown and to cover her entrances and exits from a door concealed in the blocks on stage left. Adriana was air, or wind.

Since we decided not to fly Adriana for safety reasons and to avoid triggering memories of Spider hanging dead from the rigging, the tech crew came up with the idea of flying a ball of fire to cover my third witch, Eileen Ruie. We took the time to fabricate and test it. The crew fashioned a twenty-four inch hollow ball out of eight-foot lengths of half-inch flexible irrigation tubing and added two ten-pound iron bars from a curtain counterbalance to give it some heft.

They fastened the ball to a live electric cable hanging from the top of the loft at center stage and studded it with more than two hundred red, yellow, and white mini lights plugged into the electric cable which would be turned on to simulate a ball of fire.

They rigged the ball to swing from stage right to stage left just behind the proscenium arch and in front of the blocks barely clearing Laura's stage manager's desk. A techie standing on a catwalk on the outside wall on stage right would release the ball as soon as the lighting cue came to electrify it, and another techie on the catwalk on stage left would catch the ball with a shepherd's crook and secure it until we swung it back to stage left to cover Eileen's exit.

At the lowest point of the ball of fire's swing, it barely cleared the boards at center stage. As it continued its swing, we discovered the hard way that it would hit the head or shoulders of anyone standing at Laura's stage manager's desk as it swung between the first and second curtain counterweight arbors before it got in range of the techie's shepherd's crook. Laura was going to have to step away from her desk for that effect and make sure no one was standing in the ball's path, especially anyone facing the wrong way. They wouldn't know it was coming until it clobbered them from behind.

The first time we tried it, the techie fumbled the ball at the end of its swing. Laura stuck a crutch against the curtain ropes and stopped the ball from swinging back onstage. Fortunately, the fireball didn't electrocute her or damage her crutch. She said her Lofstrands were made from carbon fiber and were lighter than aluminum, stronger than aluminum, and, unlike aluminum, non-conductive.

We costumed Eileen in a nude body suit and floor-length, hooded black cape. She slipped out in blackout from stage right and moved toward center stage and stepped up on a low block. She made herself invisible to the audience by covering herself completely with her black cape and stood with her back to the audience until the globe, ablaze with simulated fire, passed between her and the audience. As the fire ball passed, she rotated counter-clockwise, dropped her black hood to reveal her shocking, teased-out white hair, and threw open her black cape to reveal her scintillating, seemingly-nude body festooned with strategically-placed streamers of red and yellow silk that fluttered in the fan-blown fog animating her presence.

To make the effect really striking, we rigged a flash pot to fire between Eileen and the audience and set it off just as she turned. To cover her exit we set off a second flash as Eileen rotated clock-wise, closed her cape, pulled up her hood to become invisible, and then slipped back into the wings to exit. Eileen was fire.

At five o'clock we called it a day. No one was slow to leave. I walked out into the gathered gloom of the mid-November dusk to find an oyster bar and drown my sorrows in a bowl of gumbo and a schooner of beer. Alone.

On Sunday evening the entire cast and crew, Stella included, assembled for the six o'clock call. I was busy setting up the scenes in which other actors were on stage with the witches. Stella was in none of those scenes which made it easy for her to keep her distance, and keep her distance she did.

We rehearsed both of the witches' scenes with Macbeth and Banquo out of sequence to get them done so I could let the witches go home by eight o'clock. After they left, the rest of us ran through the remaining scenes in order. Because this was a technical rehearsal, I didn't expect the actors to perform with full intensity.

Even so, I was disappointed with Lance, and not from lack of intensity. That he had, but it was the unabashed intensity of a sixteen year-old bodybuilder admiring his naked body in a full-length looking glass. And then there was his whining, particularly when we got to the love scene in Shakespeare's Act III.

"Dewy, this lighting is terrible. My special is side-angled, stark white, with red shadows. Stella's special is diffused and her shadows are lavender. She looks lovely and I look like shit."

"If the light fits, wear it," I said, which brought a few sniggers from the cast. It was a cheap shot. I felt guilty for saying it, but not so guilty that I wanted to apologize.

"Come on, man," Lance complained. "You can't do this to me. I look ugly. I won't stand for it."

"You will stand for it if that's the way we light that scene."

"Give me a break, Spearman."

"I tell you what, Lance. I do want to change that lighting."

"Pete," I shouted to the light booth, "can you switch Lance's red gels for barely green? I'd like to see what it looks like. Keep his stark white, side-angled special. That's what I want."

To everyone in general I shouted, "Everybody take ten while Pete changes the gels. Ten minutes, and not a minute more."

Lance fumed.

When I turned away to speak to Stella, she wasn't anywhere to be seen. I thought about looking for her but everyone else was trying to talk to me and I had my pride to salvage.

Twenty minutes later we ran the scene again. I liked the barely green gels' shadows on Lance better. He liked them less, whined more, and threatened to complain to Clotilde Boudron, the entire board, and even to Actors Equity. No matter, I was the director and in this matter, my word was law.

We finished the technical run-through at eleven o'clock. I decided to hold over my director's notes until Monday afternoon for the technical crew and Monday evening for the cast. I sent everyone home or to wherever they were going.

The theater emptied quickly except for me, sitting in my director's chair, and Stella, standing beside the ghost light at center stage.

"Can we talk?" she asked.

"I'd like to, yes," I replied. My mouth was as dry as cotton. "Your place or mine," I said, trying to be funny but not feeling it.

"Yours, if you'll let me in."

"Why would I not?"

"You must have a poor opinion of me right now."

"I have many opinions right now, Stella."

"I'm sure you do. Let's go in silence, and let's wait until we're safely inside to say the many things we have to say to each other."

I nodded my agreement.

We walked out through the stage door in our silence. I locked it behind us. On the way, we plunged into an overflow of Bourbon Street revelers and carefully worked our way to the apartment on St. Peter's Street. My heart was as heavy as Stella's sparkle was dim.

We ascended the staircase in the silence we began at the theater.

"Leave the lights off, please, Dewy, and let's sit over by the balcony doors and talk."

She sat on the love seat. I slid into a leather-covered papasan chair draped with furry animal skins, a relic of the '70s.

"You first," I said."

"You must think ill of me, Dewy."

"I don't know what to think, Stella. I'm confused."

"I asked you not to fall in love with me."

"That's like asking a fish not to swim."

"I tried to warn you off."

"With longing looks, tender touches, and wild, passionate sex?"

"I never counted on your getting under my skin, Dewy. I thought I could control everything."

"Control is, at best, an illusion, Stella. Whom were you trying to control? Me or you?"

"Us, Dewy. Us. I was trying to keep you and me from becoming an 'us'. I knew it would end badly."

"Why, Stella? Why?"

"I told you before, Dewy. I'm not worthy of you."

"Because you're a prostitute?" I said, with an intensity that surprised me.

My words hung in the air during a lengthy silence that Stella was first to break.

"I'm not a prostitute," she said, quietly, but clearly.

I broke the next silence.

"I just don't get it, Stella. You have Val. You have me. According to what I discovered last night, you also have string of truck drivers you hook for."

"I'm not a hooker, Dewy."

"I shouldn't believe my eyes and ears?"

"You are my only lover, Dewy," she repeated, and then she looked down at the floor.

"Spare me. If you're not a hooker, you're a nymphomaniac."

Stella lifted her gaze from the floor and looked directly at me. In the dim light spilling in from the French doors I could see wet tracks of tears glistening on her face. She looked directly at me with liquid emerald eyes. She spoke slowly, quietly, and evenly.

"I am no nymphomaniac. I am not a prostitute. I did you no favor by taking you as my lover and I do you no favor by telling you the truth. You deserve much more, but you at least deserve the truth. You will hate me for it. I hope it sets you free."

"Stella, you're a damn fine actress and a beautiful woman. You're a great lover, too, but an elusive one."

I felt a sudden flash of anger, fueled by my pain, which colored my next sarcastic question.

"What can you possibly tell me about yourself that I don't already know?"

I raised my voice even louder and continued.

"What clever words can you use to falsify the inescapable facts I discovered at that truck stop? What magic spell will you weave to make me take leave of my senses, to deny the testimony of the trucker and the waitress, to set aside my sensibilities and personal observations of your hooking at a truck stop on I-10?"

With anger flashing from my eyes, I stared at her, defying her to give me an honest answer.

Tears continued streaming down her face, but her eyes burned brightly as she replied in kind.

"Can you find even one person who claims to have had sex with me? Just one. That's all I ask."

I faltered.

"Well, no, but I didn't need to. The evidence is overwhelming."

Or was it? I could hardly believe this was happening, but doubt had put its icy finger on my heart and challenged my righteousness.

"If you're not a prostitute, then tell me what you are," I said, quietly but intensely, as if the words were hissing snakes.

"Something worse, Dewy. Something far worse," she replied quietly, her anger attenuated by her interior thoughts, her gaze returned to the floor.

I did not ask the obvious question, but it was on my tongue. Perhaps she read it in my mind.

Stella looked up at my face and into my angry eyes, her own eyes wide open and glistening.

"I'm a vampire."

Chapter Twenty-Two

I was dumbstruck, witless. The silence was palpable. I let her words sink in as I attempted to retrieve my wits.

"A vampire," I said, when I found them, croaking because my mouth was completely dry. A thousand bits of information, a thousand fragmentary images, and a thousand thoughtlets crashed and jangled in my mind as they jockeyed for prominence.

"A vampire," I said, louder. "Yeah, sure. You're not a prostitute. You're a vampire. Well, missy, that explains everything," I shouted. But it didn't. Despite the literal meaning of my sarcastic words, nothing had been explained. I'd been slapped in the face, slugged in the gut, kicked in the balls, and all she could say was, 'I'm not a prostitute—I'm a vampire.' That inflamed me more.

"How do you expect me to believe something as outrageous as that, Stella? That's bullshit."

"That's the truth," she said, unwavering in her steadfast gaze.

I hurled my ultimate challenge.

"Prove it."

"Have you ever seen me out in daylight?"

"No, but you have a sensitivity to light."

"That's part of it. Have you ever seen me eat or drink?"

"We met at a dinner party. Another time you brought over a po' boy sandwich."

"You ate. I didn't. Have you ever seen me eat or drink?"

"Well, no, actually, I haven't, but you're so slender you would hardly ever eat."

"Even a slender person must have nourishment."

"O.K., so what do you do for nourishment?"

"I drink blood, human blood by preference."

"So you go around merrily killing people and drinking their blood, just like that?"

"No, Dewy. I have never killed anyone; I only drink their blood. That's what I do at the truck stop and other places in New Orleans, and in South American cities during the summer here. I cruise for men who want me for my body. When we're alone, I bite their necks and nourish myself with their blood. They become confused and can't recall what happened, so I'm relatively safe from exposure."

"You were using that truck driver for supper, not for sex?"

"Yes, Dewy. Even I have to eat."

"Then why don't they become vampires?"

"They have not drunk my blood."

"And me. Have you used me? Is that what those wounds on my neck were? Is that why I was so confused at first? Have you been stringing me along so you could suck me dry?"

"No," she said, with a look of defiance burning in her liquid eyes. "No. I haven't been stringing you along to suck you dry. And yes, I did bite you our first time together. If I am not nourished, I will wither into an undead nothingness, and you were so obliging. Yes, I used you, Dewy. I flirted with you and you flirted back. It was delicious. I haven't had such genuine male attention since my husband's stroke, long before I took up with Val."

"You aren't like those creeps who think they're going to score with me for quick, cheap sex. You aren't like Val who seduced me with his offer of liberation, a liberation that holds me captive to my induced affliction. You're real. You were genuinely attracted to me, and I responded. I liked it. It was fulfilling, but I can never be fulfilled."

"I'm weak, Dewy. I must be nourished or I will wither. I am doomed to be undead. I can't even kill myself. There's only one way I can die. At our first encounter, hunger carried me to your arms and my weakness led me to nourish myself at your expense. For that I am sorry, and I am unworthy of your love. Now, passion brings me to your bed, but knowing the truth, you will turn me away."

I felt like laughing, so I laughed. I sniggered. I chortled. I guffawed. I cackled. I howled like a hyena, like a coyote, like an alpha male wolf that has lost his mate. Stella looked worried. I'm not sure how long I howled, but it wasn't yet daylight and no one had come around to see what the ruckus was about. I stopped howling abruptly when Stella slapped my face—hard. I sat, shocked, staring at her. To this day, I don't know how I communicated to her, but she did my bidding. She crawled into my papasan chair and hugged me in a close, tight embrace. I began to sob.

"Let it out, Dewy. We'll talk later. We'll find the word we need to give this meaning. There will be time for such a word."

She held me as long as I needed to be held. In time my wracking sobs diminished. As I calmed down, I got the shivers. Shock. Stella picked up a bottle of Radu's bourbon and led me, shaking, into the bedroom. She stripped off her clothes and my clothes and got us both under the covers. She held me and she made me take a slug of bourbon. Time, the down comforter, the bourbon, and the heat of our naked bodies worked their wonders. Eventually, I stopped shaking and became semi-coherent. Stella remained beside me. I found my voice, and, in halting phrases, I spoke aloud.

"I think—somewhere, Stella—somewhere in—in my mind, Stella—I realized—realized some of—of this, Stella—but I didn't want—didn't want to—to acknowledge any of it—any of it."

"I truly am sorry I dragged you into this, Dewy. I didn't want you to fall in love with me. I didn't want to fall in love with you. But you did and I did, and now we have a mess."

She kissed me and my head spun.

"Slowly, Stella, please—I need time—to sort this out."

I took another slug of bourbon and felt marginally better.

"O.K., Dewy. I'll go slowly."

I paused for a minute or two to get my bearings. After I found some of my wits and regained much of my stride, I spoke again.

"Stella, it's time to tell me the whole story—truthfully. You've danced around many things since I met you. Just tell me the truth."

"You may not be happy with the truth."

"I'm happy now?"

Sarcasm paid another visit, but this time it was wry, not raw, and it didn't pitch a tent.

"Point taken, Dewy. Let me start at the very beginning."

"That's a very good place to start."

"Smart ass."

"O.K., O.K., but you gave me the opening."

"I'm glad to see your humor returning, even sophomoric humor. I wasn't born Stella Maris. I was born Lou Ellen Yellin. I doubt if my parents realized how hick that sounded because hick was the air they breathed and the water they drank. We were all hicks. My father was a tobacco sharecropper and sometimes coal miner in western Virginia, way back in Appalachia. Tobacco paid once a year, and whatever Pa had left after the overseer took out for expenses and rent, Pa gambled and drank away within a month, sometimes less."

"When Pa went underground he got paid every week. That took less than a day to disappear. Ma took in washing and sold dried fruit to help us get by. Neither Pa nor Ma could read, and I don't think any of us children went past the seventh grade. I didn't. In those days children were expected to work crops. Poor folks didn't see much value in schooling. It didn't put food on the table."

"You make it sound like it was the Dark Ages, Stella."

"It was, Dewy. I was born in 1926, seventy-one years ago."

That sounded strange, but I was too fried to do the math. I did want to hear her story so I pulled the comforter up to my neck and worked to listen attentively. Stella passed me the bourbon bottle. I sat up against the headboard to take another slug. The fire of the bourbon jolted me to greater awareness and my movements to raise the bottle to my lips loosened my grip on the comforter. It slipped down to our waists exposing her lovely breasts.

I was feeling warm enough, so I let the comforter lay there. I listened to her story as I watched her breasts jiggle when she moved. That gave me something to focus on.

"That part of Appalachia never has been particularly well off, and during the Depression it was terrible. Ma died of consumption, tuberculosis, when I was thirteen, and I spent the next year keeping Pa off of me. Pa had run off my oldest brother, Caleb, right after Ma died. My other brothers were too afraid of Pa to try to protect me. My younger sister, Elizabeth Ann, was barely ten. She was too little to help me even if I'd let her try."

"One Saturday afternoon, after Pa slept off his Friday night drunken card game, he pinned me down on the kitchen table and started raping me. I bit his arm, hard. When he raised his fist, I grabbed the cast-iron skillet and cold-cocked him, gathered up the few things I owned, took what little cash he had in his pockets, and lit out for Richmond. I didn't stop to see if he was still breathing."

"Did you kill him?"

"No. The son of-a-bitch didn't have the decency to die. Not then. That happened two years later. About the time Elizabeth Ann turned thirteen and Pa started molesting her, Caleb came back. He'd heard what Pa was doing. He called Pa out and he killed him with his bare hands. He had to go to prison for it, but they let him out after a year and a day. It was like he'd done a public service. Caleb joined the army and lived a decent life. He eventually became a preacher."

I took another sip of bourbon and pushed the comforter further down. I was pleasantly warm and the view was spectacular.

"When I got to Richmond I did whatever I could to make a living. I cooked, I cleaned, and I took care of children. Those were my skills. I listened to the radio while I worked and I decided to be an actress. I paid attention to the way my voice sounded and I practiced imitating their voices. After a while I saw an advertisement for domestics in New York. If you signed up with an agency, they'd give you a bus ticket to New York. I signed up."

"The agency got me all the work I could use. One job was with a theatrical family. I moved in with them. They helped me work on my voice and my acting skills. They helped me pick my stage name, Stella Maris. I am the one and only Stella Maris. I invented Aunt Stella as a cover story. How else could I explain how I haven't aged for the last thirty years?"

"Eventually, I took singing and dancing lessons and got a few entertainment jobs. Pretty soon, Hitler started gobbling up Europe and the government started building up the military to counter him. New York seemed like the center of it all. USO clubs sprang up like Johnny jump-ups. Anyone with any talent could work in a USO club. On New Year's Eve of 1943, I met a cute soldier from Georgia at a club show. One thing we had in common was no living parents. We were both orphans. We fell in love and I got pregnant. We couldn't marry because I couldn't prove I was 18. No papers."

In April of 1944, before we could overcome the bureaucratic hurdles to get married, he shipped out to England. He'd been trained as a frogman. His job was to clear obstacles for amphibious landings. He died June 6th on Omaha Beach while he was blowing up LST traps. I was the beneficiary of his G.I. life insurance."

"The red tape for an 18 year-old, single, pregnant woman to buy property in New York in 1944 was horrendous, but I did it. I used the insurance money to buy a brownstone in Brooklyn and quit domestic work. I took in roomers and continued with whatever acting work I could get, which wasn't much, until our child, Leona, was born. I passed her off as my little sister because of prejudice against unmarried mothers. Leona was nearly two years old when the war ended. New York was humming. There was always someone in the house who could look after Leona when I was auditioning or working. I managed to keep our heads above water. In a few years I got a break. I landed a job in the chorus of *Kiss Me Kate* and was understudy for Kate. That's where I met William, at the Philadelphia tryout. He was a stage door Johnny. I've already told you about William."

"Yes, if what you told me was true."

"I haven't lied about my life with William. We had a wonderful life until his stroke. After that, I coped as best I could."

"You weren't truthful about when it was. You made it sound like it was only a few years ago."

"Yes, I lied in that way didn't I? Among my other lies, I've lied about my age for 30 years, and I didn't tell you that Val is my master, not just a lover I ran away with. I lied about that. It was so exciting at first, Dewy. I was seduced by the glamour and luxury. To be fair, Val didn't really enslave me. I did that myself. Val didn't literally take me captive and hold me against my will. He seduced me. He seduced me with attention, with glamour, with power, with luxury, and with the prospect of immortality. I chose to be seduced."

"Just like Wilhemina, Stella."

"I chose unwisely. I'm weary of deceiving people. I'm bereft at not being able to visit my daughter, not being a role model for my granddaughter, and not being able to hold my great granddaughter."

"You have a great granddaughter?"

"Yes, Dewy. She's an infant. I've always looked young for my age and I literally stopped aging, but I'm old, tired, and lonely. When my granddaughter was an infant, whenever I came around she would howl and scream as if she could sense evil about me. She's never allowed me to become close to her, even as an adult."

"I won't even attempt to see her baby, my great granddaughter. Even with a Hollywood makeup job I have trouble looking like I'm seventy years old, and I can only visit at night. It's just too difficult. I've dropped out of their lives completely. I miss them terribly."

"That's hard, Stella. I don't believe I could accept never seeing my children again"

"I miss even ordinary human relationships, Dewy. That's why I was willing to drag you into my misery. I wanted joy and you wanted to share yours with me. I deceived you about who and what I am. I used you, and for that I am profoundly sorry."

"You use many people, Stella. You use everyone whose blood you suck."

"Unnourished, I wither, and they have nourishment to give."

"But you don't ask for it, Stella. You take it by deceit.

"I told you I wasn't worthy of you, Dewy. If you're over your shock, I'm going to leave. I'll finish the show, but I won't drag you deeper into my depravity."

"Don't go," I said with an intensity that surprised me. "Don't go. Let's talk about this some more."

I sat up, pushed the comforter down past my knees, and pulled my knees up to my chest before continuing our conversation. The bourbon had warmed me to almost-toasty.

"What's to talk about, Dewy?"

"What we're going to do about this. About us."

"There can't be an 'us', Dewy. This must end. Val has gone to Canada for business and to give me time, I believe, to stop this foolishness. He will return, and he will not permit this to continue."

"Leave him, Stella."

"That's easier said than done. What if I did, Dewy? What if Val would permit it? What then? You will age naturally, become an old man, and die in your time. I will still be what I am right now, an ageless, undead vampire who sucks the blood of the unwitting. No, Dewy. If I am not already repugnant to you, I will become so."

"There must be another way," I said.

"There' a way, Dewy, the way I chose years ago. You could join me. Drink my blood. Become immortal."

"Like you did with Val?"

"Yes. Only I haven't deceived you. You know the truth."

"And you didn't know the truth when you joined Val?"

Stella opened her mouth to reply, but no words issued forth. She closed her mouth. Several moments later her speech returned.

"I knew the truth, Dewy. I just didn't think through the consequences. I didn't know how worthless immortality would be compared to the daily joys of experiencing friends and family in their time. Now all I have is immortality, Val, and this bittersweet moment with you. Join me and we can make this moment last more than a lifetime."

"I love you, Stella, but this is new to me. I need time to think, but I don't believe I can do it. There must be some other way."

"There is one other way, Dewy. You can release me."

"Release you? How?"

"Drive a wooden stake through my heart."

"You're kidding."

"No."

"I don't believe I can do that either, Stella."

"Then we're doomed to continue as we are, Dewy, and I won't. I come to you only every other night because I must have time to seek nourishment, to cruise the truck stops or the French Quarter before rehearsal or after I leave your bed. I leave you before dawn, not from propriety, but from necessity, two necessities. I must feed, and I cannot remain at large during the day. Val will return from Canada soon, perhaps in two or three weeks. He is not known for his patience and he will not tolerate this much longer."

"Was it Val who tried to kill me during the apartment break-in?"

"He wasn't trying to kill you, Dewy. Not then. You interrupted him. You told us Radu had a publicity picture from *Kiss Me Kate*. That was difficult to explain away. Val knew Radu had been snooping into my past. He was afraid you might find notes Radu may have made and expose us. That would make things even more difficult. Without telling me what he was doing, he provoked you at the theater on the presumption that you would stay, either to defend my honor to the others, or to polish your own reputation. That would give him enough time to burgle your apartment."

"Val made a mistake, Dewy. He hadn't counted on my leaving in disgust, your following me, and our showing up at your apartment. He didn't take it well. Val is angry, Dewy. He is very angry. When he returns, I fear for your safety."

"And I fear for yours, Stella. I don't know what kind of future we could have. Right now have the present," I said, as I reached over and pulled her naked body to mine. Stella pushed my knees down and swiveled so she was facing me and put her legs over mine. I pulled her legs up over my shoulders, supported her buttocks with my hands, and buried my face in her warm, moist mound.

Quickly and lightly, then fiercely and firmly, I ran my tongue over her. Her musky scent inflamed my passion as my dexterous tongue inflamed hers. She began to chant in low moans punctuated by short gasps. She grabbed my legs. Her thighs, which clamped my head, were taught and stiff. So was I.

I was intoxicated by her scent and by the rhythmic chanting of her moans and gasps. I found my hands slowly and gently kneading her buttocks as I pulled her vulva tight against my face. Feral growls, muffled by her mound of Venus, escaped from my lips and resonated in my chest creating a baritone cantus firmus for her contralto counterpoint that ascended the scale to a series of soprano shrieks as she came in nine or ten heaving spasms, some light, some deep, and all with her firm thighs clamped around my head, her heels beating against my back, and her high notes piercing the November night.

As she subsided, I eased her down into a seated position between my legs with her thighs over mine. She snuggled closely pressing the underside of my swollen penis onto the sweet lips of her warm and moist mound. To keep my balance, I spread my hands on the bed just behind my buttocks and locked my elbows.

Stella reached up and began kissing and nibbling my neck as she massaged my nipples and traced intricate patterns with her fingernails on my chest and stomach. As she slowly rocked back and forth, stimulating us both, I closed my eyes and arched my neck. I was oblivious to everything but pleasure.

"Dewy, look at you. Where are you?"

"I'm here, but I'm not here, too," I murmured. "I'm transported. Is this what it's like to be a vampire?"

"Sometimes. It can be a heady experience. Is that what you want, Dewy, to be transported to immortality?"

"I don't know about that, but I know about this. Don't stop. Bite harder, bite my neck. Suck my blood. Take me."

"Oh, Dewy, I don't want to drag you into this, but I'm so excited. I can't help myself. Resist me."

"No. Bite my neck. Let me nourish you as you elevate us to ecstatic pleasure. I've spent the last several years in bed with young women and I shared pleasure with my ex-wife, but none of that was anything compared with this."

"Dewy, you make me so hot; I'm going to come again."

I felt her pierce my neck as she let out a muffled series of shrieks that coincided with her spasms. She bit down hard and I could feel a thrill, first as a wave of shock, and then as a warm, floating feeling, as if I were flying, flying with her, flying around her, flying into her, melting, melding, molding, becoming one.

Chapter Twenty-Three

The room was dark when my alarm clock buzzed at six A.M. My head was fuzzy. Small wonder. There was an empty bourbon bottle on the night stand and Stella was gone. Since I could remember that much, I figured I hadn't had my first alcoholic blackout. I just had too much bourbon.

I had a feeling somewhere in the back of my brain that I knew why Stella was gone, but I couldn't call that knowledge to my consciousness. I had a feeling we made some kind of connection, but I was confused. I just couldn't put my finger on it. Maybe I'd lay off the bourbon. Maybe I'd have another talk with Chan.

As I brushed my teeth, I noticed I had injured my neck again, this time a bit higher. My turtleneck sweater wouldn't completely cover the wound. I dabbed a bit of antibiotic ointment on the twin lesions and put on a small adhesive bandage that covered most the bruise. Whatever it was that I was confused about with Stella would have to wait. This morning I had an evil to fight.

It was obvious that Ellis had been selling theater equipment, skimming, cooking the books, and pocketing the proceeds. It also seemed obvious that Wendy Bridges was Ellis' till-tapping accomplice. She handled the cash. It was unthinkable that Wendy could tap the till without Ellis, as business manager, not knowing it. Tickets, cash, and charge accounts had to balance. Even TVC had to have an external annual audit. All 501(c) 3 corporations did.

I had asked Laura who audited TVC's books. She told me H. Willingham Fournier and Associates had the contract. Uncle Horace, the senior partner, was her mother's first cousin. He had been Ellis' business associate before Ellis went to prison.

It just figured. If Uncle Horace found anything unusual, he probably would write in his audit the typical auditor's mumbo-jumbo that, based on the sample of accounts he audited, everything seemed to be fine. That way, should the truth be known, he would have an out. He could always claim the errors weren't in the sample he drew.

If what I could see was true, a forensic accountant should be able to uncover the theft in a day or two. For that to happen, the Board of Directors would have to care enough to demand a serious audit, and then, if they were serious about faithfully exercising their fiduciary responsibility when the misappropriation came to light, to take action against Ellis.

I didn't think Madame Boudron would permit a public move against Ellis even if he were found with a sack of money in one hand and a smoking gun in the other. It would scandalize her name in society. There was always the possibility that the auditor, or even Clotilde Boudron, herself, was in on the rip-off, but that didn't make sense. Why would the accountant want to loot the theater? It couldn't net much compared to what an accounting firm could otherwise earn, even legitimately. Clotilde was rich. She personally made up for any shortfalls. Why would she steal from herself?

Ellis was the one who needed cash. He couldn't work at a public job without getting cut off at home. He was tied to his mother's apron strings and to the Boudron Trust, so he was ripping his mother off by stealing from the theater. I might be able to figure out why Wendy was helping Ellis, but right now, I had to figure out how to catch Ellis at thievery and parlay that into his confession to murder.

Piece of cake. Yeah, sure.

If I were auditing the box office I would want to see records that showed cash and credit card purchases and subscription sales reconciled with tickets sold and complimentary passes issued. For each patron attending a performance, including patrons who were attending on complimentary passes, there should be half of a ticket placed in the ticket deposit boxes by the ushers.

Those torn halves would be matched against the number of tickets available to be sold for that performance which would equal the total number of seats in the house minus the season tickets and minus the complimentary tickets.

Season tickets seats are blocked out on the chart of seats available for single sales for each performance. There would not be cash or credit card receipts in the till for them for the performance for which they were used because the revenue associated with that ticket had been collected much earlier.

Most houses use regular, assigned seating tickets as passes by marking them conspicuously as complimentary. Those tickets stubs can be identified easily. There would be no cash revenue or credit card receipts in the till for them either. The complimentary ticket I had been given for *The Passion of Dracula* was a pink piece of card stock slightly larger than a standard ticket and printed with the theater's name. The date of the performance had been written in pencil in the upper right corner. The usher had taken Chan's and my passes, dropped them un-torn into the ticket receipt box, and reminded us that seating for the preview was not assigned.

All seats that didn't belong to season ticket holders were sold through the box office on the day of the performance. All Wendy needed to do was pull unsold tickets, write their seat numbers in pencil on pink complimentary passes, hand out the passes as tickets, and collect the price of the tickets from the patrons.

Maybe she'd give them some mumbo-jumbo about season ticket holders calling in and releasing their seats for resale as a kind of donation to the theater so she had to hand out passes instead of tickets. She'd have to do it only for cash transactions so there wouldn't be any paper trace like credit card receipts or checks. She could sell as many passes for tickets as there were unsold seats for which there were customers who were paying in cash.

Simply put, she could hand out a pass, pencil in a seat number, and pocket the cash. When the ushers turned in the passes with the other ticket stubs, she could erase the penciled seat number and recycle the complimentary pass. Since no one counted the house and matched it against receipts, who would know how much was looted except the cash handler and the supervisor. I always count the house, and I would find a way to match the count against receipts.

When I looked in the box office, I didn't see a place I could hide a camera without inside help which I had no intention of seeking. So I took a different tack. The ushers were volunteers. Seeing the show for free was their compensation. If I could get two reliable people to take tickets as the patrons entered at each of the two doors, I could know exactly how many complimentary tickets were used.

To have positive identification as evidence for possible prosecution, should it come to that, we would mark each pass in a way that would show that it had been used but not in any way that would tip off Wendy or Ellis.

The obvious answer was invisible ink. I could have my two reliable undercover ushers mark each pass with the invisible ink. We could identify them later with a black light when we needed to produce the evidence. With reliable counts of the house by two or more independent sources, secretly marked complimentary passes, and an audit of the cash and ticket receipts, we should have evidence that Wendy was tapping the till.

The next step would be to tie it to Ellis. I'd figure that one out after I confronted Wendy. She was the weaker link.

All I needed were two reliable people. Perhaps I could enlist Chan and Alex. Maybe Alex would come down from Memphis for one night to help me out. After all, he was the one who sent me here. Since no one else had arrived at the theater to overhear me, I made a credit card call to Alex on the green room telephone. He answered on the third ring.

"Hello."

"Hi, Alex. It's Dewy."

"Dewy! Long time, no hear. What've you been doing? Certainly not keeping in touch with me. How's your thesis project coming?"

"It's coming along fine, Alex. Couldn't be better. I've got a Macbeth who could win a surfer boy contest without getting his swim suit wet and a leading lady with whom I have fallen hopelessly in love."

"Stella Maris? I warned you, Dewy, that if you valued your life, you would stay away from Stella. I wasn't kidding."

Chapter Twenty-Four

"Yes, Alex. Stella. I know you warned me to stay away from her, but we're like those little Scottie dog magnets. We're attracted to each other despite all obstacles. That's not why I called. I believe the business manager and the box office manager are tapping the till."

"Call the cops."

"I did. The cops said if I got any hard evidence, they'd move in; otherwise, not. It's political."

"Courageous, aren't they?"

"The Bourdons are well-connected. Ellis is the business manager and his mother runs the entire shooting match."

"Yes, Dewy, I know about the Boudron family. I believe I warned you about them, too. Yet, without the Boudron Trust and Clotilde's personal attention, the theater would probably not survive. So why is it your business, Dewy?"

"'Mankind is my business.'"

"Dickens, *A Christmas Carol.*"

"Boudron pisses me off. I don't like to see the theater so ill-treated."

"Which one?"

"What do you mean, which one? Théatre Vieux Carré, of course, and theater in general."

"No. Which Boudron?"

"Oh. Well, both of them. Ellis and his mother. Laura's O.K., but she's wary of taking on the wrath of her family. I have every confidence she'll be there when it counts. I need your help, too."

"What do you want from me?"

"I want you to usher and take tickets."

"For this I got a Ph.D.?"

"Come on, Alex. It's for the theater, and for me."

"What's the plan?"

I told Alex my plan. He suggested refinements. First, I should simply take a count of the house at the preview and try to match that with a count of the number of complimentary tickets used and with the report of the box office receipts to get some idea of how much the shortage was.

Second, he reminded me I was required as part of my graduate studies to tape a performance of the Scottish play. That would give me cover for setting up a video camera in the theater. I wouldn't have to hide it. All I would have to do is figure out how to tie it into the box office without anyone knowing.

We agreed that I would get a camera and Alex would fly down for opening night to be one of my ticket takers. I went shopping for video equipment. With an hour's help from a sales associate, I settled on two camcorders, one monitor, and an A/B switch. The first camcorder, mounted on a tripod, would be the one I would set up to record the show. The second one, a much smaller unit with a right-angle mirror attachment that offered the possibilities of concealment and misdirection, I would set up to watch the box office. Both cameras would be wired into one monitor. Which camera's signal would show on the monitor would be controlled by the A/B switch.

I bought it all and headed back to the theater. It seemed odd that I would shell out a thousand dollars to catch people who were robbing others, not me, but I was pissed off. One of those thieves had gotten away with murder, too, and that's something to get anyone pissed off. Besides, An Lin was counting on me, and I did need to tape the performance for my thesis. What's a thousand dollars compared to all of that?

Back at the theater I got help from the tech crew to set up my main camera. We decided the best place to tape the show was from the light booth which, conveniently for me, was directly above the box office. When the theater was built in the Nineteenth Century, it had gas lights and very little plumbing. Electric wiring and additional water and sewer pipes had been retrofitted in stages during this century. Two large pipes ran down the front wall of the light booth into a hole in the floor and down the back wall of the box office below.

I pulled back the flashing around those pipes and inserted my smaller surveillance camera into the space. I used the angled mirror attachment to get a view of the box office teller's station. I set my tripod and main camera up near the pipes and turned my equipment bag upside down over the mini camera to conceal it. I wired both cameras into the monitor through the A/B switch and angled the monitor so no one else in the light booth could see it. If no one in the box office below looked up at the pipes where they entered the twenty-foot ceiling and noticed the camera lens attachment in the hole around the pipes, I should be able to record Wendy's movements surreptitiously.

Laura arrived and she and I spent the rest of the afternoon working out problems we had run into during the run-through last night. Somehow I had many notes but no clear memory of making them and even less understanding of what they meant. I had a vague feeling I had forgotten something important. Fortunately, Laura was on the ball. She read each note to me. I repeated what the note said, and then I asked her how she would fix the problem. She told me what she would do and I agreed we would do it.

We wrapped things up about five o'clock. I invited her to a *table de hôte* dinner at Sebastian's Little Garden. She accepted. We caught a cab over to St. Phillip's Street. Once we had aperitifs in our hands, the conversation began.

"Since your mother's cut you off from meals at home, it seems only fair that I treat you to dinner."

"Don't let it become a habit. I don't want to ruin my reputation as a spinster."

"You're hardly old enough to be a spinster, and far too pretty."

"Thank you for your flattery, Dewy, but around here, when a woman reaches thirty without being married, she's a spinster, plain and simple."

"Rubbish."

"But true, nonetheless."

"Surely you've had your share of beaux?"

"How many is a share?"

"I'm not sure it's ever been enumerated. Besides, speaking from recent personal experience, quantity isn't all that important. Quality counts. Please tell me if I'm intruding in your private affairs, but surely in thirty years you've been in love at least once."

"Maybe."

"What happened?"

"Now you are being intrusive."

"Forgive me. I withdraw the question."

"Isn't that like un-sneezing?"

"What?"

"How can you un-sneeze? Once it's out, it's out. You can't erase it or call it back."

"I suppose not. Just ignore it."

"No. I won't ignore it. I'll tell you simply and truthfully. I'm plain, I'm crippled, and I'm rich, although you'd never prove that by how much money I can actually put my hands on. Any boy who would have been interested in me could have simply been seeking the Boudron fortune and Mother is very particular about whom we would let into the family."

"You believe the only thing you have to offer in a relationship is the Boudron fortune? What about your wit, your grace, your cool competence, and your beauty?"

"I'm not beautiful."

"*Au contraire.* Beauty is in the eye of the beholder. I behold your beauty and I care not one whit for the Boudron fortune."

"You're not available."

"I'm single."

"But still not available."

"Hmmm." I stalled, wondering exactly where my relationship with Stella stood. I had a vague feeling that we had reached some major milestone, some new level of understanding, but that understanding was not of my ken.

"So, you see, Dewy, currently, the only man who finds me attractive and who is not interested in the Boudron fortune is also not available. That's the story of my life."

"Currently? Perhaps, in the past there was another?"

"Yes. When I was young, at a summer camp Mother sent me to in the mountains."

"The Adirondacks?"

"No. The Blue Ridge Mountains in North Carolina. Mother would never let me go to Yankee Land."

"And, so?"

"I was fifteen years old and settling awkwardly into a young woman's body. I met McArthur Jefferson Randolph. He was from Virginia, from a wealthy family, but I doubt if my family and his family had ever heard of each other. All Mac and I knew of each other was that we were from families who were well-enough off to send us to an expensive camp for 'special people.' The rest just wasn't important."

"What attracted you to him?"

"I liked his smile, his un-coordination, his irrepressible exuberance, and his liking me. We had a dance on the first Saturday night and he picked me. Even though I wore a brace and used crutches clumsier than the ones I use now, Mother had made me take ballroom dancing lessons because I would be a debutante the next year. About that there could be no doubt no matter how clumsy and self-conscious I was. I had no say in the matter. I hated to dance but Mac was irrepressible—clumsy—but irrepressible. He wouldn't take 'no' for an answer. He charmed me into dancing with him and he was so bad that I looked graceful by comparison."

"He didn't care. He was full of joy and high spirits. We became as inseparable as they would let campers of the opposite sex be and more inseparable than they knew about. I helped him with his crafts because he had little fine motor control left, and he helped me with riding, canoeing, and swimming. Lord, did he love the water. He had been a competitive swimmer before his cerebellar ataxia got too bad."

"Multiple sclerosis?"

"No. Brain tumor. Slow growing, non-malignant, inoperable, and terminal."

"So he loved to swim. And you?"

"I hated swimming before I met Mac. I was self-conscious about my body, so angular, club-footed, and gawky. I was only one year away from my debut into society, I couldn't dance, I couldn't fill out a ball gown, and I had my crutches. Mac made me forget to worry about those things.

He made swimming fun. I learned how light I could be in the water and how I had more grace and poise swimming than I could ever command on land. In the water in my Prussian-blue maillot swim suit with my well-developed arms, my newly-tanned body, and my sun-bleached hair, I looked more svelte and supple than the dishwater-blond, emaciated, scarecrow persona of my normal self."

"It helped that the food and exercise began filling me out. I got so deeply tanned and my hair bleached out so nearly white that Mac said I was just like a Palomino filly, only prettier. He had horses back in Virginia, but no Palominos. One of his dreams from early childhood was to dress up in a cowboy outfit and ride a golden Palomino with a western saddle just like Roy Rogers riding Trigger."

"Once, we snuck off and went skinny dipping. Mac was beautiful, and he was kind enough to say the same about me. We became man and woman with each other. We just did it that once, well, actually three times that afternoon. At the time, I thanked God I hadn't become pregnant. Now, I regret that I didn't. It wouldn't be the disaster now that I believed it would have been then. At least I would have had some positive outcome of my only love. It's been downhill ever since that summer."

"You didn't see Mac again?"

"Once, only for a minute or two, through a window. I begged and pleaded with Mother to let me invite Mac down for my debut. After she made inquires and discovered the social prominence of his family and learned of their ancestral pedigrees and current assets, she relented, at least until he arrived. Apparently no one told Mother about Mac's brain tumor. I certainly didn't. It never occurred to me to say anything. It was just as much a part of him as my affliction is to me. It seemed normal, not remarkable."

"What happened?"

"Mac was the first one off the plane. Mother, Ellis, and I were standing inside the terminal watching like you could in those days. I lit up when I saw Mac coming down the ramp. Mother saw him too. She asked me if he was drunk. I told her he had a brain tumor. Mother jerked me out of that airport so fast we broke the sound barrier. She made Ellis stay and put Mac back on the next plane out. She wouldn't let me receive telephone calls or letters from him."

"That was fifteen years ago. Did you ever see him again?"

"No. He died about a month later. Mercifully, it wasn't the slow death he had been led to expect. He hitched a ride to California, bought a cowboy outfit, 'borrowed' a Palomino and a western saddle, took off at a gallop and tried to jump the horse over the fence. Western horses just aren't trained as steeplechasers. The horse survived. Mac didn't. A year later Mac's adult sister approached me discreetly, here in New Orleans, and told me the story of Mac's death, and that was the end of my love life."

Tears slowly and silently slid down her cheeks.

"No one has courted you since?"

"How elegantly you put that, Dewy. The few men who were socially acceptable enough for Mother seemed like fortune hunters or seekers of a marriage of convenience to me. No joy. No passion."

"Why don't you leave your mother and the Boudron fortune and just be yourself?"

"I have no self. It died with Mac. Now it's too late. Besides, I have to uphold the honor of the Boudron name."

"Forgive me for seeming dense, but what honor?"

Laura paused, placed her napkin on the table, and stood up.

"Thank you for dinner, Mr. Spearman. As a matter of common courtesy and as a personal requirement, do not cavalierly impugn the name of Boudron again. If you have substance, reveal it. Otherwise, hold your counsel. Don't get up. I'll call a cab. I'll see you next at the theater tomorrow evening for dress rehearsal."

She left swiftly and adroitly which was amazing considering her crutches and the close placement of the tables. I wondered if they mostly for emotional support.

All in all, I didn't seem to be doing well with women at the moment. Clotilde Boudron was wary of me, I had offended Laura, and Stella and I were angry at each other about something, but I couldn't remember what we were angry about. I know I saw her last night but I couldn't recall what I said to her or what she said to me. Since I had seen her last night, I guessed I wouldn't see her tonight. That was the drill.

When I walked into the courtyard, I saw a light coming through the apartment's front window. I knew I had turned off all the lights when I left this morning. On the off chance that a burglar decided to search with the lights on, as I got closer to the front door I made noise to scare him off.

I opened the door expecting trouble.

"Stella! I wasn't expecting you tonight."

"I told you last night I'd be here. I'll be here every night, at least for the run of the show. I found an extra key in the kitchen on my way out last night. Don't you remember?"

"Not really. I guess I drank too much bourbon. I can't remember much about last night."

"What can you remember?"

"I remember we fought about something and I remember that we made love. So, we made up, right?"

"We did," she said. "And we did. I should have realized that you wouldn't remember much. What we talked about last night we'll have to talk about again, but I'm just not up to it tonight. We will. We have to. And, as I promised, I'll be here every night until we've finished the show, so we have plenty of time."

"And then?"

"No more promises Dewy. We'll have to talk again, but not now. Right now we need to make love. I need you, Dewy, more than life itself."

"Don't make me that important, Stella."

"Just hold me, Dewy," she said, as tears welled up in her eyes and spilled over, wetting her pale cheeks. Just hold me."

What is it about me that makes women cry?

Chapter Twenty-Five

The technical rehearsal on Saturday and the dress rehearsal on Tuesday went well. Laura was coolly efficient as assistant director and stage manager. She showed neither signs of friendliness nor unfriendliness toward me and kept an emotional distance.

Stella, as she said she would, returned home with me every night. She was gone again each morning. I had a feeling we had talked about that recently but I couldn't remember what we said. A couple of weeks ago she said she needed to be in her own place in the morning. I guess that was still true. Now, for a while at least, I had her every night. How greedy could I be?

On Wednesday, I arrived at TVC in time for the seven o'clock call, put on my costume, went to the light booth, and switched on my video recording equipment. Since I was only in one scene midway through our first act, I stayed with the visible camera I was using overtly to record the show and I covertly watched the box office from my concealed camera. I watched Wendy hand out about twenty complimentary passes for which she received cash.

After the house manager made her obligatory announcements prohibiting photographic, audio, or video recording of the show, pointing out the exits, and telling everyone to turn off electronic devices that make noise, she left the stage. We cut the house lights and The Weird Sisters slithered, flitted, and flashed into being and opened the show.

Our preview went well. I was distracted by having to keep one eye on my monitor, but I thought Bud missed a light cue in Scene VII when Macbeth and Lady Macbeth are first on stage together. Lance looked too pretty. By the time we got to Macbeth's 'Is this a dagger I see before me...' speech, I knew something was wrong with the light cues, but I couldn't take my eyes off Wendy long enough to figure it out. I did manage to whisper a question to Bud.

"Hey, Bud. When did we change the light cues?"

"This afternoon," he whispered back.

"Why'd you do that?"

"Pete said we had to. Ask Pete. I think he's backstage."

"I will."

On my monitor I watched the ushers hand in their ticket stub boxes to the box office. Wendy calmly and efficiently went through them, removed twenty of the pink complimentary passes, erased the seat numbers from each one, and stacked them neatly in the top drawer.

She sorted the remaining passes and all the tickets into separate stacks, put rubber bands around each stack, put both stacks in a large envelope which she signed, dated, and placed in the second drawer.

From the till she pulled out two hundred-dollar bills and stuck them in her purse. She filled out a deposit slip listing each check, placed that slip in a zippered bag with the checks and the remaining cash, and stuck everything in a floor safe.

She pulled on her jacket, picked up her purse, and walked toward the door. She opened it and reached toward the light switch. Unexpectedly, she closed the door, turned, and walked toward the water pipes. If she looked up she couldn't miss seeing the camera.

I was relieved when I watched her reach out and flip the calendar to tomorrow's date. She turned again and left the box office. I hadn't been discovered, but she had.

I hurried backstage to make my entrance as the Porter. The Porter's scene is arguably the funniest monologue in any of Shakespeare's tragedies, perhaps his comedies, too. I loved playing it. Now I played it against Pete Vanlandingham as Macduff, and when my scene was over I made my exit.

Macduff is onstage almost continuously until the end of Shakespeare's Act II, so I had to wait backstage for Pete's exit after Banquo rode forth to spirit Fleance away from the treachery he anticipates from Macbeth. I caught Pete as he made his exit.

"Pete, did you change the lighting cues this afternoon?

"Yes."

"Why?"

"Orders."

"Whose?"

"Clotilde's. Didn't she tell you?"

I succeeded at not screaming. Instead, I whispered nonchalantly.

"Can you come up to the light booth at intermission?"

"Sure," he whispered back. "Right now I gotta' run go help with makeup for Banquo's ghost. See you in a few."

I went back to the light booth and watched Macbeth send forth the murderers. At least the lighting for the gloomy night scene had not been changed. Nor, mercifully, had the lighting been changed for the banquet scene which Banquo attends as his own ghost. Banquo looked ghastly in his special lighting just as we planned it.

Our first act finished with Shakespeare's third, with the gentlemen of the court telling us that Macduff had gone to England to raise an army and that many of the Scottish lords would welcome an invasion to unseat the tyrant, Macbeth. That was how I felt, too. Foul deeds have been done, and now I had to unseat a tyrant.

Pete met me in the light booth. I asked Bud to step outside. Bud looked at Pete, and when Pete nodded at him, Bud said he'd go out for a smoke.

"Why'd you make lighting changes, Pete?"

"I had my orders straight from Clotilde."

"Is she the director of this show?"

"No. But she is board's president. Besides, she told me she'd straighten it out with you. She didn't say anything?"

"No, Pete. She didn't. Why do you think she would tell you to do it instead of having me tell you to do it?"

"I dunno'."

"Come on, Pete. I know you're a member of the board and somehow beholden to Clotilde, but you're a professional. This isn't the way professionals work. Why do you think she went to you behind my back?"

"Because she knew you wouldn't make the changes."

"And she knew you would."

"You don't understand."

"Help me understand, Pete. I speak English," I said, and I stood in silence waiting for him to reply.

His face flushed, but he replied quite simply and quietly.

"I did wrong. I apologize. I'll reset the lights the way we had them originally."

"You still haven't told me why, Pete."

"Shouldn't it be obvious? Lance went crying to Clotilde that you were making him look bad. So she told me to do what he wanted to make him look good."

"And you did it without telling me and still won't tell me why."

He looked down. "I can't Dewy. I'll reset the lights tonight."

"When did you change them?"

"This afternoon when Lance brought the note from Clotilde. He walked through his blocking so we could make sure we got him in the best light."

"I'll bet he did. Do you still have the note?"

"Sure," he said as he walked over to the light booth desk and picked up a piece of lavender stationery with Clotilde's crest on it.

"May I have it?"

"Sure."

"Thanks, Pete. Don't say anything to anyone about this, please, until I give my notes tonight. After that, you can say anything you want, O.K.?"

"O.K. Dewy, I'm really ashamed. You know Clotilde's going to be furious."

"And I'm not?"

We stood there for a minute looking at each other until we were interrupted by Bud's return. He told us Laura had called places for our second act. Pete headed off backstage and I stayed in the light booth with Bud to watch the rest of the show.

Our second act went without incident except that Lance still didn't have a clue about what "She should have died hereafter" meant, and he still looked too pretty.

After the curtain call we met in the green room for notes. I let Laura go first. She noted several dropped lines and a need to repair one costume. Then she turned it over to me. I started off easy.

"Thank you all for your tireless efforts on behalf of this production. I especially thank the Weird Sisters and the entire technical crew for the great work on the special effects. Creating the fireball was a stroke of genius. I don't know who thought of it, but the idea came from the crew, not from me. Congratulations to you all."

"It was Laura's idea," Russell Prejean, the chief stage hand, said.

"Laura. Congratulations to you for a fine idea as well as for a great job of stage managing."

"I didn't really do anything, Dewy. Things just sort of took care of themselves," she said, blushing.

"That's the way it is with good stage managing, Laura. Things just seem to take care of themselves because all of the work you did beforehand to make sure that would happen. Thanks. Now, on a different note, Pete made unauthorized changes in the lighting and will stay tonight to change everything back."

Pete looked down at the floor. Lance looked up at me.

I dropped the bomb.

"Lance," I said, "now that I have everyone's attention, I have a casting change to announce. Rupert, here, has done such a good job of playing Seyton that he deserves a promotion. I am going to step out of my role of Porter and ask Rupert to play it."

Rupert Godwin, a retired high school English teacher, looked at me, flabbergasted.

"Do you think you can do that, Rupert?" I asked. "I'm sure Pete will be glad to rehearse the scene with you as many times as necessary and you can do it with the book in your hand if you have to."

"Sure," Rupert said. "Are you going to take over as Seyton, all two lines of him?"

"No. Lance is."

"What!" Lance said, rising to his feet. I can't double as Seyton. I'm Macbeth in that scene."

"You're not going to double as Seyton," I said, as gentle as a dove's cooing. "You're going to play Seyton."

"What do you mean?"

"Read my lips. You are going to play Seyton. You have two lines. You may already know them. I'm sure you've heard them two dozen times. Would you like to run the scene tomorrow afternoon?"

"Are you fuckin' crazy, man? I'm Macbeth. It's in my contract."

"No. That is not in your contract. I've read your contract. Your contract guarantees you a speaking role in every show produced by Théatre Vieux Carré this season. That's what you're getting, a speaking role with two lines: 'It is the cry of women, my good lord,' and 'The Queen, my lord, is dead.' You can do it with the script in your hands if you have to."

"You you c-c-can't do this to me" Lance said, uncharacteristically sputtering and stammering. "This is an outrage. I'll h-h-have you up before Equity. I'll c-c call Clotilde. I'll get your ass f-f-fired."

Chapter Twenty-Six

"If you read my contract, Lance, you'll find that I can be fired on-ly for misfeasance, only by majority vote of the Board of Directors, and only at any regularly scheduled or specially-called meeting. The next regular meeting is the first Tuesday in January. It takes three days' notice to call a special meeting which may be called by the pres-ident, alone, or by petition of three board members. Please, go ahead, Lance, whine to Clotilde as you did yesterday," I said, waving Clotilde's lavender note in the air.

"The Board can vote to fire me as early as Sunday if they want to, but tonight I am director of this production, and tomorrow, and to-morrow, and tomorrow, you will play Seyton. If you fail to show up at call time, I'll report you to Actor's Equity. If you refuse to per-form, I'll report you to Actor's Equity. If you merely perform badly, I'll not bother Actor's Equity. I'll let the critics and our audiences punish you."

"P-P-Pete. Are you g-g-gonna' let him d-d-o this to me?"

"He's the director, Lance," Pete said.

"B-b-but you're on the b-b-board. Have a m-m-meeting tonight."

"It takes three days' notice for a called meeting, Lance," Pete re-plied. Clotilde can call a meeting, or any three board members can call one, but they can't meet until they give three days' notice."

Lance turned to Laura. "L-L-Laura, are you g-g-going to let him g-g-get away with this?"

"Dewy's the director," she replied.

"But you're a B-B-Boudron. D-d-do something."

"I'm not on the board, Lance, and I assure you I do not speak for the board's president. She speaks for herself quite well."

"I'll go out to Maison Boudron and talk to her now. We'll get this straightened out right away," Lance said as he stomped off toward the exit.

Laura called after him. "Don't forget, call time tomorrow is seven o'clock. Let me know if you want to run through the scene."

Lance hurled a string of profanities into the air as he hurled his body through the stage door and into the night.

There was complete silence for about ten seconds and then Rupert broke it. "Who's going to play Macbeth?"

"I am." I answered. "I'm probably the only person here who knows the role well enough to play it off book and I certainly look seasoned enough to play it. Any questions?"

"Do you want to run through Macbeth's blocking tomorrow?" Laura asked.

"Yes, I would like to do that. If you're available at four o'clock tomorrow, I would appreciate your walking me through it. Anyone else who is available is welcome to come at four and help me. Some of you may not be able to make it, but it would help me immensely if you could. And, to sweeten the pot, Rupert, and everybody in the cast, I can't do anything about your honorarium, but I'll double the salary of every actor in the room who shows up early tomorrow."

Since Lance was the only actor who drew a salary, my line got a laugh and eased the tension.

"Now, back to tonight's performance. Great preview! Good night. Get outa' here you maniacs. Be back here at seven tomorrow night, four if you can make it. And thanks. Thanks a million."

As everyone started for the doors, Stella came up beside me.

"I can't be here as early as four. Maybe by six."

"I can fill in as Lady Macbeth," Laura said, not hesitating to jump into the conversation, and then hesitating, blushing, and taking a step backward. "I mean—"

"That would be great, Laura. I'm sure by now you know most of the lines and all of the blocking."

"I know all the lines."

"Then, that's settled. You can fill in as Lady Macbeth until Stella arrives. Now go home and get ready to stand in for tomorrow's special rehearsal. And while you're at it, learn Seyton's two lines. With any luck, Lance will go back to California and you'll have to play Seyton tomorrow night."

"Dewy, you're playing with fire."

"Sometimes you have to do what's right instead of what's expedient. Good night, Laura."

"Good night," she said, as she clanked off and disappeared out the stage door.

"Now, Miss Maris," I said to Stella as we walked out the stage door and headed toward the apartment, "just why is it you can't show up in the afternoon. I forget."

"I was afraid of that, Dewy."

"Afraid of what, that I'm getting senile and forgetting things?"

"I'm afraid that you don't remember things we talked about the other night."

"The bourbon night?"

"Yes, the bourbon night."

"What's to remember? You're here. That's what I want."

"This can't last, Dewy."

"So you keep saying, but it's lasted this long. Let's just keep going one day at a time and deal with problems as they arise, but not tonight. We've got a show to put on and I've got to run lines to make sure I can nail Macbeth tomorrow. I'm on the verge of cracking the box office caper, too. What a day!"

"What box office caper?"

"Oh, haven't I told you about that?"

"About what?"

"Wendy Bridges and Ellis Boudron are tapping the till."

"No. You didn't tell me. I'm not surprised. At least, not about Ellis. But, Wendy? 1 don't know."

"I do know."

"So?"

"So, don't worry about it. I've got it all under control."

"How long have you been working on this?"

"About a month."

"And you haven't told me a thing. You have your secrets, too."

"You were hardly around enough to talk to until two days ago. I only saw you every other night if I was lucky. You're always gone by morning, and you're never available during the day."

"And you don't remember why, do you?"

"Val, as I recall. Pretty soon you're going to have to make a decision about that, Stella—Val, or me."

"You're through here on the 20th. Then you'll be gone. Why should I choose you?"

"I love you, Stella. I don't have to be gone. I'm not tied down and I have no commitments. I'm a free man. I can go anywhere I want or I can stay where I am, with you. Will you stay with me?"

"Dewy, we've been over that several times before, but you don't remember, do you?"

"Come on, Stella. I couldn't have been that drunk. I can remember that every time I ask you to stay, you go, but you always come back. Why not just stay? How difficult could it be?"

Stella put her finger to her lips as we approached the courtyard. We mounted the steps in silence as we had done many times before. When we were quietly inside, she spoke again.

"Dewy, I promised I would be with you every night for the remainder of the run, and I will."

"That's what I like."

"Dewy, listen to me. "We have to talk."

"No more talk, Stella. Just be here or don't be here. That's all there is to it. Now, help me run my lines."

She helped me run my lines. We made love. I fell asleep.

In the morning, I found a note:

Dearest Dewy,

See you tonight. We have to talk.

Love, Stella

Chapter Twenty-Seven

After showering and breakfasting, I went to campus to meet Alex. A few minutes after ten o'clock, after Alex had paid a courtesy visit to Dean Halberstam, he met me at my office. When I explained the setup for catching my till tappers, he suggested not asking Chan to help because of Chan's collegial relationship to Maurice.

Alex suggested we bring in someone unknown to the theater who was also not connected to the college. I immediately thought of An Lin. She was Spider's daughter, but I didn't think anybody else knew that. While I tracked her down at her job, Alex went out to pick up a black light, the special ink, and two one-hundred dollar bills.

I met An Lin at her bar. She took a break and listened to my plan. She would meet Alex in front of the theater at seven o'clock, write her name in invisible ink on the hundred-dollar bill Alex would give her, and use that bill to buy a ticket right away. Alex would do the same about ten minutes later. As soon as both of them had their tickets, I would let them in and set them up as ushers before the house opened. She agreed, and then she returned to work.

Since all ushers were volunteers, no one would object to my bringing in two more. Wendy would be in the box office, unaware of our actions. If things ran true to form, Ellis would breeze through for a minute or so without taking much notice of anything, if he showed up at all. Besides, nothing would look unusual.

I saw only one potential problem with our plan. As Macbeth, I had to be on stage nearly to the end of our first act and Wendy might wrap things up and clear out before I could get there to confront her. I needed a way to hold her there and, if possible, protect myself in case Ellis should breeze in at the wrong time and start making things difficult. Thibodeau once said he would help me if ever I got solid evidence. Now was the time to call him on his promise.

I caught up with Alex at my office and we took a cab to the police station on Royal Street. The desk sergeant took ten minutes to reach Thibodeau by phone. Thibodeau told us to meet him just outside the

French Quarter at the bar where former New Orleans District Attorney Jim Garrison hatched his famous Lee Harvey Oswald murder conspiracy theory, another conspiracy I found lacking.

When Alex and I found the place, we went in and sat with Thibodeau and Landowski at their table. They ignored us and kept their gazes fixed out the window.

"Are we disturbing you?" I asked.

"If I say 'yes', you gonna' go away?" Thibodeau asked, not diverting his gaze one iota.

"No."

"Then why ask?"

"Common courtesy."

"O.K., Spearman, you been courteous. Now say whatcha' want and then beat it. We got a planned meet going down on the corner and we got to be there or we might lose our snitch. Spill."

"I think I can nail Ellis Boudron."

"Keep talking."

"I've got a videotape of Wendy Bridges tapping the till."

"You got a warrant to make that tape?"

"No."

"Can't use it for evidence. What else you got?"

"A plan. I've got a plan to catch Wendy red-handed."

"So, we get ourselves a till-tapper. We brace Boudron and he say he don't know nothin' about it. I'm real excited, Spearman. You excited, Landowski, or is that an oyster po' boy in your pocket?"

Landowski, with his eyes still fixed on some distant vista, replied, "I've got a hard-on to make that bust, Lieutenant, but we're weak on probable cause."

"Hey my frien'," Thibodeau said, finally looking at Alex and me, "that Landowski, he be some fine legal scholar. Say Spearman," he added, "you still shackin' with that redhead woman?"

"Yeah. What if I am?" I was angry and defensive. Thibodeau didn't think much of Stella. He said so more than once. I think he told me something important about her recently, but I couldn't remember what it was and I sure wasn't going to ask him now. "What's it to you, Thibodeau?" I said, challenging him.

"Be cool. It be your business, man. Now, 'less you got something Landowski and I can get a judge excited about, we've got to get back to work."

"Look. All I'm asking you to do is make sure Wendy doesn't leave the box office with the evidence or destroy it before I can confront her at intermission. If I get her to tie Ellis in, then I can smoke him out. Either way, I figure she'll probably walk, but I'll be able to stop the cash drain and probably nail Ellis Boudron. Is that worth a few minutes of your time?"

"So you want us to come over there with no warrant, not even a complaint, and hold a citizen in the box office against her will so you can give her the third degree at your convenience?"

"Yes."

"O.K., man. But if she don't have at least an outstanding parking ticket, you're gonna' file some kind of complaint against her so we can cover our butts. Public drunkenness ought to do."

"Do you actually prosecute people for that in New Orleans?"

"Only when we need to clear the streets and they won't move. It's no big deal. When?"

"Tonight. Be there before the curtain goes up at eight o'clock. She probably won't have everything wrapped up for at least an hour. Just make sure she doesn't do a bunk before intermission. No, wait. I have another idea."

"Officer Landowski," I said, "can you run a video recorder?"

"I'm a cop," he said, his sphinx-like gaze fixed out the window.

"Yeah?"

"I done surveillance. Yeah. I can run a camcorder. You gonna' tape something?"

"Why not? You could take my position in the light booth like you were taping the show but watch and tape Wendy instead. Be there by six-thirty. Go in the stage door. I'll set it up."

"Sure. Can't use the tape. No warrant."

"So what? I'll only use it to sweat Wendy to get to Ellis."

"O.K., man, if it's O.K. with the boss."

"Right by me," Thibodeau said.

"If Landowski sees her take money, wouldn't you have a case?"

"Not legally," Landowski answered. "Without a warrant, we'd be eavesdropping. When the box office is closed and the window's shut, whatever she's doin' in there ain't bein' done in public. It's not legal to tape her without her permission when she has a reasonable expectation of privacy, but it'll prolly' work," Landowski replied, his gaze still fixed out the window.

"O.K., Spearman, we'll back you up," Thibodeau said. "I expect to get a good arrest out of this, whatever happens. Make sure I do."

"I hope we do, but not for till tapping. I want to see Ellis busted for Spider's murder. I want to see—"

Landowski held up his hand to signal for silence. Without looking anywhere except out the window, Landowski rose and motioned for Thibodeau to leave by the back exit.

"DeLyon's on the move," Thibodeau said as he headed for the door. "Gotta' go. See you tonight. Make it good."

"O.K.," I said.

Alex and I went over to K-Paul's Kitchen for an early supper. I used their pay phone to call the theater to tell them a guy named Landowski was going to run my videotape equipment, so let him in. Alex and I caught each other up on gossip. He told me Fiona was engaged to a dental student. I told him about my run-in with Lance over the lighting. He agreed I had done the right thing and cautioned me that I'd likely hear more about it before this was over.

When we arrived at the theater, everyone had already signed in, including Lance. What a trouper. Next to the sign-in sheet was a notice of a board meeting on Sunday. Next to the board meeting notice was a notice that Madame Boudron's customary reception for the cast, crew, and season ticket holders scheduled for after tonight's show was postponed to an indefinite date. That surprised me. I thought she would have cancelled it entirely.

An Lin showed up and bought her ticket. When Alex bought his ticket about ten minutes later, I let them into the theater and quietly arranged for them to handle all ticket stubs and passes before they were deposited in the receipt boxes. They had their magic ink daubers at the ready when the house opened at seven-thirty.

I went to the light booth. Landowski was already there. He had turned on the video recorder. He motioned me over and whispered to me that Wendy was busy as a bee handing out passes instead of tickets seemingly at random. She probably had some plan which I could discover if I had long enough to study it, but we needed to act tonight. I quietly reminded Landowski to be discreet. Then I said, in a voice just loud enough for Bud Hérbert to overhear, "Since you don't know the actors' blockings, stick to wide-angle shots." I didn't want Bud to suspect what we were doing. I had a strong suspicion

Bud had received stolen lighting instruments from Ellis and might not particularly want Ellis to come to justice.

Laura called for actors to take their places, so I left the light booth and took my place in the wings for my first entrance. I was nervous. Here I was, coming to the completion of two long-time desires, directing plays that people pay to see and playing Macbeth in a first-rate production. Maybe Cap had been right to cast me as Macduff instead of Macbeth when I was not yet twenty and still in the bloom of youth. Now that I was past forty and well-seasoned, I was ripe for the role of Macbeth. I was filled with anticipation and raring to go, but I had to stand in the wings and wait for the first two scenes to play out before I could make my entrance.

As the witches finished with, "Peace! The Charm's wound up," I made my entrance with Banquo following and the magic began. As satisfying as a good rehearsal can be, there is nothing more enlivening than performing a show to a good house. This was a good house despite the absence of any patrons, save two, in the first three rows, the rows with padded chairs reserved for V.I.P season ticket holders.

Attempting to identify specific members of the audience is frowned upon because it takes actors out of the moment and misdirects their creative energy. However, since there were only two people in the otherwise-empty three row swathe of orchestra seating, without even trying, I identified Alex Righetti and Dean Halberstam. I guessed the first three rows of opening night season ticket holders were beholden to Clotilde Boudron and stayed away at her behest. I knew why Alex was there. What about Dean Halberstam? Was it possible she was there because she was her own woman and not beholden to Clotilde? The remainder of the house was packed and the audience followed us intently. I could feel it.

I focused my consciousness so completely on playing Macbeth that I forgot about Wendy until I made my last exit of our Act I just one scene short of intermission. Laura signaled me to come over to her stage manager's desk.

"The guy running your camera says, 'Get your butt in gear or he'll put your ass in a sling.' That's a direct quote."

"I'm sure it is." I covered my costume with a trench coat and dashed out the stage door to make my way around to the front door.

Thibodeau was standing in the lobby and Wendy still had the box office window open, but she looked like she was getting ready to close it and leave for the evening. Landowski came down the lobby-side stairs from the light booth, handed me the black light, and whispered in my ear.

"She handed out fifteen passes and stuck two hundreds, one twenty, and one five in her purse. I'll go back up and stay on the camera until you tell me to cut it off, O.K.?"

"Right, and thanks, Landowski," I answered.

Thibodeau signaled that he would stand where he was until relieved. I nodded, and then I stepped up to the box office window and asked Wendy to let me in for a minute.

"I was just about to leave."

"I know. I need to talk to you for a minute, and I've got to get back before intermission is over."

"Well, since you're the director. I'm not supposed to let anyone in the box office. Security, you know," she said, as she unlocked the door, let me in, and locked it behind me.

I pulled down the box office window's opaque screen so no one would see and, unless Wendy screamed, no one would hear, either.

"Security is what I'd like to talk to you about, Wendy. Someone's been tapping the till and I've got the evidence."

"I beg your pardon," she said, blanching, and clutching her purse tightly against her side.

"I believe you know what I'm saying, Wendy. In your purse, in addition to whatever you brought with you, you have several one-hundred dollar bills you did not bring with you."

"How dare you accuse me of stealing? I'll tell Ellis. Get out of my way. I'm leaving."

"Before you go, Wendy, please know that Lt. Thibodeau of the New Orleans Police Department is standing outside the box office door. He is prepared to arrest you on my complaint. Do you want to go to jail?"

"What?"

"Do you want to go to jail? Think of the scandal."

"What if I have two hundred-dollar bills? I often carry several hundred-dollar bills."

I plugged in the black light.

"Two of the hundred-dollar bills you took in tonight have people's names written on them in ink that is visible only in ultraviolet light. I watched those two people write their names on those bills. I watched them give those bills to you. If you will kindly pull the hundreds out of your purse, I'll show you their names."

I hoped at least one of the hundreds she took was one that Alex or An Lin had given her.

"The cash drawer needed change. I put in my small bills and took out two hundreds."

"You took out two hundreds, two twenties, and one five, the value of fifteen tickets at fifteen dollars each. That's grand larceny."

"What makes you say that?" she asked, in a small voice. Perspiration was beading on her forehead and upper lip.

"We videotaped you doing it."

"Where?" she said, looking around.

"Between the pipes, up high," I replied, pointing to the angled mirror attachment that barely protruded below the ceiling.

"Well, I just made change. That's all. Everything balances. You can check it out. I'm leaving."

"Do you want to leave in handcuffs?"

"You can't arrest me. Everything balances, cash, tickets, subscriptions—everything. You'll just embarrass yourself."

I heard the audience applaud the end of our Act I. I wouldn't have long to wrap things up.

"Not everything balances, Wendy. We marked with that special ink every pass that anyone used for admission this evening, too."

"So?"

"We saw you hand out fifteen passes for which you took in cash. Those fifteen passes will be mixed with the rest of the passes you put back in the supply of passes. It's a nice little scam. Take in cash, hand out a pass, retrieve the pass intact, erase the penciled notation of the seat number, put it back in inventory, and put the cash in your purse. Who would know except you and Ellis?"

"I'm leaving," she said. Her eyes, just moments ago wide open, had narrowed to horizontal slits. Muscles in her jaw were twitching.

"That's O.K., Wendy. Open the door and walk out where Lt. Thibodeau is waiting to arrest you for grand larceny. He'll handcuff you in the middle of the lobby and he'll haul you out right in front of the patrons on their intermission break. He'll take you to the police station. Your purse will be seized and searched. You'll be photographed and fingerprinted. But, it won't be so bad. Maurice will be able to bail you out in the morning, and your lawyer may be able to get the videotape thrown out. You might even beat the rap, but everyone will know, won't they? Won't they, Wendy?"

I turned on the black light. The ultraviolet light turned her English peaches-and-cream complexion into a hideous monster's hide, turned each minute freckle into a dark splotch against an eerily glowing background, and turned each piece of dandruff in her hair and each dust mote on her clothing into glowing spots that made her look like a South American poison tree frog. Her teeth, showing through tightly-stretched lips, and the whites of her eyes, showing through narrowed slits, glowed menacingly purple. Suddenly, her eyeballs turned up into their sockets entirely glowing purple for an instant, and then her eyes closed as she slumped in a faint. I broke her fall by grabbing her and collapsing with her on top of me. I called out for Thibodeau. He cracked open the door.

"What'd you do to her, Spearman?"

Chapter Twenty-Eight

"I confronted her with the truth and she didn't like hearing it. Get me some damp paper towels and keep the door closed."

Thibodeau returned quickly with wet towels and handed them to me through a crack in the door. Wendy was coming around, but I propped her feet up and put the cool towels on her face anyway.

"What are you going to do? You mustn't tell anyone. I would rather die than create a scandal. Maurice might lose his situation."

"Here's what I want, Wendy. Tell me everything, quickly. I'm needed backstage in ten minutes. Give me the whole truth and the money you took tonight, and walk away. If you don't give me the whole truth and the money in the next nine minutes, I'll let Lt. Thibodeau and the justice system deal with you."

"If I tell you, will you promise there will be no scandal?"

"I can't promise there'll be no scandal, but I'm not going to create one. Unless you tell people who turn this into a scandal, it's just between you and me. I only want the truth, Wendy, and an end to the thievery. I promise I won't tell anyone who doesn't already know."

"Does Maurice know?" she asked.

"Not unless you told him."

She seemed to calm down a little. She opened her mouth as if to speak, but she quickly put her hands over her mouth preventing herself from saying anything, and then she slid both hands up the sides of her face and began pulling at her hair. I reached down and stayed her wrists by gripping them, but not pulling them away. In a moment she relaxed her arms. I released my grip. She turned her head away from me and spoke, barely loud enough for me to hear.

"Yes. I took money tonight. I needed new clothes and Maurice said I had already overspent my budget. This is the first time I took anything and I'll never do it again. Just don't tell Maurice."

"I won't, Wendy, but I suspect he'll know before this night is done because you aren't telling the truth. I'm going to turn you over to Lt. Thibodeau."

"I am telling the truth."

"You haven't begun to tell the truth. I set up a video recording system to watch you handle tickets and cash. Would you like to see the videotape from last night and all the other nights?"

I hoped she wouldn't want to see the other nights because I didn't have anything before last night.

"Why are you doing this to me?"

"Because you're the patsy, Wendy. We know you're not stealing money for yourself. We know who you're stealing for. We even know why. Now we know how. We just don't know for how long. I knew someone was stealing back in September. How many months have you been stealing before then? A year? Two years?"

Wendy sat up. Perhaps she realized that flat-on-the-floor was a weak position from which to bargain and was making her speech sound wimpy. Her color was improving.

"Wendy. I have seven minutes left and you don't want to tell me the truth, so you can tell whatever story you care to make up to Lt. Thibodeau, Clotilde Boudron, and Dean Halberstam."

"Oh, no," she gasped. "Not them. I couldn't face them. Please give me some other way."

"The truth, Wendy. The truth is the only way. Give me the truth and the money you took tonight and you can walk out of here a free woman—but you must never come back."

"How could I," she said, tears streaming down her face. "I've made such a muck-up of things. I should just die."

"I don't think grand larceny carries a death penalty, even in Louisiana. You may make whatever amends you wish at any time, Wendy, but you have only six minutes remaining to tell me the truth, or you can say whatever you wish to the police and the press."

"Not the press." She sounded truly terrified. She looked up at me, made eye contact, and spit out her next few words.

"It's easy for you to stand there with your academic credentials and your high ideals and judge me. You're a hard man, Dewy Spearman. There's not a jot or tittle of compassion in you."

I was struck by the irony of her statement. Perhaps she should speak to Dean Halberstam about my high ideals. I could use a testimonial. But, I didn't allow my half-second of personal amusement to deter me from completing my task.

"The truth, Wendy. Five minutes for the truth."

She sat for the next sixty seconds wringing her hands, screwing up her mouth, and dancing her eyebrows, and then she popped her cork. She began spilling what could have been a long story into her remaining four minutes.

"I was a plain and shy school girl when Maurice came to take lodgings with us when he studied at Oxford. He was beautiful, witty, and charming. I loved him with a maiden's unrequited love. I didn't think he noticed me at all, other than to be polite, and I was devastated when he returned to America. I believed I would never see him again and no one would ever love me."

"When Maurice returned to England to compete in shooting matches and do whatever else he did in the Air Force and I was despairing of becoming an old maid, he came around to our house and began courting me. I was besotted. Maurice courted me, and then he proposed marriage. It was pure bliss."

"I would marry a handsome scholar and come to America. Perhaps because I was English and shy, I knew little of the ways of men and women. After my first year in this country, absorbing American culture and watching R-rated movies on the telly, I realized that neither did Maurice know much about the ways of men and women."

She paused. Her eyes glistened. I let the pause go on for thirty seconds before I spoke.

"You have ninety seconds left, Wendy. I know you're upset, but keep talking."

"Damn your bloody inquisition, Spearman. Are you really going to make me say it out loud?

"Tell me, or tell the police. It's your choice, Wendy."

She screwed up her eyes and her mouth creating a golf-ball dimples pattern on her chin as if she were going to pout and cry again, but then she took five deep breaths and resumed her story.

"After we had been in New Orleans several years I discovered Maurice knew full well the ways of men and men. I caught him in bed with another gentleman from the theater."

Not even her deep breathing could keep her centered any longer. She gasped. Her tears overflowed. They ran down her face and dripped onto the floor. She made no attempt to wipe them away.

"Maurice is afraid that he will be discriminated against for tenure should it come out that he is homosexual. That would devastate both of us."

Now came the sobs.

"It's not that Maurice doesn't love me. He does. He loves me and I love him; but, I cannot satisfy him and he will not, or cannot satisfy me."

"So you took up with Ellis."

She gasped for breath about half a dozen times. Her diaphragm distended her abdomen with each spasmodic inspiration and snot bubbled out of her nose with each convulsive expiration.

"Ellis is crass, but I am the object of his lust. I like that. He brought out my passion and allowed me to experience it fully. Ellis loves me in the way a man loves a woman. I need that."

"And Ellis needs money?"

She began to wail.

"Damn your code of honor. Ellis is not my lover because I steal for him. I steal for him because he's my lover. Don't you see?"

"Yes," I said, but I didn't see.

"It's not really stealing, anyway. His mother covers any losses. Ellis is just getting an advance on his inheritance."

"How convenient."

Despite her tears and ragged breathing, she was able to ask my indulgence.

"May I go now? Haven't you humiliated me enough?"

"Hand over the money, Wendy, and you may leave. You don't have to explain why you quit TVC, just don't ever come back. Say nothing to Ellis about this. I'll speak to him tomorrow."

"You said you wouldn't tell anyone," she said, wailing again.

"I said I wouldn't tell anyone who didn't already know. Ellis knows. He's been profiting from your larceny as well from his own."

"What?"

"Ellis is a thief in his own right, Wendy. Don't go see him tonight. I promised Laura I would confront him privately and give him a chance to take responsibility for his actions."

"I know he will. You're wrong about Ellis. He's rough around the edges, but he's not a bad man, just a defeated one. He's been crushed by his mother. He'll do right. I know he will."

"I will give him an opportunity to do right, Wendy, but don't go to see him tonight. You're in no condition to deal with anything. Go home. Have a cup of chamomile tea. Take a hot bath. Use lavender bath salts. Go to bed. Tomorrow is another day."

"All right," Wendy said, snuffling, as she fished the money out of her purse and placed it on the counter.

I heard knocking on the door and opened it only a crack.

"Spearman," Thibodeau whispered, "that Boudron girl say if you don't be in your place in thirty seconds, she's gonna' have your guts fo' garters."

"Yeah," I whispered back, "and her mother's going to have my balls for breakfast."

"What is it with you and women, Spearman? You runnin' with a tough crowd. You still shackin' with that redhead?"

"Watch it, Thibodeau."

"I'm cool man. You want to run with a pro, that be your business. You be on your way now, or that Boudron girl be after me."

"Roger that. I'm sending Mrs. Bridges out. Would you be so kind as to arrange a ride home for her in an unmarked car, please?"

"I'll put her in a cab. Hand me twenty-five bucks outta' that pile on the counter."

"That's theater money."

"Make it up outta' your pocket later."

I handed him thirty dollars from my wallet stashed in my costume purse hanging from my belt. I closed the door and spoke to Wendy.

"There'll be a cab for you out front, paid for and tipped. Go straight home. Do not see Ellis. Do not call Ellis. I'll send him a note by courier first thing in the morning asking him to meet me here in the afternoon to discuss these events. I promised Laura I'd give Ellis a chance to come clean and take responsibility for his own actions, and that's what I'm going to do. Go home, Wendy, and let me break the news to Ellis."

I opened the door and shooed her out. Thibodeau caught my eye and said softly, "Find me in the morning and we'll make a plan to confront Ellis. Now, run and strut your hour upon the stage."

"Everybody's a Thespian," I muttered as I dashed out the front door in my raincoat and headed for the stage door so Laura wouldn't write me up for missing my call.

I couldn't afford to have all the Boudrons on my case, especially not at the same time.

Chapter Twenty-Nine

The next morning I sent Ellis a message by courier challenging him to meet me at TVC at two o'clock, *mano a mano*, and hear the evidence of thievery I had against him. I had also promised Laura I would let her know if Ellis behaved truly dishonorably and allow him to clean it up himself first.

To honor that promise, I sent Laura a message, also by courier, telling her that I was going to confront Ellis with evidence of embezzlement and give him an opportunity to make it good. To keep her away from that meeting, I instructed the courier to deliver Laura's message to Maison Boudron at two o'clock.

I lied, or at least I omitted the fact that I wouldn't be alone for my meeting with Ellis. I met Lt. Thibodeau at the station on Royal and we put together a plan. Thibodeau said he had already talked with the prosecutor's office and they were looking for a judge to give them a warrant to record my confrontation with Ellis.

"I'm gonna' put a wire on you, son, just like they do on television, and we're gonna record your meet with Ellis. We got a warrant. The recording's just for insurance," Thibodeau said. "Landowski and I will get there ahead of you and conceal ourselves. That way we'll be close enough to pick up the signal from your wire and close enough to hear firsthand. Can you get us a key?"

"I'll make a copy of my key for you."

"That'll work. We'll get there early. You come in exactly at two o'clock. Don't try to spot us. Looking around might spook Ellis, and if you did spot us, Ellis might pick up a cue from your reaction and our cover would be blown."

I agreed that I would focus on Ellis and not blow their cover.

Thibodeau and a technician fitted me with a transmitter and a microphone. They showed me how to turn it on and how the indicator light would let me know it was working. The technician told me to activate it before I went inside the theater and then to forget I was wearing it.

I found an open hardware store, had them make a copy of my stage door key, and dropped it off with the desk sergeant to give to Thibodeau. Then I headed home to take a nap. I was exhausted.

Before I left for my rendezvous with Ellis at TVC, I turned on my transmitter. I didn't want to wait to turn it on at the stage door in case Ellis might be outside the theater observing me.

Precisely at two o'clock, I unlocked the stage door and let myself in. I could see no evidence of Thibodeau and Landowski on my way in and I saw none after I entered. My coming in from the bright, outside light into the darkness of the theater left me temporarily night-blind, so seeing anything was difficult. It didn't help that when I closed the door behind, me I was standing in near-total darkness. Even the ghost light was turned off. That wasn't right. As I edged my way over to the wall to turn on the stage door work light, I tripped over a large, dark lump and I nearly fell. I regained my balance and detoured around it. When I found the switch for the work light and turned it on, I could see the lump was Officer Landowski. His tape recorder lay beside him—smashed.

"He's not dead, yet," Ellis said.

His voice was coming from behind me.

"I flattened him with Thibodeau's gun. I wanted him to be alert, like Thibodeau over there by the prop room, so he could watch what happens to people who cross me. I guess I just hit him too hard. Sometimes I don't know my own strength. Don't worry. They won't tell on me. They'll both end up dead in the alley. Thibodeau clubs Landowski and Landowski shoots Thibodeau. I'll throw around a couple of packs of nose candy and two or three hundred bucks. You know, two cops kill each other over splitting up drug money."

I looked towards the prop room. Thibodeau was trussed like a Thanksgiving turkey and gagged for good measure.

"Don't bother going for their guns, Spearman. I took 'em and I've got Thibodeau's pointed at you," Ellis said, as he circled around in front of me. "Don't bother to make a dash for the door, either. You'd be dead before you could snap back the spring lock. Now, back up against the wall and put your hands on your head."

"O.K. You've convinced me," I said, and I did what he asked.

"Why don't you tell me what you and your two pals were up to? It's not like I don't know, I just want to hear it from you, Spearman.

You college boys think you're so damn smart and everyone else is stupid. I'm a lot smarter'n you think. I coulda' gone to college without even makin' Mama pay. I had the GI Bill."

"Why didn't you?"

"College is for losers and wimps like you and that faggot Maurice Bridges. I'm a man. I make things happen. I take what I want."

"And sometimes you get caught and punished. Do you think no one knows we're here?"

"That's exactly what I think, Spearman. I know these two bozos you sent on ahead. They work on their own. With all the cops getting indicted around here, Thibodeau and Landowski don't trust anyone but themselves."

"I wouldn't count on that, Ellis."

"I am counting on it, so leave that alone and tell me what I want to know."

Ellis was definitely in charge at this moment, so I figured my best plan was to stall him until I could think of a better plan, or until something shifted the distribution of power.

"O.K., Ellis. You're the man. I'll tell you the whole story. I got suspicious when my count of the house didn't match the receipts. I figured the scam was in the money-handling end. Wendy had to be the key, but I couldn't figure her for a thief. She must have been doing it for something other than the money."

"Yeah, man. She was doing it for a good dicking. That pansy husband of hers couldn't make her happy. She needed a real man."

"And you needed an accomplice."

"Right. I needed to get cash without the auditor getting wise."

"Because you aren't allowed to touch the cash."

"Ain't that a bitch? When Mama fixed things, she fixed it so I couldn't have no runnin' room. I need juice to make things work."

"So you live on an allowance under your mother's thumb and scam the theater for operating capital and for revenge."

"Yeah, man. Cool, ain't it? And it's not like I'm stealing. I mean, Mama makes it up eventually, and it don't hurt her none. Sooner or later I'll inherit, but right now, she's so tight I have to scam."

"Why don't you just kill her and inherit sooner?"

"What do you think I am, Spearman? A low-life? If Mama died under suspicious circumstances they'd bust their asses to hang it on me. I'd be back inside and it wouldn't be no Club Fed, either. It'd be Angola. Even if they was to give me parole, the governor would overturn it and I'd stay inside. I burned the governor once in a pyramid scheme. I can't do that, man. I can't go back inside."

"I'd forgotten you've already done time, but that was in a federal minimum security facility—not Angola

"You can check in to Club Fed anytime you want, Spearman. Maybe you'd like it. I didn't. But, Angola's something else. Do you know what happens to good-looking guys like me in the pen? It never happened, but I had to 'front a few people to keep it that way. Funny about that, Spearman. You defend yourself, they isolate you and give you more time. You don't defend yourself, you're fucked. Either way, you're screwed. "

"I see what you mean, Ellis. It's not fair."

"I ain't going back in, Spearman, no way. Even if that means I gotta' take crap from Mama. But I ain't going to kill her. I've got other ways to work it out."

"Scamming?"

"Yeah, man. I'm a friggin' entrepreneur; I make things happen."

"Just like your daddy."

"Leave my daddy out of this."

"Isn't that how your daddy got rich, breaking the law?"

"Law, schmaw. That stuff's for wimps. We're Boudrons. We take what we want."

"And kill those who get in your way."

"Yeah, if we have to. I got good trainin' in that in the army. It comes in handy from time to time."

"Like when you killed Spider."

"You figure I did that, huh?"

"Yeah."

"Hey, man, Spider was a drunk. Fell and broke his neck."

"It doesn't add up, Ellis. I knew you and Spider were writing off new lighting instruments as salvage and selling them for half price."

"Sure, man. Easy money. Doesn't cost nobody nothin'. All you gotta' do is keep your ears open and your mouth shut. So what?"

"I saw you and Spider argue my first day here. I found out why. Spider wanted a bigger cut. He needed money for his daughter."

"Jeez, man, go figure. Twenty years later he finds out he's got a kid and he gets righteous. What a pain. So, how'd I off him?"

"You broke his neck."

"Doc said he did that himself falling into the rigging."

"Doc's wrong. Spider had a broken neck, but not a hangman's fracture, the kind he'd get if he'd been hung. His spinal cord was severed laterally from right to left between his fifth and sixth cervical vertebrae. You did that by coming up from behind while he was seated, stabilizing his head on the left with your left hand, and thrusting his neck swiftly and forcefully to the left with your right hand."

"Then how'd he get in the rigging?"

"You locked him in the box office until everyone had gone, and then you hung him up in the rigging like you hung that cock."

"How'd you know I hung that cock?"

"It figures. At the time, I thought it was a warning to me. But now I see it was a warning to Spider, a warning he didn't heed."

"Go on, man. This is gettin' interesting, but everybody knows Spider was a drunk. He just fell, broke his neck, and hung himself at the same time."

"That's where you are completely wrong and you know it. Spider used to be a drunk. What you probably didn't know until after you'd broken Spider's neck was that he was in recovery. He'd kicked booze. The vodka bottle he carried was just for show to keep people from getting too close. Several weeks ago I saw him filling it up from the water fountain. I didn't think much about it at the time, but now it all comes together."

"Doc said Spider had vodka in his stomach."

"Yes, and in his lungs, too, but not in his blood. I'll bet you were surprised when you pulled out his vodka bottle to splash a little around and found out it was plain water."

"Go figure."

"You went out, bought vodka, and poured it down his throat while he was hanging in the rigging. You accidentally poured some of it down his trachea and you spilled some of it on his shirt front and on the floor. You wiped up the vodka because a dead man wouldn't spill vodka on the floor. Thibodeau and I both noticed the clean spot, but we didn't make the connection until we went to the coroner's inquest and talked to Spider's daughter."

"O.K., man. You're pretty smart for a college boy. Spider was skimming. He really pissed me off when I found out he was dealing directly with Bud and cutting me out. I got so mad I broke his neck. Sure, I did it. The bum had it coming. But I'm smarter'n you."

"You're right, Boudron. You are smarter than I. And there's one thing I can't figure out. You can help me. How'd you handle the lividity problem?"

"Easy man. After I broke his neck, I hung him up in the office until I could move him. I used a power cord the size of the one he was hanging from later. I take that back about you being smart. You really are a dumb shit if you couldn't figure that out."

"I guess so. You broke Spider's neck, you busted Landowski's head, and you're going to shoot Thibodeau. How are you going to kill me? The same way you killed Hammond Laidlaw?"

"Ham Laidlaw? Man, that's a blast from the past. That was near a year ago. No, that wasn't me. Laidlaw never crossed me. Whatever happened to him, man, I don't know. He fell in the river and drowned is my guess. If anybody pushed him, my money'd be on Von Dragon. Laidlaw had a hard on for Stella. He was drooling on himself tryin' to get in her pants and all. You, I'm going to skewer with this sword I got out of the prop room."

"What will that accomplish?"

"It'll make you dead."

"Sure, but how will you avoid suspicion?"

"Because I'll have an airtight alibi. Wendy will swear I was with her at the time of your death. She'll swear to anything I say. She likes my dick and she'll do anything to keep her precious Maurice out of a scandal. She knows I could get the scandal rollin'. Besides, I'm going to pin it on Sterling."

"Lance?"

"Yeah, man."

"How're you going to do that?"

"After I stick you, I'm going to open the door to the green room where I stashed Sterling, march him over here, and kill him with another one of these short swords," he said, waving a Roman gladius. "Those claymores is too big. And then I'm going to put that sword in your dying hands, Spearman. Your prints'll be on it. Everybody knows there's bad blood between you two. So, when you rehearse the fight scene, somebody starts takin' it personal."

"Sounds like you've given this a lot of thought."

"I been scheming all night. Here's how it goes down, Spearman. Sterling backs you up against the wall and stabs you through the gut, a nice clean cut through the descending aorta. A cut descending aorta is fatal, but not immediate. In your last act on this earth, you thrust up with your sword and catch Sterling under the chin, sever his esophagus, cut through his tongue, pierce the roof of his mouth, and make mush of his brain. I know that works. I did it with a bayonet in 'Nam. It's fatal, too, and it's much quicker."

On my right, the green room door opened, surprising us and spilling light into the backstage area.

"I don't think so, Ellis," Maurice said. "I have come to bring down the wrath of God upon you swift and sure."

I looked to the right. Maurice stood in the open doorway of the green room. He held a long-barreled handgun loosely in his left hand, its muzzle pointed to the floor. Behind him, inside the green room, Lance was bound, gagged, and suspended from the ceiling with his arms in the air. His feet barely touched the floor. His wide eyes, red face, and muffled cries were proof of life.

Ellis took advantage of my averted gaze. In what seemed like one quick, fluid movement, he tucked Thibodeau's revolver in his waistband, grabbed my right elbow, and spun me halfway around which put me between him and Maurice. He clamped his right arm across my stomach with his balled-up fist at my solar plexus.

With his left hand, he jammed the point of the Roman gladius under my chin. I recalled his description of how he intended for Lance to die by a sword similarly placed and my bowels roiled.

"Lower your arms, Spearman," Ellis said, jabbing the underside of my chin with his sword to emphasize his point. I did as he commanded which put my right arm on top of his.

"Maurice," Ellis said with a honeyed voice, "I didn't expect to see you here."

"You shouldn't have beaten her, Ellis. I can understand your taking her to bed. I know she has needs I can't satisfy. Why she picked you, I'll never understand. You didn't have to beat her."

"I didn't beat her, Maurice. Sure, we had a little argument last night but she was fine when she left the club. She musta' fell down some stairs or something, honest to God."

"'God and good men hate so foul a liar.' You shouldn't have beaten her, Boudron. She's going to lose her eye."

"I'm telling you the truth, man, I didn't beat her."

"'Methinks thou art a general offence and every man should beat thee.'"

"Yeah, like you're a man whose gonna' beat me, huh? Why you talkin' so funny anyway?"

Nobody spoke for a moment. Even Lance held still.

"'An eye for an eye, and a tooth for a tooth.'"

"You're making me nervous with that funny talk, Maurice," Ellis said, tightening his grip on me and pressing the sword under my chin as he continued to hold me squarely between himself and Maurice.

"He's quoting from Shakespeare and the Bible," I said, straining to get my words out without pushing my chin onto the sword.

"Shut up, Spearman," Ellis growled.

"Yes, Ellis," Maurice said. "I'm quoting from Shakespeare and from the Holy Bible, and I shall quote more from the Holy Bible before this day has run its course. But for the moment, I will quote John Milton for the benefit of Dewy Spearman whom you so cowardly hold between us. 'When I consider how my light is spent....'"

Maurice began the opening stanza of *On His Blindness*. Sometimes people get into a cognitive loop and they do things from habit or compulsion without much thought. Sometimes the things people do seem to be random, without any forethought. But, many times, people do things thoughtfully and on purpose. If you can figure out their purpose, you can come out ahead. I was interested in coming out ahead, so I listened closely as Maurice recited the last two lines.

"'They also serve who only stand and wait. They also serve who only stand and wait.'"

I figured Maurice wanted me to stand and wait. That's what I had in mind, anyway. It wasn't like I had many choices. I learned in stage combat training that you can defend yourself against being held from behind by going limp, falling to the ground, and rolling away or attacking. With the point of a Roman sword under my chin, falling down didn't seem like a good idea. Not seeing any other acceptable option, prudence dictated that I heed Maurice's poetic command.

"You're getting' weird on me, Maurice," Ellis said. "Look, I'm not holdin' a gun, man. Put yours down and we can talk this over."

"'Remember now thy Creator in the days of thy youth, while the evil days come not, nor the years draw nigh, when thou shalt say; I have no pleasure in them.'"

"O.K., Maurice," Ellis said as he maneuvered me a little to the left so he could take a quick peek at Maurice, "I don't know what you're drivin' at, but I was pleasurin' her. Lord knows you wasn't."

"'While the sun, or the light, or the moon, or the stars, be not darkened, nor the clouds return after the rain.'"

"Yeah, it was dark when she left, man. Real dark. She musta' fell down the stairs in the dark."

"'In the day when the keepers of the house shall tremble, and the strong men shall bow themselves, and the grinders cease because they are few, and those that look out of the windows be darkened.'"

Ellis was getting tense and shaky. Maurice had not moved, but Ellis maneuvered me again quickly to the left so he could peek at Maurice, and then he shifted me just as quickly back to center to shield himself with me.

"I already said it was dark, man," Ellis said, sounding exasperated. "What do you want?"

Maurice paid no apparent heed to Ellis and continued his quoting.

"'The almond tree shall flourish, and the grasshopper shall be a burden, and desire shall fail; because man goeth to his long home, and the mourners go about the street.'"

"Is that what she told you, man? I ain't never had no desire fail. She say I couldn't get it up? That bitch is lyin', man," Ellis said, practically shrieking. He was beginning to perspire heavily. "I always get it up. There's nothin' wrong with me, man. She just didn't want it last night. It was all her fault. It was her, man, not me."

"'Or ever the silver cord be loosed, or the golden bowl be broke, or the pitcher broken at the fountain, or the wheel broken at the cistern.'"

"O.K., man, so I slapped her around a little, but I didn't break nothin'. Just bitch slappin'. Bitch had it comin'. Rattin' me out to Spearman. You'd do the same if your woman ratted you out and then told you she loved her husband. Can you believe it? Bitch said she loves you. What do you think about that you dickless wonder?"

"'Then shall the dust return to the earth as it was: and the spirit shall return to God who gave it.'"

"You ain't returnin' me nowhere, fancy man. If you come here to kill me, you gonna' be suckin' wind. That little pea shooter of yours won't knock a man down, much less kill him with one shot, which is all you'll get off if you're lucky, and you'll have to shoot through Spearman. I've got Thibodeau's .38. You raise your pea-shooter and you a dead man. Jus' let it fall outta' your hand. We can work something out."

"'Vengeance is mine'," Maurice said, as he raised his pistol in his left hand, supported it with his right hand, and pointed it just to the right of my head. "'An eye for an eye....'"

"O.K., man, but don't say I didn't warn you," Ellis said, as he pulled his arm out from under mine, quickly drew Thibodeau's revolver from his waistband, thrust the gun out past my arm, and leaned slightly to the right to take a shot.

Maurice, without making any perceptible motion, squeezed off one round just as Ellis moved his head far enough past mine to sight Maurice with his right eye. It seemed like it all happened at once, but I am sure there was a sequence.

Ellis moved his gun arm out about half an arm's length in front of me as he quickly raised his gun into firing position. I heard a small pop from Maurice's gun simultaneous with a louder explosion from Ellis' gun. Ellis went slack and fell to the floor with the gun and Roman sword preceding him.

Maurice and I stood still and quiet. Maurice spoke first.

"Thanks for not moving," he said. He lowered his gun.

I looked down at Ellis. His left eye was open and rolled back in his head. Where his right eye had been only a moment before, blood pooled in an eyeless socket.

"Nice shooting, Maurice".

"That's what I trained for in the Air Force."

"I remember hearing that."

"I hope I didn't frighten you with my quotations from Ecclesiastes. I had to provoke Ellis to stick his head out to get my shot. It took a while. Thank you for your patience."

"No problem, Maurice. If it's O.K. with you, I'm going to pick up the sword. Then I'm going to untie Lt. Thibodeau."

"Yes, quite. And when you've done that, perhaps you should untruss Mr. Sterling. I'm certain he's quite vexed at this point. I'll stand here over Boudron lest he get an idea to resurrect himself."

"I don't think he's going anywhere, Maurice, but that's O.K. by me," I said, as I wobbled on rubber legs over to Thibodeau. My shaking fingers wouldn't work well enough to undo the tape that bound him, so I used the Roman sword to cut his bindings. For a theater prop, it was sharper than I thought it would be.

Thibodeau pulled off his gag and began exercising to get blood flowing in his stiffened body.

"Spearman, call this in on 911. Tell 'em there's an officer down, and tell them to get the paramedics here stat. Maybe Landowski can pull through. Tell 'em we got a corpse, too, and bring Dr. Death. And tell them to come in with their weapons holstered. I don't feel like getting shot today."

Thibodeau shifted his focus and barked an order at Maurice. "Bend down and put your gun on the floor, now."

Maurice put his gun on the floor and stared at it. Thibodeau went over and picked it up by putting his ballpoint pen through the trigger guard. He pulled a plastic evidence bag from his pocket and dropped the gun in it.

"Spearman." Thibodeau barked at me this time. "Find me a blanket or somethin' to put over Landowski. Keep him warm, but don't move him. Leave Sterling be. The bulls will cut him down when they get here. Paramedics have to look at him anyway. Then go sit by the door until my backup gets here. Tackle Maurice if he tries to make a break."

"I'm not going anywhere," Maurice said quietly, still staring at the place on the floor where his gun had been. "Where could I go?"

"Can I take this transmitter off now?" I asked.

"Sure. Too bad we didn't get Boudron's confession on tape."

"Maybe it's best we didn't, Lieutenant," I said to Thibodeau. "We can't try Boudron now. He's dead."

"And…?"

"Maurice is probably better off without the tape."

Thibodeau looked straight at Maurice and said, "Maurice Bridges, you have the right to remain silent. You have the right to have an attorney present when you are questioned. If you cannot afford an attorney, one will be appointed for you. If you give up this right, anything you say can and will be used against you in a court of law. Do you understand your rights?"

"Yes," Maurice said quietly, still staring at the floor.

"Are you arresting him?" I asked, as I spread my jacket over Landowski and went to the door to unlock it.

"Not yet. Mirandize him now; arrest him later if I need to."

"What will happen to him?"

"Depends. If the D.A. wants to push, he could go for murder one. Maurice came armed, presumably with intention of committing a felony. But, intention's hard to prove. He could go for voluntary manslaughter, or he could just come up with some bullshit weapons charge to keep Maurice on ice until things quiet down."

"Why not just let him walk? He saved your bacon, and mine, and Lance Sterling's, too, maybe even Landowski's. Why not give him a medal?"

"You can't let civilians go around taking justice into their own hands. Besides, Boudron's mama carries a lot of weight around here. There's going to be hell to pay with Clotilde Boudron."

"What about Wendy?"

"Hospital," both Maurice and Thibodeau said.

Maurice continued, "She came out of surgery for bilateral fractured orbital bones when I left to come here. The surgeon called in a retinal specialist. They saved one eye and reattached the retina. She might lose vision in the other one."

"She got a broken nose and jaw, too. Police report say she claims she fell down the stairs," Thibodeau added.

"He didn't have to beat her," Maurice said, almost in a whisper, as he stared straight at Thibodeau.

Everyone was silent for a moment.

Thibodeau look straight at Maurice and said, "How you get in here, Bridges?"

"I used Wendy's key on the front door. I got it from the hospital when she was in surgery. They made me take her things."

"That gun traceable to you?"

"It's a .25 caliber target pistol I used for training. My superior officer gave it to me and told me not to list it when I mustered out. It's a Belgian rip-off of an American model his father picked up in World War II. I've never registered it. I doubt that it's documented anywhere."

"You be willin' to give it up to stay outta' jail?"

"How would that work?"

"Spearman, I didn't see Bridges arrive with a gun. Did you see Bridges arrive with a gun?"

"I didn't see him arrive at all. He had a gun in his hand when he came out of the green room."

"So," Thibodeau continued, "Bridges comes looking for something his wife left here and lets himself in with her key. He found Boudron, a known felon just off parole, holding everybody hostage at gunpoint after he battered Landowski with intent to do great bodily harm. Maurice found a loaded gun in the office. He was trained in firearms so he took on Boudron to stop four homicides."

"Sounds good to me, Thibodeau," I said.

"D.A. will want to know why you didn't just call it in on 911, Bridges," Thibodeau added, "but that's not against the law. I'll have to take you in, anyway, to get your statement, and the D.A. might decide to charge you with something. It's not likely he could convict you on murder one. Anything else he could charge you with would be just for harassment. Any good lawyer'll get you off."

"I'll have to resign my teaching position," Maurice said, softly. "It won't do to have a killer on the faculty."

"What makes you think your faculty be so righteous?" Thibodeau sighed and shook his head. "Well, that be up to you, Bridges. None of my business."

"I'll do something to make it up to Wendy."

"That would be easier out of prison than in it." I said.

"Yes, I suppose it would," Maurice replied. "Yes, Lt. Thibodeau, I came here to fetch an earring my wife thought she may have left and I discovered Ellis Boudron in the commission of several felonies. I found a loaded pistol in the office. Believing that time was of the essence, I attempted to apprehend him. He shot at me and I returned fire in self defense."

"Think it'll fly?" I asked Thibodeau.

"What he got to lose?"

"I will repay whatever Wendy may have taken," Maurice said. "Will you charge my wife with theft?"

"That'd be up to the management of the theater and the D.A. Whatever, there'll be some kind of hell to pay with Clotilde Boudron. Count on it."

Chapter Thirty

Acting on the invitation from Dean Halberstam I received in my campus mail on Friday, I arrived at TVC on Sunday ten minutes before the announced time of the emergency board meeting Clotilde had called. Except for Clothilde, all of the board members had arrived even earlier than I and were standing in a loose group between the first row of seats and the stage.

Dean Halberstam caught my eye and nodded for me to take a house seat. She looked different. Her hair was down. She was wearing charcoal grey wool slacks and a jade-green pullover sweater with a single strand of pearls instead of her customary tailored business suit and cravat, and she wore flats instead of heels.

Pete VanLandingham and Lucien Sacristan were present. Pete was dressed in casual grunge like backstage theater personnel frequently wear. Lucian had on a three-piece gray suit with a white shirt and a powder-blue tie. Perhaps he had just come from mass.

The remaining man, Harold Ecksman, was the corporate counsel as well as a member of the board. He was dressed in brown cords and an oatmeal Aran sweater. His boat shoes and Greek fisherman's cap led me to believe he would rather be out sailing on Lake Pontchartrain than attending Clotilde's emergency board meeting.

At two minutes before the appointed hour, Harold nodded to the others. He and Dean Halberstam took the seats on the right side of a table which had been set for them on the stage. Pete Vanlandingham and Lucien Sacristan took seats on the left side.

Clotilde Boudron arrived precisely on time, and, by taking the one remaining chair at the head of the table, upstaged everyone.

"What is this odious man doing in my theater?" Clotilde demanded of the assembled board members. "Remove him."

I presumed she was speaking of me.

"I invited him," Dean Halberstam said. "Mr. Spearman, who is the source of your displeasure and the subject of this called meeting, is one of my visiting professors. His dismissal, should that happen, may reflect adversely on my college. Before we vote to terminate his contract for misfeasance, I intend to question him about his alleged misfeasance and determine, based on evidence, not emotion, that he did in fact commit misfeasance before I would vote to fire him."

"I won't," Clotilde said. "Girard," she said to her chauffeur, "forcibly remove this interloper."

"If he leaves," Dean Halberstam said, "I leave. If I leave, you can't hold a meeting because all members must be present at a called meeting for any action to be taken."

Clotilde said, in a loud, clear voice, "I call this meeting to order and note that all members are present."

She smiled broadly and cocked her head. I was beginning to think she was losing her marbles.

"Now you may leave, Inge," Clotilde said, "and we may continue to conduct our business until the question of a quorum is raised. I don't think any of these gentlemen will raise that question, will you, gentlemen?" Clotilde looked at each of the three men in turn.

"Still, Clotilde," Harold spoke up, "it will do no harm for Mr. Spearman to remain. Technically, our meetings are open to the public. Any attempt to exclude Mr. Spearman, a member of the public, could lead to nullification later of what we may do now."

"Lawyers! Arnaud never had anything good to say about lawyers. I can see why. They just get in the way and slow everything down. Arnaud managed to get things done his way without lawyers."

"With all respect to the memory of your long-departed and much-lamented husband, Clotilde, lawyers set up the Boudron Theater Trust of which we are trustees and, simultaneously, directors of the theater corporation. I believe it would be wise to proceed prudently. We prefer not to be sued, even if we would prevail."

"Cowards," Madame Boudron shot back. "Sniveling cowards. That's what Arnaud called lawyers. And worse."

Harold said nothing in reply and no one else volunteered to break the silence, so Clotilde spoke again.

"I want that man fired!"

Harold continued to hold his counsel. Again, no one broke the silence until Clotilde spoke.

"Harold, even if you're too cautious to vote my way, and Inge votes against me, too, I've got Pete's and Lucien's votes. That will make a tie. According to our bylaws, I may vote to break a tie. You may count on my voting to break the tie in my favor and get that murderer out of here no matter what you want."

"Please do not be injudicious with your words, Clotilde," Harold said. "We were shocked by learning of your son's demise, but no one has been charged in that matter. It even appears that Mr. Spearman was being held hostage by your son at the time of his death."

"Lies," Clotilde shouted. "All lies. Do I have a motion to fire that power-hungry son of a bitch, Dewy Spearman?"

"So moved," said her cousin, Lucien.

"Is there a second?"

No one spoke.

"Is there a second?" she said, speaking slowly and deliberately, without inflection, as she looked directly at Pete.

"Second," Pete said quietly. He looked down at the table.

"Call for discussion," Dean Halberstam interjected.

"Two minutes for discussion."

"Point of order," Harold said.

"Two minutes for discussion, period. The Chair has ruled."

"I appeal the ruling of the Chair."

"Shut up, Harold. This is my board. I'll run it as I see fit."

"I think you had best follow established procedure, Clotilde."

"And so do I," Dean Halberstam added.

"Very well," Clotilde said. "We'll do it properly. All in favor of limiting discussion to two minutes say aye."

Lucien Sacristan mumbled a perfunctory aye.

"The ayes have it," Clotilde said, banging her gavel on the table. "You may begin your two minutes of discussion now."

"Call for division of the house," Dean Halberstam said.

"No."

"You can't do that, Clotilde," Harold said. "You must follow appropriate parliamentary procedure as prescribed in our bylaws or risk nullification of any action taken at this meeting."

"Very well, Harold. The Chair overrules herself and will allow two minutes per person for discussion."

"Objection," Dean Halberstam said. "I appeal the Chair's ruling and call for division of the house with ayes and nays."

"This is outrageous," Clotilde responded. "We're going to fire that murdering son of a bitch anyway, so why do I have to put up with all this folderol?"

"Clotilde," Harold responded, in a lighter tone than before, "I am shocked at your language. Whatever action we take must be taken by majority vote, not by fiat. And, even if we all agree with your position, we must have a discussion before we vote on the motion."

Harold looked directly at Clotilde and spoke calmly and slowly.

"At the moment, Clotilde, we seem to have a desire among the board members to lengthen the discussion period. I recommend that you listen to what your fellow board members have to say."

"I already know what everyone will say, Harold. You'll abstain because you're a lily-livered, chicken-shit lawyer who's afraid we'll get sued. The ice maiden will vote against me because that murdering son of a bitch is on her faculty, but Lucien and Pete will vote my way. So, it'll be two to one, a majority, and Spearman will be history."

Clotilde smiled momentarily, and then she spoke directly to Harold. "And you, Harold, even if you decide to show some balls for once in your life and vote against me, it'll be a tie which I will break and Spearman will be just as gone. Too bad I can't flay him and drop him in the bayou for the alligators like Arnaud used to do. So, the motion has been made and seconded. Let's vote."

"The Chair may not call for a vote," Harold countered.

"Lucien, call for the vote."

"More details, Clotilde," Harold continued. "First, the person who made the motion may not call for the vote. Second, once a request for discussion has been made, a call for a vote must be moved, seconded, and voted upon. Then we can vote on the main motion."

"God damn motherfucking horse shit! Do I own this theater or not?" Clotilde exploded.

After a moment of strained silence, Dean Halberstam spoke.

"In the absence of a call for a vote to end discussion, I suggest we begin that discussion."

"Will no one call for a vote?" Clotilde entreated.

No one spoke.

"Pete," she commanded, "call for a vote."

Pete continued looking down at the table and said nothing.

"Let's not get out of line here, Pete. Call for a vote."

"I don't think I will, Clotilde," Pete said, quietly.

"You what!' Clotilde bellowed.

Pete lifted his head and met Clotilde's steely gaze.

"I want that motion, Pete. I want it now or you know what."

"What, Clotilde? What? You'll expose me as a fairy, a fag, a queer? You'll tell everyone that you know Maurice and I have been secret lovers for two years? Come on, Clotilde. It's a little late in the day to blackmail me again."

"Getting feisty, are we? Clotilde taunted.

"A police officer is lying in the hospital in a coma, Clotilde. Wendy is lying in the hospital with multiple fractures and one eye blind. Your precious son, who wreaked all this havoc, is lying dead in the morgue because Maurice had to shoot him down like a mad dog to keep him from killing four people. All this because we were afraid of living our truth. We all kept secrets that should have been aired."

"Half truths, Pete, maliciously spread by that arrogant asshole director, Dewy Spearman."

"Whatever fears Maurice had that he might be denied tenure for being found out to be gay, Clotilde, whatever fears I may have had at being outed and tied to a liaison with Maurice, pale in comparison to the pain we all are now suffering. Ellis blackmailed me over my secret life with Maurice so I would turn my head while he looted the theater. And you, Clotilde, blackmailed me into going behind Dewy Spearman's back to change the lighting for your precious Lance."

"That arrogant bastard is attempting to destroy Lance and has succeeded in destroying Ellis. Can't you see that?"

"By the way, Clotilde, Lance hates you. He says you're a tiresome old bitch, a wrinkled prune, a faded queen."

"Lies," Madam Boudron shouted. "Lance is grateful for my beneficence. Everyone is lying. No one can produce one iota of credible evidence," she said, her face turning a deeper hue of red, "that Ellis Boudron stole even one dime from this theater!"

"Actually we can," Maurice said, as he stepped out of the backstage shadows and approached the group.

"Get that murderer out of here! Girard, summon the police immediately," Madam Boudron shouted, spewing flecks of saliva.

"I don't think so, Clotilde," Pete continued. I think the board should hear what Maurice has to say.

"Never!"

"Don't be hasty, Clotilde," Harold said. "We have plenty of time, and Maurice is not armed or even dangerous. It's been three days since Ellis' death and Maurice hasn't even been arrested, much less charged with anything."

"Police incompetence!"

"Yes, Clotilde" Dean Halberstam said, "I, too, wish to hear from Dr. Bridges."

"Thank you, Dean Halberstam," Maurice said. "I deeply regret having focused negative attention on my department and our college by my actions. I cannot undo the damage that Wendy and I have done, but we wish to make amends in one regard."

"Can you bring my son back to life, murderer?"

"No. I cannot, but I can make restitution of stolen money. By Wendy's account, she helped Ellis embezzle up to twenty thousand dollars. She received none of it directly and little indirectly. Nevertheless, I have a check for one-half of it, what would have been her equal share had she taken one, a check for ten thousand dollars drawn on our brokerage account."

"This theater will never accept blood money," Clotilde shouted. She fixed her attention on the other members of the board one by one, and then she continued her petulant outburst.

"Ellis did not steal one dime from this theater. It's a lie. It's all lies. Restitution, hah! Did this murderer say he was remorseful for killing my son? Did he? No. He did not. What about that, Mr. Murderer," she said, refocusing her attention on Maurice.

"I regret having killed your son, Clotilde, but I have no remorse. There was no alternative. Dean Halberstam, I will submit my resignation on Monday."

"Don't be hasty, Dr. Bridges," the dean replied. "I suggest you take a week of personal leave and be unavailable for comment to the press before you consider tendering your resignation."

"Thank you, Dean Halberstam," Maurice said. He placed his ten thousand dollar check on the table and walked toward the exit.

"Vipers!" Clotilde screamed to everyone in general with seemingly inexhaustible energy. "You are all ungrateful vipers. You do not have one shred of evidence against Ellis. Not one shred."

I thought her eyes were going to pop out of their sockets.

"We have evidence of Ellis's larceny, Madame Boudron," I said.

"I will not abide this foul man's speaking!" Clotilde shouted at Harold. Her eyes looked like unlighted coals, cold, black, and hard. They wanted only a spark or lighted match to ignite them.

"I believe you will abide his speaking, Clotilde," Harold replied. "It goes to the heart of the matter. Please continue, Mr. Spearman."

"I have a videotape record of Wendy tapping the till."

"That's her, not Ellis!" Clotilde yelled.

"I have Wendy's statement that she was colluding with Ellis to embezzle funds."

"The word of an adulteress!"

"With whom was she committing adultery, Clotilde?"

She did not answer, but her rage ignited the hard, black coals of her eyes and they glowed red-hot. I risked her searing rage and spoke directly to her again.

"Lt. Thibodeau, Maurice, and I all heard Ellis boast that he had been looting the theater knowing that you would personally keep it afloat if the trust funds were insufficient."

"Lies!"

"We also heard Ellis confess to murdering Spider Slidell."

Clotilde rose and fixed her blazing gaze on Harold.

"I will not stand for this treachery. You will all bend to my will and vote to fire Dewy Spearman or I will resign from this board and take the Boudron Theater Trust with me. Then where will Théâtre Vieux Carré be? Now, is there a call for a vote?"

"Can she do that?" Pete asked Harold.

"She can. The terms of the Boudron Theater Trust are clear. The Trust will support the theater as long as a Boudron sits on the Board of Directors. Otherwise, it goes to the Ursuline Sisters."

"So that's it? Either we knuckle under and do it Clotilde's way or the money goes to some nearly defunct order of nuns?"

Clotilde rubbed her hands together and sneered. She paused a moment, and then she fixed her attention on Pete.

"It's my way or the highway."

Her sneer morphed into a leer.

Chapter Thirty-One

"I can't do it," Pete said, shaking his head. "I'll vote against you, Clotilde, even if we go belly up."

"You pathetic ingrate! You don't have the sense God gave a jackass, you little pea hen."

"And I, also," Dean Halberstam said.

"I'll vote with you, Clotilde," Lucien said.

"And you, Harold? Join Lucien and create a tie, which I will decide in my favor; or, you vote against me and bring this theater down. You may also continue your cowardly behavior of taking no position at all which is still a vote against me however you look at it."

"I abstain, Clotilde."

"That's voting against me, you gutless wonder. I will remember this, Harold. I will never forget. Very well, I resign. You can have Dewy Spearman and Théatre Vieux Carré, but you cannot have the Boudron Theater Trust. Without financial support from the trust, this theater will fail."

After a long, silent pause, Clotilde looked directly at me.

"Congratulations, Mr. Spearman. You won control of this theater, but it's a pyrrhic victory because there will be no theater to control. The joke's on you."

"Don't be too hasty, Mother," Laura said. She was speaking from behind me. I had not heard her come in which was surprising, considering the noise I would expect her to make with her brace and crutches. I had no idea how long she had been there.

"I'm a Boudron. I will humbly accept election to the board of directors should I be nominated for election."

"Don't be ridiculous, Laura, darling. You'll do nothing of the kind," Clotilde said, blanching. A sheen of perspiration spread over her lip and forehead. In a voice that now sounded small by as many degrees as it had only seconds ago sounded large, Clotilde spoke.

"Come, dear, let's go home and let these pathetic people stew in their own juices until they beg me to return."

"I'm not leaving with you, Mother, and I am quite serious about offering myself as a candidate for election to the board."

Clotilde's eyes opened wide.

"You can't do that, Laura, dear. You're not competent."

"I'm trained, Mother. And now, thanks to Mr. Spearman, I have experience in adult theater, in this theater. That's something you always denied me."

"It was in your best interests, dear. You're a cripple. Now come home with your mother."

"No, I'm needed here."

"You ungrateful child," Clotilde shrieked, venting her spleen on her daughter. "If you don't come this minute, you will never set foot in Maison Boudron again."

"As long as Maison Boudron stands, Mother, and I am not publicly employed, I have leave to live at Maison Boudron and I am allowed to draw a yearly stipend from the family trust. I hereby state publicly, in front of these witnesses, I will no longer exercise those rights, Mother. I am liberating myself. I shall leave Maison Boudron and support myself. Nonetheless, I shall continue to uphold the Boudron name in all that I say and do, both in my private life and in my work with the theater, whether I be elected to the board or not."

"You wretched girl. After all I have done for you these thirty, long years. 'How sharper than a serpent's tooth it is to have a thankless child'. You're not whole, Laura, dear. You're damaged goods. You're not competent. You're not even a—"

Clotilde stopped abruptly.

"I'm not even a what, Mother?"

Clotilde had everyone's undivided attention, but she offered nothing more. She stood, stiffened, and turned. Unsteady on her feet, she stumbled toward the exit. Her chauffeur reached out to take her arm, but she struck him. He withdrew his arm.

With her eyes fixed straight ahead, Clotilde lurched past Laura as if Laura were not there, stumbled, braced herself against the wall, and continued her halting exit. Her chauffeur followed several paces behind. Lucien Sacristan rose and followed them both.

After a moment of silence, Harold spoke.

"Since no one has raised the question of a quorum, I suggest, Inge, as Vice Chairman, you accept Clotilde Boudron's resignation and the three of us will call a special meeting three days hence to elect

Laura Boudron to fill Clotilde's unexpired term. Then, I believe we should adjourn."

"Yes," Dean Halberstam replied. "If there is no objection, I will prepare and accept the petition to call an emergency meeting to elect Clotilde's successor and then we will adjourn. I will record that for the minutes if Pete agrees. Pete?"

"Sure, Inge. That's fine by me."

"Thank you, Pete," Harold said, and then he faced Laura.

"Laura, welcome to the board, pending your election of course. Is there anything you care to say?"

"Yes, there is. First, if I am elected, I will recommend that the board accept Professor Bridges' offer of restitution. I believe we will need to offer that money to Spider Slidell's daughter to forestall her bringing a wrongful death suit against the theater. Mother can take care of any suits against Ellis' estate."

"Second, I believe Pete should begin working with a different accounting consulting firm immediately to prepare and implement improved accountability procedures for this theater."

"Third, to improve morale and limit further contention, I suggest, but not demand, that Mr. Spearman reconsider his most recent cast changes involving Mr. Sterling."

"Dewy," she said, turning to face me, "if you can find a way to give Lance a larger role without compromising your directorial and artistic privilege, I believe this theater will be better served. I will consider it a personal favor."

"How about that, Dewy?" Pete asked. "Is there any chance you could give Lance a juicer role? Maybe mine?"

That hit me hard, but I admired the wisdom of it. Laura was sound in her judgment and correct in her suggestions, but I was drunk with the spirits of retribution whose cloying sweetness had not yet soured. I wasn't sure I was ready to let go of my thirst for retribution. I mulled her suggestion in silence until Pete spoke again.

"It would give me more time to start fixing things, Dewy."

Pete's added wisdom was enough for me to put my ego in my back pocket for the moment.

"O.K., folks. I understand what you're doing. I won't let my pettiness get in the way. However, I require, *quid pro quo*, that Lance sign an affidavit acknowledging that he defied the director's authority and that he apologize for it."

"Fair enough," Laura said. "It's about time people started being accountable for what they say and do, and that includes Lance."

"Is there anything else, Laura?" Harold asked.

"Yes, there is. Dewy, I apologize for the untoward events you suffered because of your involvement with this theater. I am saddened by my brother's death. I thank you for attempting to give him an opportunity to take responsibility for his actions. I hope when you leave us, you will take with you fond memories of a good production and will consider returning in the future as a guest director."

"Yes," Dean Halberstam added. "Thank you, Mr. Spearman, Dewy, for your work here at TVC as well as for your work on campus. When you arrived, I was aware of your reputation and held an uncharitable opinion. I have since softened that opinion. I will be pleased if you call me Inge in informal settings."

"Thank you, Inge."

"Through your good work with our students, Dewy, and your improvement in deportment, you have demonstrated good character. Should we experience a vacancy in our Speech and Drama Department I will welcome your application for it."

Things were good. I was on a first name basis with all of them now, and, just as Inge had changed into a warmer and more approachable person, so had she revised her negative opinion of my character. Maybe she softened because she was at last able to see me as I truly am; or, maybe I had actually changed my character and she accurately observed it, as she said.

"Thank you, Laura, Harold, and Pete. And thank you, Inge. I am deeply touched by your demonstration of confidence in me."

"If Madame Vice-Chairman will so declare and if no one objects, we may adjourn," Harold said.

"Yes, hearing no objection to a motion for adjournment we stand adjourned until our next called meeting which is to be held three days hence," Inge declared. She stood up, shook my hand, and started for the exit.

Harold joined Inge and led the exodus to the stage door. Pete joined Maurice and filed out behind them. Only Laura and I remained.

"Laura, that was courageous."

"I take no pleasure in it."

"You stood up to your mother. Are you not proud of that?"

"I am proud of standing up for myself, but I take no pleasure in bringing down my mother."

"She was an unreasoning tyrant."

"And a reasoning tyrant is preferred?"

"I'm not a tyrant. I'm a director. There is a difference."

"Perhaps not as much as you care to think. I'm sorry if my words seem uncharitable. You're a good man, you do good work, and you mean well. You've helped me in more ways than you realize."

"I've done little, Laura."

"You've helped me liberate myself from continuing to be crippled by the conditions of my birth. Now that I am no longer crippled figuratively, I must be no longer crippled literally. I must learn to walk the walk of a competent adult. Now that I will represent the trust for the theater, I must use that power wisely. Whatever foibles and limitations Mother had, her chief flaw was faulty vision. She was often blind to things that others plainly saw, even things she was stumbling over. She believed her way of seeing things was the only way things could be seen. That was her tragic flaw."

"Her hamartia."

"Yes, her hamartia. That's also hubris, I think, believing you have the only correct vision, Godlike vision, fatal vision. Watch out for hubris, Dewy. Watch out for your own lack of clear vision. Watch out for only being able to see what you want to see instead of seeing what is there to be seen."

"Are you trying to tell me something?"

"I don't know. I have a sense that you're walking off a cliff, Dewy, because you're too busy looking off into the distance to see the abyss in front of you, but I don't know what that cliff is."

I looked at her in a way that must have signaled incredulity because she responded as if she had offended me.

"Forgive me; I don't know what I'm saying. I'm distraught over my brother's death, unseating my mother, and dishabilitating myself. I can't go home again."

"There comes a time in everyone's life, Laura, when they can't go home again. You're no longer the child you once were. You've changed. So has home. It's time to grow up. Now, what? Where will you go? What will you do?"

"I've talked the library into giving me a full-time job and I've made arrangements to rent a room from a college friend who lives here in the Quarter. I'll start there and see where life takes me. I might even be elected to the TVC board of directors."

"I have every confidence you'll do well."

"For that I am grateful. You showed confidence in me at our first meeting at Mother's dinner party, and you've always treated me as a competent person. Thank you."

"You're welcome. It was easy."

"Then why hasn't anyone else in my life ever done that?"

"Mac did."

"We were fifteen year-old adolescents in love at summer camp. Why no one else?"

"Maybe you wouldn't let anyone else."

"Perhaps not. I'll work on that. Meanwhile, I have every confidence that you will successfully resolve your struggle."

"What struggle?"

"I'm unsure. I don't understand what you're wrestling with, only that you are wrestling. Changing the subject, when are you going to tell Lance he can take over as Macduff?"

"I'm not going to tell him. You are. You're the stage manager. I suggest you do it at call tonight. He can go on tonight if he feels confident he knows the role."

"Have you ever seen Lance lack confidence in his ability to play a role?"

"No, but I haven't always shared his judgment of his capacity to play it well."

"But, he's always O.K. on confidence, right?"

"Yes."

"I'll go write my curtain speech announcing the cast change. See you at seven."

"See you at seven."

As I walked from the theater to my apartment, I turned several thoughts over in my mind. Laura stood up for herself and her birthright at the cost of bringing her mother down. I always thought that boys were supposed to do that with their fathers, or fantasize about it anyway. I didn't know about what girls do.

Laura asserted herself and saved my job at the theater which, technically, was over anyway. Once a show goes into production, the stage manager takes over. The director is finished. It was only my last-minute directorial decision to take the role of Macbeth that required my presence at the theater for each performance.

Laura would be well within her rights as Stage Manger to put Lance back in as Macbeth. I could turn my attention to other things, like polishing off my master's thesis or working on my relationships with Stella.

Stella. *Mia bella,* Stella. What the hella'. Now I was making bad puns to myself. I must be the one losing his marbles. It must be stress, the stress of starting a new career, a new job, two productions, Stella, Spider's murder, burglary, embezzlement, Lance, Ellis, and Clotilde. What a quarter. Had it been a quarter?

Yes, three months, with only two weeks remaining until *Macbeth* was finished, two weeks until the school term was over, and two weeks until I was free to go if I wished, or stay, if Stella would stay with me. Only two weeks left in the time span of Madame Claire's Tarot reading. Only two weeks remained for me to live in hope, and in denial.

What was two weeks? I had proved myself in my new profession. I produced both a student show and a semiprofessional show to favorable reviews and popular acclaim. I resisted the charms of my nubile young student. I broke up a criminal enterprise that was sapping the vitality of the theater. I brought a murderer to poetic justice. And, I encouraged the belated coming to adulthood of Laura Boudron, a woman of considerable talent and character.

So what if my relationship with Stella was more of an alliance than a partnership—ambiguous and impermanent. Although Stella was also looking stressed, at least she was with me every night after the show. We never seemed to have time to talk, but the sex was good. All in all, things seemed to be going my way. So I went home, content for the moment.

I had two weeks left to make my choice: take Stella from Val, or let her go. That must be the choice Madame Claire said I'd face.

When I opened the apartment door I saw the message light blinking on the answering machine. I picked up the phone and listened. It was a message from Radu.

Chapter Thirty-Two

"Professor Spearman," said the disembodied voice on the answering machine tape. "This is Radu...I have some bad...." The message faded out and then back in. "...quality of the connect...I'm calling...remote place in Romania...lucky...phone...wrote me...theft of the L Daybook and Stel...know who did it...been suspicious for some...is the one...illed Ham Laid...sure of...and he...all his action...is what she...I've...away from...of them...I will be back in Buda... days...try again...stay...ert "

The message ended and left me listening to a dial tone. It sounded like Radu figured out who stole the L volume of his journal and probably the photograph of Stella's aunt Stella. That struck me as odd that he could figure it out from there. I had the feeling I already knew who stole the journal and the photograph but I just couldn't remember. It was like it was on the tip of my tongue but I couldn't say it. And Radu figured it out from Romania.

What was Radu doing in Romania? Wasn't Romania many miles from Budapest? Maybe he was on holiday. Oh, well, I thought he said he would try me again when he got back to Budapest, whenever that might be. If it was important, he'd call back. I couldn't call him. He didn't leave his number.

I was weary of thinking. In two hours I would return to the theater for tonight's performance. It would be interesting to watch Lance play Macduff.

I set my alarm for six-thirty and lay down. Sleep eluded me. I kept turning over in my head the idea that I knew more than I knew. That might sound crazy to anyone else, but it made perfect sense to me. Somewhere in me was knowledge that I simply could not access.

I thought I had not slept at all, but I must have fallen into a dreamless sleep because the alarm woke me with a jolt—and with a piece of recovered memory. Val Von Dragon had stolen the picture and the L Daybook. I could see it now, now that I knew it was Val. I could see Val standing in front of the window in the study dressed in his show costume: black swallowtail coat, white boiled shirtfront, starched French cuffs protruding fashionably from the coat's sleeves, and pearl-grey gloves.

I saw Val holding the photograph of Aunt Stella and two volumes of the Daybooks in his left hand as he swung the J volume at me with his right hand. Why had I not been able to recall this before? How did Radu figure it out at that distance? What else did he know? What else did I know?

Maybe I should talk to Stella about this. And then again, maybe not. Maybe I didn't want to know. Maybe I just needed to cruise on automatic pilot for a while longer until some mountain or storm necessitated a course or altitude change. Maybe I should just finish my classes, finish my show, and finish—I broke off my own thought. It was going to take me to, 'finish my relationship with Stella,' and that's not where I wanted to go. That was unthinkable.

I got off the bed, walked to the theater, and put on a show. Even Lance was O.K. in this performance. After the final curtain, Stella returned to the apartment with me.

For the next two weeks Stella came home with me after the show and we made love every night. Her ardor seemed undiminished, even increased, but she was growing weaker. Stella had never looked robust, never close to rubenesque, but each day she looked paler and thinner than the day before. Her pallor and frailty added gravitas to her portrayal of Lady Macbeth as victim but frightened me as her lover.

I thought Stella was not eating well and that worried me, too. She always told me she had eaten before the show and late night snacks like I had were not to her liking.

She was always gone in the morning before I woke up. I know she didn't leave just after I fell asleep. Sometimes I would wake up and find her sitting up in bed, looking at me. Other times, she would be stroking my face or my hair. Sometimes she would lean over and kiss me. Then we'd make love. One night, just before the end of the run, I woke up in the dark and heard her crying. I asked her why. She told me she was so happy it made her cry. I wanted to believe her, so I did. And in the morning she was gone—again.

For two weeks I played three roles, scholar, actor, and lover. By day, I was scholar. I taught class and thought about my thesis. Certainly I had shown that Lady Macbeth was no bloodthirsty virago; she was a faithful and loving companion who took it upon herself to have the strength to do for her companion that which he must do but lacked resolve to do.

By evening, I was actor. I continued to play Macbeth to Stella's Lady Macbeth. Each evening I was better able to portray Macbeth as a man who lacked the final strength to seize that which was foretold as his to have, and, even without the courage to admit it to himself, as a man who pressed his lady to hearten him to fulfill his own ambition. Each evening Stella was better able to portray Lady Macbeth as a loving, but distorted, reflector of her husband's ambition, reflecting an image of ruthless power with all doubts filtered out so she might act, not for her, but for him, so his conscience would be clear because it was she who had acted, not he. And each evening I was better able to deliver the line, "She should have died hereafter. There would have been a time for such a word."

Even Lance came to see that Macbeth recognized that his lady had sacrificed herself to be for him what he must be, but on his own could not be—ruthless. By the words Lance had so aptly butchered a month ago, Macbeth acknowledged his debt to his lady, acknowledged his sorrow, and acknowledged his awareness that, having been deprived even of sleep "to knit the raveled sleeve of care," only death could release her from her torment. Since she was not a warrior, she had no honorable means to seek death; she had to wait for death to kindly stop for her.

By night I was lover, Stella's lover, and she was my lover—until our final performance.

On the night before our final performance, Stella looked more distrait than usual. When I awoke in the deepest hours of the night she was sitting up in bed staring at me and stroking my head. Tears flowed down her face. She had done that before, so I didn't make anything of it except to kiss her, rub her neck and shoulders, and make love until, my passion drained, I drifted back to sleep.

When I awoke a second time, Stella was sitting at the desk, writing. I asked her what she was writing. She said she was writing a letter. She said she couldn't sleep, but if it bothered me, she would stop. I told her it didn't bother me and rolled over and dropped off to sleep. When I awoke a third time, at first light, Stella was gone. She'd left the letter. It was for me.

Dearest Dewy,

I love you. Whatever you may think, or say, or do, I love you, so I must leave you. I will be in seclusion, hidden from everyone.

Much of what I write you already know. Some things you have forgotten because you received the kiss of forgetfulness. I will explain later in this letter. At this moment, you are in grave danger and in even graver danger if I remain here. Val killed Hammond Laidlaw. Val returned from his trip last night and told me this, although I had suspected it at the time. Hammond had been closing in on the truth of Val and of me, and he had shared his suspicions with Radu.

Val did go to Canada. He also went to Europe. While he was in Europe, he did a horrid thing. He attempted to kill Radu, about two weeks ago, when Radu was on a research trip to the Borgo Pass between the Transylvanian Alps and the Carpathian Mountains.

Val was interrupted in his heinous task by local residents who knew and understood what Val was about. Radu did not die. Those people drove Val off. The people who now care for Radu guard him carefully so Val will not succeed at killing him. Radu is delirious and debilitated from acute loss of blood. He also suffers from the "kiss of forgetfulness." But Radu is no fool, and he is on to Val.

In his L Daybook, Radu wrote of his suspicions. In the mountains of Romania, Radu confirmed them. Val is known as Vlad Dracul, a son of the one known in the West as Vlad the Impaler. These things you know but cannot recall because you have been "kissed" by a vampire. We spoke of these things after you and your policeman friend saw me at the truck stop. "Prostitute" you named me. "Whore," you implied. Were that the truth of it, Dewy, were that all it was, everything would be simple and we could love in the natural flow of life. You will begin to recall these things when I am no longer with you and your senses completely clear. I don't need to retell you everything in this letter.

I am no prostitute, Dewy. I am much worse than that. I am a vampire. Not only am I a vampire, I am the consort of Vlad Dracul, Dracula, as you are wont to say. I am his Queen of the Night, his favorite among many, although I am not much favored in this moment, nor shall I be favored in the future.

Radu will recover. When he does, he will expose Val. Val won't be able to remain in New Orleans. He must leave and reestablish himself elsewhere. He requires that I go with him and he plans for us to leave before dawn tomorrow, December 21st. I shall not go with Val so I must hide in my secret place. I will miss our last performance. You will not see me again unless you seek me. I will be open to discovery by you but to no other, especially Val.

I love you, but I cannot be what I am and also be what you need me to be. I no longer want to be what I am, but I crossed my Rubicon. My choice cannot be unmade. Like your Lady Macbeth, I cannot even seek death for release. It must find me, and there is only one way.

When your head clears, you will recall that twice I said, "If you love me you must join me or release me. The first time you did not understand what I was asking. Nor did I explain. You have forgotten the second time because of my vampire's "kiss." Now I ask you a third time. You no longer have the excuse of not knowing or not remembering.

If you love me, join me or release me, but if you love yourself, release me. There is only one way. I have every confidence you will be equal to the task.

I do not lightly love. In my desire for companionship, joy, and love, I hope you will join me. Together we will be immortal. We will find a way to deal with Val.

If you release me, you will release me from a life where I am anathema to all who come to know my true identity, where I am estranged from my daughter, where my grandchildren cannot abide me, where I can only appear by night, where I take no pleasure in food or drink, where I survive only by deceitfully sucking the life blood from unwitting victims, where we can never "grow old together, you and I."

I will say, in my own pathetic defense, I never killed anyone, I never turned anyone, and I never used anyone more than once, with one exception. No, I did not turn you. You are not a vampire. You must desire it, and you must drink my blood.

You twice refused me. I used you twice. I am disgusted by my own wretchedness, but I must use people to survive. In truth, I only used you once, the night we went to hear jazz and ended up here. We did not make love. That came later, but I used you to feed myself, and in spite of myself, I fell in love with you.

The second time was after you saw me at the truck stop and confronted me about being a 'prostitute.' We had it out and I told you everything. It was a tempestuous and passionate night. In the heat of our passion, you demanded that I bite you so you could nourish me, and I did. I was weak.

I regret biting you that second time because it clouded your memory. The 'kiss of forgetfulness' usually serves me well, but this time it failed me. I wanted you to remember, to know what I am, so you could choose with a clear head.

You forgot, and I feared I would lose you if you remembered, so I kept quiet. I did honor the agreement we made that night. I stopped cruising and I stopped feeding. That's why I'm so pale and thin.

I shall continue like this until you join me or release me. It is the only honorable choice I have. On my own, I cannot die, but I can waste away to nearly nothing. That is my choice. What is yours?

Love, Stella.

The writing wavered in front of my eyes; I couldn't tell whether the tear stains on the letter were hers or mine.

Chapter Thirty-Three

I cried; I sobbed; I howled. Memories came flooding back. The truck stop. Our confrontation. Her story. Her confession. Her age. Her invitation. My refusal. My invitation. My pleasure. Her bite. Her body. Her pain. As I exhausted myself and wound down to mere whimpering, I heard someone banging on my door. I looked through the peephole. It was Madame Claire. I let her in

"You are in grave danger. We must protect you. We will keep you safe. Come to my kitchen and have tea and toast."

I wasn't sure how tea and toast would protect me, but I went.

"Don't worry,' she reassured me, "I heard from Radu. He told me to come see you. He was injured but he's recovering. He's in good hands back in the old country. Soon, he'll recover his strength, and he will fight the evil he has uncovered."

She put her tea kettle on and continued. "I sense trouble. It involves a woman. You have stolen this woman and made an alliance with her. Deception and illusion are clearing. Now you're beginning to see clearly. You have a choice to make. Whatever you choose, you will lose something precious, no?"

"Yes."

"I sense your pain. It will become greater. Your pain will be so great that you will shut down and take the inner way. You face the question of your life, no? I am sorrowed that you have so much pain. It's the woman or your life, no?"

"You're probably right."

"How so?"

"Read this," I said, handing her Stella's letter. She read it carefully and then she spoke to me.

"You no longer doubt your Tarot reading, yes? You continue to be in grave danger. You will be safe by day, but you will be at peril at night. Go away, now."

"No. I'll finish the show, and I have my final grades to turn in."

"Is there no one who can perform in your place?"

I thought of Lance. "No, Madame Claire. No one."

"Then we shall protect you well as well as we can."

"With voodoo?"

"I do not practice voodoo, Monsieur Dewy. We will protect you by staying close. I will be with you at the theater tonight. I'll see for myself if you are as good an actor and director as you think you are."

"Thank you, but I'm a big boy. I can take care of myself."

"You are truly the innocent fool, Monsieur Dewy. You've been fortunate so far."

"It's in the cards," I said.

"You need help beyond your own strengths and abilities. Today, go see my old friend, your priest friend, Dr. Fellows. He will be your help and your moral guide."

"Both you and Chan will be my protectors?"

"Yes, and see if your policeman friend will help you, especially to-night. Your enemy is desperate and has little time to act. Keep your-self safe tonight and he may be gone tomorrow, no?"

"Possibly."

"The difference between a fool and a hero is that the hero asks for help. Be a hero, Monsieur Dewy. Ask for help."

"O.K., Madame Claire, I accept help, your help, Chan's help, and Thibodeau's help if he agrees. You'll have a complimentary ticket waiting for you at the theater. With three of you looking out for me, I should be safe until the show is over."

"Yes. And you will come back here with me after the show."

"Do you think your spiritual powers would be enough to hold Val, I mean Vlad, at bay?"

"I was planning to use my Remington 870. I keep it in my shop to chase away robbers."

"If what Stella says is true, you can only kill a vampire with a wooden stake through the heart."

"Perhaps yes, perhaps no. One blast from my shotgun at close range will kill a mortal man. For Vlad, maybe I need two, perhaps three shells. I have two boxes. That is well with you, yes?"

"Yes."

"I'll see you at the theater. Go see Dr. Fellows and call your po-lice lieutenant. Tell Dr. Fellows everything but tell the police lieuten-ant only that Monsieur Val Von Dragon comes back to town to seek revenge on you for stealing his lady. He will believe you."

"How do you know that?"

"Never mind. Just do it. I am sorry I didn't warn you well about the woman, but I think you would not have listened, no?"

"No. I heard what I wanted to hear and I saw what I wanted to see. Now I'm ready to hear and see the truth."

"When the student is ready, the teacher will appear."

"I guess so."

"She loves you, no?"

"Yes."

"And you love her, no?"

"Yes."

"May the Lord have mercy on you both, guide you in the right paths, bless you, keep you safe, and give you peace."

I went to Gudrun Hall to see Chan by way of the Café du Monde where I stopped for coffee and beignets.

"Aren't you Professor Spearman?" said a female on my left."

"Yes, I am," I replied to a young woman who looked as if she could be one of my students.

"I've seen you down at Jackson Square more than once. I've heard about your production of *Macbeth*. I'm sorry I haven't been able to see your production, your performance in particular."

"Do I know you from school?"

"I'm Susannah Coumo. I'm a theater major. I'm not in school this term but you've seen me perform."

I looked at her intently, and then I let my mind go blank. "Crimson Liberty!" I blurted out when I realized who she was.

"Yes. That's me. I do that by day."

"Why aren't you performing this morning?"

"We rotate. It's regulated so there won't be too many of us down there at one time. Today I work the afternoon slot."

"Since you aren't performing after dark, Susannah, why haven't you been able to see us perform one evening?"

"I work banquets out in Jefferson Parrish most nights. Also, it's a matter of money. If I save it, I'll have enough to enroll next term."

"You're the one Radu recommended for Delia in *Four Plays*. Since you weren't at auditions, I cast someone else."

"You might not have cast me anyway, even if Radu recommended me. No matter, I needed to build up my funds."

"If you're free tonight, be my guest. It's our last performance."

"Sure, if I can get someone to pick up my banquet shift. Does that mean I'll be your date for the cast party?"

"No, it doesn't. You're an attractive and talented young woman, but a young woman. I'm a middle-aged man who's freed himself from chasing young women."

"You're not chasing me. I'm coming on to you."

"Thank you for finding me attractive, Susannah, but we'll not connect on that level. Should you decide to come see the performance anyway, a pass in the name of 'Crimson Liberty' will be waiting for you at the box office. I hope you enjoy the show."

"Me too. May come backstage?"

"If the stage manger lets you."

I gave her my third beignet, made my adieu, and walked to the college knowing I was forever beyond chasing young women. I'd taught my last class and there were no final exams in the ones I was teaching. All that remained was for me to calculate my students' final grades and turn them in by the end of the week.

I called Chan from my office and made an appointment to see him at two o'clock. That gave me enough time to calculate and record my students' grades before our appointment but not enough time to turn them in.

As soon as I walked into Chan's office, he motioned for me to sit, and he started speaking before I could utter a word.

"Madame Claire filled me in."

"Are you clairaudient, too?"

"No. She telephoned. We're old friends. May I see the letter?"

I handed him the letter. He sat silently and read it. When he finished reading it, he folded it closed and continued his silence.

"Well?" I asked.

"Well, what?"

"What do you think?"

"More importantly, Dewy, what do you think?"

"I think I'm in danger."

"From...."

"From Val, Vlad, whatever."

"And from whom else are you in danger?"

"From Stella?"

"I'm asking you. Do you feel you are in danger from Stella?'

"No."

We sat silently for a moment.

"Not exactly," I said, but Chan didn't respond.

"Damn it, Chan. Say something."

"How 'not exactly?'"

"I don't know. I don't feel any threat from Stella. She wouldn't harm me. If she was going to harm me she would already have done it, wouldn't she?"

"Would she?"

"How do I know, Chan? Fat lot of help you are. You don't know anything."

"Who does?"

"Stella. And Vlad."

"And...."

"Me, I guess. O.K. Chan. Me. Are you happy?"

"My happiness is not the issue Dewy. Yours is. Why don't you tell me about it?"

"At last, something I can sink my teeth into," I said, lapsing into silence again as I contemplated my unintentional but ironic pun. At least I hadn't resorted to sarcasm.

"Dewy," Chan said, breaking the silence, "I can't listen to you if you're not talking. I'm not here to judge you or anyone else. I'm here to listen and to help you get things straight in your mind. If you find that helpful, then tell me what's on your mind. If not, remain silent, but un-helped by me. It's your choice."

"'A hero is a fool who has learned to accept help.' That's what Madame Claire told me this morning."

"Do you find wisdom in her words?"

"Yes."

"Good, Dewy. You finally said something non-evasive. Now perhaps you can tell me what's on your mind."

"I'm confused."

"I shouldn't wonder."

"Un-confuse me."

"What are you confused about, Dewy?"

"My feelings for Stella."

"Tell me about your feelings for Stella, Dewy."

"I love her."

"You love her?"

"Yes."

"What does that mean to you, Dewy?"

"It means I want to be with her, Chan. It means I want to protect her, to encourage her, to be with her."

"She offered you that opportunity more than once."

"I know, damn it. That all I've ever wanted my whole life, to love someone and to be someone's beloved, to be together forever."

"For eternity?"

"'Therein lies the rub,' Chan. I had never reckoned on forever being forever. I was thinking of a natural lifetime."

"And?"

"What Stella offered me is an unnatural lifetime. Do you realize the disgusting things she has to do to survive? For what? To be immortal? Big deal. Who wants to be miserable forever?"

"It sounds like you have strong feelings about that."

"I think it's disgusting. I wish I had never known about this. Now I recall the first time she told me we could be together forever. I didn't understand what she meant then, or I don't think I did."

"Your memory's coming back."

"Yes. I recall, now, the second time she asked me. At the time, I knew what she meant, but I would not choose. I wanted to have her, but I didn't want to become her kind of 'immortal' to do it. I chose to do nothing except to live for the moment. Yet in the heat of love and passion, I asked her to bite me so I could nourish her with my blood, and then I forgot everything until now."

"You wanted to nourish her?"

"Yes. I love her. I was floored by what she told me, shocked, but, somehow, crazy as it seems, it all made sense. I still love her, and I want to nurture her, maybe to save her."

"To save her?"

"Yes. To keep her from having to deceive people and drink their blood to survive."

"You offered her your blood and she accepted."

"Yes."

"And how long will that save her?"

"Not long."

"How long can you keep that up?"

"Not long."

"Then what?"

"Then I'll have to make a choice. I can join her or I can release her. Or I could ignore the whole thing, which is what I've decided to do until after we close the show tonight."

"Dewy, it comes down to this. You get to chose for yourself what you will or won't do and you will receive the natural and logical consequences that follow. You get to ask anyone you want for help, and they get to decide for themselves whether or not they will help. You have no control over how anyone reacts to your request. That's their choice. Your choices are how you react and what you do. That's all you control."

"So, it's up to me?"

"What you choose is up to you."

"Will you help me?"

"Yes. Was that so hard?"

"Yes, particularly since I don't know what I'm going to do."

"Well, Dewy, I know what I'm going to do. I'm going to the theater tonight with you."

"You and Madame Claire?"

"Yes. She and I agreed on that today. At the very least, I'm going to stick with you until you're out of immediate danger. Vlad is just one step away from being discovered, and I think he would be looking for cover or relocating soon."

"You know, Chan, there's only one way to release her."

"I know, Dewy."

"O.K. I'll go call Lt. Thibodeau and then go to the theater before dark, so I should be safe enough. When will you come?"

"Before dark. So will Madame Claire."

"O.K. In fact, I'm leaving now. I'll call Thibodeau from there."

I left Chan and headed for the theater. On my way, I picked up two hot dogs from one of those hot-dog shaped carts that are a New Orleans fixture, but I couldn't eat them once I had them in my hand. I feared this night would go badly, and the sight of ketchup dripping from my hotdogs killed my appetite.

I arrived at the theater long before dark, just for safety, and made my telephone calls from there. I left Laura a message on her answering machine telling her to replace Stella for tonight's performance. I called Lt. Thibodeau, told him that Val had come back to New Orleans, passed along Stella's warning about Val's intention to thrash me, and asked him to come to the theater this evening for backup. He agreed. I issued backstage passes for Susannah Coumo, Thibodeau, Chan, and Madame Claire

Tonight was closing night. We'd had a good run. Reviews had been excellent. My thesis was secure if unwritten. The house had sold out every night despite Clotilde's attempt to organize a boycott. Receipts were up, Laura was officially a board member, and Clotilde had not set foot in the theater since she resigned. I was delighted.

When Laura arrived at six-thirty, she brought bad news.

"No one within driving distance is available to play Lady Macbeth tonight, Dewy."

"You'll have to do it, Laura."

"Me?"

"Yes, you. You know the lines. You know the blocking."

"But I'm crippled."

"How do you know Lady Macbeth wasn't crippled?"

"They didn't have Lofstrand crutches in those days."

"Laura, they used something. People have been using crutches and walking sticks since prehistoric times. They probably weren't made of carbon fiber like yours, but they were crutches. Crutches or not, you're the only one who can play Lady Macbeth tonight."

She stared at me for a moment. I met her gaze and held it. She must have sensed the level of my resolve because she nodded her head in agreement and said, "I'll get a costume together."

After settling that, Russell Prejean, the chief stagehand, brought even worse news. Lance had just called on the green room phone and Russell answered it. Lance was admitted to Tulane Medical Center with a broken leg and lacerations on his neck and he couldn't remember how it happened. It was a bad situation, but Laura and I handled it. We persuaded Pete to step back in as Macduff and sent Russell to help Bud Hérbert in Pete's place. Luke Martingale stepped in to replace Russell. A good save all 'round.

The rest of the cast had settled into a finely-tuned ensemble. Pete had played Macduff before and Laura knew Lady Macbeth's lines cold. Everything thing was going to be O.K. After all, what else could go wrong?

And then I saw Vlad in the house.

Chapter Thirty-Four

Once the Weird Sisters slithered, flitted, and flashed to begin our performance, my fears lost their potency. Our first act went smoothly, intermission passed without incident, and our second act, beginning with the cauldron's rising, was working like a charm. Pete performed Macduff probably better than I did in college, and Laura was a natural as Lady Macbeth. Pete and I had no opportunity to rehearse the fight scene in Act V, so I did have that to worry about.

When, as Macbeth, I received news that my lady had died and I uttered that famous line, "She should have died hereafter. There would have been time for such a word," I heard sniffling in the house. I had heard sniffling in the house nearly every night since I replaced Lance as Macbeth. I took that as a sign the audience identified Lady Macbeth as victim of her lord's insatiable ambition and grieved her untimely death. My thesis was confirmed. I was on cloud nine. I love it when things come together.

Until they fall apart.

When Macduff made his entrance, it wasn't Pete, it was Vlad. Vlad was wearing Pete's Macduff costume. I looked into the wings toward the stage manager's desk to see if anyone there was trying to explain this to me, but all I could see was Laura Boudron in her Lady Macbeth costume with her face buried in the script. No help there, but the show must go on.

Vlad acquitted himself well as Macduff. His diction was precise. When he challenged me, as Macbeth, he spit out his lines crisply and his elocution was appropriate to the occasion.

Ever the trouper, I soldiered on; and, on cue, I delivered Macbeth's famous line, "Lay on, Macduff, and damned be he who first cries, Hold, enough." At that point, Vlad lit into me with the passion of blood vengeance and he didn't follow the blocking that Lance and I had carefully choreographed so no one would get hurt. He wielded his claymore as if he meant to do me grievous bodily harm, which likely was his intention.

Lance and I had staged the fight so Macbeth would be on the defensive, fighting what he knew to be a losing battle; hack, thrust, parry, retreat, hack, thrust, parry, retreat, and repeat until we were offstage. That's exactly what I was doing, hacking, thrusting, parrying, and falling back, and not only because the script called for it, but I held my own.

Vlad attacked me and I defended myself. As we had originally staged the fight, Macbeth gradually falls back until both he and Macduff are offstage. After some dialogue among the king's retinue who had taken the stage for their brief, triumphal scene, Macduff would march back onstage to show King Malcolm that he'd slain Macbeth. He would raise a pike with Macbeth's head stuck on it to prove his triumph. Bloody warriors, the Scots.

Since the show must go on, my only hope was to keep fighting to stay alive as I retreated offstage using all my skill and strength to ward off Vlad's mighty blows in what truly would become a losing battle unless someone came to my aid, but no one seemed to realize my fight was real or raised a hand to help me. I needed a helping hand, but it would have to come from some unexpected quarter.

Vlad drove me offstage with his unrelenting attack. The standers by didn't seem to become alarmed, perhaps because a fight should continue offstage, but diminish and quickly cease. This fight intensified and continued.

I fully believed Vlad intended to put my real head on that pike instead of the prop head we had prepared, but I continued to hold out valiantly until I tripped. I toppled backwards between the first and second curtain counterweight arbors and landed on my back beside the stage manager's desk. I could roll neither to the right nor to the left. I was pinned between the two arbors, but I still had my sword. Vlad took a mighty swing at my neck. I raised my claymore and deflected his blow, but not by much. Then he kicked me in the groin. While I was racked with pain and nausea, he kicked the sword from my hand. I figured was a goner.

Vlad raised his claymore over his head preparatory to one final hack. He paused momentarily to channel all his strength and coordination into his task, and then he launched his downward stroke.

Immediately, two things happened simultaneously. First, Laura cried out, "Mr. Von Dragon, you can't do that," and slapped one of her carbon-fiber crutches across the tops of my two flanking counterweights, spanning them, about two feet above my supine body. Vlad's swing brought his claymore down on the crutch and splintered it. The crutch absorbed much of the force of Vlad's blow and deflected it, giving me a glancing blow to the deltoid of my left arm, a painful, but not mortal, blow. Vlad had not drawn blood.

Second, the fireball swung across the stage and struck Vlad from behind just below his neck. He hadn't seen it coming. His claymore flew from his hand. He staggered from the blow and fell on me. Before anyone could secure him or pull him off, he bit me.

Chan and Thibodeau attempted to restrain Vlad, but he sprang up, shook them off, and bolted out of the theater.

I looked over to stage right, the direction from whence my help had come, my saving fireball. The only person on the catwalk was Susannah Coumo, my Crimson Liberty. She waved. I hadn't seen her come, but there she was.

I was not able to move unaided. Laura reorganized the final scene without me. As Luke rushed out on stage to secure the errant fireball, Laura pulled off parts of my costume and grabbed enough bits of other actor's costumes to send Mojoe Watkins, the property master, out on stage with Macbeth's virtual head on the pike.

Vlad was gone, I couldn't speak, and Mojoe didn't know the lines, so Laura handed her script to Chan and had him yell Macduff's lines from the wings. Following King Malcolm's speech, she brought down the show curtain and then she reorganized the curtain calls.

Laura sent Mojoe out as Macduff, but when it would have been time for Lord and Lady Macbeth to make their curtain calls, Laura stepped into the breach. She walked out on stage with her remaining crutch. After taking three steps, she stopped, turned, smiled at me, and tossed her crutch into the wings.

"It's time to stand on my own," she said, and hitched herself to center stage unaided. The audience, many of whom had known Laura from childhood and had known of her disappointments and struggles including the present rift with her mother, applauded wildly.

Laura raised both hands to the audience, palms outward, soliciting their silence, and she waited until it came.

"Ladies and gentlemen, we've had an outstanding run with an outstanding cast. This would not be possible without loyal and appreciative patrons such as you. Unfortunately, Miss Maris was unable to appear this evening. I so appreciate your kindness and forbearance in allowing me to make my acting debut. I apologize for our technical error with the fireball."

"Mr. Spearman is indisposed and will not take his curtain call. Both Ms. Maris and Mr. Spearman asked me to tell you how much they love you and to ask you to return to Théatre Vieux Carré in February for *Agnes of God*. Speaking on behalf of myself, I am happy to be here, and I thank you for your support."

She took her bows to a standing ovation. The show curtain closed raising one of the the counterweights that Laura had so recently used as an anvil for her now-splintered crutch, the crutch that prevented Vlad from separating my head from my body.

Chan and Madame Claire helped raise me into a sitting position. Thibodeau stepped away to call in an all-points bulletin for the arrest of Vladimir Von Dragon. Josephine Toulouse, the wardrobe mistress, came rushing up and told us she found Pete sitting in his underwear in the storage room with blood oozing from a wound on his neck and babbling incoherently like he was drunk.

Chan and Madame Claire helped me to my feet. Laura wanted to call the paramedics, but I insisted that Chan and Madame Claire would see to my health and safety. As they helped me to Chan's car, I asked Madame Claire, "Will Vlad's bite make me forget?"

"I have no vision of that, Monsieur Dewy, but I know that you must not allow yourself to forget; you must fight to remember."

Right now, all I could fight was unconsciousness, and that was another losing battle.

"First, I must sleep," I whispered, cotton-mouthed.

Chapter Thirty-Five

Bats swarmed around my head and bit my face with razor-sharp teeth. I couldn't breathe. Vlad was in my face, laughing. He held me by my shirttail as I tried to flee on a floor slick with blood. My blood. The faster I ran, the faster I got nowhere.

My body flashed hot and then cold. Thirst. I was thirsty. When I raised my glass to drink, blood poured out and ran down my body. Rats came to lick the blood. My hand turned to dust and the glass fell and shattered

Vlad shrieked as he tormented me, raking my flesh with his fingernails and throwing brine and vinegar on my wounds. Thousands upon thousands of cockroaches crawled across my body, up the wall, across the ceiling, down the wall, across the floor, and back across my body in a never-ending, perfectly symmetrical procession while Vlad ran shards of the broken glass across my chest and naked, black-haired women with ten-inch tongues licked the blood seeping from my wounds.

Stella floated in front of me in a sea of crimson blood on a slab of white marble. She floated in front of a soldier mounted on horseback, his saber held high above his head. Her thoughts came to me.

"Join me, or release me, but if you love yourself, release me. Fight Vlad. Steel your mind against him. Focus on the white light."

I saw a white light tracing a path through a maze of avenues lined with trees and small houses, but Vlad threw blood in my eyes, blinding me. He raked my body with iron grappling hooks and let the blood drip for the cockroaches to enjoy, the cockroaches that invaded my body and oozed out with my blood.

"Defy me and die, mortal," screamed Vlad's contorted life-mask.

Stella returned in the white light in a travertine limestone building to which the soldier pointed. She lay on an unblemished white marble table, this time in the clear, and whispered to me.

"Find me, Dewy. Hide your thoughts from Vlad. Find me. Follow the path. The soldier points the way. It's in your hands, now."

I collapsed in a haze of sweat and blood as the ordeal began again. With each repetition, I focused more on the white light. With each repetition, Stella waxed and Vlad waned until Vlad imploded and Stella, once dressed in white and now dressed in in crimson, flowed out of my consciousness until only the light remained, and in that white light I awoke.

I awoke fresh and clear. The terrors that had enthralled me had dissipated. The nightmares that gnawed my nerves were gone. I was in my own bed. I was alive. I was awake. I knew what I must do.

It was so simple, so clear. How could I have ever thought anything else? I had to help Stella, and I would need help.

Chan could help. I struggled to the telephone and dialed his number.

"Hello."

"Chan?"

"Dewy? It's four A.M. Are you O.K.?"

"Yes. My night terror broke. Everything is clear. I know what I must do. I have 'screwed my courage to the sticking place,' but I'll need help. Can you come over right now?"

"You've decided."

"No question. I must act now while my thoughts are clear. Vlad is messing with my mind. I need a guide and helper. I've never done this before."

"Nor have I, but I'm here. More importantly, I'll be there. Madame Claire will be looking in on you. She's been checking on you every hour. I'll collect a few things and be there soon. In the meantime, light all the white candles you can find, put on a pot of coffee, take a purifying bath, and read Matthew 26:39."

"Madame Claire has a key and will let herself in. Otherwise, don't open your door to anyone except me. Just so you know it's me, I'll use the secret password for the theater honorary fraternity. I doubt if Vlad has ever been tapped into Alpha Psi Omega."

"O.K., Chan, but don't you think you're being paranoid?"

"Where have you been for the past five hours, Dewy?"

"Right here. Going crazy, having night terrors. Vlad was here torturing me."

"I'm certain Vlad was in your dreams, and I'm not certain they were only dreams. Apparently he can project his image, some sort of astral projection, but I don't believe he can actually pass himself through physical barriers. If you don't let him in, he can't come in unless he breaks down the door."

"You think he might try?"

"Maybe. Even though Madame Claire has been checking on you hourly and taking precautions on your behalf, I'm sure Vlad was there with you, not in corporeal form, but in some psychic sense, some kind of apparition or projection into your subconscious mind. He's working to control your mind. There's something Vlad wants of you, Dewy, and he wants it mightily. So far you've resisted his powers of mind control so he may try to take you by brute force. Vlad has survived for centuries and he didn't do that fighting by the Marquis of Queensbury's rules. He's vicious, ruthless, resourceful, and relentless in pursuit of his goals."

"Let me remind you, Dewy. During these last twenty-four hours, Vlad has severely injured both Pete Vanlandingham and Lance Sterling , he attacked you, and no one has seen Stella. Now do you think I'm paranoid?"

"I guess not, Chan. Stella said Vlad was the one who killed Hammond Laidlaw."

"Why am I not surprised?"

"I think I know why Vlad's after me. It's because of Stella. Stella defied him. Stella left, and Vlad wants her back. He must not know where she is. She must be resisting his power, defying him. But I know where she is. She called to me in my dreams and showed me the way to find her. That's exactly what I'm going to do."

"Don't tell me where she is until I get there. I don't want to know until then. Vlad might grab me if he thought I knew. If he grabbed me, it's certain he would get it out of me if I knew. I'll bring what's necessary. Just don't let anyone in without the password. And light those candles."

"Will that help?"

"Couldn't hurt."

I hung up and spent the next five minutes finding and lighting about two dozen white candles. Radu had them in abundance. I guess he burned them too. Or, maybe Madame Claire brought them up. Garlands of garlic had been hung on each window and on the door, no doubt the work of Madame Claire.

I started a pot of coffee and headed for the shower. I ran the water as hot as I could stand for as long as I could stand it, and then I turned down the hot water and turned up the cold water until I shivered. A brisk rubdown with one of Radu's oversized towels brought me back to life.

The doorbell rang. I wrapped the towel around my waist and headed to the door. It was difficult to make out Chan's face because of the distortion of the peephole's fisheye lens.

"Dewy, move that silly garlic that Madame Claire has foolishly placed on the door and let me in."

"I'm sure Madame Claire was acting out of concern," I said, as I put the night chain on so I could open the door a crack to get a better look.

"Perhaps so, but she is only a foolish and superstitious woman. Hurry and open the door before Vlad appears."

Something wasn't right. Chan respected Madame Clare, and those weren't respectful words. I temporized.

"Hold on, Chan. These locks are complicated. Besides, you haven't told me the secret password."

"Bugger the password. Just open the door. I feel Vlad's presence and I'd rather be in there than out here."

That didn't ring true, either. I heard Chan's voice, but I didn't believe those were Chan's words. I rattled the night chain without turning the deadbolt to open the door as I peered intently through the peephole at Chan's face.

"What was that, Chan? I couldn't hear what you said."

Chan's voice said, "Forget the password. Just open the door, man, there's danger close at hand," but Chan's lips were mouthing "nine, one, one."

I had thought Chan foolish when he insisted I not open the door except with the password, but here he was, his voice saying "Open the door," but his lips mouthing "nine, one, one."

I went to the phone, picked it up, and started dialing. I heard a loud thud against the door followed closely by a second thud. Someone was trying to kick in the door. Brute force. By the third thud, I had reached the emergency operator and told her someone was battering down my door. The operator told me to stay on the line, but after the fifth thud, I heard two explosions, so I broke the connection, ran to the door, and looked through the peephole.

I saw Madame Claire with her shotgun. Chan was leaning against the stair railing clutching his throat. Password or not, I unlocked the door and demanded to know what Madame Claire was doing with her shotgun.

"I wounded Vlad but he is getting away," she said, pointing to her right. Vlad's foot was clearing the edge of the gutter as he clambered onto the roof and disappeared into the night. "I knew I couldn't kill him," Madame Claire said to me, "but I did drive him away. He's now favoring his left shoulder. Now, quickly, before he comes back, help Dr. Fellows move inside. Give him coffee with brandy. I'll go down to the street and take care of the police you called."

I didn't even ask how she knew.

I helped Chan inside. I added some of Radu's brandy to the pot of coffee and made Chan drink it. When color returned to his face, he leaned close and whispered the secret password. No one outside of the theater world would know that. In a croaking voice, Chan told me that when he reached my door, he was seized from behind in a grip so powerful he could neither break it nor could he summon the will to try, and some force had seized his throat, paralyzing his vocal chords. He was only now beginning to get his voice back.

"It's good that Vlad didn't paralyze your brain. I was getting suspicious, but if I hadn't seen you mouth 'nine, one, one' while I heard you telling me to forget the password and open the door, I might have done it. And, thank God for Madame Claire."

"Yes, thank God for Madame Claire. That was Vlad talking, not me. He made his voice sound like mine. He has great powers. We must take care. Are you still up for the task?"

"Absolutely. Are you up to it?"

"More than ever, Dewy, more than ever. I have what we need in this bag, but I'd like to stop by the theater, if you can get in, and pick up a couple of claymores. If Vlad shows up, they might come in handy. I know we can't kill him with them, but you did a serviceable job of holding him off with your claymore at the theater."

"And maybe I should get Laura Boudron's other crutch, too. It might come in handy."

Except for the white part of his clerical collar, Chan was dressed entirely in black. Even his bag was black. So, I dressed in black: black trousers, black turtle-neck sweater, black boots, and black leather jacket. It would be little more than an hour before the sun rose to offer its weak winter warmth and the night was cold, even if it was New Orleans, so I knew I would need my jacket.

We slipped quietly through the courtyard to the street. Madame Claire had pulled the policemen into her shop. When I opened the door to Chan's car, I saw the shotgun and box of shells Madame Claire had left for us.

We drove the six blocks to the theater where I picked up the swords Vlad and I had fought with only hours ago. I wondered if Atlanta Costume Company would care that they had been used in real combat.

I told Chan to drive us to Racetrack Cemetery. My progression would begin at the statue of a mounted soldier, sword raised, on top of the monument to the Confederate States. Chan parked the car and we climbed over the gate into the cemetery. I let my mind go blank and walked a path according to my memory of the white light's tracery. I sensed that Stella was calling me and I trusted my feet to find the way.

The mausoleums looked like little houses, some large, some small. Leyland cypress trees lined the paved paths. As was the custom in New Orleans, a custom borne by necessity, people were often buried above ground in mausoleums. Dig more than a few feet down and you might hit water. After a few minutes of walking through the maze, I saw the mausoleum I had seen in my dreams, if they were dreams. This is where I would find Stella. This mausoleum was large and built of travertine limestone.

I was glad I was wearing my leather jacket. It was still a good half-hour before the sun would rise and begin to warm us with its pale solstice light, and the unusually clear night was cold, especially cold for New Orleans. With the north wind chilling us, I recalled Madame Claire's Tarot image of King Lear and his fool tramping across the desolate wastes into the teeth of the freezing wind, but which one of us was the fool, Chan, or I?

Polaris, the North Star, seemed particularly bright. The remaining stars appeared as silver points studding the obsidian sky which, tinged only the palest of gold at the rim of the eastern horizon, offered the sweet promise of dawn. As I stood under that sparkling, gilt-edged welkin, the dew turned to frost before me.

Chan motioned for me to circle around the mausoleum and check it out. That's what they had taught me in the military: reconnoiter, and secure the perimeter. Maybe Chan had served, too. I made a mental note to ask him sometime.

The mausoleum was about ten paces long on each side and had a domed roof. The double doors, cast bronze with an overlay of wrought-iron grillwork, were on the west side. The original lock, of Nineteenth Century vintage with a pencil-sized pinhole and a narrower, two-inch vertical slot for the wards, had been supplemented by a modern Yale lock. A separate brass padlock secured a chain that wound through the bars of the wrought-iron gates.

The single window was on the east side. In the fading starlight, I could see that the window was glazed with irregularly-shaped pieces with cames between them. The window had been painted over in black, overlaid with wrought-iron grillwork, and covered with hardware cloth, probably to keep vandals from breaking the glass. The double front doors were the only way in or out.

I scanned the area and had not seen anything move. Chan seemed satisfied with our security, so we moved to enter. Chan produced a two-pound blacksmith's hammer from his black bag and gave the padlock a solid whack. Obediently, it fell open, but the Yale lock on the bronze doors presented a bit more difficulty.

"Do you know how to pick a lock?"

"No, Chan, I don't. Do you?"

"Haven't a clue," he said as he pulled a pry bar out of his bag, "but I don't have to. I have a universal key."

I stood guard with two swords at my feet and a loaded shotgun in my hands while the Reverend Doctor Chandler Fellows alternately pried things with his pry bar and smashed things with his blacksmith's hammer until the locks were defeated.

The mausoleum was completely dark. Neither the fading starlight nor the barely-present light of the eastern sky illuminated the apparent void. Chan pulled a pen light from his pocket and shined it around. I was behind him watching his back.

"Give me the swords, Dewy. You keep the shotgun. Let's step inside and close the doors. Once we're inside I'll light candles."

Chan pocketed his pen light and received the swords I held out to him. I held on to the shotgun and stepped quickly inside. My ears were straining to hear sound of any kind, but the only sounds I heard were the echoing sounds of our feet moving across the limestone floor, our breathing, and the sounds of Chan closing the doors.

I strained my eyes to see something, anything, but it was velvet-black, darker than any darkness I had ever known, so it came as a shock when Chan struck a match to light a candle and the cream travertine limestone walls fairly glowed. I could hardly believe what I saw. Stretched out on top of a carved, white marble table was a recumbent statue of a woman in a flowing white gown. But it wasn't a statue. It was Stella.

Stella was laid out on the white marble slab. Her white gown, molded to her lithe, supple form, spilled onto the surface of the stone and her apricot hair framed her face and fanned out in a radiant halo. Her eyes were closed. Her face was drawn as if she were concentrating on something. Chains and cables wound around her and pinned her to the marble table.

"Look, Dewy, the chains. Do you suppose Vlad did that?"

"I don't know, Chan, but I think not. Look at those cables. They're antitheft bicycle cables with tamperproof locks. Those things are virtually tool-proof. The students say they can't be cut with a hacksaw. See how the combination locks are close to her hands. My guess is that she locked herself up, and, by sheer force of will, is refusing to unlock herself."

The bronze doors suddenly banged open.

Chapter Thirty-Six

I felt a rush of numbingly cold air.

"That is precisely correct my dear Mr. Spearman," Vlad hissed. "Your precious Stella foolishly attempts to defy me. She found love, she says, for the second time in her life. That's ludicrous. What could this magnificent woman, my queen, to whom I have given immortality, find with a puny mortal like you? You are so pathetic that you even refused her misguided offer of immortality."

"Stella cannot escape me. She is destined to be my Queen of the Night—forever. I have willed it. No one can circumvent my will. Her pathetic attempt to hide from me and suspend her animation has failed. You have saved me the trouble of finding her, and Dr. Fellows has eliminated my need to bring tools to free her from her self-imposed bondage. Hand me the tools, Dr. Fellows. Now!"

As if he were in a trance, Chan moved to obey.

"And you, my dearest Dewy, you will hand me the shotgun. It is of little use. You cannot kill me with a shotgun. Nevertheless, it is a noisome and irritating thing. Hand it to me, now!"

I couldn't believe what was happening. In spite of my decision, my resolve, and my interest in self-preservation, I meekly handed the shotgun to Vlad. He extracted the shells and tossed the gun on the floor. Likewise, Chan handed over his black bag. Vlad was messing with our minds. I couldn't resist. I could hardly even think, but in the deep recesses of my brain, I heard Stella speak.

"Find your power. Resist. Fight. Overcome."

Vlad closed the doors and commanded Chan to sit with his back against them. From Chan's black bag, Vlad extracted a sharpened wooden stake and hurled it against the wall.

"A puny attempt by a feeble mortal, my dear Dewey. Do you actually think you have the intellect, the cunning, and the cajones to kill me, a son of Vlad Dracula III, Vlad Tepes, whom you know as Vlad the Impaler? Know my name, mortal. I am Vlad Dracul, *Printul de Întuneric*—the Prince of Darkness!"

I summoned every ounce of resistance I could muster and croaked a reply.

"It wasn't for you."

Vlad seized me by my jacket-front and hurled me against the wall. Stars appeared in the mausoleum as a familiar metallic taste arose in my mouth and Vlad's raging faded into the distance, three signs of incipient shock and imminent unconsciousness.

I must have blacked out. As my head begin clearing, I became aware of Stella's words in my head. "Liberate me, Dewy. Find your power. Resist. Fight. Overcome." I lay still for a moment to get my bearings. I figured out who I was and where I was, good signs that I wasn't concussed. I was acutely aware of the sharpened stake Vlad had hurled against the wall because I was lying on it. It hurt.

I covertly moved every joint and flexed every muscle to see if they still worked. The front of my left shoulder felt stiff and the front of my left thigh, my point of contact with the stake, was going to have a deep bruise, but everything moved. Vlad had taken the two-pound hammer from Chan's black bag and was attempting to smash the locks that bound Stella to the table. Chan, glassy-eyed, remained immobile. He was sitting against the closed doors holding his throat. Had Vlad bitten him while I was unconscious?

Stella remained motionless in her self-imposed trance, but her voice spoke loudly in my head. "Resist. Fight. Overcome."

Vlad had the hammer in his hand. I was woozy. Not only was Chan was out of action, he was sitting on both swords. I wouldn't be able to get them before Vlad got to me with the hammer, or worse. The shotgun was out of reach—and unloaded. Two loose shells lay on the floor. The box of shells was in the black bag at Vlad's feet.

That left the stake. I surreptitiously moved my hand under my thigh and gripped the stake. It was substantial, about as long as my thigh and as thick as two fingers, oak from the feel of it, sharpened to a good point, not that a good point would do me much good. I doubted I had the strength to drive it barehanded through Vlad's ribs and into his heart, but I could use it as a club. Maybe I couldn't kill him with a club, but Susannah Coumo had knocked him down with a fireball to his back at our last performance of *Macbeth*.

Madame Claire's shotgun blast slowed him down for a while, too. Maybe I could slow him down with a club. That's all I needed. Just slow him down. Soon it would be dawn and he would leave.

Maybe he wouldn't leave. Maybe he could stay in the dark mausoleum all day. Maybe daybreak would bring people to the cemetery, people who would hear the ruckus and come to my aid. Maybe I could load the shotgun. Maybe I could grab the swords. Maybe. Maybe. I was growing weary of maybe. It was time to act.

I gripped the stake and rose silently to my hands and knees, pausing to make sure my body would obey my brain. My left thigh and shoulder were arguing with me, but I willed them to work. Quietly, I rocked into a crouch and, with a blood-chilling yell, sprang at Vlad and whacked him hard across the back of his head.

He staggered, but he did not stay his hammer swing. I gave him a backhanded whack to his left kidney with the stake. He listed, but he reached back with his left hand and gripped the stake. Even though he was shaken, he was still strong. He jerked the stake down and held on, making us adversaries in a tug-of-war. He pivoted on his left foot and swung the hammer at my head.

I stepped in close, raised my left arm to meet his right arm and deflect his arm and the hammer, and then I ducked. The force of his swing carried his body to the left. I let go of the stake and let the force of his swing overbalance him, grabbed his right wrist with both hands, pulled him onto my back, raised up to my full height, and threw him over my shoulder, slamming him to the floor—right on top of the shotgun.

Vlad was momentarily stunned. Even so, with the hammer in his right hand, the stake in his left hand, and the shotgun under his body, he still controlled the weapons and I was unarmed.

Slow him down. Slow him down? What would slow me down? Doubt. Fear. Injury. How could I bring Vlad to doubt? What could I do to create fear? What could I do to injure him?

Vlad already doubted his power, his hold on Stella. Partly because of me, Stella was defying him, and he was using a bully's tools to reclaim her. Despite his arrogant assertions to the contrary, Vlad already feared me because I had frustrated and hindered him.

That left injury. What could I do to injure Vlad? Continue to attack him? Yes, that's what bullies respond to. That's what they fear most, pain, getting hurt. That's what I had to do to resist him, to increase his fear and his doubt—hurt him. But how?

As Vlad lay on the floor, acting on impulse, I stepped closer to him and raised my foot to smash it down on his wrist to loosen his grip on the hammer. If I had the hammer, I'd have a weapon. Vlad anticipated my move. He released the hammer and shot his hand upward to deflect my foot even before it began its downward arc.

Vlad pushed up against my upraised foot, overbalanced me, and propelled me, arms pumping to maintain my balance, toward Chan. When I fell, I managed to avoid landing on Chan, but not by much.

"Resist. Fight. Overcome."

Stella's voice spoke to me in my mind. I looked at her lambent form recumbent on the marble table. She had lost her earlier sepulchral visage of deep concentration and now appeared serene, glowing, despite the turmoil surrounding her, as if she had turned over her struggle to me and to my resolve to liberate her.

I picked myself up from the floor and checked Chan. He was still sitting on the swords and clutching his throat but he was breathing easily and coming out of his catatonia. He looked at me and gave me the barest of nods."

To give the bully his due I challenged Vlad directly.

"If you're so powerful why don't you take me on, *mano a mano*, just like we did in the theater? You against me, winner takes all."

"I already have it all, mortal. I take what I want. There is nothing you can do to stop me."

"It looks like I've been slowing you down," I said as I pulled the claymores out from under Chan and slid one across the floor to Vlad. At least we'd both be armed.

Using a claymore is a physically exhausting process of hacking and chopping. The idea is to clobber your opponent before he clobbers you. The edge of a claymore doesn't need to be particularly sharp because the sword has such great mass that, when wielded in an arc that ends at your opponent's leg, or trunk, or neck, it does considerable damage even if your opponent is protected by clothing or light armor.

It takes a normal man both hands to wield a claymore so there is no hand free to hold a shield. It is blade to blade, man to man, or perhaps in this case, man to beast.

Vlad was giving as good as he got and probably a little better. I thanked my guardian angel for the stage fighting training I had taken at the Shakespeare Tavern in Atlanta and the experience I had gained working with Vic Lambert in stage fighting and in interactive theater, but Vlad was well-schooled, too.

He landed a blow to the back of my left shoulder, the one that was aching from his having thrown me against the wall. I landed a blow to his leg. He pulled back. I no longer entertained any thought of taking him if I had ever thought it possible before, but as long as I could stand, Vlad could not win.

My objectives were to survive until we were discovered or until sunrise, whichever came first, although I was beginning to wonder if sunrise would make much difference.

I didn't know how long we had been fighting, but the sun must have risen by now. Then why was Vlad still here? Was that the purpose of the blackout paint on the stained glass window, to keep out the sun, to provide a daytime resting place for creatures of the night? If that were true, I had only two options. I could fight to the death, which would likely be mine since I could not kill Vlad with a sword, or I could hope someone would discover us and give me help.

I confirmed the rising of the sun when I saw light beaming through pinholes in the black paint covering the stained glass window. That light illuminated the window just enough for me to make out the picture in the glass: Samson bringing down the pillars of the Temple. I wished it had been Samson slaying the Philistines with the jawbone of an ass. That would inspire me.

Vlad was limping and he was favoring his left shoulder, the one Madame Claire had blasted with her shotgun. Perhaps the increased illumination from the partly-occluded sunrise was slowing him down, or perhaps I was engaging in wishful thinking because, however slowly Vlad was moving, I was moving slower.

I continued to meet Vlad stroke for stroke as we danced around the marble table. I juked to avoid tripping over Chan. My sword grew heavy and my dancing devolved into shuffling. I was the aging prize fighter who still had the capacity to take the blows but lacked the strength to knock his opponent down or the wisdom to end the fight.

Were it not for Stella's voice inside my head reinforcing my resolve, I would have flagged completely. Fear of dying was no longer enough to sustain me. Only my motive to save Stella kept me going.

Motivation notwithstanding, mortality caught up with me: I no longer yelled, I wheezed; I no longer danced, I shuffled; I no longer attacked, I defended. I could only stand my ground for a moment at a time until I fell back again. I could raise my claymore no more.

I halted. My chest was heaving and the tip of my claymore was resting on the mausoleum's white limestone floor.

Vlad capitalized on my weariness and his unnatural strength. He held the stake in one hand and his claymore in his other hand as a matador holds his two swords at the ending of a bullfight when the bull, injured from the lances of the picadors and exhausted from his waltz with the toreadors, drops his head. The matador boldly inserts one sword, and then the other sword, into the bull's massive neck between the fifth and sixth vertebrae and brings the bull to his knees in the white, sun-bleached sand that eagerly accepts his warm, flowing blood and provides him an incarnadine repose as his life force bleeds away.

I took a step back to create enough space to attempt one more swing with my claymore, but I was so weary and clumsy that I tripped over the black bag, fell backwards, and landed sitting down with my back against the marble table. Vlad threw down the stake and made a two-handed swing with his claymore. It connected with my claymore and knocked it from my hand.

I was weaponless and exhausted, but proud. I refused to bow my head to accept my *coup de grâs*. I continued to entertain the nearly-impossible hope that help would come.

Vlad stood with his back to the stained glass window, raised the hilt of his claymore to the level of his burning-red eyes, and held it with both hands as if it were a long dagger poised to pierce my chest with one powerful, two-handed stab

I prayed for deliverance, and I heard it coming. I heard the unmistakable sound of a shell entering the chamber of a shotgun.

Chan!

Vlad heard it too, grimaced with horror, and ducked. The blast nearly deafened me. Chan missed Vlad, but he hit the window, taking out all of Samson and most of the Temple. The early morning sunlight streamed through the hole.

Vlad screamed.

"Quickly, Chan," I said, laboring for breath sufficient to speak, "open the doors. Lord knows, I can't."

The doors swung open. I felt the rush of chilled air as the morning light from the clear, western sky illuminated the interior of the mausoleum with defused light. I looked up and saw cherubs painted on the ceiling. Maybe I wasn't done for just yet. I redirected my attention from the cherubs to Chan. He was loading another shell into the shotgun.

"Shoot him, Chan," I wheezed, even though a second blast would likely be too little. Vlad shrieked again and I looked in his direction. He shrank in upon himself, writhing in agony, until nothing remained but black clothing on the floor. Not only too little, another shotgun blast would also be too late.

Vlad, or what was left of Vlad, had flown out the open doors. I attempted to spring up to follow, but my spring was sprung.

"Let it go, Dewy. You've done well to survive. Vlad is a formidable adversary. Perhaps you will meet again, but Vlad is not why you came to this place. My confusion is lifting and my voice is returning. Quickly, while we're alive and alone, be about your work."

"Vlad didn't bite you?"

"No, but he made me speechless again. I'm recovering. Quickly, it's full daylight outside. People might start coming around."

Chan closed the doors. I summoned my residual energy and crawled over to retrieve the hammer and stake. As Chan returned to the marble table, he mumbled parts of various church rituals I had heard before, "Ashes to ashes, and dust to dust," words like that.

I couldn't focus on what he was saying. I could only focus on what I was doing and what I was feeling. Slowly I rose to my knees. I planted one foot on the floor. Holding on to the marble table, I pulled myself up.

Stella's body was before me. She was beautiful and I loved her.

"Release me," I heard her say with unmoving lips. I leaned over and kissed them. They were warm.

I heard more bits and snatches of Chan's ministrations as I went about my work. "Let this cup pass from my lips....Not my will but Thine be done...."

Before my knees buckled, before my resolve dissolved and doubt clouded my brain, I centered the point of the stake between Stella's breasts and raised the hammer above my shoulder. With the mightiest blow I could summon, I drove the stake into her heart.

My right hand dropped to my side and the hammer fell to the floor, but I kept my left hand on the stake between Stella's breasts as crimson blood flowed from her mortal wound and set her at liberty. Her blood was warmer than her lips had been. Tears dropped from my face and mingled with her flowing blood, salt tears into salt blood. How many tears and how much pain had I released in that crimson flood?

Chan's ministrations crept into my consciousness.

"A Buddhist practice, Dewy. The body does not die all at once. It dies in stages from the root chakra to the crown chakra. I must tell the soul what is happening to it, particularly where Stella may have a karmic block, so her soul will not be frightened. We can ease her transition."

I couldn't speak. I simply listened as Chan spoke to Stella, now dead as far as I could tell.

"You are experiencing the overlapping of your consciousness and universal consciousness. Try to hold that."

Chan paused for a moment before he spoke again. "If your soul is lodged in your crown chakra, then you have already ascended, but if you have missed that, try to bring into your consciousness the Lord God who has been of your worship in your lifetime...."

My mind faded in and out as Chan continued.

"...the fourth Buddha of the throat chakra. If your karma is blocked here, you struggle with the lesson of learning to love by letting go. The five Buddhas will smash your ego with terror. Let go of your ego and let these radiances hold you."

Perhaps I was imagining things in my shock, exhaustion, and emotional overload, but when Chan finished these last few words, I saw something move from Stella to the window, and I was seized in my throat.

I was seized in my throat, but there was nothing there, nothing I could taste or feel, but that's what happened. I was not seized by my throat; I was seized in my throat, and I began sobbing.

Chan's voice became increasingly faint as I sank to the floor and into oblivion.

Chapter Thirty-Seven

I close my eyes and vivid images overwhelm me. I can't sort out which ones are memories, stories Chan and Madame Claire told me, or my own phantasmagoric creations. I hardly need to close my eyes to see Vlad's face. I see it sometimes in my wakeful mind and often in my dreams. It's a hideous face, full of hatred and contempt, not his *faux masque charmant* fashioned to seduce the unwary. I don't know if Vlad is reaching out to find me or I if carry him with me. Some things I don't want to think of at all.

Madame Claire told me I was catatonic for three days and semi-conscious for another seven before I came around. Chan turned in my grade book fulfilling my duties to Gudrun Hall.

My daughter called on Christmas day, but I was semi-conscious and hardly coherent. Madame Claire told her some half-truths about my having laryngitis. Chan composed a brief, upbeat letter to Elizabeth and had me sign it before I slipped back into near-catatonia.

Even when I was lucid I had difficulty speaking, but I reacted so violently each time Chan and Madame Claire attempted to take me to a hospital that they continued to nurse me in Radu's apartment.

I would have to vacate Radu's apartment soon. The woman who was hired to fill in for him next semester had also been promised his apartment and she was expected on January 15th.

Chan brought over the Book of Kells and a Joseph Campbell piece on death. When I discovered the ceremony Chan performed at Stella's release, I wept. At first I was wracked with silent sobs, but soon I wailed and howled, just as I had done when Stella was with me and I became consciously aware of the truth of our existence and of our relationship. For some reason Chan and Madame Claire were pleased. I was miserable.

Chan arranged for me to stay at a lamasery in California to complete my mourning, recuperate, and, as I was able, write my master's thesis. He put my car in storage, shipped my papers to the lamasery, and flew out there with me on January 10th.

Under the head monk's guidance, I worked in the garden and I read. I made desultory attempts at journaling. Staring at blank pages was the best I could do at writing my master's thesis.

I could not dismiss Stella from my mind. Even now, I have but to un-focus my eyes to see her green eyes, her apricot hair, her fair skin, and her crimson blood flowing over my hand. I would never be at peace with this until I wrote the story.

For two months, other than receiving three letters, one from Alex inquiring about my health, one from Inge inviting me to teach on a one-year appointment, and one from Laura offering me a one-year contract as artistic director of TVC, I had no contact with the outside world.

On a fine mid-March afternoon, when the California poppies were shining gold on the hillsides, the head monk summoned me to his quarters and handed me his telephone.

"Dad, is that you? How are you feeling?"

"Much better, Elizabeth. Thanks for calling. How did you get the number here?"

"Dr. Fellows gave it to me. Why are you there? Are you O.K.?"

"I'm O.K. I just had a mid-life crisis, that's all. This is a peaceful place to be. I'll write my thesis before I leave. I'm O.K., really."

"If you're sure. Listen, Dad, I've got wonderful news. I'm pregnant. I'm due in September, around the 21st."

"That's wonderful. You sound so happy."

"I am, Dad, but I'm a little spooked, too."

"Worried about parenting?"

"Not that. I know it's a big responsibility. Thanks for doing as well as you have with me."

"You're welcome. Your mother and I had two really good babies to work with."

"Dad, let it rest. Mom and I will work things out eventually. Just don't push me.

"O.K., then, what's got you spooked?"

"A dream. I had a weird dream. In my dream my guardian angel, Michael, appeared and told me I was with child. You know, just like when Gabriel appeared to Mary."

"Did Michael also say that you were a handmaiden of the Lord?"

"No, he didn't. David definitely is the father of this child. We can even name the day and hour. David had been working on call day and night and sleeping at the hospital since December 9th. I stayed out late at a solstice party on the 20th. I figured I could stay out late because there was no one to go home to and I'd be able to sleep in the next morning. I didn't have to show up at the library until noon on the 21st."

"At least, that was my plan. David got a break at the hospital and came home about midnight. I wasn't there, so he crawled into bed and fell asleep. I got home about an hour later and didn't have the heart to wake him up."

"He woke up on his own, about daybreak, with passion on his mind, and we made a baby. Around noon he got called back to the hospital and didn't get home again for another ten days. I had Christmas dinner with him in the hospital cafeteria right after I called you and spoke with Mrs. Claire."

"Soon after daybreak on December 21st had to be the moment. In my dream, Michael said it was the right time to give us a baby, a Star Child, and she would bring joy into our lives."

"She?"

"It's too early to confirm that one-hundred percent, but in my dream, Michael said our baby would be a girl—with green eyes."

"Green?" I asked, my voice choking.

My eyes unfocused. Stella was there.

"Yes, Dad. Green eyes. I don't know how I'm going to explain that since my eyes are blue and David's are brown."

"Lots of people have green eyes, Pumpkin. Your mother's eyes are hazel."

"I know that, Dad. Why are you calling me Pumpkin? You haven't called me Pumpkin in a dozen years."

"Not since you turned thirteen and told me you weren't a little girl anymore."

"Maybe I grew up too fast, Dad. You sound wistful. Are you missing Mom?"

"I was thinking of green eyes, Pumpkin."

"How much longer are you going to stay at the monastery?"

"Lamasery. It's a lamasery. I'll stay a few months more. I don't need to worry about money and I'm accomplishing things here. I'm working on a manuscript I am compelled to write, and then I'll turn my attention to writing my thesis. The guy I was filling in for at Gudrun Hall decided to stay in Hungary permanently. They want me to be a visiting professor for a year starting next fall, and Théâtre Vieux Carré asked me to come back as their artistic director on a one-year trial."

289

"That's wonderful, Dad.

"I'm thinking over both offers. I plan to stay here through May, and then I want to visit you and David. As good as I may have been as a dad, I have a feeling I'm going to be an even better grandfather. It's important to be present for your family in their time."

"I don't have any complaints, Dad."

"Thanks, Pumpkin. Will you tell your mother, soon?"

"It's hard for me to talk to her. She's still acting weird."

"Maybe an impending granddaughter will give the two of you something to talk about. She's had experience with pregnancy and childbirth. As I recall, she was present at yours."

"Oh, Dad, don't be so corny. I'll call her too, soon."

"Good, Pumpkin. I know she'd like to hear from you even if she seems unable to make a call herself. Give her a chance to find her way. Maybe she's going through her mid-life crisis, too."

"O.K., Dad. I'll try."

"O.K., Elizabeth. Anything else?"

"Just one more thing, Dad. In my dream, Michael told me we will name our baby Stella because she's a Star Child. That's not a name from anywhere in our family, or David's, so I'm hesitant. What do you think?"

With my last ounce of courage, I controlled my voice well enough to fool Elizabeth, but on the inside I could hear it crack. Loss welled up and nearly engulfed me. All I could say was, "Let it go."

"What? Oh, let go of my resistance. Maybe so. Stella is a nice name. I'll think about it. Thanks, Dad. Thanks for being there, and thanks for letting me go without abandoning me. Write me when you can. I love you. Bye."

"I love you," I croaked, and I managed to click off before the sobs began wracking my body.

Nobody warned me that letting go would hurt so much.

~~~

Coming in the fall of 2013 from Georjes Press

The Cuban Connection

I came to loathe three things in the army—getting waked up by fly-boys at O-dark hundred, getting pushed around by the brass, and being shot at. I learned to ignore the flyboys. I've almost learned to ignore the brass. I've never learned to ignore being shot at.

I was rudely awakened by airplane sounds bouncing off the rock face on my right. I turned my head left, toward the valley, to discover the source. In the pre-dawn light of the longest day of the year, I could just make out a multi-engine plane heading toward me with its nose at a fifteen-degree take-off angle. I could handle that annoyance as long as the brass didn't push me around or someone shot at me.

The plane swooped up over the narrow valley of the roadbed, gained altitude, and cleared the trees my jungle hammock was tied to by about ten meters which is about ten yards on a football field. As the plane climbed over the rock face on its way to the crest of Turkey Knob, its engine noises vanished, consumed by the dense vegetation of the Smoky Mountain National Park.

Even though I was irritated, I had to admit the pilot was pretty good, but foolish, to fly that close to the rock face. I wondered if it was the plane I heard coming though earlier going the other direction.

It must have been one of those low-level military flights I read about in the *Knoxville News-Sentinel*. Sometimes they flew right into the side of a mountain usually no more than ten meters short of the crest; but, generally it happened to flights coming up from the coastal plain and flying over the mountains from the leeward side, not from the Tennessee Valley side like this fly-boy had just done. The crashes probably had to do with faulty altimeters and prevailing air currents.

The prevailing winds came from the Tennessee Valley and passed over the ridge of the Smokies toward North Carolina and squeezed enough water out of the air to make the western side of the Smokies a virtual temperate zone rain forest. That same wind made hang gliding so good when it wasn't raining. On a great day, the mountain ridges created standing air waves that could keep a hawk aloft for hours without having to do so much as flap a wing. It could keep a hang glider aloft, too. I'd been thinking about taking up hang gliding and I had two months of summer left to do it.

As I drifted in and out of my semi-reverie, visions of hang gliding over the Smokies pushed me to commit. I would master hang gliding by the next new moon, or at least before fall semester began.

My reverie was shattered by the familiar clunk of single-lens reflex camera's mirror locking up. The sound had come from below me. Looking down the slope I spotted a photographer in camouflage clothing crouching behind a blooming Catawba rhododendron that rose a full meter above the edge of the slope.

I followed what I judged to be the photographer's line of sight. Looking further down the steep slope in the burgeoning daylight, I saw the small paved road that ran just on the far side of Harmon Branch, a creek that drains Harmon Cove.

Across the road were two buildings. One building had automobiles, trucks, and assorted vehicle parts scattered about. Further up the hill I saw a small cabin and immediately spotted two men standing on the porch. They were looking in the direction the plane had gone. One of the men wore a campaign hat like marine drill instructors wear and looked as if he might be in some kind of uniform. The other man looked completely civilian and appeared to be wearing a light grey or silver skull cap.

Just below the porch sat a green and white sheriff's car complete with red and blue bubble-gum lights on a rack. I followed the line of the road and saw that it angled down the hill toward the cove, made a sharp turn, and came back down to a parking lot beside the second of the two buildings at the bottom of the hill.

I didn't have the foggiest idea of what was going on, but I didn't intend to lie in my hammock wondering about it forever. In a normal tone of voice, I spoke in the direction of the photographer's back.

"Do you think they've seen us?"

The photographer jumped up like a startled jack rabbit, slipped on the steep slope, and skidded, feet-first, into the rhododendron making a racket that caught the attention of the two men across the way.

The silver-crowned civilian stepped into the cabin. The uniformed man snatched up a rifle and squeezed off a round in my direction. I heard the slug splat on the rock face about three meters above my jungle hammock. The uniformed man bolted to the cop car, pulled out a bullhorn, and sounded out across the valley.

"This is Chief Deputy Crawford. You, up there on Turkey Point, stay where you are. I'm coming up to talk to you."

As I lay there forgiving the relatively mild rudeness of the early morning flyboys and vowing to even the score with the uniformed bully who shot at me, I heard a woman's voice speak from the bush.

"Horse feathers," she said. "Listen, whoever you are, who are you? Are you with Chief Deputy Crawford? What are you doing up here? Trying to scare a girl half to death?"

She stuffed her camera into an equipment bag and pulled out something that she held near her face. Whatever it was didn't look like a gun and she wasn't pointing it at me, so I felt fairly safe.

"No, I'm—"

"Never mind that just now. What I really need is a park ranger. Do what I tell you, please. I'm not a crook, I'm a photographer. I've been working on a moonshine story, you know, illegal whiskey. Chief Deputy Crawford told me to keep my dirty-words nose out of his county. I don't think he's positively identified me this morning and I'd like to keep it that way. I'd advise you to do the same. Some folks around here are downright mean. Have you got a hat?"

"What?"

"A hat. You know. You wear it on your head. Have you got a hat?"

"Sure."

"Can you put it on before you get out of that green thing you're trussed up in?"

"No. I stuffed it in my pack. Why?"

"So they won't get a good look at your face."

"No problem. This thing zips on the other side. I'll just slip out and use the hammock for a screen until I can properly disguise myself."

"Great. Then come down here and help me out of this rhododendron. My feet skidded up into some branches and I've got another branch across my tummy that won't let me sit up to untangle my feet. I may have turned my ankle, too. Anyway, it's wedged in."

I guess her piece of equipment wasn't going to help much because she stuck it back into her bag. I slipped into my tan slacks, my wool socks, my boots, and slipped out of my jungle hammock. I pulled a well-crushed golfer's hat from my pack and jammed it on down to my ears. For added measure I tied a bandanna around my neck and pulled it high up under my chin. To ward off the early-morning chill I pulled on a dark green wool shirt. When I stooped to tie my boot laces, I saw that Chief Deputy Crawford was nearly down to Harmon Cove Road.

"What happens when that cop gets here? Won't he recognize you?"

"With any luck, he'll change his mind about making the climb. If not, I'll keep my hat low and my mouth shut. We can stick my equipment bag in your pack and tell him we were just camping out."

"With only one jungle hammock?"

"Tell him we were sleeping together. People do that, you know. If you have to say my name, call me Sally. Sally Lucille Fowler. I came up here from Atlanta to go camping with you. I got laryngitis and can't talk. Then I fell in the bushes and hurt my ankle. Okay?"

"Okay, Sally, but there's barely enough room in there for me."

"We're real close."

I lifted the branch that held her down, undid the forked branch that wedged in her ankle, and helped her scramble out of the bush. She rotated her ankle tentatively and only winced a little.

"It moves, but I don't think I can make a run for it. Help me up the slope to our hanging love nest. Did you really sleep in that thing?"

"Yes, and so did you as far as Chief Deputy Crawford is concerned. Anyway, aren't we still in the park? This isn't his territory, is it?"

"Sort of. Harmon Cove and everything you can see looking towards that cabin is inside Luther Crawford's county. So is everything across the state road. Turkey Point is technically in his county, but it's also inside the park. The rangers generally look after things up here. But, jurisdiction or not, I don't want Crawford to recognize me."

I stood up and shaded my eyes with my hand, mostly to hide my face, and looked across the valley at the cabin on the opposite slope. I spotted the double glint of field glasses staring back at me. I also saw a light-green sedan make the turn off the state road into Harmon Cove, pull over to the side, and stop.

The man who emerged from the sedan looked like a park ranger. He crossed the creek and headed in our direction. I lost sight of him as he approached the trail head to Turkey Point. A few minutes later Chief Deputy Crawford appeared where the ranger had disappeared and headed back to his cop car. I guess the park ranger must have won the jurisdictional dispute.

"Well, Sally, or whoever you are, it looks like the Lone Ranger rides again. A park ranger just headed off the sheriff at the pass."

"Chief Deputy," she corrected.

"There's still a watcher across the way. Act normal. Come on, I'll help you up the slope and we'll make lemon tea."

"Lemon tea is normal?"

"Normal enough. Just sit still and watch," I said, as I helped her up the slope to a fallen tree where she could sit with her back to the cabin and her leg propped on a rock. We were in the morning shadow of the rock face. Even so, she pulled her wide-brimmed camouflage hat far back on her head so even her neck was hidden from the watcher. I put half a liter of water to boil on my butane stove and chose this moment to answer my early morning call of nature.

"Excuse me for a minute, Sally. While the water's heating, I'll step behind a convenient tree and answer nature's call."

"Don't mind me, but remember, you're being watched."

I couldn't forget. I didn't know why we were being watched, but I was going to find out one way or another and do something about it.

When the water came to a boil, I dropped in two tea bags and eight lemon quarters. Three minutes later I removed the tea bags and gingerly squeezed the hot lemon quarters until most of the juice and pulp oozed out. I dumped the tea bags and lemon rinds into a self-sealing plastic bag and dropped the bag into my portable stainless steel garbage canister. I opened a similar canister and drizzled out Tennessee sour gum honey into the hot infusion.

"I only have this one pot for cooking and for eating. If you care to join me for a cup of tea, we'll need to share it. I don't have any contagious diseases. Do you?"

"You mean like syphilis or herpes?"

"Or influenza, scrofula, or areopagitica."

"Hold on," she said. "I've heard of scrofula, although I can't recall what kind of disease it is, but I know *Aeropagitica* isn't a disease. It's an essay by John Milton. It was his attack on censorship.

"I guess you don't have it, then," I said, rather pleased with my cleverness, as I handed her the pot. "Neither do I."

She took a long, slow slip. "This is a lot better than I thought it would be. It really hits the spot. In fact, it's absolutely delicious. I may not leave you any."

"You may not have time to finish it. Here comes the ranger."

"Good morning," the park ranger said to us as we sat sipping our lemon tea. "The chief deputy wants to know if you saw or heard anything suspicious this morning."

"Why didn't he come up and ask us himself?" I asked.

"Jurisdiction. I was on my way to inspect fire road out of Harmon Cove. To humor our good neighbor, I'm making a small detour to ask if you two saw or heard anything suspicious this morning."

I wondered if I should say something about the woman. She was suspicious, well, maybe just bodacious. I thought better of it.

"I heard a low-flying airplane, likely one of those military training flights. What would the chief deputy be suspicious of, moonshiners?"

"As a matter of fact, that's exactly what he said he was looking for. How'd you know?"

"Lucky guess. As you can see, we don't have a still here. Moonshiners don't actually set up in the park, do they?"

"Not often. By the way, I'm Ranger Norton. May I see your back country camping permit?"

I fished out my permit and handed it to him.

"We're running an ecological survey of park use this week. We call in every contact we make to see how closely back-country hikers stick to the plans they filed at the ranger station."

Ranger Norton unhooked a small radio from his belt and called Cosby Sector HQ. When he got a go-ahead, he announced that he made contact with Freidrich Schiller Gilmore of 178 Euclid Circle in Knoxville at the rock face of Turkey Point on Turkey Knob.

"I'm actually from Gatlinburg," I corrected. "I'm building a log house there on Persimmon Court. I've mostly moved in,"

"Thank you, sir," Norton said, "but I have to call 'em as I see 'em. That's part of the research protocol."

The voice on the other end of the radio transmission came back. "Say, Norton, is that Professor Gilmore?"

"Assistant Professor, actually," I said.

"He says 'Yes,' Norton said back into the radio.

"I had a class under him at the university. Best damn' professor I ever had. And right on his plan, too. Over and out."

"Well, professor," Norton said, "your first unsolicited testimonial of the day." He turned to Sally. "May I see your permit, too?"

The woman lifted her face and looked squarely at Ranger Norton.

"I'm Sam, the photographer from Gatlinburg. You must have seen my pictures around there. I'd prefer that Chief Deputy Crawford not know it's me up here. I hiked in from the Mountaintops Lodge parking area just before dawn. I wanted to get some sunrise pictures looking out over the Tennessee Valley. You don't actually think two people could sleep in one jungle hammock, do you."

"I've seen stranger things tried around here," Norton said.

"Since I wasn't camping, you won't have to call me in, will you?"

"No."

"So much for protocols," I said. "It reminds me of what some researchers used to do with oppositional laboratory rats, the ones that refused to make the correct turn in maze, the ones that failed to confirm the researcher's hypothesis."

"What was that?" Norton asked.

"Let me put it this way. Have you ever seen a starving laboratory cat?"

"I give you my word, Professor Gilmore; I won't feed anyone to the predators. I'm required to call in contacts with campers I encounter away from the shelters, not hikers. No camp, no call. I told them they would undercount off-trail use if they ignored the day hikers but I do what I'm told. Besides, the main focus is to see if back-country campers stick to the plans they file at the ranger stations."

"No offense intended. I see lots of research proposals. I'm expected to look for defects in them. It's an occupational disease."

"I hope it's not contagious," the woman said, laughing. Her green eyes sparkled.

"None taken, professor," Norton said. "Now, if you'll excuse me, I've got to go down and chat with Chief Deputy Crawford for a bit and then make my rounds. I'll tell him a couple of campers fell into a rhododendron thicket and they didn't see or hear anything suspicious."

As Norton turned to leave, he said, "Good day."

Good day, indeed. It wasn't much of a good day so far, but it could turn out to be a good day. I could be starting on an adventure with an attractive woman. I'd like to see her in something more revealing than her camouflaged fatigues and jungle hat, but I had caught the sparkle in her eyes when she laughed and that attracted me.

I saw from the odd wisps of hair slipping out from under her hat that her hair was dark brown. I saw no freckles on her fair skin. She probably weighed about one hundred and fifteen pounds or so. I was certain I could carry her for a couple of miles, but it wasn't my idea of the most fun thing we could do together.

I asked her about her ankle.

"It'll do, more or less. Are we still being watched?"

I sneaked a look at the cabin. We were. I told her to sit still while I broke camp. I put two trail bars in my pocket, packed everything else, and carefully lashed the pack fly to the D-ring with my personal favorite pack-fly-lashing knot, two half hitches.

I hoisted the pack onto my shoulders, grabbed my walking stick, and assumed command.

"Let's move out," I said.

"I need to eat something to have enough energy to hike out."

"Here," I said, fishing out a trail bar from my pocket and handing it to her. "Eat this. It'll keep your backbone from rubbing your belt buckle." Sometimes I say the classiest things.

I held my walking stick out to the woman.

"Here, take this. Let' get moving, and then you can tell me all about it starting with your real name."

Contact the author at
MorrisonGW@aol.com